Terry McMillan, the author [KU-594-399] acclaimed novels, *Mama* and D..... (both available in Black Swan), was born in ... Huron, Michigan, and studied at the University of California and Columbia University. She lives with her son outside San Francisco.

INTERNATIONAL ACCLAIM FOR
WAITING TO EXHALE

'McMILLAN IS AN ENGAGINGLY FRANK, UNPRETENTIOUS AND ENTERTAINING STORYTELLER . . . DELICIOUSLY MEMORABLE AND FUNNY AS WELL AS FULL OF PATHOS. SHE HOLDS UP A CANDID MIRROR TO THE OFTEN LUDICROUS FLAWS AND SELF-DELUSIONS WE ALL SHARE'

Sunday Times

'HER CHARACTERS' VOICES ARE HONEST AND TRUE, AS THOUGH SHE'S WIRETAPPED THE DEEPEST FEELINGS OF THE HEART'

San Francisco Chronicle

'*WAITING TO EXHALE* DESTROYED MY SLEEP PATTERNS. I WAS UP AT 3 A.M. FOR THREE NIGHTS IN A ROW READING COMPULSIVELY. TERRY HAS A WONDERFUL EAR FOR STORY AND DIALOGUE. SHE GIVES US FOUR WOMEN WITH RAW, HONEST EMOTIONS THAT BREATHE OFF THE PAGE'

Amy Tan

Also by Terry McMillan

DISAPPEARING ACTS
MAMA

and published by Black Swan

Waiting to Exhale

Terry McMillan

BLACK SWAN

WAITING TO EXHALE
A BLACK SWAN BOOK 0 552 99503 7

Originally published in Great Britain by Doubleday,
a division of Transworld Publisher Ltd

PRINTING HISTORY
Doubleday edition published 1992
Corgi edition published 1993
Black Swan edition published 1993
Black Swan edition reprinted 1993

Set in Linotype Melior by Phoenix Typesetting
Ilkley, West Yorkshire.

Black Swan Books are published by Transworld Publishers Ltd,
61–63 Uxbridge Road, Ealing, London W5 5SA,
in Australia by Transworld Publishers (Australia) Pty Ltd,
15–25 Helles Avenue, Moorebank, NSW 2170,
and in New Zealand by Transworld Publishers (NZ) Ltd,
3 William Pickering Drive, Albany, Auckland.

Printed and bound in Great Britain by
Cox & Wyman Ltd, Reading, Berks.

This one's for you, Daddy
Edward Lewis McMillan, 1929–1968

If there was any other way . . .
Don't you think I've tried to find it . . .

'(If there was) Any Other Way' (P. Bliss)
Celine Dion

Acknowledgements

I'm indebted to quite a few folks who hung in there with me during the writing of this book. I can't thank my best girlfriend in the world – Doris Jean Austin – enough, for being hard on me, giving me solid criticism. I still have to mail back a million of her paper clips. I'm grateful to Monica Stewart-Ferris, my brand-new neighbor, who stopped painting to read it; my sister, Crystal Joseph, who told me she loved it (but she's my sister). I have to thank Blanche Richardson, the owner of Marcus Bookstores in Oakland and San Francisco, who kept rushing me, calling after every hundred pages to see 'what happened next.' My girl, Rasheedah Ali, who gave me constant pep talks when I got scared; Gilda Adams, for saving me in Tucson; and Terence Pugh for 'hooking up' my hair. And I'm grateful to my legal buddies, Oliver Jones and Janis Wiggins, for all their advice. I'd also like to thank Fletcher Diggins, for being my friend for forty years; Charles 'Box' Smith, a real-life victim of Alzheimer's. I'm forever grateful to my agent, Molly Friedrich, for her continued faith in my work; my editor, Dawn Seferian, for relentlessly being in my corner, but mostly for her patience. And last but not least, I want to thank my son, Solomon, for trying so hard not to disturb Mommy while she sat in front of her computer for months. I'm all yours.

The Women

Savannah Jackson
Bernadine Harris
Robin Stokes
Gloria Matthews

Contents

Not Dick Clark

Right now I'm supposed to be all geeked up because I'm getting ready for a New Year's Eve party that some guy named Lionel invited me to. Sheila, my baby sister, insisted on giving me his phone number because he lives here in Denver and her simple-ass husband played basketball with him eleven years ago at the University of Washington, and since I'm still single (which is downright pitiful to her, considering I'm the oldest of four kids and the only one who has yet to say 'I do'), she's worried about me. She and Mama both think I'm out here dying of loneliness, which is not true. I mean, I have my days and I have my nights, but I haven't gotten to the point where I'll take whatever I can get. There's a big difference between being thirsty and being dehydrated.

But Sheila and Mama have always thought that something was better than nothing, and look where it's gotten them. Mama, who thinks she's an expert on everything, hasn't had a whole man in her life for seventeen years, and if I knew where my daddy was, I'd probably kill him for making her such a bitter woman. He broke her heart, and she's never recovered. And Sheila? She files for divorce on an annual basis and calls me collect from some cheap motel where she and the kids are hiding out until she can serve the papers on Paul. I listen to her whine for hours about how sick she is of him and that there's nothing he can do or say that would make her go back this time. But then, like a fool, she turns right around and calls him up, repeats her long list of needs that aren't being met, and he promises to give her anything she wants. She refuses to believe him, so he begs on a daily basis for two weeks, and by

1

then he's convinced her that he means it, so she gives in and goes on back home. I rarely hear from her while they're 'honeymooning,' except maybe a three-minute synopsis of how hunky-dory everything is now, and because he's given her permission to go ahead and rip out the old carpet or buy some new dining room furniture, she's watching her money, which is why she can't talk long. One of my brothers is in prison for doing some stupid shit, passing counterfeit money, but he's not a criminal; and the other one's a lifer in the Marine Corps. So as far as taking advice from *any* of them goes, I'm skeptical.

The deal is, the men are dead in Denver. Which is only one reason why I'm leaving. I'm tired of this altitude, all this damn snow, and this obsession with the Denver Broncos. For the last three years, my life has felt inconsequential, like nobody really gives a shit what I'm doing or how well I do it. From the outside, everything looks good: I've got a decent job, money in the bank, live in a nice condo, and drive a respectable car. I've got everything I need except a man. And I'm not one of these women who think that a man is the answer to everything, but I'm tired of being by myself. Being single isn't half as much fun as it used to be. Ever since I broke up with Kenneth, I haven't even come close to being in love, and that was almost four years ago, when I lived in Boston. I miss that feeling, and I want it back. But I'm also not the type to sit around and wait for too much of anything. If I want something to happen, I know I have to make it happen. And as hard as I've tried, nothing unforgettable has happened to me since I've been in Denver, which is why I'm getting the hell out of here.

My baby sister has also never appreciated or understood taking real risks, so she wasn't all that thrilled when I called her two weeks ago to tell her I was moving to Phoenix. 'Why would anybody in their right mind want to live in Arizona?' she asked me. 'Are there any black folks out there? And isn't that where that governor rescinded the King holiday after it had already been passed?' I had to remind her that my best friend, Bernadine – the girl who was my roommate in college, the girl whose wedding I drove sixty miles in a snowstorm to get to because I was her bridesmaid – lives in Scottsdale. She's been black all her life, and she seems to like it there. And as far as the King holiday goes, all I could say was that I'd be one of the first people at the polls when the time came.

Bernadine had talked me into coming out there to spend my birthday, which I had to remind Sheila was October 14 and not the twenty-second, which was the day I got her card. She damn near has a stroke if hers is late. Anyway, I couldn't believe how pretty and warm and cheap it was to live there. We went to this Urban League affair, and I got to talking to one of Bernadine's husband's friends, and he told me about this opening in the publicity department at one of the local TV stations, so I applied, and after flying back and forth for three different interviews, I had just found out that I got the job, and hell, it's a welcome change from the gas company, and plenty of opportunities to advance. What I didn't tell her was that I was taking a twelve-thousand-dollar-a-year pay cut, which probably would've sent her soaring through the roof, because I'm the one who's basically been supporting Mama for the past three years while everybody else just watched. Mama gets a whopping $407 a month from Social Security and $104 worth of food stamps, but who the hell can live off of that? She lives in a Section Eight apartment, I pay her portion of the rent and send her a few extra dollars a month so she can at least go to a movie, but all she does is spend it in thrift shops or put furniture on layaway that'll take years to get out. If my condo doesn't sell, I'll be up shits creek. I'll be cutting it close as it is, but I'm hoping it won't take me that long to get into producing, which is what I really want to do.

Sheila's got three kids, doesn't work, and has never lived anywhere except Pittsburgh. 'This'll make the

3

fourth city you've lived in in fifteen years. I can't keep track, Savannah. When are you gonna be still long enough to settle down?' All I could say was, 'When I find what I'm looking for.' I didn't feel like telling her for the umpteenth time what it was, because she doesn't understand it: peace of mind; a place I can call home; feeling important to somebody; and just trying to live a meaningful, significant, and positive life. Of course she didn't bother asking this time. But Sheila did manage to remind me for the zillionth time that I'm running out of *time*, because here I am all of thirty-six years old without so much as a prospect in sight; and on top of that, she said that my swinging-singles life style doesn't amount to shit, that I run the gamut when it comes to stereotypes of buppiedom because I put too much energy into my career, that without a husband and children my life really has no meaning, that I'm traversing down that road less traveled, and that by now I should've been divorced at least once and be the mother of at least 2.5 children. Sheila said I'm too choosy, that my standards are too high, and because they seem to be non-negotiable, she swears up and down that if I don't loosen up, the only person who'll ever meet my qualifications is God. I love her to death, but I swear, she gets on my last nerve.

It was right after Thanksgiving when she called to tell me about this Lionel. I had just finished hanging a painting I'd bought by Charles Alston: a watercolor of a black man and woman jitterbugging in the 1940s. It took me six months to pay for it, and I was so excited to finally have it on my wall that I was standing there grinning at it when the phone rang. I sat down at the dining room table and looked out the window. It was snowing again, but it was beautiful. I swear, sometimes it feels like heaven up here. I live on the twenty-third floor and have a 180-degree view of the Rockies and downtown Denver, which is right downstairs. I lit a cigarette and rested my elbows on the glass tabletop. 'So how old is he?' I asked.

'Forty-one,' she said.

'Forty-one? That old?'

'Forty-one is not old, Savannah. You're almost forty, so be quiet.'

'Look, Sheila. I've been out with enough of these over-forty-year-olds to last me awhile. Most of them come in five minutes, are out of shape, sound like they're your daddy, or so set in their ways they act like old ladies. And personally, I can't be bothered.'

'You're starting to sound like your mama.'

I resented that shit, but Sheila doesn't know *what* kind of men I've been dealing with since I left Boston, and I didn't feel like telling her. She's accused me of judging them too fast, but hell, I know what I like and don't like, and it doesn't take that long for me to tell if there's any chemistry at work or not. I've met a whole lot of educated, successful, handsome black men who don't turn me on. Riffraff comes in all kinds of packages. 'So,' I said, and took a long drag from my cigarette, 'what's wrong with him?'

'Nothing is *wrong* with him.'

'If he's forty-one years old and still single, something's gotta be wrong with him.'

'He's divorced.'

'How long?'

'Paul said four years. He's got his own business.'

'And what exactly is his line of business?'

'He sells fire trucks.'

'He sells what?'

'You heard me: fire trucks.'

'Wow, how exciting.'

'Don't be cynical, Savannah.'

'I'm not being cynical.'

'Anyway, he owns his own home and even has some rental property.'

'Did I ask you for his résumé?'

5

'No. Which is why I'm giving it to you. You never seem to find out that a man doesn't have anything going for him except what's between his legs, but by then it's always too late.'

I didn't even feel like responding to that because Sheila doesn't know what the hell she's talking about. I think she ran a TRW on Paul before she married him because as far as she's concerned, if a man doesn't have good credit and isn't making six figures, then he's not worth your time and energy. 'And just what does this prize look like?' I asked.

'Would you stop being so sarcastic! According to this picture, he's handsome.'

'How old is the picture, Sheila?'

'I don't know. Ten years, maybe.'

'Ten years can destroy anything.'

'Well, let me say this. Paul said he runs five miles a day, restores vintage cars, drives a jeep, has a college education, is six one, and that's all I know.'

I had to admit that my curiosity was sparked a tad, but I knew enough not to get excited. I'm tired of getting pumped up for nothing. But I called him. And he wasn't home. So I left a message on his machine. He had a civilized voice and Grover Washington playing in the background. I like Grover Washington. We played machine tag for three weeks. As the media representative for the gas company, I travel off and on, and Lionel told my machine that he'd been traveling too, trying to secure more backing for some new business ventures he was trying to launch. Well, at least he's industrious, I thought. And then a few days after yet another solo and boring Christmas, I came in from work and there were two messages on the machine. One was from Mama, asking if I could please Federal Express her ninety-five dollars so she could take some crocheting class and pay her light bill, which was past due, and the other was from Lionel. He said that he and some of his racquetball buddies were throwing a New Year's Eve party at some spiffy hotel and that I should come.

6

So it wasn't like I had a date. But what I did have was something to *do*. It was better than sitting in this apartment with my cat on my lap, purring. I haven't *purred* since I met Fred, but that only lasted a week, because the wife he forgot he had came back from a business trip. But hell, that was three months ago. Wouldn't it be ironic if this Lionel Playworld turned out to be Mr Right? Just because I'm moving. I just hope he's socialized, moderately charming, halfway articulate, and doesn't spend half the night trying to convince me how he got to be so goddamn wonderful.

What I do know is this: If my mind wanders when he talks, or if what he has to say sounds like some more superficial rehearsed bullshit, I'll do my best to be as gracious as I can and shine him on. One way I can always tell if I'm at least interested on a primal level is if I find myself wondering how he looks without any clothes on and imagining how good he is in bed. But. If I don't even entertain the thought, it means he's not generating any heat. And no heat means no interest.

I had just gotten out of the shower when the phone rang. I was hoping it'd be him, calling to make sure I was coming. I answered the phone in the voice I use at work. 'Hello,' I said.

'Savannah?' Mama asked, like she was expecting somebody else to answer my phone. I pulled up the antenna and immediately went to find my cigarettes.

'Yes, it's me, Mama. How you doing?'

'I'm fine. Thanks for the money. The lights didn't get cut off, and that class is too hard. Seems like I got new stitches to learn every night, and with Sheila and the kids being here, I can't hardly get to it.'

'Sheila's staying with you?'

'Yeah. I thought you knew. Don't tell her I told you. She claims this time she's divorcing him for real. But I don't pay no attention to that girl. She don't know whether she's coming or going. I think she's one step away from a nervous breakdown.'

'Mama, you say that every time she leaves.'

'Well, he's been calling, and they've been talking. She'll be home in a minute, mark my words. Anyway, I hope you're not sitting in that apartment tonight of all nights.'

'I'm not, Mama.'

'Good. Are you going to a party?'

'Yes.'

'What you wearing?'

'Why, Mama?'

'I just hope it's something sexy and not any of those office getups you've got a closet full of.'

'Mama, what difference does it make what I'm wearing? You're two thousand miles away, and I don't exactly need your approval, now do I?'

'Look, you don't have to tell me where I live. And no, you don't need my approval for anything, but I'm still your mother, so watch the tone of your voice. You didn't answer my question.'

'I'm wearing a skin-tight dress with the back cut down to my behind and the front slit almost to my navel. How's that sound?'

'Good. Just wear a warm coat. Do you have a date?'

'Sort of.'

'Either you do or you don't – which is it?'

'No, but I was *invited* out.'

'Male or female?'

'Male, Mama.'

'Then why ain't you going with him?'

'Mama, it's a long story, and look, I'm trying to get dressed. What are *you* doing tonight?'

'Staying home. It's too much violence going on to be out on New Year's for me, so me and Sheila's cooking some black-eyed peas and chitterlings for tomorrow, and the kids rented some videos and they're making popcorn balls.'

'Well, tell everybody Happy New Year for me.'

'Wait a minute! Don't hang up yet! Do me a favor.'

'What's that, Mama?'

'Try not to swear.'

'I won't, Mama. And give me *some* credit. I don't use the same kind of language around men that I do when I'm with my girlfriends – at least not until I get to know him better.'

'You still smoking?'

'Every once in a while,' I said.

'Well, if you have to have a cigarette, smoke it in the bathroom and keep some breath spray in your purse.'

'I will, Mama.'

'And please try to smile, Savannah.'

'I will, Mama. I'll grin all night.'

'And put on a little extra makeup and wear your best cologne.'

'I am, Mama, I am.'

'Good, and just remember: Every man you meet don't have to be a potential husband. If you ain't exactly thrilled about him, be nice and act friendly anyway. He might just have some friends you like better.'

'Are you speaking from experience?'

'What did you say?'

'Nothing.'

'Bye, baby. And you have a Happy New Year.'

'You too,' I said, and hung up. I poured myself a glass of wine, lit another cigarette, and stood over by the window. Now it was snowing hard and horizontally. I couldn't see anything except lights from office buildings, red taillights and yellow headlights moving on the freeway. Mama just doesn't know. I'll be glad when I *can* pick up the phone one day and tell her I want her to meet my future husband. Maybe then she'll give me a break.

I went into the bathroom and plugged in the curling iron, and without even giving it a second thought, I found myself splashing on puddles of Joy. After I blow-dried my hair, I turned the fan on because it was getting too hot. My cat, Yasmine, followed me into the bedroom and sat down next to me on the bed. I put my panty hose on, then slipped into my new purple suede pumps so I could break them in. I stood up and looked down at my stomach. It was so bloated it looked like I was about three months pregnant. Yasmine looked at me like she agreed. I don't know how I could forget that my period was due in four days, which should explain why I'd been such a bitch at work and why I spent half of last night crying for absolutely no reason I could think of. This PMS shit is definitely for real, and it's getting worse every year. I wish I knew what to do about it. I took the panty hose off and rummaged through my top dresser drawer until I found some with a control top. They didn't help all that much, which means I'm going to have to hold my stomach in when I walk, because I'm wearing this dress tonight and that's all there is to it. And I lied to Mama. The only thing that's true about this dress is that it's tight. It's also teal-blue suede, and since I don't have any cleavage, my ass is about the only thing that makes a statement in it.

This hair is tired, but I was doing the best I could with the curling iron. I took another sip of my wine, hoping it would help me get in some kind of festive mood, and turned on the little radio sitting on the back of the toilet. I was singing 'How Will I Know' right along with Whitney Houston while I put on my makeup. I took my time because I didn't want to look like I was wearing any, except for the lipstick. I love lipstick but wear only three colors: red-red and fuchsia, and orange in the summer. After I blotted my lips, I got a bottle of red nail polish out of the medicine cabinet to add a new coat to the two that had already dulled since yesterday. Then I put a pair of these drop-dead crystal earrings on and looked at myself in the mirror. I thought I looked pretty good, but my feet were already killing me. Hopefully, in another hour or two these shoes'll be looser. I went into the living room and turned on the TV. Somebody was asking all these celebrities about their New Year resolutions. As if anybody cared.

I shook the bottle of polish and started with my thumb. Then, as corny as I know it is, I actually found myself thinking about a few resolutions of my own. On the top of my list is finding a husband. I promise myself that in 1990 I will not spend another birthday by myself, another Fourth of July by myself, another Thanksgiving by myself, and definitely not another Valentine's Day, Christmas, or New Year's by myself.

I also need to quit smoking. But not tonight. I have to be realistic about this shit. But before my thirty-seventh birthday, which is ten whole months away, I will. I just pray I don't get fat. So far I've been pretty lucky. I look and feel almost as tight as I did when I was thirty, and the most exercise I get is walking to my car. That's pitiful, when I think about it. I know I'm at that age when my body is going to start corroding if I don't do something to slow down the process. I remember the day I turned thirty. I was getting out of the shower and I stood in front of the mirror and stared at myself for a long time. I examined every inch of my body and appreciated the fact that I finally looked like a grown woman. I also assumed that this was how I was going to look for the rest of my life. The way I saw it, I was never going to *age;* I'd just look up one day and be old. And Lord only knows what'd happen to my body if I were to have a baby about now. It looks like somebody stenciled beige skid marks all over Sheila's breasts, stomach, and hips. I can't imagine having a baby at forty. That's too old to be bringing anything into the world if you ask me. But let me shut up. If I was still able, the right man could probably talk me into having one at fifty. Anyway, when I get to Phoenix, I'm joining a health club and'll start doing aerobics and ride that bike I spent a fortune on and have only ridden around the block. So maybe by the time I quit smoking, I'll have already replaced one bad habit with a good one. Shit, I feel better already.

After I finished both hands and started blowing on them, I was wondering: Is it really possible to want something so bad that you could make it happen just by *thinking* about it? I mean, could I just dream myself up a husband? Wouldn't it sort of be like praying? A long time ago, I asked God to please send me a decent man, and one by one, what I got was Robert, Cedric, Raymond, and Kenneth. Unfortunately, I left out some very important details: like how about a little compassion, some pride as opposed to cockiness, some confidence as opposed to arrogance. Now I'm more specific: Could You make sure he talks about what he feels and not just about what he thinks? Could he have a genuine sense of his purpose in life, a sense of humor, and could he already *be* what he aspired to? Could he be honest, responsible, mature, drug-free, and a little bit spontaneous? Could he be full of zest, good-enough-looking for me, and please let him be a slow, tender, passionate lover? It takes me forever to say my prayers these days, but I don't care, because this time around, I want to make sure God doesn't have to do any guesswork.

The truth of the matter is, I've spent nine years of my adult life living with three different men that I'm glad I didn't marry because all three of them were mistakes. Back then, I felt like I had to live with them in order to find out that *I couldn't* live with them. However, I refuse to live with another one unless I'm married to him: That much I do know. I'll take my chances the next time around. People aren't so quick to call it quits when they're married. I'm also willing to spend the rest of my life alone if I have to, until I find someone that makes me feel like I was born with a tiara on my head. People like Sheila and Mama are beginning to make me feel as if I should be embarrassed or ashamed for not having a husband by now. Mama's got about ten empty pages in the family scrapbook set aside for my wedding pictures. At this point, they'd rather see me settle for some lackluster man with the right credentials: put my yearnings for love a little lower on the totem pole and just be done with it. But I can't do

12

that. All I've got is *one* life, and this is one area that's too large for me to compromise.

As a matter of fact, most of the men I've met over the last few years have been boring, selfish, manipulative, or weak. Worse than babies. Got an excuse for everything. Some were just plain lost. Of course the flip side is the die-hard buppies, who think that the true measure of success is how much money they make, what kind of car they drive, how big their house is, and how much pussy they can get before they die. Their priorities are all fucked up. And the more successful they are, the more arrogant they are. They've taken these stupid statistics about *us* to heart and are having the time of their lives. They do not hold themselves accountable to anybody for anything, and they're getting away with murder when it comes to women. And *we* let them. They lie to us without a conscience, they fuck as many of us at a time as they want to and then cry that 'I'm not ready to make a commitment yet' bullshit as soon as you act like you're serious about them. They have done one helluva job convincing themselves – and a whole lot of *us* – that we *should* feel desperate, which is why so many of us are willing to do damn near anything to snag one of them. Well, not me. I don't need a man to *rescue* me or take care of me financially – I can take care of myself. What would be nice is to know you're with one who's looking out for your best interests, one who makes you feel special, safe, and secure. And one who excites you. I'm tired of being the thrill*er*, always trying to prove myself. Shit, I want to be the thrill*ee* for a change. I want a man to go out of his way for me. It would also be nice to meet one who understands that it takes more than a stiff dick to keep a woman happy. But most of the ones I've met don't have a clue.

What I want to know is this. How do you tell a man – in a nice way – that he makes you sick? Cecil was so vulgar when he drank that I had to drive his ass home after we went out. Which was all of three times.

He still doesn't understand why I didn't want to see him anymore. Bill just irritated the hell out of me. I think he got a real charge bringing everything he thought I did wrong to my attention. He corrected me whenever I mispronounced a word and told me that I watered my plants too much. He wouldn't eat my jelly because some dots of butter were in it. And he insisted on showing me how to get more dishes in the dishwasher. He was always right, and everything had to be done his way. He made me want to throw up. And what if a man's a drag in bed? This list is too long to name names, but of course all black men think they can fuck because they all have at least ten-inch dicks. I wish I could tell some of them that they should start by checking the dictionary under *F* for 'foreplay,' *G* for 'gentle,' and *T* for 'tender' or 'take your time.' I've wanted to tell some of them that acrobatics and banging the hell out of me is not the same as making love. I've had enough bladder infections to last the rest of my life. And boring? John and Elliot were beyond dull. All they ever talked about were their jobs and sports. At first I thought this shit was masculine, but they lived and breathed for ESPN. Both of them had satellites, which is why neither one of them lasted longer than a baseball season. And what about Sam and Arthur and a few others, who were 'recreational' drug users but couldn't do anything unless they did a few lines or smoked a joint first? I made the mistake of telling them that right after college cocaine became my drug of choice but I stopped doing that shit years and years ago. Now that we're all damn near middle age, I don't want to be around *anybody* who's still into drugs. And I'm not interested in rehabilitating anybody, either. I've tried it, and it doesn't work. And Darrell. The wimp. He was scared of damn near everything: spiders, snakes, mice, heights, and he wouldn't drive at night and couldn't fix shit. And then there're the rest, the ones who wanted to own me after I slept with them two or three times, or the ones who were just too stiff and IBMish, or so married to their jobs that they hardly had any time left for themselves, let alone me.

I have tried being honest, telling them as diplomatically as I possibly could that they just weren't right for me, that they shouldn't take it personally because there was somebody out there for everybody. Which is how I became 'the bitch.' They couldn't stand the thought of being rejected, that I didn't want them, so of course something had to be wrong with *me*. I *know* I'm not perfect, but I've spent tons of energy trying to be. I wanted to tell all of them to come back and see me after they grew up or got some serious counseling. Unfortunately, most men are deaf. They hate advice. Especially if it's from a woman. They get defensive as hell if you so much as suggest that there's a few things they might try doing that would truly please you. 'Fuck you' is what they ended up saying to me, because they didn't want to be *told* what I liked or needed; they preferred to guess. Well, I'm here to tell you that at least seventy-five per cent of the ones I've met were terrible guessers.

All I've had in the three years I've been in Denver are dates from hell in one form or another. I'm sick of dating. All through college I had a *boyfriend*. All my girlfriends had *boyfriends*. We didn't date. White girls dated. You met a guy at a party or a club or somewhere, and if you liked the way he looked or danced or smelled or what he had to say and how he said it, the next thing you knew you went out, then you slept together, and if he made you feel all tingly inside and made you smile and even laugh, and if on top of this he made you come, the next thing you knew you were going together until some lengthy or unforgivable bullshit happened and you broke up. Then you started all over. I had four contiguous boyfriends in college and never went more than two weeks without having an orgasm. I had no idea what loneliness felt like, because somebody was always waiting in the wings to fill whatever's-his-name's shoes if he blew it.

15

Times have damn sure changed.

And I can't lie. Now I worry. I worry about if and when I'll ever find the *right* man, if I'll ever be able to exhale. The more I try not to think about it, the more I think about it. This morning, I was drinking a cup of coffee, when it occurred to me that my life is half over. Never in a million years would I have ever believed that I would be thirty-six years old and still childless and single. But here I am.

I turned the TV off because I was making myself feel too sad and wishy-washy, and I hate it when I get like this. Now that my nails were dry, I went into the bathroom to comb out my hair. The black lace bra I had put on was damn near empty, and I don't even know why I bothered wearing it. If I had the nerve, I swear I'd buy me some bigger breasts instead of walking around all these years with this big ass and big legs and these little sunny-side-ups on my chest.

I put my dress on and got my coat and walked out to press for the elevator. Please God, I said, as I stood there, if this man isn't The One, at least let me have some fun tonight. Let me dance so hard that I sweat. Let me laugh. Hell, let me feel something.

When the elevator doors opened and I started going down, I couldn't believe it when Gerard – my high school sweetheart – suddenly popped into my head. He was the first major love of my life. The one who sat on the couch with me while I baby-sat and kissed me during *Shock Theatre* for two years in a row; the one who caressed my breasts through my blouse and then stopped because he respected me; the one who looked for me in the crowd when he scored a touchdown, gave me Valentine candy, and worked part time at McDonald's so he could help take care of his mother. He was *already* a man at seventeen years old, and I never even slept with him. He ended up going to Vietnam, I went away to college, and I never went back to Pittsburgh. I felt myself smiling, remembering how pure and innocent he used to make me feel. I had no idea where he lived now or what he was doing, but for some reason I couldn't even explain, something told me I probably should've married him.

When I pulled into the parking lot of the hotel, I was nervous and my heart was racing. I got out of the car, and my eyes started watering. My cheeks felt like they were being pulled away from my face; my lipstick felt like Chap Stick. It had stopped snowing, but now it was reportedly a whole twenty degrees. I knew I should've worn a hat and my down coat, but noooooo, I just had to look cute. By the time I made it to the lobby, the soles of my feet were frozen and my corn was already killing me.

I got on the elevator with three couples. I decided right then and there that I wasn't going to let them bother me. Not tonight. If I'm lucky, next year I'll be one of them. They mumbled a hello, but I said a loud and cheery 'Happy New Year!' I was taking off my leather gloves when the doors opened and we were facing a man sitting behind a long table. He was putting money and tickets into a metal box. Lionel didn't mention anything about having to pay. 'How much is it?' I asked the man.

'For you, sister, twenty dollars.'

I handed him a twenty and smiled. Then I went to check my coat and walked over to the doorway that led to a huge ballroom. There were balloons and crepe paper everywhere and about two hundred people. I saw the DJ perched on a platform. The music was loud. It sounded like he was playing oldies but goodies. Only a few people were on the dance floor. I stood there and prayed that this wasn't going to turn out to be one of those over-thirty-five networking parties where folks sit around and make small talk all damn night because they think they're middle-aged and therefore no longer entitled to get loose. Hell, it was New Year's Eve.

17

All Lionel said was that he'd be wearing some snake-skin cowboy boots and one of those cowboy ties with silver tips on the end. It had a name, but I forgot what it was. I thought about how so many men here ride horses, and I prayed that his boots wouldn't have spurs and he wouldn't be wearing one of those stupid ten-gallon hats.

I took a deep breath, sucked in my stomach, pretended I weighed ten pounds instead of a hundred and thirty-five, looked around the room for a vacant seat, and, when I saw one, headed in the direction of a big round table. The music stopped, and I was now in the middle of an empty dance floor. There were three nondescript couples at the table, and I politely asked, 'Is someone sitting here?'

'No,' one of the men said. 'Please join us.' All three women gave me a suspicious once-over, and then those phony smiles that even a fool can see through. They didn't say a word, not even so much as a nod. I wish I knew why some women are so damn catty or feel threatened by the presence of an unescorted attractive woman. Shit, it's not my fault that I'm not fat and ugly. The way they were sizing me up, you'd swear I was wearing a sign that said, 'Hell, yeah! I'm single and desperate and I have no morals and as soon as you turn your back or go to the bathroom, I'm going to flirt with your man and try to take him!' I hope I never get this insecure.

I sat down anyway, since I was there, but after ten or fifteen minutes I started feeling uncomfortable, unwelcome, like an intruder or somebody with the plague. Black people didn't use to treat each other like this. Where I came from, folks talked to you even if they didn't know you. When these women started whispering and giggling, I decided to walk over to the bar, get myself a drink, and see if I recognized anybody or if I could identify this Lionel along the way.

The DJ was playing Michael Jackson's 'Don't Stop Till You Get Enough,' and it seemed like everybody migrated to the dance floor at once. This time I walked around, sliding through one crowd after another. 'Yo, Mama, can I follow you?' I heard, but I didn't bother to look up. Then a few more steps. 'How'd you like to bring in the New Year with me, babeeee?' I kept walking. 'Sister sister sister. You wearing the hell outta that blue suede dress. Can I take you home with me?' I ignored them and worked my way through the crowd until I finally came to the bar. I'll be glad when these men learn that if they want to get a grown woman's attention or if they want to give you a compliment, this is not the way to do it. 'Yo, Mama' and other such phrases are not only a sign of poor upbringing, they're tacky and downright insulting, and if I had any guts, I'd love to say, 'Do I look like your mama?' I wonder if 'Hello, how are you, I'm Carl or Bill or James, and you sure look nice tonight' has ever occurred to them. That's what I want to hear. I also want to know what they'd do if just *once* I actually called their bluff and said, 'Yo, baby, I've been waiting for you all my life and I'd love to fuck your brains out right now. Let's go!'

I ordered a white Zinfandel and saw an unoccupied window seat across the room, so I walked over and sat down. Within a few minutes, this man who looked like Barry White's twin sat down next to me and smiled. That gold tooth was already working against him, and I gave him the same phony smile those women had given me. Then that bottle of Polo he was wearing started making me sneeze. 'Bless you,' he said, and I thanked him. He was wearing a diamond ring on each pinkie, and he tried to cross his legs but couldn't, so then he ran his hand over his Jheri-Kurl and leaned toward me like he was settling in for the night.

That's when I got up. 'You have a Happy New Year,' I said, and walked away. I really felt like dancing, but I didn't dare ask anybody, not knowing if he belonged to somebody or not. I didn't want to get my feelings hurt tonight. I decided to find the ladies' room, smoke a cigarette, and check my makeup. It was really an excuse to circulate, but I needed a destination. There was one thing I did know. If I didn't see this Lionel in the next twenty minutes or if nobody decent asked me to dance, I was going home and watch Dick Clark.

The bathroom was packed with rhinestoned, sequined, glowing, glittering women. Everybody was in front of the mirrors, spraying or squeezing drops of breath spray on their tongues, adding more lipstick and blush and perfume when they didn't need it. pulling their boobs up, fluffing, spraying, and picking out their hair. Some were simply admiring themselves. I took off my shoes and lit a cigarette. All of a sudden I did have to go to the bathroom, so I got in line. That's when I felt somebody tap me on the shoulder. I turned around and faced a woman who probably would've been even more beautiful if she wasn't wearing so much makeup. And if she would get rid of some of that hair – which I could tell right off the bat was a weave – maybe you could actually see her face. 'That's a bad dress, girl, and you're wearing the hell out of it,' she said. 'That's the truth,' somebody in front of the mirror said. 'Thank you,' I said, and smiled. When a stall opened up, I went in, and when I came out, I checked myself in the mirror, said Happy New Year to everybody, and headed out the door.

I walked over to the entrance of the ballroom and stood near the doorway. A trillion couples were all locked up on the dance floor, because Lionel Richie's 'Truly' was playing. I felt like a fool standing there by myself, but now I was praying no-one would ask me to dance; I don't like dancing close to strange men on slow songs.

I was shifting my weight to my right foot – the corn on my left toe was throbbing – when I felt a wide run in my panty hose zip down my thigh. Shit. That's why I hate these things. If I could get back half the money I've spent on panty hose, I'd be rich. I looked down to see how far it had gone, and with my peripheral vision saw a pair of cowboy boots minus spurs, attached to a set of rather long legs. I looked up and saw this hunk, this handsome hunk with mixed gray hair, a mixed gray mustache, and a neat mixed gray beard. He was wearing a cowboy tie with silver tips. This couldn't be Lionel, I thought, but he smiled at me with his pearly whites and gave me that 'Are you who I think you are?' look. I smiled back. He was talking to a bunch of guys, and he patted one on the shoulder, then walked over toward me.

'Savannah?'

'Lionel?'

Instead of shaking my hand he gave me a hug, which shocked the shit out of me, because I wasn't exactly prepared for this. During the two seconds that he squeezed me, I was thinking: There is a God, and he's watching over me tonight.

'Well. Finally, we meet,' he said, and let me go carefully, as if I might fall. 'What a pleasant surprise. So. How long have you been here? Are you enjoying yourself?'

'I've been here about an hour, and yes, I'm having a pretty good time. It's a nice party.'

'Good, good, good,' he said, looking at me as if he hadn't expected me to look quite this way, either. I sucked in my stomach and tried to poke my chest out as subtly as I possibly could and prayed he wouldn't ask too many questions that would require me to breathe in order to answer them. At least not until I sat down. 'Can I get you a drink?' he asked. 'Where you sitting?'

I'd never seen anybody smile and talk at the same time, but he was doing it. 'Well, I'm not sitting anywhere in particular, and sure, I'll have a glass of wine.' I looked down and took a quick breath.

'White or red?'

I was thrilled he had sense enough to ask. 'White Zinfandel. Thanks.'

'Be right back,' he said. 'Don't move.'

I had no intention of moving, and I could tell right off the bat that there was something different about this man. First of all, he was polite and clearly articulate.

21

Plus, he was the only one in here who wasn't wearing a suit. He had on faded blue jeans, and I don't think I've ever seen a man look so good in a white shirt. I watched him walk away, and he moved like a man who was sure of himself. Like he knew his own power. And I swear, if I wasn't mistaken, it seemed as if a clearing was made for him to pass right on through. I already liked his style.

I was trying not to fidget, and I needed a cigarette about now, but instead I reached inside my purse and got out two Tic Tacs, popped them into my mouth, and started sucking real fast. Then, so as not to look nervous, lost, or bewildered, I pretended I was looking for somebody. I was still concentrating on finding this invisible person when Lionel came back.

'Looking for somebody?' he asked.

'No. I thought I saw somebody I knew, but I didn't.'

'You sure look beautiful tonight,' he said, and I thought I would go right through the floor. I blushed and said the softest thank you known to mankind.

'Would you like to join me at my table?'

'Sure,' I said, and followed him. There were a few more obvious couples and three empty chairs. We sat down, and I put my purse in my lap and let it lean up against my stomach, then I crossed my arms in front of it.

'So,' he said. 'How long have you been in Denver?'

'Three years.'

'Do you like it here?'

'It's OK, but I'm moving to Phoenix at the end of February.'

'Phoenix? Why Phoenix?'

'Well, I got a better job offer.'

'What kind of work do you do?'

'For the last three years I've been doing PR for the gas company, and technically I'll be doing the same thing, except at a television station.'

'Interesting,' he said, while nodding his head in slow motion. 'Not many of *us* out there, is it?'

22

'Not many of *us* in Denver, either, but that didn't stop us from coming, right?'

'You've got a point. Well, I hear Arizona's beautiful. You sure you can take that heat?'

'Let me put it this way. I'd rather be too hot than too cold any day.'

He started laughing. I didn't think that what I'd just said was all that funny, but I started laughing too, like a fool. I was about to ask Lionel exactly what he did for a living, since he had mentioned something about starting some new business ventures, but I decided to wait. I hate asking men that question right off the bat, because I'm sure they're probably thinking that you're just trying to figure out how much money they make, not that it doesn't matter. The main reason I usually ask is because what a person does for a living tells me something about them.

'So did you make your New Year's resolution?' he asked.

'I did,' I said, and took a sip of my wine.

'Are you gonna keep it?'

'I'm working on one of them right now,' I said.

'Are you giving up something?'

'It depends.'

Then both of us started laughing.

'How about you?' I asked. 'Did you make one?'

'I make affirmations,' he said. 'Every single day.'

Just then, Billy Ocean's 'Caribbean Queen' came on. I used to love to dance to that song.

'Would you like to dance?' he asked.

'Yes,' I said, and got up. We squeezed our way on to the dance floor, and for forty-one, this man could still dance. His movements were strong and smooth, fluid, and I kept looking at those athletic hips and thighs, imagining how hairy and tight they probably were, and what a dream he must be in bed. He smiled at me through three more songs and looked me in the eye until I thought mine were just about ready to cross. When I heard 'If Only for One Night' by Luther Vandross come

23

on, I was just about to head off the floor, when he reached for my hand and said, 'One more. Please?'

Thank you, Jesus, I thought. Lionel put his arms around me and held me close, so close that to keep from getting lipstick on his shirt I had to turn my head to the side, and what else could I do but rest it on his chest, which was firm and hot? His hands circled my back, and I heard him say, 'You sure feel good.'

I lifted my head and looked up at him. 'You don't feel too bad yourself,' I said. He sort of laughed and pressed my head back down. That's when I went ahead and closed my eyes, feeling the run run down my leg, but I didn't care. I exhaled and pretended that this man was mine. That he was everything I'd ever dreamed of, that he was the one I'd been waiting for all my life.

When the record ended, Lionel walked and I floated back to his table, but now the other empty seat was filled with the woman who had given me the compliment in the bathroom.

'Savannah, I want you to meet a good friend of mine. Denise, Savannah.'

She smiled at me and said, 'We've sort of already met.'

'Hello again,' I said, and didn't know if I should sit down or not. But I sat down.

Lionel looked a little bewildered. Then Denise scooted her chair as close to his as it would go, put her arms around him, and said, 'You haven't danced with me all night, Lionel.' She got up and stood directly in front of him and took him by the hands. He got up and looked at me as if he was apologizing. I gave him what I thought to be an understanding look and tried not to stare at them as they headed out to the dance floor. I couldn't even hear the song, because I was hypnotized watching him hold her the way he had just held me. Before I knew it, I had reached into my purse and lit a cigarette and forced myself to look in the other direction, because I couldn't stand this. When I went to uncross my legs and the run zipped down to my ankle and I felt my heel pop through the hole and stick to the lining of my shoe, that was my cue. I put out my cigarette, picked my purse up off the table, and headed for the coatroom. If I was lucky, I could still catch Dick Clark.

Suddenly Single

Right after Bernadine's husband told her he was leaving her for a white girl, she stood in the kitchen doorway, snatched the eighteen hot rollers out of her hair, and threw every last one of them at him. A few loose curls fell over her eyes and into her mouth, so she pulled them behind her ears.

'I'm sorry,' John said, and finished the last of his coffee. 'You can have the house, but I want the condo.'

'House?' she said. 'Condo?' Bernadine tried to look directly into John's eyes in order to figure out if this was some kind of joke, but for some reason her vision was blurred. He was out of focus, and she couldn't tell if the expression on his face was fear or relief. They had both known for over a year that everything between them was wrong. There weren't any more excuses, apologies, or explanations for his not coming home. Intimacy was out of the question. Neither desired the other. And when they did sleep in the same bed, their backs barely brushed.

Rows of perspiration had trickled down the nape of her neck into her hair and soaked through the top of her nightgown. A lone stream was making its way down her spine. But Bernadine didn't care. She squinted, hoping to get a closer look at John. It was indifference she saw all over his face. His shoulders were so erect when he popped a Pop-Tart into the toaster that she knew he didn't really give a damn how she felt or what her reaction to his announcement would be. She couldn't decide what else his face carried. Now she was trying to remember just how he'd said it. It seemed as if he'd told her with the same tone he used when he'd say, 'I'm going to the store, do you want something?' or, 'Is anything good on HBO tonight?' But then again, Bernadine really couldn't be sure, because she felt stoned, as if she'd smoked a good joint. But she hadn't. Still, something was pushing her shoulders down, while what felt like helium was escaping inside her head. She couldn't move. She was sinking and floating. Felt heavy, then light. And this scared her.

She tried to get her feet to move, to turn and walk down the hallway, but they were paralyzed. She tried to raise her arms, to dismiss this whole thing, but now they were frozen too. She couldn't even move her fingers. And then, for no apparent reason, Bernadine remembered feeling helpless like this before. It was the time she had almost drowned.

She had swum out into the middle of the lake to a raft with a girlfriend who was six months pregnant. Being a pack-a-day smoker and not a very good swimmer, Bernadine was so out of breath she was panting by the time she climbed up and collapsed on the wooden slats. The sun was turning orange behind her closed lids, and she was just getting comfortable, when she heard a voice say, 'Ready?' She opened her eyes and saw a big belly hovering over her. 'Race you back,' her girlfriend said, and dove back in. Bernadine sat up slowly and tumbled over the side of the raft. She cut through the water without grace. She could see her girlfriend up ahead. For five or six yards, Bernadine did the crawl stroke, but when she went to pull her right arm up over her shoulder, she had no strength. She tried treading water but had no strength to do that, either. She tried twisting over on her back to float, but the thought itself tired her even more, and finally she gave in and let her body sink. With her eyes open, Bernadine dropped down, watching the golden water swirl in front of her, thousands of bubbles engulfing her, and she felt as if she was flying. She went ahead and surrendered, gave in to what felt like complete grace, as close to peace as she had ever come, when suddenly it occurred to her that she was in fact drowning. She panicked. Took water into her lungs and was coughing, when her feet touched the bottom of the lake. Bernadine pushed down hard, forcing her body to jet up through what seemed like miles of water, where she was surprised to learn that she could now stand. The water barely covered her shoulders. She stood there for a few minutes, long enough to catch her breath, then started walking to shore, the water pulling at her breasts, thighs, and calves. She didn't bother telling her friend, who was waiting on the blanket, that she had almost given herself permission to die.

Now she looked over at her husband, thinking she had wanted to be rid of him, had been trying to conjure up the courage, the nerve, the guts, to tell *him* to leave, but she didn't have that much courage yet. All she wanted to do was repossess her life. To feel that sense of relief when the single most contributing factor to her uttermost source of misery was gone. But he beat her to the punch. Not only was he leaving *her.* Not only was he leaving her for another woman. He was leaving her for a *white* woman. Bernadine hadn't expected this kind of betrayal, this kind of insult. John knew this would hurt me, she thought, as she tried to will the tears rolling down her cheeks to evaporate. And he'd chosen the safest route. A white woman was about the only one who'd probably tolerate his ass. Make him king. She's probably flattered to death that such a handsome, successful black man would want to take care of her, make her not need anything except him. She'll worship him, Bernadine thought, just like I did in the beginning, until the spell wore off. Hell, *I* was his white girl for eleven years.

It's sad, she thought, as she stared at specks of what had to be Kathleen's dandruff on the lapels of John's black suit, that when you finally come to understand the man you love, that's when you realize you don't love him any more. As a matter of fact, she couldn't stand John. It had taken years for her to see that he was nothing but an event junkie: marriage had been an event; the business had been an event; and the kids had been events too.

And just as he'd promised, he had conquered the American dream: built a dream house in a picture-perfect neighborhood and filled it with picture-perfect furnishings. Since they lived in the desert, John wanted the yard to look like one, so he spent a fortune on mature palm trees, ten-foot saguaro and ocotillo and mesquite trees and almost every other form of desert vegetation the landscaper had shown him. Neither of them played tennis, but there was room for a court, so he put one in. And a lap pool, which he'd been in maybe three or four times. Since the time she had almost drowned, Bernadine was scared of water and had never done more than put her feet on the steps in the shallow end. And John just had to have what Bernadine thought of as Hollywood cars: he had bought her a BMW, a Porsche for himself, and the Cherokee for hauling the kids around.

Only private school was good enough for the Harris children, even though they lived in one of the best school districts in Scottsdale. And there were only four black kids in the whole school, but that's the way John wanted it. 'They'll get a solid education and be exposed to all the right things. And we won't have to worry about them being badly influenced,' he'd said.

Over the last five or six years, it became apparent to her that John was doing nothing but imitating the white folks he'd seen on TV or read about in *Money* magazine. At first he thought he was J. R. Ewing, then a black clone of Donald Trump, and finally he settled on Cliff Huxtable. And he was good at it. He loved to entertain. At least once a month they had a dull dinner party, where Bernadine, who had long since transformed herself into Martha Stewart, would spend hours preparing exotic meals she had memorized from countless gourmet cookbooks. He had a vintage wine collection stored in the underground bin that he'd had specially built. But John didn't drink.

Of course John was also a shrewd businessman. He believed that money should make money. For that reason, he'd always handled their financial affairs. They had liquid accounts with Lehman Brothers and Prudential Bache; CDs and IRAs and zero coupon bonds, and savings bonds for the kids. What Bernadine didn't know about were the two hundred acres of farmland John owned in California or that he was a fifty per cent owner of a vineyard in Arizona. She had no idea how much stock he owned, because she wasn't allowed to open his mail. She didn't have a clue about the three-week time share in Lake Tahoe or the apartment building he'd just bought in Scottsdale. If Bernadine hadn't trusted John all these years, she'd have known about his Subway franchise and the brownstone he owned back in Philadelphia, both of which were in his mother's name. If she hadn't trusted him all these years, never doing anything more than signing their joint tax returns – because what was the point; they always had to pay up the ass anyway – she would've known about all these enterprises. If she hadn't trusted John all these years, she would've known that he'd just sold his half of the software company to his partner for a mere three hundred thousand dollars, even though its market value was well over three million. But John's partner was also his friend, and although John was now just a salaried employee, his partner had agreed to 'take care of him' down the road, once Bernadine was out of the picture. However, John still had use of an unlimited expense account. If Bernadine hadn't trusted him all these years, she'd have known that all of this had been carefully planned and calculated. Now – on paper – John's income would drop from four hundred thousand dollars a year to eighty. But Bernadine *had* trusted him all these years, and she had no idea how much it was going to cost her.

It's unfortunate, she thought, as she watched him take a sip of his coffee, then gritted her teeth to stop them from chattering, that he never understood or appreciated the virtues of patience, the sanctity of stability, or the sheer comfort of knowing that you have some level of control over what happens next. By the time John knew he had clearly *arrived,* when everything had fallen into place and there wasn't much further he could go – when the routine had become too much of a routine, when even making money became predictable – John needed another event. Enter Kathleen. His boredom with Bernadine and their life had set in like gangrene, and she knew there was no antibiotic strong enough to cure it. She almost wanted to warn the white girl.

And she wasn't hurt. She was mad. So mad that now her temples were twitching and it felt as though somebody was tightening a rubber band around her forehead. She wanted to say something, but she couldn't get her mouth to work. She took a deep breath, and kept inhaling until finally she managed to get a small tunnel of oxygen into her lungs.

'Take it easy, Bernie. You knew this was coming, so let's not get theatrical.'

She exhaled slowly, then said, 'Theatrical.' It sounded like she was singing it soprano, so she said it again, like an alto. 'Theatrical?' Bernadine wanted to tell him that he could take his little Barbie doll and leave now. But she couldn't say it, because her mind kept getting tangled up and now she couldn't stop blinking. She collapsed against the doorframe for support and waited for her muscles to work.

So this is how a bookkeeper keeps books, she thought. This is what happens after eleven years of marriage. This is how it can all end, just like this, on a Sunday morning when you wake up, getting ready for church, and you put your rollers in and go in the bedroom to check on the kids and decide to let them sleep a few more minutes and your husband calls you out into the kitchen, where he's drinking coffee, wearing the same clothes he'd worn yesterday when he left, and of course you can see that he's not going to church and he tells you, 'We need to talk,' and you dread this because talks always lead nowhere and they always end up with John telling you what you're not doing right or what you're not doing enough of or what he would prefer that you be doing. He hands you a cup of coffee and does not prepare you for anything except some more minor bullshit, but then he just blurts out, 'I've filed for a divorce because I want to marry Kathleen.' You are glad you didn't sit down. You drop the cup on the floor, and the hot coffee splatters all over your ankles and the hem of your nightgown. At first you don't feel it, but you do feel the heat from the rollers, so you yank them out two at a time and hurl them at him. You know who Kathleen is, and you know you heard him right. Kathleen is twelve years younger than you. She is twenty-four. She is white. She is your husband's bookkeeper. At his company, where he sells computer software. The company you helped him start. The company you worked your ass off to strengthen, because right after you went back to school and got your degree in business, you became his secretary, his office manager, his computer, his consultant, his accountant, his *bookkeeper*, his wife, and his lover. You did everything for him at once.

And then he grew. He got a partner and a real office and real employees and, later, Kathleen the bookkeeper, who was fresh out of some two-year college and California pretty and blond but not at all a threat because, number one, she was white and you knew John would never look at a white girl and, number two, he loved you and the kids.

Of course this is all your fault, Bernadine, because like a fool you acquiesced too soon and gave up too much. You fell right into the blueprint of *his* life and gave up your own. Let him talk you into leaving Philadelphia and moving out here to Phoenix, where the overhead was supposedly low. He knew you had always wanted to start a catering business, but John said to wait. Wait to see how well his business did before taking on any more unnecessary risks. While you waited, you took the first boring job offer you got, at a nursing home. Then he had this house built on a mountainside acre in Scottsdale because he wanted privacy. You got lonely up here on this mountain in this big-ass house. You began to ignore the city lights you could see from every room; the sunsets began to vex you because they were so predictable. You even prayed for a few overcast days, just to break up the monotony of all this damn sunshine. And on top of everything, all your neighbors were white and not all that neighborly.

So you put your dream on hold and learned how to decorate. For a while, all you thought about were French doors and Mexican tile and window coverings and Kohler toilets and Sub-Zero refrigerators and porcelain vs. stainless steel and Casablanca ceiling fans and recessed lighting and verde light fixtures and pickled oak and cool decking. Everything in your house was south-western. But you started to loathe anything that was pastel and everything that had a coyote or a cactus on it.

You had enough equipment in the kitchen to open a restaurant: Krups coffee/cappuccino/espresso maker; four different sets of pots and pans: Calphalon, white and orange baked enamel, stainless steel; and you had woks, a Belgian-waffle maker, deluxe blenders, an Acme juicer, and everything Cuisinart ever made. You even joined a cook-book club and spent years in the kitchen teaching yourself how to prepare even more exotic meals. To get out of the house, you took a cooking class. Then an entrepreneur class for women. You had tons of books on catering, but then John thought it would be a good idea for you to become a CPA, so you took the test and failed two parts on purpose because you did not want to become an accountant.

And you didn't need to drive a BMW – you had loved your Legend. You didn't want to store your art deco posters in the garage simply because they weren't originals. You didn't need two-hundred-dollar shoes or Louis Vuitton luggage or somebody's name on the label of every piece of clothing you bought. You didn't need that ugly Rolex, either – your Seiko was just fine. You thought gold was boring, that silver was prettier and looked purer, but thanks to John, you owned more gold than Mr T. And you had never been turned on by diamonds; you loved stones that had some cultural value: lapis, jade, turquoise, carnelian, ivory, onyx, and obsidian. But John wanted you to look rich, and for the past eleven Christmases and birthdays, every box he gave you was small enough to fit in your palm and you didn't have to guess what was inside. And the kids. They were spoiled rotten. Too many expensive toys, which, for the last four years, you'd given to the children in Mexico at Christmas, along with tons of shoes and clothes, some of which had never been worn.

What it all boiled down to was that you didn't need to live in all this luxury to be happy. Because you weren't. You didn't need to be rich in order to appreciate the 'finer' things in life. Right after you got married, John started his litany. 'One day I'm going to have exactly what they have,' he'd say. 'They' being rich white folks. He had taken it to the extreme, gone completely overboard, but you couldn't tell him that. You didn't know *how* to tell him. You·didn't know then that you had no courage, or that you'd need so much of it, at least as far as dealing with your husband was concerned. When you told him you wanted to cut your hair, he told you he would leave you if you ever came walking in here with it short. So you let it grow. You had to wear number 30 sun block or avoid the sun altogether, which was pretty hard to do in Phoenix, because John didn't want you to get too dark. And more important than anything, you didn't tell him how damaging you thought it might be to your kids to go to a school where there were only two other black children. But you were his wife, and you had done what you'd been taught to do: let him take the wheel while you took the back seat.

You fool. You didn't even realize that you had stopped looking at the road, until John got bored watching the fish multiply in the ponds he'd had dug in the backyard and said he thought it was time to start a family. So you got pregnant. Your blood pressure skyrocketed and you had to quit your job, but John said it was better this way. You *should* be at home. So you followed both his and the doctor's orders. You stayed in a horizontal position for six months and read Dr Spock and every baby book on the market until you felt like a child expert.

When John junior was born, you poured all your energy into motherhood and watched your husband's business prosper. You believed in him, in the safety of his plans. And at his request, before John junior could say a complete sentence, you had another baby. John insisted on naming the first child after him, and you insisted on naming the second one. But he didn't want any child of his to have an African name. He wanted to name her Jennifer or Kristen or Ashley or Lauren, but you had made a deal, and you kept it. By the time you were weaning Onika off breast milk, you started feeling restless and bored and got tired of staying at home with the kids all day long. You started watching those stupid soap operas and game shows and got a prescription for Xanax because you were screaming all day long. And your brain, it felt as if it was shrinking.

Every single time you said you were ready to start your catering business, John would think of something else for you to do with the kids that would usurp your time. He wouldn't let you put them in day care, because he thought those places were dangerous. So you spent your afternoons taking John junior to piano lessons, karate, Cub Scouts, T-ball, and soccer. You dragged Onika to ballet and gymnastics when the child could barely walk straight. He had convinced you that being a *good* mother meant staying at home with the children until they were at least school age.

So you postponed your dream again. For five more years. But you felt like a single mother, because John worked long hours and the kids were always asleep when he got home and barely saw him on weekends. It was you who read them bedtime stories. You who took off work to take them to the doctor, the dentist. You who stayed home to nurse them when they were sick. It was you who didn't miss a recital or a game. It was you who took them to school and picked them up. It was you who got the wax out of their ears, made sure they took their vitamins, and later made sure they did their homework right. And it was you who took them trick-or-treating, you who dressed up like the Easter bunny, and for the last eight years, it was you who coordinated their birthday parties and sat through hundreds of others.

And then there were the conventions. The conferences. The trade shows. The potential-client dinners. Potential-client meetings. John went everywhere he could so he wouldn't have to come home.

And sex. It became almost irrelevant, almost an after-thought, because when it did happen it was as if John was doing you a favor, and even then he tried to overcompensate. So you stopped wearing the garters, the G-strings, the lace, and those four-inch heels. You hid all those videos that had given him most of his ideas. You stopped pretending to enjoy it altogether and started giving him mummy pussy. You simply stopped moving. Of course by then you knew something was terribly wrong, but you didn't know how to fix it and didn't want to.

And last year, right after Onika had started first grade, John had a brainstorm. He wanted another baby. For the first time in years you felt strong enough and told him no. That you had not been educated to become a permanent housewife, that you needed more stimulation and you were going to get it. He got mad and you got your tubes tied. You complained to Gloria, your crazy hairdresser, who told you that one sure cure for chronic boredom was to get involved in something worthwhile. She belonged to Black Women on the Move, a support group that held workshops for women who wanted to do more with their lives than cook, clean, and take care of the kids; for women who weren't moving but wanted to move; for women who had already achieved some measure of success but wanted to find a better way to deal with the stress that came with it; for women who wanted to be more than role models, who were willing to make the time to do *something* for black folks whose lives – for whatever reason – were in bad shape. So you joined it.

Gloria introduced you to everybody she knew, but Robin was the one you hit it off with. She was so unlike you: bold and zany, optimistic about everything, and she talked a mile a minute. She didn't have a drop of class, no sense of style, but it was clear that she tried hard. And you didn't care, because what you liked about Robin was the fact that she knew who she was and what she wanted, which turned out to be a baby. She ordained herself 'Auntie Robin' and started taking your kids to the park, the movies, the zoo, roller-skating, to anything 'on ice' – and anyplace else she saw in the Sunday paper – so you could have some time to yourself and she could get some maternal experience. You thought she was a little on the fickle side when it came to men, because that boyfriend of hers was giving her a run for her money. He treated her worse than a stepchild, but you kept your mouth shut and your thoughts to yourself, because you now had something you hadn't had in a long time: somewhere to go, something to do, and somebody to do it with.

When John had eventually refused to give you the money to start your catering business, claiming it was just too risky, you took another boring job, as a controller for a real estate management firm, and lied to him about your salary. You began to put money aside so one day you could start your business anyway. He had a series of fits after you went back to work, because now not only did you have your own money but for the first time in years you had interests outside of him and the kids and this stupid house.

From there everything had gone downhill.

'I'll be back next Sunday to get my stuff,' you heard him say. 'You'll be hearing from the lawyer soon too.'

This was entirely too easy for him. And like everything else he did, you could tell that he'd been creating the software for this program for some time. But he'd computed wrong. You wanted to catch him off guard, remind him that you also knew how to exit DOS, how to search and replace, how to merge, but when you thought about it, you realized you didn't have to prove anything to him any more, so instead you simply moved your cursor. You cleared your throat and summoned your mouth to work. 'What about Onika and John junior?'

'I love my kids,' he said. 'And I'll make arrangements.'

'Arrangements?'

'You'll get some money, don't worry.'

'Money?' That's what this was really all about. Division. Dollars. Divvying. He's scared I'm gonna take his ass to the cleaners. Bernadine felt as if she'd been plugged back in. Her fingers twitched and her feet tingled. But now that she could talk, she didn't have a damn thing to say to him. She turned her back and walked through the living room, up the two steps into their bedroom, slammed the door, and locked it.

She surveyed the room. A room she felt could easily be part of a funeral home. The mahogany bed was too ornate and looked like a giant sleigh. She had never seen a burgundy flower before in her life, but the comforter was full of them. There were too many goddamn pictures on the wall. Ugly oil paintings of things she didn't give a damn about, in those ugly gilded frames. She wanted white bookcases, but John had insisted on maple. And that Chinese rug. She hated that damn rug because she hated green, and besides, there was nothing in this room, nothing in this whole house, that would indicate that black people lived here. She jumped over the rug, and the tiles made her feet cold, but Bernadine didn't feel like putting on her slippers. She headed for the bathroom.

Once in there, she stood stock-still and looked at herself in the wide mirror behind the two sinks. Sunlight poured down over her from the skylight. Her eyes were puffy, her lips were chapped, and four red splotches had formed on her left cheek. She looked terrible. She turned around to face the mirror on the linen closet door and, for no apparent reason, lifted up her nightgown. Her breasts had shrunk. They didn't look the way they did before the kids. They were thin and almost flat; her nipples were on the verge of pointing downward. The contour of her body was a short soft curve, her skin a dull brown, except for the beige stretch marks on her hips and belly. Bernadine felt old. She looked old. Older than thirty-six. She got closer to the mirror, so close that when she breathed, two small circles of fog formed. She studied her face. Bernadine knew she'd never been pretty, and she reconfirmed it now. She stepped backward and stopped. Her eyes grazed up and down her body once more, because she was trying to imagine if anybody might still think of her as attractive, since right this minute she was ugly. She let go of her nightgown until she felt the hem hit her knees. She said, 'Cheese.' Her teeth looked yellow, although it had been 106 days since she'd quit smoking. But damn, that was what she needed right now. A cigarette. A cigarette would help her believe this. A cigarette would help her understand that her life had just been revised. A cigarette would help her decide exactly what to do next. How to proceed. She already knew she would no longer have a husband. Then she thought about that. Not have a husband? She sat down on the toilet and put her face in her lap. It seemed as if she'd always had a husband. Now all she knew was that she was going to be a thirty-six-year-old divorced mother of two. Which meant she was going to be single. 'Single?' Her face sprang up, as if she'd just remembered something she'd forgotten.

'You son of a bitch!' she said, and jumped up from the toilet to look at herself again. Who's gonna want me? How am I supposed to start over, when in fact I'm not starting over? This is the middle of my damn life! And I've got two kids! Bernadine opened the medicine cabinet and looked at a row of prescription bottles. She was looking for an *X* for Xanax. When she found the bottle, she opened the top and popped two of them dry. She'd never taken two before. They were dissolving on her tongue when she realized she should take them with water. She turned on the faucet, placed her palms on her side of the vanity and stared at the gold-and-black speckles on the cultured marble. She pushed all her weight on her hands and felt her shoulders drop. I hadn't planned for this, she thought. Never even anticipated what I'd do if my marriage didn't last. It was *supposed* to last. She filled a Dixie cup with water, swallowed it like a shot, threw the cup in the trash, then felt even more enraged for having been this presumptuous. She wanted to punish herself for being so damn naive, but all she could do right now was kick the hell out of the mirror on the door. A spiderweb spread across the silver surface and made her body look as though it had cracked into hundreds of broken pieces.

'A pack of Kools, please,' she said to the man behind the counter at the Circle K.

'You ain't got nothin' smaller?' he asked, trying to give her back the hundred-dollar bill she had handed him.

'I don't know,' she said, and didn't bother to look. He was staring at her rather strangely, because although he saw crazies up here from time to time, this one looked sane, except why was her hair in them Shirley

40

Temple-looking curls, like she just took out her rollers and didn't comb it? And why was she wearing a bathrobe and fancy bedroom slippers and a diamond ring what looked as big as that one Liz Taylor got? It looked like she'd been crying, 'cause her eyes was blood red, but then again, he thought, it could be drugs. That's probably it. She ain't been to sleep. A whole heap of these rich white women what live up here don't do nothin' but pop pills and drink all day long, 'cause they come in here to get their liquor and I see them little white bags with the writing on 'em from Walgreen's when they open their purses. That's a shame, he thought, as he watched Bernadine try to stuff all those bills inside her wallet. This one here's black.

Bernadine had not remembered leaving the house, or driving, or the fact that John had left before her. She did not remember falling down the two steps outside her bedroom when she had gone to look for her purse. She didn't know that right this minute the kids were still asleep, alone in the house, nor did she realize that for February, it was a record 90 degrees outside. When she got back into her car and turned on the ignition, not only did she not hear it, but her hands didn't feel the steering wheel, and the music coming out of the radio sounded muffled and distant, even though it was loud. Bernadine was trying to keep her eyes open, and when she looked out the window, everything she saw was gray. She knew that heat was silver, but when she blinked, everything was still gray. She pushed in the lighter and ripped the cellophane off the pack. When the lighter popped out, she lit her cigarette and sucked in the cool smoke. She did not cough. She sank into the sheepskinned seat, pushed the gear in reverse, pulled out of the parking space without looking over her shoulder, and tried to remember which way led home.

41

Forget What I Just Said

They say love is a two-way street. But I don't believe it, because the one I've been on for the last two years was a dirt road. I finally gave up on Russell – a lying, sneaky, whorish Pisces – after realizing he was never gonna marry me. The first time I asked him about it, he said, 'Just be patient, baby.' And I was. Six more months went by, and he never once brought the subject back up. That's when it dawned on me that I could be living with him for the rest of my life.

Last January, we went to see *The Accidental Tourist* and came home and made some serious love. I knew Russell was in a luscious mood, so I figured this was the perfect time to bring it up again. And you know what he said? That marriage was a scary thing and he still wasn't ready to 'make that move' yet.

I pushed him off of me and sat up. 'What's so scary about it?'

'Everything,' he said, and started stroking my breasts.

'Russell, it's not prison,' I said, and brushed his hand away. 'We've been living together a whole year. What's the difference?'

'There's a *big* difference.'

'Russell, do you *really* love me?'

'Of course I love you,' he said, and started kissing my arm.

'Don't I make you happy?'

'Very.'

'Don't I satisfy you?'

'Definitely.'

'Then I don't understand what the problem is. You're thirty-seven years old, Russell.'

'I know that.'

42

'And I'll be thirty-five in six months.'

'I know that too,' he said. Now he was circling my belly button with his index finger.

'Well, when do you think you'll be ready?' I said, and slapped the top of his hand.

'Soon,' he said, and rolled over. 'I do wanna marry you, Robin. But it's a big commitment, and I'm just trying to get used to the whole idea. And as soon as I am, believe me, baby, you'll be the first to know.'

So, like a fool, I kept my fingers crossed and hung in there another six months. I didn't wanna lose Russell. I'd had five serious relationships over the last seven years, and two of them ended because they met somebody else. I was determined not to let that happen again. I did everything in my power to make sure Russell would keep loving me. I kept myself up. Worked out four days a week, and he hardly ever saw me without my makeup. I spent a fortune on this weave, and mine looks as good as – if not better than – Janet Jackson's. I used to do my own press-on nails, but I let Gloria give me some acrylics after Bernadine finally told me how tacky they looked. My polish was never chipped, I always got a fill when I needed one, and my feet were never crusty because I got a pedicure once, sometimes twice, a month. I kept this apartment spotless, and Russell never had to so much as empty the trash. I warned him ahead of time that I couldn't cook, but he said he didn't care. He was also the outdoorsy type, liked to go camping, hiking, and fishing. I hated sleeping outside, not being able to go to a real bathroom, and fishing was totally boring, but I didn't complain. I went anyway. And on top of everything else, I gave him as much pussy as he wanted, whenever he wanted it, even when I was dead tired. What more could a man ask for?

When I first met Russell, he was living with some woman in this super-deluxe apartment complex, but he came home from work one day and she had moved out. Took everything. I hate to say it, but I was glad.

I was tired of 'laying low' and sneaking. Tired of him getting up in the middle of the night to go home, and really tired of not being able to call him except when she was out of town. He worked on a train, for Southern Pacific Railroad, so I couldn't exactly call him at work. I went over there a few times, but I never slept with him in their bed. That I refused to do. I did have some pride. Russell said that even though he could afford to keep the apartment, what was the point? He had told me at least a hundred times that as soon as he could figure out a way to end the relationship amicably, he would, because he loved me and couldn't wait until the time came when he could be with me twenty-four hours a day. 'I guess things happen for a reason, don't they, baby?' he said. This psychic I go to, who's also a numerologist, had just told me something similar the week before: 'Timing is everything,' she said. And since I was entering a four personal month, she told me that 'some mistakes would soon be corrected.' She didn't say whose, but look at how things turned out.

I didn't want to know why that woman had left him, and didn't ask. I was just happy to have him all to myself, which is why, four days later, I let him move in with me. I felt like I had finally been blessed, because Russell was so fine that every black woman in America in her right mind probably wished she could have him. But he was mine now.

He did have a few problems. Problems I thought I could help fix. First of all, Russell was in so much debt I borrowed three thousand dollars from my parents and lent it to him so he wouldn't have to file Chapter 11. He got in a minor car accident, and as it turned out, his insurance had just been canceled, but since I work for one of the biggest insurance companies in Phoenix, I made a few phone calls and was able to get him a backdated policy, and at a cheaper rate than he was paying before. He was having a string of bad luck, because then somebody stole his car, so I cosigned for him to get another one, because he couldn't go to work on his motorcycle.

To make a long story short, everything was fine until I found that half-slip in his gym bag and noticed quite a few of the Calvin Klein briefs I'd bought him started disappearing. And just like they do on TV, he started playing poker every Friday night with the fellas. Well, color me stupid, because I didn't want to believe he was seeing another woman. My mother always told me that things are never as bad as they look and to always give a person the benefit of the doubt. So I didn't mention the slip to Russell. I racked my brain trying to figure out what I wasn't doing enough of that might make him want to stray. Bernadine said I should just blow his brains out, because that's what she'd do if she ever found out John was cheating on her. Gloria told me to open my eyes and stop acting like I was blind. My mother said to make sure he used a condom from now on, and my daddy, who has Alzheimer's, didn't understand what the big fuss was all about.

I couldn't give up without a fight, so I tried harder and harder and even harder than that to please him. I loved Russell and wanted him to marry me so I could have his baby. I'd had a million dreams about it. But I know what my karmic lessons are. My numerology book says I'm too decentralized and will have a tendency to fight to express myself, because I'm always going to meet opposition. It also said I might want to consider changing my name in order to get a better vibration, because I'll never be able to 'see the woods for the trees' as long as I'm a five. But I can't do that. Russell's numbers are worse than mine. He's full of fours. Which means he's irresponsible, tends to be scattered, restless, and dissatisfied, and in case of fire, he would seek all doors at once and, finding none, would run around in circles, screaming. Until he learned his karmic lessons he'd be a pleasure-seeker, constantly demanding change. But our Life Paths added up to the same number, so I figured he

45

was supposed to be a part of my destiny, which was one reason why I couldn't let him go.

The next thing I know, some woman starts calling the house and hanging up. Then I get this anonymous letter at work, marked Confidential, but my secretary claimed she didn't see that, so she opened it. I didn't know what to think after I read it. It was typed. And it said this: 'You're one stupid woman. Do you realize that the only reason Russell moved in with you was because the woman he was living with took his name off the lease, and since his credit was so bad, they evicted him? Did you know that? Did you know that a totally *different* woman helped him buy that 325i and when he got behind three payments she took his name off the title and reclaimed it? I bet he told you somebody stole it, didn't he? How much have *you* lent him? Has he promised to marry you too? Do you get the feeling that he's stalling because he keeps coming up with all kinds of lame-ass excuses why he can't "make that move yet"? Dream on, honey. Dream on. You better get out now while you can.' Whoever it was signed her name: 'Burned Once But Not Twice.'

I tore it to pieces. But I told Russell about it, and you know what he said? It must be some disgruntled woman from his past, trying to get back at him. He said he had no idea who it could be, and if I believed that bullshit, then it just meant I didn't have very much faith in him, and how could he think of marrying somebody who didn't have any faith in him? A few weeks went by. It was the Fourth of July weekend, and we had just come back from tubing on the Arizona River. We went on Russell's motorcycle, and when he pulled into the parking space next to our cars, somebody had slit the top of my 5.0 to shreds. That was the last straw. I didn't want to hear another one of his tired excuses. He couldn't apologize his way out of this. So I packed his clothes and put his ass out.

Once it sunk in that he was really gone, it felt like there was this big hole in my life that needed to be filled. I was a mess. I lost eight pounds in two weeks, and still haven't been able to gain it back. I didn't have that much ass to begin with, and now it's *gone*. I don't know why I didn't get fired: I forgot about meetings I had with brokers and couldn't come up with quotes I'd promised. At night I sat by the phone, waiting for it to ring, and when it did, it was never him.

But I got tired of being depressed, so to make myself feel better, I went on an extended shopping spree: from July until right after Christmas. If somebody was having a sale, I was there when the doors opened. I also became the queen of mail order. At least two or three times a week the UPS man would ring my doorbell or leave the packages behind the big pot of jumping cholla outside my front door. It felt good coming home and finding these boxes waiting for me. Half the time I forgot what I ordered, but I made a game out of trying to guess what was underneath the tissue paper. I ran all of my credit cards up to their limit, which was why I had to get that consolidation loan last month. The bank made me cut all nine of them up, right there in that office, but thank God they let me keep my Visa and Spiegel cards. Russell still hasn't paid me back a dime.

I did not like being by myself and wasn't used to it. I can't remember the last time I didn't have a man in my life. I needed some form of male stimulation and companionship before I went crazy or bankrupt, so I started making myself visible and accessible again. It didn't take long for me to find out that the pickings were slim, and I didn't know how rough it was 'out there' until I found myself out there. But this time around, I was determined to learn how to tell the difference between the Real Thing and the Pretenders, and in the course of doing this, I spent many an evening with quite a few understudies. I call it trial and error.

These New Men of the Nineties are scared of women like me. I thought if I was honest and told them what

I wanted, then all the cards would be on the table. Silly me. All I did was tell a few of them I was interested in having a serious relationship because I wanted to get married and have a baby. They ran like mice. What was the big deal?

I have always fantasized about what life would be like when I got married and had kids. I imagined it would be beautiful. I imagined it would be just like it was in the movies. We would fall hopelessly in love, and our wedding picture would get in *Jet* magazine. We would have a houseful of kids, because I hated being an only child. I would be a model mother. We would have an occasional fight, but we would always make up. And instead of drying up, our love would grow. We would be one hundred per cent faithful to each other. People would envy us, wish they had what we had, and they'd ask us forty years later how we managed to beat the odds and still be so happy.

I was this stupid for a long time.

Lately, though, I've had to ask myself some pretty tough questions, like, What am I doing wrong? And why do I keep picking the wrong men to fall in love with? I don't know what I'm doing wrong, to tell the truth, but I do know that one of my major weaknesses has always been pretty men with big dicks. And Russell definitely fit the bill. I've been trying to figure out a way to get over this syndrome, but it's hard, especially when that's all you're used to.

I should've paid closer attention to what Linda Goodman and the Chinese astrologers have been saying all along. That I should stay away from Pisceans, Virgos, Aries, Libras, and Geminis. They're a disturbed group. And forget about those Boars, Cocks, Dragons, and Rats. I've had it with men born under these signs, I don't care how good they look or how big the bulge is in their pants. I've dated at least twenty or thirty of these weirdos, enough to notice similar patterns in their behavior, and it's taken me a long time to gain this astrological insight: Pisceans are habitual liars, lazy, irresponsible, and have no willpower; Virgos are perfectionists, obsessive about *everything*, and freaks in bed; Aries are egomaniacs, narcissistic, and have run-for-your-life tempers, but they're exquisite lovers; Libras are too sentimental and jealous, and so possessive you end up not wanting to sleep with them at all; and Geminis are boring as hell, but they think they're deep, and I've never met one who could fuck.

I can't say I haven't been tempted to take Russell back, especially since he's been bugging me these last couple of months to do just that. He said he missed me something fierce and had mended his ways. But he couldn't prove it. I admit that I made the mistake of letting him spend the night a few times during the siege of my first dry spell, but last week Gloria told me something that made me want to spit nails. Desiree, the girl down at Oasis Hair who does my weave, told Gloria she saw this woman named Carolyn driving Russell's car, the car I basically bought him, and if she wasn't mistaken, when she got out, the woman looked pregnant. I told Gloria that Russell wasn't the only one in Phoenix who drove a black Z. 'I know that,' she said, 'but who else do you know whose license plates say SUAVE?'

Now I knew I didn't have dibs on him any more, but I wanted to hear it from the horse's mouth, so I left an urgent message for him at his job. He didn't call me back until two days later. He said he didn't know anybody named Carolyn. And as far as he knew, no woman was carrying his baby. But I knew he was lying through his teeth. I called him a low-life, garbage-eating javelina and hung up on him. He called me right back and said he didn't know who was spreading all these lies about him, but I could believe it if I wanted to. He said he was still interested in marrying me, as soon as he got his finances together, which he hoped would be some time this year. And maybe we could work on having a baby too. But he sounded like a damn fool. He had humiliated me for too long and now embarrassed me no end. What I *would* like to do is give his ass to the dog pound so they could make soap out of him, or call the FBI and tell them he's responsible for those ax murders I just read about in the paper. I wish there was some way I could give him life imprisonment, because he needs to be stopped. He needs to suffer for a while, long enough for him to realize that a woman's love is a privilege and not his right.

There's no sense in me lying about it. I'm desperate. I haven't been 'out' with a man now in over a month. I've been trying to convince myself that I'm still a good catch, but I can't pass a mirror these days without staring at myself. All I do is look for new flaws, trying to forgive myself for not looking twenty-four any more and apologizing for being a six instead of a ten. I know I've limited myself by only dealing with pretty boys, which is probably the main reason I'm going to the other extreme tonight.

Right now I'm sitting here waiting for Michael, this man who's coming over for dinner. Michael is not pretty, but he's available. He's also a half hour late, and you think he's called? Maybe something happened to him. I hope nothing's happened to him. This is our first date. We work at the same insurance company, but in different departments. To be honest, Michael never dredged up much in me until I'd gone through my old phone book and noticed that all the men I used to date had been crossed off: the ones who'd gotten married or moved or were so pitiful in bed that I didn't have any other choice but to draw a line through their name. So when I saw Michael's picture in our newsletter sitting at his desk, saying he'd been promoted to marketing rep, which was why I hadn't seen him on the elevator lately, and it was clear that he wasn't wearing a wedding ring any more, and since I'd just finished this assertiveness training seminar at Black Women on the Move, I decided to be assertive and sent him a note of congratulations. It couldn't have been more than two hours after I'd put it in our interoffice mail that he called and invited me to lunch. In his office. Needless to say, I accepted his invitation without thinking of the consequences, because I've never dated anybody I worked with. Well, once, but he doesn't count.

Anyway, he had already ordered two turkey and Swiss sandwiches, diet Pepsis, and Doritos. I must admit that his presumptuousness turned me on in a weird sort of way. I like men who take control. His teeth were obviously all capped, so they were nice and white, and he had sleepy eyes, which some women would call sexy bedroom eyes, but he looked like he'd had too much to drink to me. I put him at about thirty-eight or thirty-nine, because he was starting to get those laugh lines when he wasn't even laughing. Michael also had the shortest, fattest little hands I'd ever seen on any man, and I've heard all the stories about short men with thick fingers before, but there's a whole lot of lies floating around in the world that have become myths that ignorant folks believe. I say make me a believer.

After the small talk about his two diseased marriages, two consequential children, dialing-for-dollars divorces, office politics, and what have you, it was clear to me that he was what teenagers call a nerd. But when Michael leaned forward in his chair and said, 'So tell me, Robin, why isn't a beautiful woman such as yourself happily married?' he got my deepest attention, and all I could say was, 'Because I haven't met a man I want to marry yet.' I didn't dare tell him the truth, that no-one had ever asked me, and Russell's phony little lightweight desperation plea doesn't even count. I couldn't believe Michael called me beautiful.

'What about you, Michael? Do you think you'll ever say "I do" again?'

'Certainly,' he said. 'It's not that marriage itself is bad; it's the people we marry who give it a bad name.' Then he sort of chuckled. 'I think I'm wiser now, so I'll make a much better assessment the next time.'

Assessment? Is that what you guys do, I thought, assess us? Well, if I had to *assess* him right now, on a scale of one to ten, I'd be generous in giving him a five. First of all, he's definitely not my type. He's light-skinned — pale when you get right down to it — and how about those freckles? His hair is that rusty reddish-brown, and he's about two inches shorter than I am, which would make him a whopping five foot seven. He's obviously not spending any time at the gym, because he's leaning toward pudgy. But I will say one thing. That baritone voice and those juicy lips could tip the scale in his favor.

So I had lunch with him again the next day, because he asked me. This time we went out to eat. Most men usually talk about themselves until you don't have any questions left to ask, but not Michael. He was actually curious about me.

'So, Robin,' he said. 'Tell me a little more about yourself.'

I had already told him that I graduated from ASU and majored in anthropology, that I grew up in Sierra Vista because my daddy was in the army, and that I was an only child. 'What else do you want to know?'

'How old are you?'

'How old do you think I am?'

'Twenty-seven. Twenty-nine at the most.'

He got three points for that. 'Thirty-five,' I said.

'No kidding.'

'No kidding,' I said.

'Where's your family?'

'In Tucson.'

'So at least you get to visit them.'

'Yeah, I do, but it's not all that pleasant. My parents've been through living hell these last few years. My mother had to have a double mastectomy, and then two years ago my father was diagnosed with Alzheimer's.'

'I'm sorry to hear that, Robin. Is he still able to be at home?'

'Yeah. Which is one reason why I try to get down there at least twice a month to help my mother out. He can't do too much for himself any more. Look, can we talk about something else?'

'OK,' he said, and took a sip of his coffee. 'Do you have any hobbies?'

'Hobbies?'

'You know, things you like to do on a regular basis.'

'I used to sew a lot, make quilts, but I don't have much time for it any more. I do collect black dolls, though.'

'Really? What's your favorite color?'

'Orange.'

'Favorite place?'

'Hawaii.'

'Fruit?'

'Plums.'

'Movie?'

'I don't know. What is this, *Jeopardy*?'

He laughed. 'I'm just trying to make getting to know you more fun, that's all. If it bothers you, I can stop.'

'No. Let me think. One of my favorite movies of all time was *Body Heat*, and I have to put *Raging Bull* in there and *Raiders of the Lost Ark*.'

Michael smiled. I didn't notice until now that he had a rather sexy, self-assured smile. 'So do you have a steady?' he asked.

How corny, I thought, but at least he wanted to know, and for that reason I thought it would be smart not to tell the truth. 'Well, I've been seeing someone on a regular basis, if that's what you mean, but how serious it is, I'm not sure yet. Why?'

'I just wanted to know if I was walking in on something.'

Had I opened a door and said, 'Michael, come on in,' without knowing it, or was I projecting that hungry

53

look? He looked me dead in the eye, and I noticed that they were a soft brown, the whites were milky white, and they *were* kind of dreamy. Maybe he had some other redeeming qualities that weren't so visible to the naked eye. But enough already, Robin. The last thing you need is to get yourself all tangled up with a chubby little dweeb from the office. However, since he'd started this conversation on hobbies and what have you, I felt obligated to ask him. 'So, Michael. Do *you* have any hobbies?'

'As a matter of fact, I do. Drag racing, for one.'

I almost choked on my diet Pepsi. Michael a drag racer?

'And deep-sea fishing and scuba diving.'

'Where do you do all of these things?'

'Mexico. I also have a boat that I like to cruise around in when I can.'

I swallowed hard. This was unreal. 'Here in Phoenix?'

'No; I keep it up in the White Mountains.'

'You're not making this up, are you, to impress me?'

'There's a whole lot of other things I'd be more inclined to lie about if I was just trying to impress you, Robin.'

Then he started talking about the insurance business. He wanted to know how long I'd been in underwriting, but I didn't want to talk about insurance, so finally I just interrupted him and came right on out and asked him. 'When's your birthday?'

'June second,' he said, and sprinkled some salt on his french fries. 'Why?'

'I was just curious.' I found a slice of avocado in my salad, pierced my fork into it, and sighed. Another Gemini. By anybody else's standards, Michael would be considered a good catch – as catches go. He appears to be intelligent, tries hard to be witty, has a good job, and hell, he's available. So far he has been kind of charming and somewhat interesting and definitely a gentleman, which was a nice change of pace. I looked at him a few more minutes and didn't feel any disgust whatsoever. If I'm lucky, maybe his rising and moon signs are in Scorpio or Aquarius. Should I go ahead and give Michael a chance? I asked myself. Should I just forget all about astrology and try not to judge the man before I get to know him?

My questions were answered when I got to work the following morning and found a big bouquet of spring flowers on my desk. I hadn't decided if I actually liked Michael or not, and when I decided that I did like him a little bit I couldn't put my finger on why. I knew I wasn't attracted to him physically, but maybe that's what I needed: the kind of man every woman wouldn't be drooling over. Somebody decent and ordinary. But shoot, he could still turn out to be another Pretender. However. There was one way to find out.

So here I am, waiting.

I'm wearing bright orange tonight because I had my color chart done and Sunanda told me to wear warm colors if I want to emit warmth. I do. I definitely do. But maybe this color is too strong for Michael. Maybe he'll think I'm a hot number right off the bat and read me the wrong way. I ran into the bedroom and changed into a soft yellow sweater, then slipped a lace handkerchief into my skirt pocket. I was staring at myself in the mirror, trying to give myself approval, when Gloria and Bernadine popped into my mind. While I fastened all but the top three pearl buttons, I heard them cackling. They think I have poor taste in men (they despised Russell), and they also think I'm a nymphomaniac, which is why they jokingly refer to me as 'the whore.' But they're just envious. Bernadine has a husband she doesn't want to fuck, and Gloria doesn't know anybody who wants to fuck her. We fight like sisters, but I don't know what I'd do without them. When my mother was in the hospital, Bernadine and Gloria were right there. And when we found out that Daddy had Alzheimer's, my mother asked me when I could pay her back the three thousand dollars because they'd be needing that money real soon. Of course I didn't know when I'd have it, so Bernadine just wrote me a check and told me to forget about it. And when me and Russell broke up, it was Bernadine and Gloria who dragged me out of this apartment and treated me to a Beauty Day at Canyon Ranch and called me every three hours to make sure I was holding up OK. They're the ones who always send me flowers on my birthday, and we draw names at Christmas. They're both older than I am, which is why they're always offering me advice I don't need. And by their account, you'd swear I've slept with half the men in Phoenix, Scottsdale, and Tempe. But that's not true. I've slept with my share, mind you, but hell, this valley is pretty small.

I can't deny that before I met Russell and right after I broke up with him I was a little generous in the loose-sex department. And I admit that I sometimes find myself at parties and other social functions where I can count how many of the men in the room I've slept with. Unfortunately, in some rare instances, more than one is aware of the other. It's a small world.

I really have no business getting involved with somebody from my office, now do I? Especially since Michael already told me he thinks my being an underwriter is great, based on how fast I've moved up in the company. But he just doesn't know. I'm living from paycheck to paycheck and am scared to answer my phone sometimes because I know it might be the student-loan people. Since my daddy's been sick, the money he and my mother had put away for their retirement is dwindling fast, and I'm not in any position right now to help them out. And they need help. Plus, I'm tired of working ten- and twelve-hour days. I'll be the first to admit it: I would be content being a housewife if I could find the kind of man who wouldn't treat me like one. I want to know what it feels like to be pampered, to not have to worry about how high the phone bill is or if the rent is going up. I would like to have at least two

56

kids before menopause sets in. I don't want to have to drag them to the Before School Program at seven-thirty in the morning and have to break my neck in rush hour to pick them up before six, like Bernadine and some of my other girlfriends do. Their kids spend more time away from home than they do at home. I'd also like to have some time to work on my quilting again and do laps and read books and take my kids to ballet or karate and piano lessons after school and still be home in time to grin in my husband's face. I'd like to go to the gym and work out when everybody else is at work. Shoot, I'd like to do some charity work. Take weekend trips. And I'd love to be able to go to the grocery store any weekday afternoon I choose instead of on Saturday mornings. And I want to live in a house, because now that I owe the IRS every year, I don't know when I'll ever have enough money for a down payment.

I just heard the doorbell.

Before I answered it, I checked to make sure the flowers I bought myself with the card signed by a man I made up were prominently displayed. I want Michael to think he's got some competition. I also took off Reba McEntire and put on Freddie Jackson. I'd already sprayed some Glade Spring Fresh throughout the whole apartment and sprinkled a few drops of Halston on all four of my pillows – just in case. I blotted my orange lips on a tissue so that when he kisses me it won't be smeared all over his. I opened the door. 'Hi,' he said.

Michael looked taller, and he didn't look quite so dorky, either. Why was that? I wondered. 'Hi,' I said.

'I'm sorry I'm late. I was stuck in traffic and couldn't call,' he said, and walked right past me. What about my kiss?

His hair was different. It was slicked back and had little ripples of waves in it. Not bad, Michael. 'I was getting worried that something had happened to you.'

'Well, that was sweet,' he said, and walked over and sat down on the couch. 'Something sure smells good.'

I'd almost forgotten about dinner and had to think for a minute what I'd bought. Stuffed shells from the Price Club, smothered in Classico basil and tomato sauce, along with Italian bread sticks. I had two bottles of wine and had opened one. I made the spinach salad myself.

'Your place is very nice,' he said.

'Thank you, Michael.'

'Beautiful flowers,' he said, touching a gladiola petal. Then he looked at me with a smile on his face and said, 'So, Robin, did you buy these for yourself, or do I have some fierce competition out there?' He winked at me. 'You don't have to answer that,' he said.

'Are you hungry?' I asked.

'Starving.'

I betcha, I thought, but I just said, 'Good, then let's eat!'

We ate. And went through a bottle of wine before I even thought to pull out the Price Club cheesecake. Freddie Jackson was sounding even better, now that Michael and I were both feeling pretty mellow. 'Dessert?' I asked him.

'Yes,' he said, but before I could get up from the table to get the cheesecake, he said, 'I'd like to taste you.' His bushy eyebrows moved up and down.

'Me?' I said, unable to think of anything better.

Michael got up from the table and took my hand, then led me to the couch.

'You're a great cook,' he said, and I just said thank you, because I felt like taking the credit. Before I knew it, he was kissing me. For such a short man, he had an awfully long tongue, and a wild one at that. I pulled away, then pressed my lips on the side of his and tried not to let the saliva running out the corners of my mouth distract me. I repositioned myself and went to put my tongue in his ear, but it was full of this hard hair that made me change my mind. I rested my chin on his shoulder and pressed my breasts against his chest. For a minute there, I thought I was hugging another woman. I felt these two soft spongelike things on his chest. So I backed away, unbuttoned his shirt, and put my hand inside, only to feel this fatty substance that should've been muscles on his chest. Michael was about a 38B. I was repulsed, but I couldn't say anything, because he was kissing me again and pulling me down on top of him. When I looked at him, his eyes, of course, were closed, and I closed mine for different reasons: I was trying to pretend that he was Russell. But Michael was too soft. What had I gotten myself into?

'You feel better than I thought you would,' he said.

I didn't say anything, because I couldn't think of anything to say. I would have loved to say, 'Let go of me and go home and don't come back, you tub of lard,' but you just can't say that kind of thing without hurting somebody's feelings.

The next thing I knew, Michael was lifting me up and carrying me into the bedroom, just as I was entertaining the thought of how to stop him altogether, but once I saw the sweat beads popping off his temples and heard him panting like an asthmatic and what have you, I felt sort of sorry for him. So when my foot crashed into the bathroom door, I just said, 'Wrong room,' and pointed to my bedroom. The room was dark, but after we got inside, he bumped into the bed and sort of dropped me on it. I whispered, 'Just a minute,' and out of sheer habit, went to the bathroom and put in my Today sponge. When I came back, I lit my fat scented candle, and Michael was almost completely undressed, except for his boxer shorts. Since he didn't look like he wanted to do it, I unbuttoned my own sweater and took off my bra. When I saw his eyes grow as big as saucers, I worried about my breasts. With his shorts still on, Michael slid under the covers before I got a chance to see what he had to offer.

'I knew you were going to be beautiful all over,' he said, after I got under the covers. 'And you smell so good.' He put his little fat hand over one of my breasts

59

and squeezed. My nipples immediately deflated.

'Do you have protection, or should I get it?' I asked.

'Right here,' he said, pulling it from the side of the bed. He took his shorts off and threw them on the floor. Then he put his hands under the covers, and his shoulders started jerking, which meant he was having a rough time getting it on.

'Do you need some help?' I asked.

'No no no,' he said. 'There.' He rolled over on top of me, and since I could no longer breathe, let alone move, I couldn't show him how to get me in the mood. He started that slurpy kissing again, and I felt something slide inside me. At first I thought it was his finger, but no, his hands were on the headboard. Then he sort of pushed, and I was waiting for him to push again, so he could get it all the way in, but when he started moving, that's when I realized it was. I was getting pissed off about now, but I tried to keep up with his little short movements, and just when I was getting used to his rhythm he started moving faster and faster and he squeezed me tight against his breasts and yelled, *'God this is good!'* and then all of his weight dropped on me. Was he for real? I just kind of lay there, thinking: Shit, I could've had a V-8. I mean, did he really think he just did something here? A few minutes went by, and he lifted himself up, looked me in the eye, and said, 'I knew you were somebody special. How do you feel?'

'About what?' I asked.

'Me. This. Everything?'

'I feel fine, except I feel like I could use a cigarette.'

'I don't mind a woman who smokes,' he said.

I wanted to say, 'Did anybody ask you?' but instead I said, 'It was just a compliment. I don't smoke,' then I got out of the bed and went into the kitchen to get myself another glass of wine. I drank the whole thing, poured another one, and went back and stood in the bedroom doorway and stared at this human submarine sandwich sitting in my bed. How am I going to get rid of you? I wondered. And God, am I going to have to face you at work too?

'What are you thinking about?' he asked. He was smiling, of course.

'Oh, nothing,' I said.

'You know what?' he said.

'No, what?'

'I like you, I like you a lot.'

'You don't even know me, Michael.'

'I like what I know so far.'

'But you might not like me if you *really* got to know me.'

'Tell me what you want, what you need.'

'What?' He had this satisfied look on his face, like he had the goods on me or something.

'What's your fantasy?'

'What are you talking about, Michael?' I took another sip of my wine and found myself walking over toward the bed, which I had had no intention of doing. For some reason, this didn't feel real, it felt like . . . like a movie. I put my wineglass down and started running my hand through the few curls I had left, and all of a sudden I felt so sexy and aroused it was scary, because I was actually seeing myself outside myself, like I was on a big screen or something, and if I was, this is how I would act, this is what I'd do. So I licked my lips and looked down at Michael until he started to look like Russell, but then I remembered that I hated Russell. Denzel Washington would do, so I thought about him and gave him a wicked grin. The whole time I was rubbing my other hand up and down my thigh, and breathing so hard I could see my breasts rise and fall. This was just great.

'I mean, ideally, what do you want from a man? What would you want a man to be able to do for you?'

Michael was messing everything up, and I wished he would just be quiet. 'Are you serious?' I said, snapping back to reality.

61

'Very.'

'Everything,' I said, trying to recapture my persona, but it was too late. It was gone.

'Be more specific.'

I looked at him sitting up in my bed and realized that this man was dead serious. I moved the glass from the night table and put it on the floor, then sat down at the foot of the bed and said, 'Are you sure you want to hear this?'

'It's the reason I asked.'

He clasped his hands together and put them behind his head. For some weird reason, Michael was starting to look better. Why was that? I wondered. Since he was asking, I figured I should go ahead and tell the truth, because when I got right down to it, what did I have to lose? 'I want to live in a house,' I heard myself say.

'That's easy enough.'

'In Scottsdale.'

'I own a house in Scottsdale.'

'You do?'

'Yep. What else?'

'I'd like to go away for long weekends.' That's when I felt his foot ease under my crotch through the sheet, and then his big toe pushed up and made a tent inside me.

'What else?'

'I'd like to be able to eat out at least once or twice a week.'

'And?'

'Get married and have a baby. Two or three.'

'And?'

'Quit my job until the kids are at least seven.'

'What else?'

'That's enough for now, don't you think?'

'You don't need much,' he said, and motioned for me. Now I was slippery where I should've been earlier, and I sat up and walked on my knees toward the rest of him. I looked down at Michael hard, then harder, and he smiled at me. He's not *that* bad, I thought, and let's face it, Robin, he *is* a good catch, and hell, he's available. I lifted the covers and sat down on his now limp lump. Maybe I could get him to go on a diet. Maybe I could teach him how to fuck. How to use his tongue more efficiently. Maybe I could get him to go to a tanning salon, join the gym, and we could work out together. I could trim those hairs in his ears, couldn't I? I slid my hand between his legs and touched what he obviously assumed was a lethal weapon.

'I could sure get used to you,' he said. He put his arms around me and closed his eyes. Then he fell asleep. I was thinking about waking him up and making him go home, but for some stupid reason, I changed my mind. It felt good having a man in my bed, even if he wasn't exactly my Dream Man.

I fell asleep too, and when I woke up, I decided that I wasn't letting him get out of here without at least giving me some iota of satisfaction. Too many of them get away with this shit as it is. So I rolled over, lifted my hips up, and reached underneath them until I found what I was looking for. I worked it until I got a rise out of it, then I sat down on it and pushed.

'What do *you* want?' I asked Michael, staring down at him and massaging my breasts so he could at least see how it's done.

'I think I've found it,' he said, smiling.

'How can you say that, Michael?'

'Because I've been out here a long time, Robin, and I haven't felt like this in years.'

'Like what?'

'This needed.' After that, he nuzzled me in his arms, and for a minute I let my head rest on the cushion that was his chest. 'I can give you everything you want, everything you need, if you'll let me,' he said.

Without even thinking, I said, 'Are you sure you know what you're saying?'

'I know exactly what I'm saying,' he said. 'I've been watching you for three years. Waiting for this opportunity. So yes, I'm sure.'

I was so flattered that I didn't even realize what my body was doing. It pressed down hard and squirmed, then I leaned forward and whispered in his ear, 'You want to make me happy right now?'

'Yes, I do,' he said.

'Really really happy?'

'Really really happy,' he said.

I leaned back and rocked forward again, this time gently pushing both nipples into his mouth. 'You can start by sucking them gently and slowly.' And he did. And he did it right, and I felt like silk, and for the next few minutes Michael wasn't fat or short or pale and I felt young and beautiful and sexy and desirable, and when I squeezed my pelvis and eyes real tight and my body exploded from the inside out, Michael felt just like the Real Thing and everything was just perfect. For once.

Unanswered Prayers

'Tarik!'

'What?'

'Turn that music down!'

'What'd you say?'

'I said turn that damn music down!'

Gloria was yelling from the upstairs landing, right outside her bedroom doorway, where she was standing butt naked, and didn't move until she could barely hear Run-D.M.C. 'Now would you please call the shop and tell Phillip I'm gonna be about twenty minutes late.'

'Ma, why can't you do it?'

'Because I'm getting ready to take a shower, and look, Tarik, don't give me a hard time today. Just do it!'

'I'll be glad when I'm old enough to get my own pad so I can stop being your slave.'

'What did you say?'

'Nothing.'

Gloria swallowed her blood pressure pill dry, put her bathrobe on, tied it as far as it would go, and stormed downstairs. She was perspiring, mostly because she was about sixty pounds overweight. Tarik's saxophone was hanging around his neck. She felt like strangling him with it, but instead she put her hands on her hips and glared up at him. 'Look. I don't know where you're getting this nasty little attitude from, but you better get it corrected. Today. Is something bothering you, Tarik?'

'Ma, why does something always have to be bothering me? I can't find the phone.'

'Forget it.' She walked over to the couch, flipped all four pillows over until she saw the portable. As always, he had been the last one to use it. She started punching the buttons on the phone so hard that her index finger slid between them, and she had to hang up and dial all over. 'I know one thing – if you don't watch the tone of your voice and change this attitude, the only way you'll see Public Enemy is if they come to this house. And come Friday, if that report card looks anything like it did last time, you'll be using Morse code to talk to all your little girl-friends until I see some improvement. Do I make myself clear?'

Tarik, who was well over six feet tall, looked down at his mother and said, 'I'm doing the best I can, but it's never good enough, so why don't you just go ahead and ground me now?'

'Hello, Phillip?'

'Gloria, sweetheart, what's up?'

'I'm running late. Would you check to see what time my first appointment is?'

'Do not fret, honey. I've got everything under control. Sister Monroe already called and said she'd be a little late, and I told the old biddy if she had any errands to run, to take all the time she needed and go ahead and do 'em. Just kidding,' he said. 'Bernadine had to cancel her eleven o'clock appointment. She said Onika was sick and she had to take her to the doctor this morning. And, honey, some drunk driver hit Gwen's son on his motorcycle last night, but he's OK. Just a few cuts and bruises. And if you ask me, I think they should outlaw those damn things, they're too dangerous, and anybody in their—'

'Phillip?'

'OK. I moved Sister Monroe into Bernadine's slot.'

Gloria looked at the clock above the fireplace. It was nine-fifteen. 'What about Desiree? Is she there yet?'

'Take a wild guess.'

Gloria just shook her head. Desiree was starting to get on her nerves; she was always late, always backed up, and lately the customers had been complaining to Gloria about her. Gloria had hired her less than a year ago, because all of a sudden it seemed like half the black women in Phoenix wanted more hair, and Desiree specialized in weaves. So Gloria didn't want to lose her; she brought in too much money. But with Joseph gone all this week, she'd been shorthanded. 'Thanks, sugar,' she said, and hung up. 'Tarik?'

'Yeah, Ma.'

'What?'

'I mean, Yes, Ma.'

'Look. Who was it that asked if he could drive his own car in his senior year?'

'Me,' he said, lowering his head.

'And who was it that's gotten almost straight A's for the last five years?'

'Me.'

'And now, all of a sudden, whose last two reports cards had too many C's, and a D plus in gym?'

'Mine.'

'So what am I supposed to think?'

'Eleventh grade is harder, Ma.'

'That's horseshit, and you know it. Tarik, sit down for a minute.'

'Do I have to?'

'I said sit your behind down.'

Tarik walked over to the sofa and picked up a peach-colored pillow and put it in his lap.

'Put that pillow down.'

He slung the pillow back where he'd gotten it and then looked bored.

Gloria sat down in the leather chair opposite him and just looked at him for a minute. She wasn't thinking about her shower now, or what time she'd make it into the shop. 'At the rate you're going, if you don't hurry up and clean up your act, you may not see the inside of a college.'

'So?'

'So?' Gloria felt like slapping him across the room, but she hadn't hit this boy since he was thirteen, when he started looking down at her and his hands were already twice the size of hers. 'Oh, so now that you're grown, you've decided you don't want to go to college, is that it?'

'I think I want to go into the navy.'

'The what?'

'The navy. What's wrong with the navy?'

'Nothing is wrong with the navy, but you still have to have a high school diploma. They don't want any dummies in the navy.'

'Oh, I get a couple of C's and one lousy D, and now all of a sudden I'm a dummy?'

'Did you hear me call you a dummy?'

'No.'

'You're a smart boy, Tarik, and I don't want to see you end up like some of these hoodlums out in the street. I just wanna know why your grades are going down.'

'I just told you.'

'Does your daddy's coming here tonight have anything to do with why you're being so testy?'

'No.'

'Then what's bugging you?'

'Nothing's bugging me, Ma.'

'Did he say something on the phone that upset you?'

'No!' he said, and jumped up from the couch. 'Look. I haven't seen the man in two years and he calls and just decides he can fit me into his schedule and I'm supposed to stop everything because he wants to see me? For what? We don't have anything to talk about, and it's not me he wants to see; it's you.'

'That's not true, and you know it. He didn't *have* to call. He didn't *have* to offer to take you to the Grand Canyon, but he did.'

'Where did he sleep when he was here last time?'

'You better watch your mouth. Where he slept was none of your business.'

'He's nothing but a pretty boy who can probably get any woman he wants. I hope you don't think he wants you.'

Gloria picked up the phone and threw it at him, but he was too quick. He ducked out of the way, then rolled his eyes at her and ran upstairs to his room. She heard his door slam. What was she supposed to do with this boy? For fifteen of his sixteen years, she couldn't have asked for a better son. She should've never taken him out of that Christian school. Now he's talking like a hoodlum, dressing like a hoodlum – the boy won't wear shoes, he's got at least seven or eight pairs of leather sneakers – and everything he wears is too big. All he listens to is rap music, as if there's no other kind, and he wears two earrings in one ear and one of those flat-top haircuts with lines zig-zagging all across the back of his head. She went upstairs and knocked on his door. 'Tarik?'

'Yes?'

'Would you open this door for a minute, please?'

'I can hear you.'

'Open this damn door, Tarik.' Gloria, who swore only when she was mad, opened the door herself. 'Look. I don't like all this arguing we've been doing. Let's call a truce.'

'I'm not the one arguing, Ma. You've been jumping on my case about every little thing I do.'

'I don't mean to, and I'm sorry. But, Tarik, we used to talk about everything. We used to be just like friends. But you're changing, and I don't know how to talk to you any more.'

'I'm not changing, Ma. Look, if you want to talk, talk.'

He was making this too hard. She took a deep breath and just blurted out what she was thinking. 'Remember when we talked about drugs?'

'What about drugs?' he asked, while he took off one pair of sneakers and changed into high-tops this time.

'Remember when we talked about peer pressure?'

'Yes.'

'Didn't we agree that if you ever felt inclined to try any, we would talk about it? You could come to me.'

'Oh, so now I'm on drugs, right?'

'I didn't say that, Tarik. But I don't know what to think. You're acting so cocky, and your attitude's getting—'

'I'm not using any drugs, Ma. Believe me. I'm not that stupid. I wish you would give me some credit,' he said, and tied his thick shoestrings twice, then pulled the knots extra hard.

'You're doing something, and whatever it is, I hope you can talk to me or your father about it.'

He bolted straight up and flung his arms into the air. 'You don't get it, do you? That man is not my *father*, he's my *daddy*. If he was my *father*, he'da been here to help you take care of me. If he was my *father*, he'da done more than drop a check in the mail. He'da taken me to my baseball games, to the movies, somewhere – anywhere. I know a whole lot of dudes out here making babies and bragging about it. When Reverend Jones took all of us boys on that camping trip last year, he told us that anybody can *make* a baby but it takes a man to be a father. I see this bastard every two years, and I'm supposed to get excited? *You* get excited, Ma. Can I go to the arcade? Please?'

She knew if she said no, as soon as she left he'd go anyway. 'Just be back in the house by six.'

'I will,' he said, and put his Walkman on. 'Can I get ten dollars?' he asked. 'Please?' Gloria got ten dollars out of her purse. 'Thanks,' he said, and bent down and gave her the habitual kiss on the cheek. She was surprised that he'd done it, and relieved, as she watched him trot down the steps to a beat, his right arm punching the air rhythmically, while he talked or sang – whatever they called it.

She walked back to her bedroom, switched on the ceiling fan, then went into her bathroom and turned on the shower. What was she going to do with this

70

boy? She hoped he wasn't messing around with drugs, especially that new one that's out there: crack. It was treacherous. Too many of her regular customers had had some kind of tragedy happen in their family because of it. Gloria didn't know what was in this stuff, but whatever it was had to be powerful, because it seemed like everybody who tried it got hooked. When she was growing up in Oakland, heroin was the culprit. But she didn't remember heroin becoming an epidemic as fast as this crack mess was. And as usual, it seemed to love black people more than anybody else.

As a matter of fact, the main reason she bought her house in this subdivision was because it was a safe, clean, middle-class neighborhood that happened to be predominantly white. But that's what she felt she had to do to keep Tarik off the streets and get him into one of the best school districts in Phoenix, away from those schools that were already drug- and gang-infested.

Gloria took her robe off, put on her shower cap, and got in the shower. She would die if anything happened to this boy. She had been his mother for almost seventeen years. And for most of those years she had worried. She worried when he was late coming home and would sit by the phone, contemplating when to call the police, because she just knew he was dead, in a gutter, or on the side of a deserted highway somewhere. And she worried about whether or not she'd been doing a good job. She had introduced him to God a long time ago, but she still worried whether or not she had taught him the right things at the right time: manners, kindness, generosity, respect for others and respect for himself; pride in the color of his skin; how to eat at the dinner table and how to act in restaurants; why she'd refused to buy him any kind of guns except water guns; how to talk like he had some sense; how to stick up for himself and fight if talking didn't work; and when he was hurting, she didn't care if it was a scrape or a fall or his feelings, she had told him it was OK for him to cry and to ignore the

71

little boys that called him a sissy. But she wasn't sure if she'd done enough, or if she was doing it right.

She wanted to be a good mother, wanted to expose Tarik to as many different kinds of cultural experiences as she could manage. When he showed an interest in music at seven, she gave him piano lessons; when his lungs got stronger and he said he wanted to learn how to play a horn, she bought him a clarinet; and in high school, he fell in love with the soprano saxophone, so she got him one. Over the years, it was when she watched him do little things – eating without spilling, tying his shoe for the first time, riding a two-wheeler, his first recital, his first nosebleed from a fight – it was during these moments that Gloria would become overwhelmed with the anxiety of being a mother, because it dawned on her that she was responsible for molding and shaping another human being's life. And later, when she watched him make his first basket, his first touchdown, when she saw the first signs of hair on his chin and above his lip, when he backed her car out of the driveway the first time, Gloria developed a different kind of anxiety, the fear of knowing that she was the person who was preparing her son for manhood. What if she forgot something crucial? How would she know? And when would she know it? Who would tell her? And what if she was raising him to be a mama's boy? She regretted all those years she let him sleep with her, but she couldn't help it. Those first few years were lonely, after she moved out of her parents' house and got her own apartment. Her bed was always cold. And Tarik's little body was so warm, and when his tiny feet would rub against her leg, Gloria knew she wasn't alone in this world.

She was in her last year of college when she got pregnant. Most of her girlfriends who'd gotten 'caught' had run straight to the abortion clinic, but Gloria couldn't do that. She had been baptized Catholic, and even though she hardly ever went to church any more, she knew she'd committed a major sin by having sexual intercourse before marriage; there was no way she could commit another. Her girlfriends tried to talk her into getting rid of the baby, telling her how safe and easy it was, and in this situation she shouldn't worry about God, because she was the one who was going to have to take care of it. But Gloria was too scared. And decided that a child's life wasn't such a high price to pay for a sin.

Her parents had insisted that she marry the father, but Gloria couldn't do that, either. First of all, she hadn't exactly been David's girlfriend. She'd been out with him a few times – like half the other black girls on campus. And like them, Gloria had secretly craved him. But who wouldn't, after watching his strong legs jump over those hurdles so fast that his blue-and-white jersey looked like a purple blur; David looked like a floating ballerina when he pole vaulted, a beautiful kangaroo when he broad jumped, and black lightning when he ran the 400. Gloria, who was one of the most striking girls on campus and, at that time, a perfect size nine, had prided herself on resisting David's overtures for two years. She didn't want to be part of his stable. And he seemed to like the chase. But finally she gave in and had coffee with him one afternoon; they went bowling and then to an early movie. When David asked if she'd be his date for one of the biggest frat parties, Gloria was so flattered to have been chosen, she went ahead and accepted. It was a wild night, so wild that she'd had four beers and two rum and Cokes, and she didn't know what to think when she woke up the next morning in his dorm room. She was three months pregnant before she got the courage to tell him, and David was in shock. 'Why didn't you use something? And why didn't you tell me this sooner?' he said. All she could say was, 'I don't know.' David, who was on a track and field scholarship, had been selected to participate in the '72 Olympics. Gloria didn't want to spoil his life or ruin his future because of her own mistake, her own negligence, so she asked if he would do her one favor: after the baby was born, would he just acknowledge that he was the father? She told him she would never ask him for anything except his whereabouts over the years, so that whenever the child was old enough, or curious enough, it would know how to find him. At first David was reluctant, but his parents had laid such a heavy guilt trip on him for being so irresponsible, he agreed to it.

She had majored in theater arts, but Gloria couldn't act to save her life. She yearned to do something involving the theater: set or costume design, lighting, or even stage makeup. After she graduated and had Tarik, Gloria couldn't find a theater job anywhere in the Bay Area that would support her and a child, and by the time Tarik was three, he was severely asthmatic and had so many allergies he could hardly play outside.

They were at their church's Fourth of July picnic in 1975 when Gloria's mother reached for a bowl of potato salad, dropped it on the grass, and said she felt dizzy. Like she was choking. Pearl suffered from high blood pressure and couldn't seem to keep it under control. Before the ambulance made it to the site, she was dead. Gloria's daddy was so distraught that a week after the funeral, he couldn't stand being in that house alone and decided to drive down to Alabama, where his people were. Gloria told him she didn't think it was a good idea; but he insisted the drive would do him good. On the way there, he fell asleep behind the wheel. His car overturned and crushed him. Shortly afterward, Gloria decided to leave California. She didn't have any reason to stay there now. She picked Phoenix, not knowing anybody there and not caring. At least Tarik would be able to breathe.

She sold her parents' house, donated some of the money to their church, put the rest in the bank, and enrolled in cosmetology school. Gloria had always cut and styled and dyed the hair of half the women in her neighborhood anyway. It seemed as though doing hair was as dramatic as she was going to get.

Over the next few years, David sent money and came to see Tarik a few times. Tarik's asthma got less severe, and the allergy shots he had to get once a week helped, but he still couldn't play in the grass, and his first furry pet, which was a rabbit, had to be his last. By the time he was five, Tarik had no memory of his daddy. David had suffered some kind of knee injury that prevented him from becoming a professional athlete; he had gone back to school, gotten his master's degree, and become a physical therapist for other injured athletes. He lived in Seattle and was still single. He traveled year round and only managed to see Tarik every couple of years.

At six, Tarik started asking for a daddy. He had memorized how to say his prayers, and Gloria had always told him that if he wanted something special but reasonable, he should ask God for it; if God felt he deserved it – or he had earned it – He would answer the boy's prayers. So Tarik started praying for a daddy – every single night. It broke Gloria's heart just to listen to him. 'Don't worry,' she'd say. 'One day, Mommy'll get a husband, and you'll have a daddy that lives with us.'

'How come he's not here yet?' he kept asking.

'You have to give God time,' she'd say.

By the time Tarik was seven, he had already lost some of his faith in God, since God hadn't delivered. And that's when he started asking Gloria for a baby sister or brother. She explained that she needed a husband first. 'But you don't got one now and you got me,' he said. She told him that it would be too hard having two kids and no husband, and then she'd look over at his bookshelf and pick out a book, he'd get excited, and that was the end of it, till the next time.

Gloria had no idea how much her life revolved around her son, until he reached that age where he preferred playing with his friends instead of spending his free time with her. Which was when she learned that food was good company. Back then, it was Bernadine who told *her* she needed to get out of the house and branch out socially. But Gloria had lost her social skills, especially when it came to men. She didn't know how to respond to them, so she treated them as if they were children; made herself indispensable and saw that their every need was taken care of. Gloria didn't know a thing about protocol.

She started with the phone calls. She didn't wait for them to call or ask her out a second or third time; she solicited them. Volunteered her services: cooked them meals and would freeze them if they weren't around to eat them; she would rearrange their furniture, clean their apartments, take their clothes to the cleaners and pick them up, and sometimes she even footed the bill for weekend getaways that she had suggested. She thought they would appreciate all these gestures, but the gestures scared most of them away. And by the time Tarik was nine, he was getting all his uncles mixed up.

It took years for Gloria to realize that she was going about this all wrong. Robin, who Gloria knew wasn't the wisest person to take advice from, made a valid point: 'You can't buy a man's love.' But Gloria wanted to know what being in love felt like; she'd read about it in magazines, seen it on TV, heard Robin rant and rave about how good some man had made her feel and how Russell had made her toes curl. For a long time, Gloria waited for her toes to curl. But they never did. It finally got to the point where she got tired of waiting for love and divided all of her attention among God, hair, and her son.

She also got fat. Food became her salvation, her elixir, her husband, and the orgasms she'd never had. She forgot all about men, forgot that she was still an attractive woman, and became a supermom. It was Gloria who took half the neighborhood boys to Little League and soccer practice, flag football, Boy Scout meetings, karate class, puppet shows, and Saturday afternoon movies. And when Tarik had sleepovers, she cooked. She always served his friends homemade waffles and blueberry pancakes for breakfast, and hot lunches: grilled cheese sandwiches and hamburgers and thick soup; and for any occasion she could think of, she baked pies and cakes and cookies. For years, Gloria's house was full of children.

But God and hair and kids turned out not to be enough. And Tarik grew up. And Gloria got fatter. Now it was clear that her reign as mother was almost over, because her 'baby' would be out of high school next year and then he'd probably go away to college, not anybody's navy. What was she going to do with herself then? How was she going to survive? And just how do you go about making a life for yourself when you've been socially crippled and emotionally bankrupt for years?

As Gloria got out of the shower, she was thinking about what Tarik had said this morning: that David really wanted to see her. But Gloria knew that wasn't true. When he was here last time, he had done her a favor by spending the night, because she had damn near begged him. He had done it out of pity, but she didn't care. Though it was obvious that he hadn't enjoyed it, Gloria was grateful that he had been kind enough to touch her. Grateful that after four years, somebody had finally touched her. As she dried herself off, she said a silent prayer that in spite of her weight, maybe he'd have some more mercy for her tonight.

Gloria was coloring Sister Monroe's hair Flame Red.

'Could you leave it in a few minutes extra?' she asked. 'The missionaries are going to Las Vegas next week, and I want to look extra good.'

'Yes, ma'am,' Gloria said, and looked over at Phillip, who was cracking up. Sister Monroe, who was in her late fifties, was a true size twenty-two and wore three-and-a-half-inch heels at least six out of seven days. Her shoe size was six and a half, and she looked like Little Lotta, but you couldn't tell her she wasn't fine, that she didn't look thirty years old and a size fourteen. If so much as a strand of gray hair popped up through that whorish red Gloria'd been putting on her hair for the last four years, she'd run in for a touch-up. 'Get this mess off my head,' she'd say, and wait hours if she didn't have an appointment.

Gloria's rubber gloves were too tight, so she smeared the thick dye on to Sister Monroe's roots as fast as she could, then asked her to sit at an empty dryer, so she could at least start pressing and curling little LaTisha, who'd already been waiting close to an hour. There were at least eight other women and men waiting; a few of them were asleep, the others were reading *Jet, Ebony, Essence* magazine, or an old *National Enquirer* that somebody had left. The reason people didn't mind waiting was that Oasis Hair was one of the few black shops in Phoenix that had a consistent reputation for keeping up with all the latest hairstyles and techniques.

Desiree, who did nothing but weaves, was her own best form of advertising. Somebody had made the mistake of telling her years before that she could be a model, and she'd never forgotten it. Even though she was clearly in her late late thirties, she wore miniskirts when her thighs should've told her it was too late, leggings and crop tops, with a thick belt of fat in between that apparently everybody could see except her. There was no such thing as too much makeup to Desiree, and no-one knew how she did those weaves, considering how long her acrylics were. Cindy was much pleasanter to work with. At twenty-four, she was already divorced and taking care of three kids. She dressed as if she was going to a nine-to-five, which had always been her dream, and although she specialized in individual braids and cornrowing, her own hair was cut short. And no-one seemed to care (considering how everybody was so paranoid about catching AIDS) that Gloria's two best stylists – Phillip, whose hair was platinum, and Joseph, who wore black every single day of the year – were gay. Now she had two full-time manicurists, since it seemed like everybody and their mother couldn't live without acrylics or silk wraps.

Gloria loved the atmosphere of her shop. The place was sort of funky chic – everything was silver, black, purple, and white – and full of hanging plants, all of which were fake. There were huge, colorful posters of black models, male and female, wearing the latest hairstyles. She sold custom-made costume jewelry, T-shirts she made in a class she'd taken, and Brown Sugar panty hose that nobody ever bought.

Most of the people who came to her shop either knew each other or knew of each other, and Phillip and Joseph knew *all* the gossip – a.k.a. dirt – about all of them and usually kept everybody in stitches in the absence of that person on that day. Gloria also had a little TV in the back room, and when it was slow during the week, particularly on Wednesday, which was Senior Citizen Day, they dragged it out front so folks could watch the soaps and game shows. On weekends the shop felt more like a nightclub, because Phillip – who was in charge of entertainment – played nothing but music videos on BET, and Gloria served wine, which she was beginning to think was not such a good idea, because some of her customers were drunk by the time they got in the chair.

'So did you hear about Bernadine?' Phillip now asked Gloria. He was combing Lustrasilk through Sandra's hair. Sandra, who was LaTisha's mama, looked in the mirror to watch Gloria's face.

'No, what? Sit up straight, baby,' Gloria said to a sinking LaTisha.

'John left her, honey. Get ready for this: for a white girl!'

'No, he *didn't*.'

'If you don't want your neck burned, you better stop being so nosy and be still,' he said to Sandra, then turned to Gloria. 'Would I lie about something like this? Tell her, Joseph.'

79

Joseph, who was working at the station next to Cindy, was putting a male customer's hair on rods for a Jheri-Kurl. 'I saw her coming out of a Circle K in Scottsdale last Sunday, and the chile had on her bathrobe and was all messed up. I couldn't believe it was Bernie – I mean, she was so out of it. Anyway, I asked her what was going on. I don't know if you know it but she takes those pills sometimes for her nerves but anyway her speech was slurred and I was scared to death so I told her to drive slowly and I followed her home. She was smoking those disgusting cigarettes again, and she was doing so good, chile. Anyway, she told me that John left her for some white wench named Kathleen. His bookkeeper. And guess what? When we got to her house, the kids were watching cartoons, girl, and had been in the house all by themselves. Can you believe it? Does that tell you what shape our girlfriend was in? Anyway, I hung around there most of the day, fed those kids, made her sleep off them pills, and then called a cab when she woke up and acted like her head was back on straight. So,' he said, after a long sigh, 'you just never know.'

Gloria was shocked. So that's probably why she canceled Onika's appointment this morning. Bernadine was not only one of her best clients but one of her closest friends. They had met six years before, in church. Gloria was sitting next to her and couldn't help but notice how dry and brittle Bernadine's hair was. After the service, she asked Bernadine who did her hair, and Bernadine said she did it herself, so Gloria gave her her card and recommended that Bernadine let her give her a good conditioning. And when women sat in *her* chair, they usually told Gloria all their business. Bernadine was no exception. She had told Gloria how bored she was with her life, and especially with John, but all Gloria could think of was suggesting that she join Black Women on the Move, since Bernadine never mentioned anything about getting a divorce.

'Do you think she's OK?' Gloria asked.

'Well,' Joseph said, 'I haven't talked to her since then, but hell, how would you feel if your husband just came home and told you he was leaving after a million years of marriage — for a white girl?'

'I couldn't imagine,' Gloria said. She put the last curl in LaTisha's hair and picked up the phone. Sister Monroe cleared her throat about ten times. 'I ain't got all day, Gloria, and Lord knows I been patient. Now please get this stuff out of my hair before it goes up in flames for real.'

'Just wait a minute,' Gloria said, and dialed Bernadine's number. Phillip and Joseph put their heads down to hide their laughter. Desiree, who thought she was Miss Sophisticated, ignored all the conversations that went on, because she was 'above' petty gossip. Cindy was listening too, but she never had any comments to make, one way or the other. It was no secret that Phillip and Joseph couldn't stand Sister Monroe, because they thought she was a hypocrite. She was the only Pentecostal they knew whose missionary work always seemed to take her to Las Vegas.

Bernadine's answering machine came on. 'Hey, girl, this is Gloria. What's wrong with Onika? You know what that child's hair looks like if she misses an appointment. Call me.' She didn't want to make mention over the phone that she knew anything. After she hung up, she wanted to call Robin, but when she looked over at Sister Monroe, who was now fuming, she decided to wait.

Tarik wasn't home when she got there. It was almost seven. Before she put her purse down, she called Bernadine and got her machine again. 'Look, Bernie. I hope you're all right. Joseph told me what happened, so call me. I'm worried as hell about you, and I won't be able to rest until I know you're OK. So call me. I don't care how late it is.' She called Robin next but got her machine too, so she asked if she'd talked to Bernadine and, regardless, to call her as soon as possible. It was urgent.

David was supposed to be here around eight. She thought about dinner and realized it would be tacky not to have anything prepared if it turned out he was hungry. And there was Tarik to think about. But she didn't feel like chopping, slicing, or dicing anything. Before Gloria heard about this business with Bernadine, she'd been praying all day that David would spend the night. But right now she didn't care one way or the other. She just hoped nothing terrible had happened to her friend.

She got up and went out to the freezer in the garage and pulled out some spaghetti sauce she'd made. She put it in the microwave to defrost, then went into her bedroom to make sure she looked OK. There were tiny hairs on her blouse, so she dusted them off. Her hair, which was dyed jet black and blunt cut, hung below her jawbone. If her face weren't so fat, she'd cut it all off. Phillip always teased her. 'So what if you're a little on the heavy side, sweetheart. You're still pretty. I'd kill for those cheekbones. So flaunt everything you've got.' Gloria looked at the picture of her and Tarik hanging on the wall. She had to have been a size twelve in that picture, and now she was an eighteen, although twenties felt better. She'd tried every diet on the face of the earth, but starving herself to death off and on for the last two years made her too miserable. It wasn't worth the aggravation, so she stopped trying and accepted the fact that she was fat and was probably always going to be fat.

Gloria was snacking on some cheese and crackers and washing it down with a sixteen-ounce tumbler of diet Pepsi when the phone rang. It was Robin. 'What's so urgent?' she asked.

'Have you talked to Bernie?' Gloria said, and took a sip of her Pepsi.

'Not since last week. Why?'

'You don't have any messages from her at all?'

'No. Gloria, stop beating around the bush. What's going on?'

'John left her.'

'Say that again.'

'John left her.'

'I told you he was an asshole, didn't I?'

'For a white woman.'

'I *know* you're lying, Gloria.'

'I'm dead serious. And Joseph said he saw her last Sunday at a Circle K and she was so out of it that he had to drive her home, but nobody seems to have talked to her since. I wish I knew her mama's last name; she lives out there in Sun City. Anyway, I've left two messages on her machine, but I haven't heard from her yet.'

'Well, I'll keep trying her. I'll call you as soon as I find out what's going on. Wait a minute. Isn't Tarik's daddy coming tonight?'

'He should be here soon, but where that son of mine is, Lord only knows.'

'Look, call me after he leaves.'

'I *was* hoping he doesn't.'

'Listen to Miss Frigid, would you? Well, if something weird has happened to Bernie, I'll just have to interrupt you. You've waited a hundred years to get some, a few more minutes won't kill you.'

'Shut up, Robin. I just hope Bernie's OK.'

'Me too. Talk to you later.'

After she hung up, Gloria walked outside to look for any sign of Tarik. None. She heard the timer for the sprinkler system come on, and found herself staring at the desert flowers and vegetation in her front yard: jumping cholla, ocotillo, prickly pear, organ pipes, purple and pink verbena, Mexican bird of paradise, and mesquite trees. She remembered when she used to think the colors of the desert were ugly, but now this yard looked like an oasis.

She walked back into the house, put a pot of water on for the spaghetti, then made a salad. She was buttering the French bread when the phone rang again. She hoped it was Bernadine.

'Ma, can I spend the night at Bryan's?'

'Don't be ridiculous. Your daddy should be here any minute, so get your behind home. Now. I mean it, Tarik.'

'I don't want to see him.'

'What?'

'I said I don't want to see him.'

'Tarik, all you're doing is making a bad situation worse. Don't make me come over there. Put Bryan's mother on the phone.'

'She's not here. And if you come over here, I'll be gone by then.'

'Why are you doing this, Tarik? What's it proving?'

'It's proving that this man hasn't been in my life for my whole life, so why's he keep making special appearances and thinking I'm supposed to be so happy about it? What does he want from me? That's what I want to know. I don't know him and don't want to know him.' He was quiet, and then he said, 'I just hope he doesn't spend the night.'

So that's what this was about. Now Gloria knew why he'd been acting so ugly all week. 'Well, look, I don't want to force you to see him, but why didn't you tell him yourself?'

'Because I couldn't, Ma.'

'Well,' she sighed, 'go ahead, stay on over there. I'll figure out something to tell him. But what about the plans he made for you tomorrow?'

'Tell him to cancel them or go down to Big Brothers of America. They're looking for stand-ins down there.'

'Watch your mouth, Tarik.'

'I'm sorry, Ma. And thanks for listening to me this time. Will you do me a favor?'

'What's that?'

'Don't have too nice an evening.'

He hung up before she could answer. This was all her fault, really. All she ever wanted was for him to know who his father was. That's all. Now she realized that it was causing more harm than good. She didn't know what she was going to tell David.

Gloria was stirring the spaghetti sauce when she heard a car pull into the driveway. She ran over to the sink and peeked through the mini-blinds. He was still gorgeous, she thought, as she watched him get out of the car. Tarik was built just like him. Strong and muscular. Since she didn't want to appear eager, she stepped away from the window. When the bell rang she counted to three before walking over to the door. She took a deep breath and opened the door slowly. 'Hi, David,' she said.

'Hello, Gloria,' he said, and gave her a weightless hug, then he walked over and sat down in a chair. 'So how are you?'

'I'm fine,' she said.

'You're looking healthy,' he said.

She knew he meant fat, but she said, 'Thanks,' anyway. He was wearing a navy-blue suit with a pale-pink shirt and what she knew was a silk tie and real lizard shoes. He was clean-shaven now – she'd never seen him without a mustache – and he looked like one of those men on the cover of *GQ*.

'I must say your landscaping is stunning,' he said, and crossed, then uncrossed, his legs. He sounded so formal, she thought. No, it wasn't formal. If she closed her eyes, she'd have sworn he was white.

'Thank you,' she said.

'So,' he said, and started drumming the arms of the chair, 'where's Tarik?'

'He's not here right now.'

'Well, I can see that. When will he be back?'

'I'm not sure.'

'Didn't you tell him what time I said I'd be here?'

'Yes, I did.'

85

'Is there a problem, Gloria?'

'Well, he's feeling a little awkward about seeing you.'

'I'm feeling pretty awkward myself. I mean, I don't even know why I continue to do this. I don't know the boy, and he's almost an adult now anyway.'

David was obviously feeling uptight; Gloria saw his jawbone jumping. It also looked as if he was grinding his teeth.

'I made spaghetti, if you'd like to have some dinner,' she said. Now she sounded like him.

'No, thanks. I'm not hungry,' he said. His tone was strained, and it was clear that he was annoyed, but Gloria couldn't much blame him.

'Would you like a glass of wine?'

'A glass of wine would be perfect. Exactly what time are you expecting him?'

'Tomorrow,' she said, and darted toward the kitchen.

'Wait a minute, Gloria. Did you say tomorrow?'

'Yes,' she said.

'Forget about the wine,' he said, and got up.

Gloria turned around to face him. She had a mournful look on her face. 'Are you leaving now?' she asked.

'Yes,' he said.

'You're welcome to stay here.'

'Here?' he said.

'Well, I just thought, maybe, that because last time, well, I just thought that you'd like to stay with us.'

'Look, Gloria. I might as well be honest with you.'

'About what?'

'About me.'

'What about you?'

'Do you remember what happened when I was here the last time?'

'Of course I remember.'

'Do you remember how I didn't respond to you?'

'Well, yes.'

'Did you have any idea as to why?'

'I thought it was because I'd put on so much weight.'

'That was only part of it.'

'Well, what was the other part?' she asked.

'I've been bisexual for some years,' he said, and didn't flinch.

'You've been what?'

'You heard me right. But I'm not any more. I'm gay.'

'You're what?'

'Don't sound so shocked. You're the last person I had to tell, and now it's done.'

'Look, you don't have to go to this extreme just because you don't want to spend the night. I understand.'

'I don't have to lie about this, Gloria. I'd been lying too long as it was, but I thought it was time you knew. By the way, I'm staying at the Biltmore,' he said, and walked toward the door. 'If and when Tarik gets home, tell him where I am. If I don't hear from him by noon, I'm checking out. I mean that literally and figuratively. When and if he ever wants to see me, he'll have to make the next move.' He opened the door, started toward the car, and got in. Then, before he started the engine, he turned and looked at Gloria. There was no expression on his face at all. She watched the wheels of his rented blue Celebrity back out of her driveway, and her eyes followed that car until it turned the corner. The sprinkler clicked off. Gloria backed inside the doorway and closed it. When she sat down, the top button of her blouse popped off, but she didn't get up to find it. Because she couldn't.

Fire

After Joseph left, Bernadine put on a pair of shorts and a T-shirt, packed the kids' overnight bags, told them to get in the car, and headed for Sun City.

'Why come we're going to Granny's?' Onika asked.

'*How* come. Because Mama and Daddy are going on a trip.'

'Why can't we go?' John junior asked.

'Because where we're going is only for grownups.'

'Can't Auntie Robin baby-sit us?'

'No, she can't.'

'I don't want to go to Granny's,' he said.

'And why not?'

'Because she's too mean.'

'She is not mean,' Bernadine said.

'Yes she is.'

'The only reason you think she's mean is because she doesn't let you do whatever you want to do.'

'Uh uh. She yells at us all the time, doesn't she, Onika?'

'Not all the time,' Onika said.

'She does too!'

'Look. Your granny's just got a heavy voice, and you might think she's yelling, but she's not.'

'She won't even let us play in the front yard.'

'You're not supposed to play in the front yard.'

'Or the back.'

'I don't believe you.'

'Uh huh. She won't let us pick the oranges or the grapefruit, and she won't even let us climb that big tree.'

'The fruit's not ripe yet. And that tree is dangerous.'

'She makes us go to bed too early, and she doesn't

have Nintendo, and it's boring at her house.'

'That's just too bad. So stop whining.'

John junior let out a defeated sigh.

Bernadine knew they were telling the truth. Her mother could be a bitch sometimes, but Geneva loved her grandchildren. She just had a strange way of showing it. After driving a school bus for twenty-eight years, she was sick of kids. Her grandchildren were the two exceptions, although sometimes Geneva had to remind herself that they were blood.

'Ma, Onika doesn't have her seat belt on.'

'Onika, put your seat belt on.'

Bernadine pushed the CD button for George Winston's 'Autumn.' She always played him when she needed to relax, but right now she couldn't really appreciate the beauty of much of anything, let alone piano playing. She had forgotten to do something important, but she couldn't remember what it was.

'Ma, do we have to listen to that piano music again?' John junior asked.

'No,' she said, and pressed it off.

'Raffi, Raffi, Raffi!' Onika shouted.

'Stop screaming. I can hear you,' she said. She was not in the mood for kiddie music, but what the hell. She sifted through a stack of tapes until she found it. John junior was now searching for Waldo. 'There's Waldo! I found him again, Ma!' Onika could never find Waldo, and John junior wouldn't tell her where he was when he knew where Waldo was and she'd cry and Bernadine would have to threaten to take the book away and then he'd still only tell his sister if she was getting warm. But *Where's Waldo?* kept them occupied when she drove.

'Good, good, good,' she said to John junior. 'Now let's see how long we can be quiet.'

One whole minute went by.

'Mama, look! McDonald's!' Onika yelled. 'I'm hungry. And I want a toy. Can we have a Happy Meal, please, Mama, please?'

'I'm hungry too,' said John junior. 'But I just want McNuggets with barbecue sauce and french fries and a vanilla shake.'

'All right, all right, all right. Now settle down.' Bernadine didn't have time to put on her blinker. She turned the car into the entrance and whipped up to the drive-through window and gave her order.

'Mama, can we eat it here? I wanna play on the balls,' Onika said.

'I don't want to eat it here. Inspector Gadget is coming on in a few minutes, Ma. Ma, can't we eat it at Granny's?'

'Be quiet! We're already at the drive-up window, I'm in a hurry, and I'm in no mood to sit. You will eat these Happy Meals in the car and enjoy them. Do I make myself clear?'

'Yes,' Onika said.

John junior didn't answer but flipped the large page of his book. 'There's Waldo again!'

When Bernadine handed the kids their boxes, she realized that Onika's hair was a mess. She hadn't combed it in two or three days, and the child looked wild. She wanted to let Gloria give the girl a perm, but John had refused to let her put any chemicals in his daughter's hair. Onika had enough hair for two grown women. Her braids were long and thick. She was so tender-headed that when she even heard the word 'hair' she'd start wailing. A few months ago, Bernadine had finally reached the point where she couldn't stand the squirming and crying any more and started letting Gloria wash it and run a warm comb through it every other Saturday morning. And now that John was gone, Saturday after next, which also happened to be Onika's seventh birthday, she was getting this girl a perm.

Bernadine was on the last long stretch that led to Sun City, a two-lane highway usually filled with old drivers who were afraid to do the speed limit. Traffic was backed up, and Bernadine went through two or three cigarettes just waiting to get to her turnoff, which was five miles up ahead. Thank God it was dinnertime, she thought. Sun City was a sterile place, where mostly retired people lived. For some reason, her mother loved it there. Right after Bernadine's daddy died two years before, Geneva sold their home of forty-two years and bought a town house out here. She said she wanted to be near one of her children in case anything happened to her. Bernadine's two brothers lived in Philadelphia, less than a fifteen-minute drive from Geneva.

As usual, there were no people on her mother's street. Not even so much as a leaf was on the sidewalk. The lawns, manicured to perfection, looked like green velvet. The palm trees all had bushy heads and were straight in a row. Not a single car was parked next to the curb, because it wasn't allowed. Bernadine pulled in front of her mother's town house and honked the horn. It was an adobe, a reddish-brown brick that looked as if it had been dipped in acid. All the houses on the block were identical. When her mother first moved here, the same white-haired white woman answered the door on three different occasions before Bernadine realized she had rung the wrong bell.

Geneva came to the door and put her hands on her hips. As warm as it was, she was wearing a lavender jogging suit. It looked like she had on new glasses too. At sixty-four years old, if her hair hadn't been completely silver, Geneva could probably have passed for fifty. There was hardly a wrinkle on her face. Last year, Bernadine had convinced her to stop dying and relaxing her hair, and now it was natural, curly and short. She'd always been a husky woman, so Geneva watched what she ate, walked a mile every other day, and went to a water aerobics class three times a week. She practically lived at the mall, and Bernadine was glad when somebody there finally showed her how to put her makeup on right. These days, Geneva always looked good. Bernadine found it truly amazing that her mother was better-looking than she was. Wasn't it usually the other way around?

'Well, this is a surprise,' Geneva said. 'What happened? You called and there was no answer?'

'No,' Bernadine said, and got out of the car. The kids were already running toward the door. 'Hi, Granny!' they both yelled.

'Hello, my little dumplings. What's wrong with this girl's hair?'

'I didn't have time to comb it.'

'You have time for everything else. You need to make time.'

Bernadine didn't want to get into it with her today. She was not in the mood and wanted to nip this in the bud now. Geneva was always finding fault with her parenting skills and brought it to Bernadine's attention every opportunity she got. 'Would you mind if the kids stayed with you for a few days?' she asked.

'Where you going?'

'Sedona. John and I are taking a little hiatus.'

'How many days is a few?'

'Four or five.'

'And what are they supposed to do about school? You know I can't drive that far two days in a row, let alone four.'

'I'll call the kids' school and tell 'em they'll be out for a few days.'

'It's Rodeo Days, Ma,' John junior said. 'We only have three days of school next week.'

Bernadine had forgotten, but that wasn't what she was trying to remember. 'Good. Then you guys can have the whole week off.'

John junior jumped up and down, but Onika was clearly upset. 'I wanna go to school,' she said.

'Be quiet,' he said to her. 'First grade isn't a big deal.'

'It is too, and I'm the Special Person this week.'

'It's week after next,' Bernadine corrected her. 'Two days after your birthday.'

'Is everything all right?' Geneva said to Bernadine.

'Everything is fine. We just need a break.'

'Now tell me again. Exactly what day are you planning on coming back?'

'Late Friday or the first thing Saturday morning. Is that OK?'

'My golf lesson is at eight on Saturday, and I won't mind so much if I miss that, but don't make me miss that bus to Laughlin. It leaves at ten sharp.'

'You're going to Laughlin again?'

'Why not? Last time, I won ninety-three dollars. I have a good time in Laughlin.'

'Believe me, Ma, I know. I'll be back – I mean, we'll be back long before your bus leaves.'

Geneva gave her daughter a questioning look. 'You coming in, or are you gonna stand out here and burn up?'

'I think I should head back. I need to pack.'

'Where's John?'

'He should be on his way home.'

'You sure you're gonna be able to stand being up there by yourselves for four whole days?'

'Yes, Ma.' Bernadine knew what she meant. Her mother never liked John from day one. Geneva wasn't one to bite her tongue and, a couple of years ago, came right out and told Bernadine that she let John control her too much. 'Some women just let a man take over their mind. If you do that, what's left? I'm just waiting for the day to come when you tell me you're divorcing him. But knowing how he is,' Geneva had said, 'I figure he'll probably be the one to leave.'

'Get away from those flowers,' she said now to John junior. 'And come here.' He sauntered over to his granny, and she ran her hand roughly over his head. 'You need a haircut. When was the last time your daddy took you to the barbershop?'

'I don't know,' he said.

'Did you bring these kids something to wear?'

Bernadine reached in the back seat and got Onika's

Barbie overnight case and John's Spider-Man back-pack. The kids ran over to the car and grabbed their respective bags. 'All right, you two. I want you to behave, listen to your granny, do whatever she asks you to do, and don't get on her nerves.' She bent down and gave them both a kiss. 'I'll see you in a few days. Love you.'

'Bye,' they said, and ran back toward the house.

'Stop that running,' Geneva yelled.

Bernadine waved as she drove off. She popped Raffi out and put George Winston back on. The whole car smelled like barbecue sauce. She turned around; Onika had smeared it all over the back seat. French fries were on the floor, and those Happy Meal boxes were sitting side by side, next to a few loose McNuggets.

Before she got on the freeway, she stopped at a Circle K and bought three more packs of Kools. It seemed as if it took her only a few minutes to get home, but it was closer to forty. When she got near her house, she reached up to the sun visor, pressed the Genie, and turned into her driveway as the garage door opened. She parked next to the Cherokee, which was next to John's 1949 Ford, which he kept covered. Bernadine sat there listening to the car idle for five or six minutes. Her hands were gripping the steering wheel. She didn't want to get out. Didn't want to go into that house and face the empty rooms. But she had to. She wanted to know what being by herself was going to feel like. She started crying. Then stopped. Then she cried until her heart literally hurt. She took a napkin from the glove compartment, blew her nose and wiped her eyes, and said, 'Get out of this car.' She grabbed her purse, pressed the Genie again, and heard the garage door slam shut before she got inside the house. 'Hello,' she yelled. The reply she got was her own echo, because the great room – the south-western term for a gigantic room in the middle of the house that served as the living, dining, and family room – had brick walls, sixteen-foot ceilings, and thick concrete beams.

She sat down on the couch, feeling the leather stick to her thighs, opened her purse, and got out her cigarettes. She lit one. And smoked it. Then she lit another one and slid the pack of Kools and the matchbook in her shorts pocket. Bernadine looked at the stone fireplace, which was almost big enough to stand in. There wasn't a trace of ash in it. She scanned the entire room but then stopped. Everything was too goddamn perfect. She was tired of seeing it all, so she stood up and looked down, counting fourteen of the rust-colored tiles before she reached her bedroom. She shut the door, fell on the bed, kicked off her sandals, and closed her eyes, but they popped back open. She was staring at the ceiling. Bernadine saw the number 732. It wasn't written on the ceiling; it was written in her mind. That was how many times John had told her they had made love. She remembered when the figure was 51, and how shocked she was that he'd actually been counting. But after a while, nothing he did surprised her.

She couldn't keep her eyes closed, because they weren't tired. Feeling antsy, she got up and took a Xanax, came back out, and looked at the bookcase, which took up a whole wall. Close to a thousand books, most in alphabetical order, sat on the shelves. John insisted that this was the only way he'd know how to get his hands on a book if he wanted it. There was too much order in this damn house. Everything in the right place. She opened John's closet. His shoes were all lined up nice and neat. His shirts were grouped by color: white, beige, light blue, pink. The suits were in order by designer, starting with Adolfo; sports jackets, trousers, ties too. He had a fit once when he discovered one of Bernadine's blouses mixed in with his shirts.

Now she found herself standing inside the closet, snatching his clothes off the hangers and letting them drop over her arm until she had so many she could hardly carry them. She left the bedroom, went through

95

the great room, picked her keys up from the kitchen counter, and pressed the garage-door button on the wall. She walked out into the driveway, dropped the pile of clothes on the pavement, went back into the garage, got behind the wheel of the BMW, rolled all the windows down, then backed the car out and away from the house. She opened the rear door and threw the pile of clothes on the seat. Bernadine made six more trips before all of John's hangers were empty.

At his side of the dresser, she opened the top drawer. His underwear was folded nice and neat, just the way he liked it. And she should know, because it was her job to make sure his sleeveless undershirts weren't mixed up with the undershirts with sleeves. The V-necks not mixed up with the crew necks. Boxer shorts not mixed up with briefs. Socks were arranged from their opaqueness to their brightness. She put them all in a trash can and proceeded into the bathroom, where she threw every toiletry he owned – including his toothbrush and electric shaver – on top of the socks. When she came back out into the bedroom, she spotted an empty shopping bag, went over to the dresser, and pushed all his bottles of cologne inside it. She heard glass break. On this trip she ran through the garage, before the wet bottles could fall through the bottom. When she hit her baby toe on John junior's roller racer, she remembered the shoes. Onika's little red wagon was over in a corner, so she made three more trips and, on the last one, stopped to pick up a can of lighter fluid. She threw the shoes on the floor of the car, then squeezed at least half the can over the huge heap that had formed in the front and back seats. She pulled the wagon back into the garage, went into the laundry room, washed her hands, and walked outside again. Bernadine then reached into her pocket, got out a cigarette and the pack of matches. She struck the match, tossed it inside the front window, and stepped away from the car. On her way back, she struck another match and lit her cigarette. She

96

heard the fire erupt but wasn't interested in seeing it, so she pushed the garage-door button and returned to the house. When she got to the bedroom, Bernadine picked out a book – *Almost Midnight* – climbed back in bed, and finished her cigarette.

She must have dozed off, but she heard the sirens. One of her nosy neighbors up the road had probably driven by, and thinking the car was going to explode, the way they always do on TV, called the fire department. But Bernadine hadn't heard any explosion. When the doorbell rang, she got up to answer it. She peeked through the glass and saw a fireman standing there. After she opened the door, she smelled smoke. Hot metal. Burnt rubber. Fumes. But the car was still black and recognizable.

'Ma'am, were you aware that your car was on fire?'

Bernadine didn't answer him.

'Did you start this fire, ma'am?'

Bernadine didn't answer him.

'Well, ma'am, it's against the law to burn anything except small amounts of trash in your own yard.'

'It is trash,' she said.

'You know what I mean, ma'am. It should be in some kind of receptacle.'

'I wasn't aware that burning your own property on your own property was against the law.'

'Yes, ma'am, it sure is. Why would you want to burn up a brand-new BMW?'

Bernadine didn't answer him.

He looked at her apprehensively, because he knew exactly what she'd done. 'Look,' he said. 'This is a pretty nice neighborhood you live in, and one of your neighbors was kind enough to notify us, because they thought no-one was at home.'

'I'm grateful,' she said.

'You know your insurance won't cover this.'

'I'm aware of that,' she said.

'And it's a good thing we got here in time, but there's

97

still considerable damage to the interior, as you can see.' He put his hand on his chin and rubbed it. Then sighed. 'Would you do us and your neighbors a favor? The next time you want to set a fire, could you pick something smaller, less expensive, and do it a little more discreetly?'

'It won't happen again,' she said, and closed the door.

The following morning, Bernadine made three phone calls. She called her office and told them there'd been a family emergency and she'd be out for the rest of the week. Her boss asked if there was any possible way she could make it in on Thursday, if only for a few hours, because the Langone property, which had been in escrow for the last twenty-eight days, was scheduled to close that afternoon. After all, they were her client, and she was the one who'd been instrumental in making this whole deal happen, and the Langone people were adamant in their request that she be at the closing. Bernadine said she was sorry, but somebody else would have to do it.

She called Gloria, knowing she wouldn't be home. Gloria always did her grocery shopping on Monday mornings, so Bernadine left a message. 'I know Joseph told you what happened, but I'm all right. So don't be worried about me. I'm going up to Sedona for a few days, and I'll call you as soon as I get back. I mean it, I'm fine. A little shook up, but I'm fine.' Robin was at work, so she called her at home and basically left her the same message.

Over the next four days, Bernadine did not leave the house. She read six books, none of which she could remember. She did not bathe, because she thought about how each and every time she and John had made love he'd made her shower first and sometimes afterward. She was sick of being clean. And the house. She'd kept it spotless for years, but for these four days, whatever she picked up, she left wherever she felt like leaving it. Newspapers were everywhere. Food that she'd decided not to eat after all filled the counters, alongside the box of Pop-Tarts John had left out. She watched TV and played the stereo at the same time. She even spent hours playing Nintendo. The phone had been ringing off the hook, but she didn't dare answer it. Not yet. She didn't feel like talking to anybody. Didn't feel like explaining this shit. And what was there to explain? She had taken the last of her Xanax, and although she was entitled to another refill, she didn't feel like going to get it.

On Friday morning, Bernadine sprang up in bed and realized she'd been in the house for five days, had not bathed, had not brushed her teeth or combed her hair, had hardly eaten, and this bedroom smelled like a pigsty, and so did she. 'I won't let you reduce me to this,' she said out loud, and got up.

The first thing she did was call AAA and have them come and tow the car away. Then she brushed her teeth, took a long shower, washed and conditioned her hair, and pulled it into a ponytail. She put on some clothes and fixed herself two soft-boiled eggs, grits, bacon, and toast. She ate all of it. When she walked back into the bedroom, she emptied the overflowing ashtray, threw the cigarette pack in the trash, but changed her mind and retrieved it. When she saw John's jewelry box sitting on the dresser, she was mad that she'd forgotten to put it with the rest of his stuff.

She spent all day cleaning because the housekeeper came only twice a month. When she finally dragged two giant trash bags into the garage, she looked around and saw so much junk – most of it John's – that Bernadine had a brainstorm. She dropped both bags into the trash container, ran back to the house, got the number for the newspaper, and called the classified section. 'I'd like to place an ad in tomorrow's paper for a garage sale,' she said. 'Yes, I have a credit card.' She gave them her Visa number, address, and phone number, and told the man how she wanted the ad to read: 'Fantastic Estate Sale: Saturday Only. Eight to one. Bargains Galore! Scottsdale! Everything: $1.00. Come see for yourself!' The man asked if she really meant to say a dollar, and Bernadine said yes, and he said that he might just stop by himself. After she hung up, she dialed the number for Merry Maids, and told them she wanted to change her schedule to every week.

The ceiling fan was spinning quietly, and as Bernadine sat on the stool, she remembered what she'd forgotten to do. She had meant to call Savannah and tell her that maybe it wasn't such a good idea for her to stay with them, but now she was glad she hadn't called. She could use the company, especially the company of a good friend. Bernadine loved Gloria, and Robin too, but Savannah was the one person who would understand how she was feeling. She wouldn't have to apologize for it. She was one of those glass-is-half-full people. Always was. Yeah, she thought, Savannah would definitely cheer her up. Bernadine grinned and looked at the calendar. She'll be here about the twenty-sixth. Hallelujah.

The message light on the answering machine was blinking like crazy, so Bernadine pressed Play. As it rewound, she knew most of the messages were probably from Gloria and Robin. And she was right. Robin volunteered to come and get the kids, and said she hated to say it, but she was glad the bastard was gone. 'I know this may not be the best time to tell you, but girl, guess what? I met somebody. He's so nice. And the complete opposite of Russell, that's for sure. He's not much in the looks department, he's a little on the chubby side, and unfortunately he's a Gemini, but so far he's treating me the way a woman should be treated. So call me.'

Bernadine chuckled. Robin with a man who wasn't completely photographable? Please. And Gloria: 'I still don't believe this, but I'm glad to hear you're all right. And don't lie to me, Bernie. This isn't something you take lightly, so let me know if you want me to come over there. By the way, you know you missed the Black Women's Achievement Awards luncheon. I'll tell you all about it. Anyway, the first advisory board meeting for Sisters' Nite Out isn't until sometime next month. I know you'll be able to make that. You can bring your girlfriend. She is still coming, isn't she? Call me as soon as you can.'

Bernadine had forgotten all about the luncheon. Thank God the meeting was a long ways off. Sometimes all the petty gossip that went on made her sick: who's making more money than whom, and who's got a bigger house. But Black Women on the Move did take care of business, which was why she was still a member.

She made herself a cappuccino, and while she steamed the milk, she couldn't understand why she felt so relieved. She felt lighter, almost graceful. But then, when she really thought about it, she did understand. She was free. Free to do anything she pleased, the way she pleased. Once this mess was all resolved, she'd be able to start her catering business, or anything else she wanted. John had always made it sound like such a shaky idea, but now she didn't have to consult John, did she? Bernadine was tingling when the phone rang, and without thinking, she answered it on the first ring.

'You're back?' her mother said.

'Yep,' Bernadine said. 'I was just about to call you.'

'Did you have a good time?'

'I had a lovely time.'

'Good. And what time were you planning on picking these kids up?'

'I was about to come get 'em now.'

'Well, they've been begging for pizza all day, so I might as well take 'em. I'll meet you back at the house. You've got your key, don't you?'

'It's on my chain with the rest of my keys, Ma. I'll be there in a half hour, but I can't stay long.'

'What you fixing to do now?'

'We're having a garage sale in the morning.'

'You just don't know what to do with yourself, do you?'

'Ma, please. There's so much stuff in the garage we don't use, I figured this would be a good way to get rid of some of it.'

'Knock yourself right on out, then. Anyway, I washed Onika's hair and French-braided it, so you won't have to be worrying about that for at least another week.'

'Thank you, Ma. I'll see you in a few minutes,' she said, and went to get the keys to the Cherokee.

After she brought the kids home, Bernadine had them help her get things ready for the next day.

'Ma, why are we having a garage sale?' John junior asked.

'Because your daddy doesn't want any of this stuff any more.'

'Not even his golf clubs?' Onika asked.

'Nope.'

'What about these tennis rackets?'

'Put those out here too,' Bernadine said.

'Are we just selling Daddy's stuff?' Onika asked.

'Yes.'

'Why come?'

'*How* come. Because he asked me to.'

'He did?' John junior said.

'Yes, he did. He said he doesn't want it any more. And all it's doing is collecting dust.'

'Who gets to keep the money?' he asked.

'We do,' Bernadine said.

'Good,' he said. 'Is Daddy going to help sell it too?'

'No,' she said.

'Is he on another trip?' Onika asked.

'I guess you could say that,' Bernadine said, and left it at that. For now.

It was 7:00 A.M. Bernadine looked out at the driveway. She had set up a card table and put all of John's jewelry

102

on it. She took the cover off his old Ford. The kids had taken turns bringing all one hundred and ten bottles of vintage wine out of the wine cellar and broken six or seven of them, but Bernadine told them not to worry about it. She got his Rossignol skis and his Salomon ski boots and poles and laid them down in the driveway. She took his eight-hundred-dollar mountain bike and put it out there too. She got his power tools, most of which had never been used, and set them next to the skis. She sorted through the winter storage closet, which was also in the garage, and took all his good wool suits and cashmere coats, which he hadn't worn since they lived in Philadelphia, and laid them side by side on a king-size sheet. When it seemed like she had everything he cherished, everything he would miss, out on the pavement, she sat down in one of the card-table chairs, smoked a cigarette, and waited.

Folks started arriving about seven-thirty. They acted as if they'd won the lottery or something. Some squealed. Some thought surely Bernadine was off her rocker, especially when a man handed her four quarters for John's antique car and she handed him the pink slip and he drove it away. By ten minutes after nine, Bernadine had made a hundred and sixty-eight dollars, and the driveway was empty, except for the card table, which wasn't for sale. The kids were so excited that they asked if they could have another one next week. Did Daddy have anything else he wanted to sell? She told them no, that this about covered everything. Bernadine had a smile on her face a mile wide. When the kids dragged the table back into the garage, she told them to go on in the house, divide up the money, and put it in their banks. She was standing on a puddle of old oil, in the space where the Ford used to be. Now the kids would have some room to play. As she wiped her feet on the doormat, she said out loud: 'Since you want to start a new life, motherfucker, see what starting from scratch feels like.' She pushed the garage-door button, but this time Bernadine watched it close.

Fat

Gloria hardly slept a wink. The last time she looked at the clock, it had said 5:36. It was after ten when she woke up. She checked Tarik's room, saw that he wasn't home yet, and since she still hadn't heard from Bernadine or Robin, decided to do something she hadn't done in a while: go to church. She got there late and had to sit in the back. She dozed off in no time. The sermon was boring, because the guest minister couldn't preach. Gloria dreamed she was in church, and a woman she didn't know had to nudge her to tell her the service was over. It was on the drive home that she decided not to tell Tarik about David.

The garage door had come off the hinges again, which meant it wouldn't open, so Gloria parked in front of the house. Tarik's saxophone was hanging over the corner of the downstairs bathroom door. His dirty sneakers were lying on their sides. She went upstairs to change her clothes, heard him in his bathroom, and came back downstairs and started dinner. Last night, after David left, she had poured the spaghetti sauce down the garbage disposal, broken the French bread into bite-size pieces, and pushed it down there too. That was all she could manage. The salad was still sitting in the bowl on the counter, the lettuce dark green and soggy. She dumped it down the drain now, then took the thawed-out liver from the refrigerator and seasoned it. She was flouring the last piece when Tarik entered the doorway. He was wearing green sweat pants and a white turtleneck. He held the Sunday paper under his arm.

'I'm sorry, Ma,' he said.

'You don't have to be sorry,' Gloria said, and dropped

a piece of liver into the skillet. 'It's over. Done. Finished.'

'Was he mad?'

'No, he wasn't mad. Just disappointed. He'll get over it.'

'Did he spend the night?'

Gloria gave him a piercing look. 'No, he did not.'

'Good,' and he sat down at the table, opened the paper, took out the sports section, and started reading.

'Did anybody call?' she asked him now.

'Yep.'

Gloria stopped moving. 'Bernadine?'

'Nope. But Miss Robin called and said she went by Miss Bernadine's and nobody was home. She said she was driving down to Tucson to spend the day with her parents. That lady from your women's group called, but I forgot her name 'cause she was talking so fast I couldn't hardly write everything down. She said some meeting about some sisters is being postponed until April fifth, and she said she hopes you wanna chair some exhibit committee again this year and to start thinking about a theme for something. I forget. Oh. And Phillip called and said he thinks he's got the stomach flu and may not be in on Tuesday. Depending.'

'That's it?'

'Yep.'

'So how was your night at Bryan's?'

'I didn't spend the night at Bryan's.'

Gloria dropped a piece of liver on the floor and left it there. 'You didn't what?'

'I spent the night at Terrence's.'

'You asked me if you could spend the night with Bryan.'

'No, I didn't, Ma. I said I was *at* Bryan's, but I wanted to spend the night with Terrence.'

'Are you trying to tell me I'm crazy or something?'

'No, Ma. You're just not remembering right.'

'Look, boy. You said *Bryan*, or my name ain't Gloria.' She bent over to pick up the liver and, when she did, got a sharp pain in her chest. Gas, she thought. 'Come here,' she said, ushering him with her index finger.

Tarik walked in front of her and looked down.

'Do I look like a fool?'

'No.'

'I was a teenager myself not too long ago. What's Terrence's sister's name?'

'Felicia.'

'That's the one you've got a crush on. Now tell me I'm wrong.'

'You're dead wrong, Ma. I can't stand that girl. She's whacked.'

'You mean she's on drugs?'

'No. It means she's a no go. Ill. As in ugly.'

'I've seen that girl before. And she is not ugly.' But she knew what he meant. Felicia was fat. When Gloria first started putting on weight, every time a new diet came on TV, Tarik would drop hints. 'Look how skinny that lady is now, Ma. Why don't you try that one?' Gloria had ordered so many $19.95, $79.95, and $129.95 diets that she turned into a bitch and almost drove the boy crazy, trying to function on liquid food, no food, tiny portions of food, and stuff that didn't look like food. One day, Gloria just got pissed and told him to buzz off. 'I'm not a goddamn whale,' she said. 'When I get up to a size twenty like Sister Monroe, that's when you can talk about me. But for now, keep your mouth shut.' When she got up to a size eighteen, every now and then she'd accidentally lose five or six pounds, and she'd mention it to Tarik. 'That's great, Ma,' he'd say. Gloria knew she embarrassed him, because one time he came right out and asked her if she just had to wear her dresses so tight, with her boobs pushing all out like that. How did she ever expect to find him a father or get a husband, being so fat? Hadn't she noticed that since she got this big, the men stopped coming around? In church, Tarik looked for men who weren't wearing wedding bands, hoping Gloria would introduce herself, but no-one except deacons' wives ever paid her much attention. 'Don't you get tired of going out with your girlfriends?' he asked her. And sometimes Tarik looked at her with pity. 'You're too pretty to be this fat, Ma,' he'd say. 'I wish you could look like you used to.' All Gloria could say was that even if she lost a hundred pounds, she could never look the way she used to.

'Tell me something else,' she said to him now. 'Why is it that it's damn near ninety degrees outside and you're wearing a turtleneck?' Before he had a chance to answer, Gloria reached up and pulled the neck of his shirt down toward his shoulder. Sure enough, two round strawberries were engraved on Tarik's neck. 'Did *Terrence* do this to you?'

Tarik dropped his head and stepped backward, bumping into a chair at the kitchen table. 'No,' he mumbled.

'Speak up; I can't hear you.'

'No,' he said clearly.

'Tarik. Sit down. And don't say two words to me until I tell you to.'

He looked at the clock. It was two-thirty. 'Ma, I'm supposed to meet my homeboys on the court at three.'

'That's not my problem, is it?' she said, and went on about her business. It took Gloria four minutes to put the rest of the liver in the skillet, switch the dial from high to medium, get two pots out of the cabinet, measure the water, and stir in some rice. Tarik watched his mother's behind jiggle as she shook the frozen vegetables from the bag, and when she bent down to put the biscuits in the oven, the skirt she had on looked as if it was busting at the seams.

'So,' Gloria finally said, as she sat down at the table. 'Are you having sex these days?'

'Sort of,' Tarik said, and pushed the newspaper aside.

'Sort of?'

'Yes.'

'Since when?'

'Ma . . .'

'Ma, my ass. Since when?'

'Since last summer.'

Gloria thought about that. It was the middle of February. Damn. She pushed the chair away from the table and went to turn the air conditioner up, because the oven was making the room too warm. Her thighs kept sticking together as she walked. She turned the thermostat to seventy degrees, then stood there for a minute. Her *baby* was fucking? That's probably why his grades have dropped, she thought, and wanted to chuckle but didn't dare. He's pussy-whipped. Coming had affected the boy's brain. They're all alike, she thought, as she wiped the smirk off her face, did a quick squat so her thighs could breathe, turned the corner, and sat back down. 'Do you think you know what you're doing?'

'I think so,' he said, and tried not to grin.

'Oh, you do, do you? Look. It's been a while since we talked about this, Tarik, and I never really expected you to come up to me one day and say, "Yo, Ma, I'm doing the wild thang now," but my Lord, Tarik. This is just one reason why I've always wanted you to have a father. Let me ask you something. And don't lie to me. Are you using condoms?'

'Most of the time.'

Another gas pain shot through her rib cage and settled in her heart. She took a breath, then exhaled. Gloria eased out of the chair, got the Pepto-Bismol from the refrigerator, and took two tablespoonfuls. The liver was sizzling, and the rice was about to boil over, but Gloria couldn't move another inch until this pain passed. She leaned on the countertop for support. 'Most of the time?'

'All the time,' he said. 'Are you all right, Ma?'

'It's just indigestion. I'll be all right in a minute. Don't lie to me, Tarik. You can't lie about this kind of stuff.'

'All right, all right. Most of the time,' he said, and stretched his long legs out.

'Most of the time isn't good enough, and you know it. You know how many diseases there are out in the streets these days?'

'Yeah, but, Ma, I don't mess with those kind of girls.'

'Those kind of girls? *Anybody* can get VD. I've had it.'

Tarik looked at his mama in total disbelief.

'And now there's AIDS. You young people may think you're immune, but this is one disease that can kill your black ass.'

'I know, Ma.'

'You ever heard of crabs?'

'Crabs? Yeah, you eat 'em?'

'You don't want to eat these,' she said. The pain had started to let up, so Gloria sat back down. 'Half of these young girls out here don't know when to change their Tampax, let alone what the word "douche" means.'

'What does it mean?'

'A douche? Ask one of them to explain it to you. How many?'

'How many what?'

'How many have you slept with?'

'I haven't *slept* with anybody.'

'Don't get cute with me, Tarik.'

'Nine.'

'Nine! Nine different girls? Just since last summer?'

'That's not a lot. You should see how much action most of my homeboys get.'

'I don't give a damn what your "homeboys" are getting. It's *you* I'm concerned about. I want you to listen to me, and you listen to me good. You do not – you understand me – you do not walk out of this house from this day forward without your house key and a condom in your wallet. Do you understand me?'

'Yes.'

'And you do not, under any circumstances, believe a damn word any of these sweet little innocent girls tell you when they say they're using something.'

'But they are.'

'How do you know that?'

'Because they're all on the pill.'

'You can believe that shit if you want to, but, Tarik' – she took her first smooth breath; the Pepto-Bismol had worked – 'listen to me. You're a handsome young man. Until recently, you were a straight-A student. You're a decent athlete, a fine saxophonist, and I'd like to think you've got a future – and I'm not talking about this navy business, either. This phone rings off the hook with nothin' but girls on the other end, and I'm not saying anything is wrong with that. I'm not saying having sex at your age is wrong, either. But some of these teenage girls are dizzy as hell, their mamas don't teach them anything, and some of them don't think any further than today, let alone tomorrow. That includes you and whatever it is you're doing that you think is so great between their legs. Having sex without any protection makes babies. Get it? Like one plus one equals two. For some of these girls, the only thing in their future *is* a baby. And Lord knows you could make some pretty ones. I just don't want you to be so naive and take their word for it when they tell you they're on the pill or any nonsense like that. You protect yourself, you hear me?'

'Yes, Ma.'

'I don't care if they're using a diaphragm, the pill, that damn sponge, and foam all together – you put your business on regardless. Do I make myself clear?'

'Yes, Ma.'

'So back to one of my original questions. Did Terrence put that hickey on your neck?' Gloria was laughing now.

'No,' he said, blushing, then he started laughing too.

'Then who did?'

'Michelle.'

110

'Michelle?! That itty-bitty white girl who lives two doors down?'

'You asked, so I'm telling you.'

'You mean to tell me you're screwing a white girl?'

'What's wrong with that?'

Gloria had to think about how to answer this one. The first thing that popped into her head was Bernadine and John. Was this shit catchy or what? In the seventies, when she was still living in Oakland, everywhere she went she saw black men with white women on their arms. Back then, the men seemed to be doing it more to prove a point. Then things cooled down for a few years. Now Gloria was wondering if 'our' men were running to white women again because *we* were doing something wrong? Her son wasn't even a man yet, and he was already on his way. What was the deal here? Did white women have something we didn't? Were they doing something to these boys and men that we couldn't? 'Look,' she said. 'All I'm saying is that I just assumed when you started liking girls that they would be black.'

'This is the nineties, Ma. What have they been teaching us in church all these years? Didn't Reverend Jones say that people should like each other because they like each other, not because of the color of their skin?'

Gloria said, 'That's true. But look. I don't have anything against most white folks, and who you like is your business. I want you to know that. If I had a real problem with 'em, we wouldn't be living in this neighborhood. Do you like this girl?'

'She's pretty def.'

'Wait. Don't tell me. I know the girl can hear, so I suppose this means you like her.'

'She's all right.'

'Are there any *black* girls you like?'

'A few.'

'But you like white girls better?'

'I like *this* one.'

'Why?'

'Ma, what is this, the third degree or something? I just said I liked her. What's wrong with that?'

'Nothing is *wrong* with it, Tarik, but how old is this girl?'

'Her *name* is Michelle.'

'Whatever. How old is she?'

'Eighteen.'

'Eighteen! You're only sixteen.'

'Sixteen and a half. So what?'

'Doesn't she go to your school?'

'Yeah.'

'I hope she's a senior.'

'She is. But what difference does age make, Ma?'

'None, Tarik. None. But I bet her parents don't know you're tiptoeing over their house at night, do they?'

'Yeah, they do.'

'Do I look like a complete fool to you? Don't answer that. Just let me say this and get it over with. If I ever hear from her parents that they've busted your black ass in their house in bed with their daughter, that'll be the end of it, do you understand me?'

'Yes, Ma.'

'Tarik, all I'm trying to say is there's a right way to do things, and there's a sleazy way to do things. If you don't know it, it's called discretion.'

'I'm always careful, believe me. I don't want to get caught.'

'You've already been caught.'

'I don't mean like this.'

'You just better watch your step and be careful where you put that *thing*.'

'I am, Ma.'

'Tarik?'

'Yes, Ma?' He was looking at the clock now. Three o'clock had come and gone.

'I hope you don't get any happier about this newly discovered feeling than you obviously have already, 'cause I don't want to see you bringing home any more

C's and, Lord, please not another D. Can you promise me you'll try to concentrate on *one* thing at a time?'

'Yes, Ma.'

'And believe me: If somebody ever comes knocking on this door telling me their daughter's pregnant by my son, it'll not only break my heart but it'll mess up everything for you, everything I've tried to do for you. Do you understand what I'm trying to say, Tarik?'

'Yes, Ma.'

'Do you *hear* what I'm saying?'

'I do, Ma. And I promise. I'll be extra careful, and you'll see, my grades'll improve. I guarantee it.'

'Thank you,' she said, and got up. 'Thank you. Now let's eat.'

Tarik and Gloria agreed that the liver and rice and mixed vegetables and biscuits were good. After he emptied the trash, Tarik went upstairs to his room, and Gloria heard him playing his horn. He always left his door open, because he knew she loved to hear him play. She was putting the leftovers into plastic containers, stacking them inside the refrigerator. She scraped the gravy off the plates, rinsed out the pots and pans, and put them in the dishwasher. While she poured the detergent in, Gloria was thinking about what Tarik had told her. She was wondering what kind of lover her son could possibly be at sixteen and a half years old. Shaking her head from side to side, she pressed the On button and heard the water spraying out. She put her elbows on the counter and crossed her arms. Through the window she could see that For Sale sign in the front yard of the house across the street. It had been there for ever. Gloria dropped her chin in the palm of her right hand. After a while, she couldn't see that house or that sign. She was trying to picture her son on top of some girl, with his clothes off, giving her pleasure. She hated to admit it, but she envied him. She stayed there for another ten minutes, staring at the glare on the glass. But now Gloria was

113

thinking about Gloria. Wondering if she'd ever get a chance to welcome a man into her life. If she'd ever get a chance to say 'I love you' or if somebody would ever say it to her. She didn't even want to think about the area between her legs.

Interstate Lust

I was all set to let the phone ring, because here it is two days before I'm supposed to be moving, and the girlfriend who had promised to help me drive just flaked out on me. Her boyfriend waits until this morning to tell her he doesn't think it's such a good idea. And to top it off, the sale of my condo fell through, so for now I'm stuck with this damn place.

'Hello,' I said in a hostile voice.

'Savannah?'

'Who is this?' I asked, even nastier.

'This is Lionel, but if I've caught you at a bad time, I can call back a little later.'

'Lionel?'

'Have you forgotten me already?'

'No. I'm sorry for yelling. It's been a rough day.'

'Well, I was trying to catch you before you left. I wanted to take you out to dinner, since you disappeared on me so fast New Year's Eve.'

'I just had another party to go to, and I wanted to get there before midnight.'

'Well, can I at least take you out for a farewell dinner?'

'The movers'll be here tomorrow, and I was just on my way out to get something.'

'Can I meet you somewhere?'

Why not? I thought. 'Do you know where Yamashita's is?'

'Yep.'

'I'll be there in about ten minutes.'

'I'll see you in fifteen.'

I was sitting at a table by the window when he walked

past. I waved and smiled. Steam was jutting out of the tea spout, but I decided to wait until Lionel sat down before I had some.

'So hello and goodbye,' he said, and took off his coat and gloves. Before he sat down, he rubbed his hands together.

'Hi, Lionel,' I said.

'I could use some of that tea to warm me up,' he said.

I wanted to say I could warm you up faster than some Japanese tea, but instead I said something deeper. 'It *is* freezing out there.' Then I poured us both a cup.

'So are you all set to go?' he asked.

'Sort of. This girlfriend of mine who volunteered to help me drive can't go now.'

'Does that mean you're driving by yourself?'

'It looks that way. I mean, I can *do* it. I just wasn't prepared to drive a thousand miles by myself.'

'I'll help you.'

I almost choked on the tea. 'What did you say?'

'I said I'll help you. It shouldn't take more than sixteen, seventeen hours.'

'But you don't even know me, Lionel. And I don't know you.'

'Well, from what Paul told me, and from what I've seen, you seem like a pretty nice lady. I give you my word, I'm not a serial killer or a rapist,' he said, and held up his hand like a Boy Scout.

'Look, I really appreciate this offer, but do you realize what you're saying?'

'I do.'

'But what about work?'

'I work for myself.'

I swallowed my tea and started playing with my chopsticks. Hell, it might just be fun. Sharing a drive this long with a real man. It's not like he's a complete stranger. I mean, after all, my brother-in-law knows him. Right? 'Are you sure about this?'

'I'm positive,' he said, and brought his little cup to

116

his mouth and drank it in one swallow.

'Don't you sell fire trucks?'

'No no no no no. I haven't done that in five years. I import all kinds of doodads and trinkets from Korea and Japan, but I'm working on some other things too.'

'Well, let me say this, Lionel. I could fly you back to Denver the same day if you need to get back.'

'That won't be necessary,' he said. 'I've always wanted to see Phoenix. I've never been to Arizona, so I might just take a few days and check the place out. I've heard a lot about this place called Sedona. And hey,' he said, leaning forward, 'let's play it by ear.' He looked at me like it was all settled, then at the menu, and said, 'So what're you gonna have?'

I wanted to say that what I wanted wasn't on the menu, but I ordered ginger beef, and Lionel said he didn't eat red meat, so he ordered vegetarian tempura. While we waited for our food, we talked about how great it was that after twenty-seven years, Nelson Mandela had finally been released from prison yesterday. We spent an hour talking about apartheid in general, and then we lightened up the conversation and talked about how boring Denver was. By this time, it had registered that in two days this man was going to be sitting next to me in my Celica for one whole thousand miles of interstate highway.

He insisted on walking me home. When we got inside the lobby, I thanked him for dinner, said good night, and he kissed me on the cheek. I guess I was somewhat smitten, because when I got on the elevator, I visualized us turning off some deserted road, not being able to contain ourselves, and making passionate love in the back seat of my car. But I forgot about that hump in the middle. Damn. Now I wished I drove something big. Like a Buick.

Bernadine had left a message and said it was important, so I called her. 'Hey, girl,' I said, when she answered.

'Hey. I've been meaning to call you,' she said in a tired voice.

'What's wrong, Bernie?'

'Girl, John left.'

'I *know* you're lying.'

'It's going on two weeks now.'

'And you're just now telling me this shit?'

'I was fucked up, girl.'

'So why didn't you call me? I'da caught the next plane out of here, and you know it. Damn, Bernie.'

'I'm OK now. Really.'

'Wait a minute. Back up. Where'd he go? And why'd he leave? Wait. Let me guess. Another woman?'

'A white one.'

'Get the hell out of here!'

'Anyway, now that it's sunk in, I'm glad the mother-fucker's gone, but I just didn't want you coming here not knowing what the deal was.'

'Are you sure you're OK? You don't sound so hot to me.'

'I was out there for a minute, but I mean it, I'm fine. Just tired. I'll be glad when your black ass gets here, though.'

'Me too. What about the kids?'

'I haven't told 'em yet. They think John's on another one of his business trips. I'll tell 'em. As soon as I figure out the best way. Anyway, I've got a lot to tell you when you get here, girl.'

'I really don't believe this shit.'

'Believe it, girl.'

'Well, guess what?'

'What?'

'My so-called girlfriend flaked out on me, so now this man named Lionel is helping me drive.'

'The one you met at that New Year's party?'

'Yep. And we may have to spend the night at a motel, but we should be there sometime on Friday. As soon as we hit the city limits, I'll be at your front door.'

'Then I'll leave the key under the mat. I'm taking the

day off. I have to talk to my lawyer about John's and my financial disclosure statements. She said she found some discrepancies. I don't know what that shit means, but I'm sure it's probably some more of his bullshit. I hope it won't take long. I've got errands to run, have to pick up the kids and then stop by my mother's.'

'I still don't believe this shit, Bernie.'

'Girl, some days it's hard for me to believe too.'

'Did you tell Geneva?'

'Not yet, but you know she'll be glad to hear it.'

'You're not sitting around that house going crazy by yourself, are you?'

'I was, but remember I told you I wanted you to meet Gloria and Robin?'

'Yeah.'

'Girl, you'd swear I was dying and they were trying to save my life. Robin took the kids this past weekend, and Gloria dragged me to see *The War of the Roses* because everybody had said how funny it was, but halfway through it, I walked out on that shit and went two doors down and *Men Don't Leave* was playing, so I kept right on walking until I came to *Steel Magnolias*. It was good, girl. Anyway, they won't let me do too much of anything by myself. But I've gotta go. I've got to read Onika *Messy Bessey* for the zillionth time and then help John junior with his science project, something with vinegar and baking soda. So I'll see you when I see you. And don't worry about me. You just have fun getting here.'

After I hung up, I watched Yasmine jump across some crates and boxes, and all I could say was, 'Damn.'

I pulled in front of Lionel's house at 5:30 A.M. Yasmine was in her travel carrier, and I stacked her on top of a suitcase on the back seat. The trunk was full. I'd bought some toys for Bernadine's kids, which was stupid, because they took up most of the space. I had filled a thermos with Five Alive and crushed ice, bought some plastic cups, a big bag of potato

119

chips, and a few pieces of fruit, which I put in an Igloo.

His house was tiny, and there was a rusty old car hiked up on stilts – or whatever they call them – sitting in the snow-covered driveway. I didn't see a jeep. I was looking for the doorbell but couldn't find one, so I knocked. Lionel came to the door in a hooded black sweatsuit, and even in twilight, with a mouth full of toothpaste, he looked good. 'Come on in,' he mumbled. 'I'm almost ready.' I sat down on his sofa, which was really a futon. It was so low I almost broke my neck when I landed. There wasn't what I'd call a color scheme or a 'look' he was aiming for in here, but everything looked clean. Bachelors, I thought, and chuckled. There was also a musty odor that I couldn't quite identify because the mist of some kind of air freshener still hung in the air.

I looked around the room. His stereo looked just like the one I had in college. There were hundreds of cassettes stacked on top of each other. Books were opened, lying in a variety of places, and right next to me was *The Art of the Deal*, by Donald Trump. Two sets of weights lay in the middle of the floor in the next room, which, if it had had a table in it, would have been the dining room. Men. I shifted my weight to get more comfortable, and that's when I saw two over-stuffed gym bags sitting on the other side of the front door. How long was he planning to stay in Phoenix?

'Are you making fun of my bachelor pad?' he said, coming from the back of the house.

'No. I was trying to figure out how we're going to get your bags in my car.'

'Don't worry. I'll get 'em in,' he said.

He put on one of those sleeveless down vests, picked up his bags, locked the front door, and went outside. He turned to face me and was grinning again. 'You look like the kind of lady who'd drive a red car,' he said, and opened the passenger door. 'What's that in the cage?' he asked, while he stuffed his bags in the back seat.

120

'That's Yasmine, my cat. Please don't tell me you're allergic to cats.'

'No,' he said. 'I just can't stand 'em.'

We gassed up at a Chevron station, went across the street to a Circle K, bought some coffee and doughnuts, and hit Interstate 25. He insisted on driving, which was fine with me.

'Don't you drive a jeep?' I asked.

'Not any more. I sold it a few months ago.'

'Oh,' I said, and decided not to ask why.

The first two hundred miles were enlightening. Lionel did most of the talking. He told me he used to be in real estate and had acquired some property, but when he discovered how much money there was to be made selling fire trucks, he disposed of it and used the money to buy two trucks. Things went well for a couple of years, but then the bottom dropped out: too much competition, and fire departments weren't replacing their trucks as fast as they used to. He said he could only sell in his region – which was shrinking. That's why he bailed out and went into business with a buddy, who had convinced him that importing Korean and Japanese 'junk,' as he called it, would be even more profitable. But over the past year, things weren't going so hot. The market for junk had also become saturated, and his partner wanted out because he and his wife were opening a bed-and-breakfast near one of the ski areas. Lionel had to buy him out. It took all of the money he had on hand, and after that, most of his 'backers' backed down. He tried to convince them that African art was about to become a big thing in the States, but they didn't go for it. So now, he said, he was stuck between a rock and a hard place.

'So what's your next step?' I asked.

'Pork,' he said.

'Excuse me?'

'Pork. There's a lot of money in pork.'

'I thought you said you were vegetarian.'

121

'I am, but what's that got to do with anything?'

'Well, if you wouldn't eat it, how could you sell it?'

'Do you think that everybody who owns a liquor store is an alcoholic?'

'Of course not.'

'I know this guy who's one of the biggest pork exporters in the country, and I've been trying to get in touch with him for months. I met him at a ranch in Cheyenne, and he told me if I ever wanted to get into pork, to give him a call.'

'And?'

'He hasn't called me back. As a matter of fact — and this is so coincidental I can't believe it — right after I got home from dinner with you, a good source told me this guy's gonna be in Phoenix day after tomorrow. I know the hotel he's staying at and everything.'

I must have looked like a fool to him. But I didn't know what to say. Lionel just kept right on talking, while I looked out the window at the mountains. I was thinking about my new job. Not the job itself but the opportunities that lay ahead. At my interview, I was straightforward and told them I was also interested in producing, that I didn't want to stay in publicity for ever. They assured me that their policy was to promote from within whenever possible, and since I knew I was good at what I did, I wasn't worried. I had already proved myself at the gas company. I had produced quite a few public service announcements and instructional films, but I'd reached my peak as far as promotions went. I didn't like the idea of making less money, but I knew television stations didn't pay much unless you were in front of the camera. It just meant I was going to have to work my ass off and, in the meantime, cash in some of my bonds and CDs to cover my mortgage and take care of Mama.

'Am I boring you?' I heard him ask.

'No, Lionel. I'm sorry, I guess I'm just a little tired. I'm not used to getting up this early.'

'I am,' he said. 'I usually run about six every morning.'

'So that's how you manage to stay in such great shape, huh?'

'That's one reason,' he said, and winked at me. He pulled my ashtray out, and the smell of old ashes filled the air. 'You mind if I smoke a joint?'

'Not in the car. Please. I'm allergic to it,' I said, lying. 'Why don't you pull over?'

'I can wait,' he said. 'I'm allergic to cigarette smoke myself,' he said, and pushed the ashtray back in. 'What kind of music you got in that box?'

I picked up the cassette case and started going through it. He didn't want to hear Phyllis Hyman or Simply Red or Anita Baker or Tracy Chapman or The Whispers or Stevie Wonder or Michael Jackson, and had never heard of Julia Fordham, and when I finally said Tchaikovsky, he laughed.

'Here,' I said, putting the case between us. 'Why don't you pick out something you like.'

'No. Keep going.'

'Tell me what you want to hear.'

'You got any Kenny G?'

'Yes,' I said, and took it out and pushed the tape in. I turned it up loud enough so that if he said something, I wouldn't hear his ass. Then I decided the only way to ensure this was to pretend like I was asleep. Which I did. Apparently I dozed off for a few minutes, because when I felt the car stop, it startled me. We were at a gas station.

'How much does it take to fill up your tank?' he asked.

'About fifteen dollars.'

'We're only on half, but we don't wanna get out in the middle of nowhere and can't find a gas station.'

I handed him a twenty-dollar bill. Lionel got out and put the gas in, and as I watched him clean the front window, steam was coming out of his nostrils. He wasn't as handsome as I'd thought he was. As a matter of fact, he looked sort of like a horse. I was wondering how many more miles we had to go, so I looked at the map. We were almost in Trinidad, which meant we still had close to eight hundred left.

It took seven dollars and thirty cents to fill up the tank, but when Lionel got back in the car, he didn't give me my change. 'You want me to drive yet?' I asked.

'No. You just sit back and relax.'

By the time we reached New Mexico's border, I was starving and needed a cigarette bad. We stopped in a little town called Springer, and Lionel pulled over to the side of the road, stood in what was left of the snow, and smoked his joint. I smoked my cigarette. We walked to a diner, and I ordered a tuna fish sandwich. He ordered a hamburger and fries and a strawberry milk shake. I gave him a funny look. 'I still eat a hamburger every once in a while,' he said. Once we'd finished, he said he was still hungry and ordered a slice of apple pie. When we got back outside, I insisted on taking the wheel, because I didn't know how stoned he was and didn't want to find out.

By the time we got to Santa Fe, the weather had changed dramatically. Everything was green. I wanted to stop, since I'd never been anywhere near here and I knew Santa Fe was known as a haven for artists. I'd never seen a real adobe, either, and was interested in buying some turquoise jewelry. But Lionel didn't want to stop. 'Why not?' I asked him.

'It's nothing but a tourist trap. They put everything on the streets so you'll spend all your money, and they jack the prices up sky-high.'

'So what?' I said.

He seemed agitated. 'I don't like stopping and starting when I'm on the highway, that's all. And besides, I thought you were in a big hurry to get to Phoenix.'

'I am, and you're right,' I said. 'The sooner we get there, the better.' He sort of smiled, and I wanted to push him out of the goddamn car.

124

It was getting dark by the time we made it to Gallup, and I was tired of driving. I ran out of things to talk about with Lionel. To break up the monotony, I suggested we spend the night at a motel.

'We're less than five hours from Phoenix. I'm not tired, and I can take over,' he said.

'Lionel, we've been on the road for twelve hours. I could really use a shower, and I would love to brush my teeth and lie down for a while.'

'I hear you,' he said.

'I'll get us separate rooms.'

'Come on, Savannah. Why you wanna throw your money away like that? I don't bite,' he said, and smiled.

We drove a few more miles, and I turned off at the exit when I saw a Great Western. I got two rooms anyway. Poor Yasmine – I had almost forgotten about her – but then again, I'd drugged the cat so she could tolerate being caged. I brought her in the room and got a few toiletries and a change of clothes out of the trunk. Lionel didn't take anything up to his room. He was pouting.

When I opened the door, I sat Yasmine down on the floor. She was awake now, so I let her out and gave her some food I'd put in a Baggie. I had barely sat down, when Lionel knocked on the door. I opened it. 'I'm sorry if I was a pain in the ass,' he said.

'You weren't a pain, Lionel. I think we're both just tired.'

'I'm not all that tired,' he said, and smiled at me. For some reason, now he looked as tempting as he did on New Year's Eve. 'Don't you need somebody to keep you warm?' he asked.

'I brought my pajamas.'

'I think I feel better than pajamas,' he said.

I thought for a minute. Part of my fantasy was to get myself a little piece out here on the road. And hell, I hadn't had any in five months, and even though Lionel had gotten on my nerves, maybe he communicated better in bed. I didn't have to be in love with the man to do this, and my poor body'd probably be grateful to get fed, since it'd been on such a starvation diet. I can block his bullshit out of my mind, because I've done it before. I should go ahead and get me some. If I'm lucky, I may never see this man again after tomorrow. 'Come on in,' I said, and turned on the television. 'I need to take a shower. I feel yucky.'

'Take your time,' he said.

So I took one. When I came out, he was lying on the bed, butt naked. Hair was everywhere, but it couldn't hide the beauty of this man's body. I wanted to say, 'Damn, Lionel,' but instead I dropped the towel I had draped around me to the floor. If this was going to be a fantasy, I wanted to start it on the right note.

'You want to take one too, don't you?' I said, as he looked up at me. I swear I wished I had big luscious breasts, because when he got up and walked toward me, he kissed them, and his entire lips covered one. I felt my body heat up, just that quick.

'I'll be right out,' he said.

I fell on the bed and, through the open door, looked at his steamy silhouette in the mirror, feeling my body's growing excitement. Thank God I didn't pack away my diaphragm, I thought. When the water in the shower stopped, he came out and went over to the sink and picked up my toothbrush. Was he crazy? I was about to say something, but I swear, I couldn't. I just watched him squeeze the little tube of toothpaste and then commence to brushing.

By the time he finished, I had dried up. I was trying to force myself to feel lustful again, because I wanted to do this, I needed to do this, but when he put his pants back on and then his jacket and said he'd be right back, it was all over for me. I didn't even have to ask where he was going.

I could smell the reefer on his breath when he came back. He took his jacket and pants off and threw them

126

on a chair, then came over to the bed and got on top of me. His hands were ice cold, but he was kissing me so hard I couldn't say anything. The next thing I knew, I felt this big thick stick trying to force its way inside me, but I couldn't help him out. As a matter of fact, the shit hurt. 'Lionel, did you bring a condom?'

'I've got it on,' he said.

I felt down there just to make sure. When did he put the shit on? I wondered. 'Well, you can slow down. We've got all night.'

'I'm just excited. I've been thinking about what I'd do to you ever since New Year's, and I guess I'm just a little anxious, but I'll slow down, baby.'

I might as well have been talking to myself, because when he pulled away, I thought he was going to take it from the top, but instead he put his face between my legs and started licking and chewing like a wild animal. I guess he thought I was aroused because of the way I was grabbing on to the headboard, and all the twisting and wiggling I was doing, but I was scared he was going to bite my clitoris off – if and when he found it. I wanted to get this shit over with before I was raw, so I took my hands and put them firmly on his head and pushed it away. Then I moaned. I gripped him by the shoulders, pulled him up on top of me, and, in an exasperated voice, yelled, 'Please, put it in!'

'I'm on my way, baby,' he said, and jabbed me worse than he had the first time. I held my breath until I felt him sink into a soft, warm place. He went to work, and during this whole ordeal, not once did he kiss me. When I finally looked up at his face, he was gazing at something on the wall with unbelievable intensity, and all of a sudden his face became monstrous and contorted, and the next thing I know, he started growling like a bear. Really, fucking growling. 'Grrrrrrrrrrr,' he said, and when I looked at him, he was gritting his teeth and his eyes looked like red lasers. 'Grrrrrrrrrrr,' he said again, and I thought his penis was going to come out through my chest. I was about to push

127

him off, but I was scared, and he did it again, even louder and more piercing this time. 'Grrrrrrrrrrr,' he screeched, and then, thank God, collapsed. I lay there as still as I possibly could, because I was terrified. I didn't know what I was sleeping with: a man or a beast. Shit. I could've handled this highway by myself and done without this detour of the goddamn zoo.

Lionel rolled over and sighed. I was dripping with his sweat, but my forehead and armpits were dry. 'That was good,' he said. 'And I want some more before the night is over.'

I thought I would gag. 'That felt like it might last me awhile,' I said.

'No no no no no,' he said, grinning triumphantly, and turned toward me to kiss my shoulder. 'It gets better.'

When I heard him snoring, I thought about putting my clothes on, grabbing Yasmine, running out of this damn room, and leaving his black ass right here. I tried to go to sleep, but I couldn't. So I dragged the phone into the bathroom, closed the door, and called Sheila and cussed her ass out. 'Thanks a lot for introducing me to this asshole,' I said, after I told her what had happened. She apologized between outbursts of laughter. I started cracking up too. She wanted to tell me all about their new van, but I was tired and told her to tell me another time. I got back in bed. I was not going through this shit again and wanted to be up and ready to leave before he opened his eyes. Luckily, God was on my side, because I had already showered and dressed and was taking two Advils when he sat up in bed the next morning.

'Savannah?'

'Good morning,' I said.

'What you doing?'

'I'm getting ready to go downstairs to the coffee shop to get us something to eat.'

'Don't they have room service here?' he asked.

'I don't know, but I need to take Yasmine out for some air anyway. By the time you shower and get dressed, I'll be back.' Before he had a chance to respond, I was already out the door.

I drove.

When we got to Flagstaff, I called Bernie. She wasn't home. I left a message: 'You will not even be meeting Lionel, girl. He is one weird motherfucker. An impostor from the word go. I'm taking his ass to a motel. There's no way I'm spending another night with this reptile. See you later.' I was also glad I didn't have to start working for almost two weeks. Lord knows, I'd need to chill out after this ordeal.

When we passed the sign that said Sedona was however many miles, Lionel said, 'You wanna check it out?'

'No,' I said.

'Why not?'

'It's a detour, Lionel, and second of all, my girl-friend's waiting for me.'

'Girlfriend?'

'Yeah, didn't I tell you I was staying with a girlfriend when I got here?'

'No, you didn't.'

'Well, that's the plan. I'll put you up in a motel for tonight, and we can check to see how much it costs to fly you back tomorrow, just like I promised.'

'I was hoping to spend some more time with you, Savannah. I'm enjoying your company. Immensely.'

'Well, I've been enjoying yours too, Lionel, but I start my new job in three days, and I've gotta find a place to live.'

'I didn't know you were starting work so soon.'

'Yep.'

'Well, look,' he said, appearing rather worried. 'What line of work is your girlfriend in?'

'Why?'

'I'm just curious.'

129

'She's a controller for a real estate management company.'

'What about her husband?'

'She doesn't really have a husband. They're going through a divorce. But he owns a software company.'

His eyes lit up. 'You mean as in computer software?'

'Yes,' I said.

'Look, when we get to Phoenix, do you think you could introduce me to him? I'd like to ask him a few things about how you go about getting into the software business. I know a lot about computers myself, and I've always wanted to throw my ideas back and forth with somebody who knows the ins and outs of the business.'

'Didn't you hear what I just said?'

'Yeah, but just because they're going through a divorce doesn't mean you can't talk to him.'

'Look, Lionel. It would be kind of tacky for me to deal with him under the circumstances, circumstances that I don't fully understand myself.'

'Can I stay with you?' he asked.

I just looked at him like he was crazy.

'So it's like that,' he said.

'I'll drop you off when we see a motel that looks like it's in the middle of town.'

'Drop me off?'

'Yeah.'

'Don't you want to spend a little more time together?' he asked.

'I would love to, but I'm tired and I've got a million things to do in the next few days. We'll see each other again, won't we?'

'I hope so,' he said.

When we got inside the city limits, we stopped at a gas station and asked for directions to central Phoenix. We drove until we came to Camelback near Twenty-fourth Street, which was lined with one beautiful hotel after another. I kept driving. 'Where you going?' Lionel asked.

'There should be a travel agency around here some-where,' I said.

'Why are you looking for a travel agency now?' he asked.

'To get your airline ticket, Lionel.'

'But we just got here. I wanted to at least check the city out.'

'What's to stop you?'

'Well, it seems like you're in a big hurry to get rid of me or something.'

'That's not true. I'm tired, Lionel, and I've got a lot of business I have to take care of.'

'Well, I'm a little tired of Denver myself, and from what I can see already, Phoenix doesn't look too bad.'

I couldn't even twist my mouth to respond, so when I saw a travel agency, I turned in. We got out of the car, and I left the windows down so Yasmine could breathe. It was actually pretty warm here. Hallelujah. We walked inside, and an agent was able to help us right away. I asked her how much a one-way ticket to Denver would cost. Leaving tomorrow. When she told me two hundred and nine dollars, I felt like screaming.

'Shall I book that for you both, ma'am?'

Lionel bent down and said, 'Can I talk to you over here for a minute?'

I excused myself, and we walked over by the door.

'Look. Could we do this? I really don't wanna miss this pork guy, but he won't be here for another two days. Could you just let me have the plane fare, and I'll hang out at a cheap motel for a couple of days and take the bus home?'

'Are you serious?'

'I'm serious.'

'Don't you have any money?'

'I've got about sixty dollars in cash on me.'

'Haven't you got a credit card?'

'Not any more. I got rid of 'em. Look, Savannah, things have been tough for me for a while. And I'm trying to see if I can get something going in the pork business. If you could introduce me to your friends, or if I can catch up with this pork guy, my luck might change.'

I wanted to vomit, but instead I told the reservationist that we wouldn't be needing her services after all. I got behind the wheel and looked for the closest bank that took my ATM card. I withdrew two hundred dollars, handed the money to him in silence, then drove until I spotted a cheap motel, where I politely dropped his ass off. When he asked me for Bernadine's phone number, I made one up. 'Can I at least get a kiss?' he asked.

I took a deep breath, rolled my window halfway down, and let him kiss me on the cheek.

'I'll call you tonight,' he said.

'You do that,' I said, and put the car in first gear and sped off.

Discovery

Bernadine was steaming. She'd just left her lawyer's office and was on her way to the bank. She was trying to maintain her composure. 'You lying, sneaky, conniving bastard!' she yelled, and bit down on her cigarette. She replayed what Jane Milhouse had told her: According to John's financial disclosure statement, his annual income was eighty thousand dollars – nowhere near the four hundred thousand Bernadine had estimated it to be. 'He's lying through his teeth,' she had said. 'How in the hell did he come up with that figure?'

'Well, it appears that John sold his half of the partnership late last year and is now a salaried employee.'

'He's what?'

'That's what it says here,' Jane said. 'He claims to have sold his interest in the company to his partner for a mere three hundred thousand.'

'Three hundred thousand! Dollars?' Bernadine lit a cigarette, even though Jane Milhouse had a No Smoking sign in her office. 'Now I know why women kill their husbands,' she said.

Jane went on to say that since John's income was significantly lower than his last year's tax returns reflected, and his income-to-debt ratio was exceedingly high, his lawyer claimed that John was unable to meet Bernadine's support request. Jane said there had clearly been some level of deceit on John's part, as it was obvious that he'd sold the business to reduce Bernadine's community property interest. It sounded like 'a scam,' Jane said. She believed the reason John had been so eager to sign the deed to the house over to Bernadine was to abrogate his equity, which in turn

133

could be 'exchanged' for partial value of the sale of the business. Bernadine was confused, but a few minutes later it all made sense. He was trying to get over on her.

In listing his assets, Jane said, he had also failed to comply with the court's standard discovery order, because he hadn't provided the required evidence to substantiate his claims. She suggested that Bernadine go to the bank today to make sure John hadn't made any major withdrawals. If he had, Jane advised her to withdraw half of what was left and put it into a new account. In her name only. 'I don't trust him. If he sold the business without your knowledge, and at such an unreasonably low price, then there are probably other things he's hiding.' She said it was common practice for spouses with considerable assets to use any tactics they could to protect themselves financially.

Jane also felt it would be wise to hire an investigator to do an asset search, which would enable them to assess everything that was on his statement and, possibly, things that weren't. She advised Bernadine not to discuss *any* of this with John, and under no circumstances should she try to negotiate with him on her own.

As a matter of fact, Jane urged Bernadine to stay as far away from John as possible until after the custody and child support hearing, which was two weeks from now. At that time, Jane planned to ask the judge for four things: to challenge the authenticity of John's financial disclosure statement; to invoke an order that would basically 'freeze' his assets; to secure temporary support and visitation privileges; and to grant her request for a six-week continuance, giving her time to conduct a full and thorough examination of John's financial assertions.

'How much more will this cost me?' Bernadine asked numbly. Jane said that would depend on how extensive the investigation became. She told Bernadine not to worry. If the judge granted her requests – and she was positive he would – and if John failed to comply with any of the court's orders, he could not only be forced to pay her legal fees but be held in contempt, and even go to jail. 'Right now,' Jane said, 'the most important thing for us to do is get the company appraised so that we can determine why and how he sold the business for less than market value, what he did with the money, and if there are any other assets he may have that he hasn't disclosed.'

But Bernadine was worried. What if the judge only made John pay her support based on the income he claimed he was making now? There was a big difference between eighty and four hundred thousand. And what if they got this continuance and she had to wait it out? What was she supposed to do in the meantime? Their living expenses ran close to sixty-five hundred dollars a month. She brought home about fourteen hundred dollars every two weeks. How would she pay her bills?

Bernadine was on her third cigarette by the time she pulled into the bank's parking lot. She put the car in Park and sat there for a few minutes. What kind of man would stoop this low to avoid paying for his kids? And how in the hell could she have ever fallen in love with somebody who had absolutely no respect for anybody but himself? If she had known this was the kind of man she was marrying, she would never have said 'I do.'

'I'd like to open a new checking account,' she said to the bank officer, 'but first I'd like to know the balances in these accounts in order to determine how much I want to transfer into the new one.' She handed him the account numbers for the money market, two CDs, and a checking account.

The officer started punching his computer keys, and Bernadine saw her and John's name appear in orange on the top of his monitor. 'Oh, dear,' he said.

'What's wrong?' She leaned over his desk to get a closer look.

'I'm afraid these accounts have been closed, with the exception of the checking account.'

'Closed?' she said, and leaned even closer. 'What do you mean, closed?'

'I see here that Mr Harris closed them out earlier this week, but he's left the checking account open; it has a balance of three thousand ninety-two dollars, and there's three thousand available in the overdraft as well.'

'But he can't just close these accounts without my signature, can he?'

'Well, yes, he can and he did.'

'But I'm his wife,' she said.

'I understand that, Mrs Harris, but these were the terms under which the accounts were set up, and I'm not sure what to say, except that I'm sorry you've had to discover it this way.'

You motherfucker, she thought. And then panicked. Last week, she had given her lawyer that five-thousand-dollar retainer, which she must not have deposited yet, and yesterday she'd paid bills as usual. She had written close to three thousand dollars' worth of checks, which didn't include the mortgage. It wasn't due for two weeks. 'But I've got checks – bills – that are going to bounce.'

'I wish there was something I could do,' he said.

'I'd still like to know how much was in these accounts before they were closed,' she said. 'The combined total.'

He got his calculator out and looked at the monitor and started punching. A few seconds later, he wrote a figure on a piece of paper and handed it to Bernadine. It said thirty-two thousand dollars and some change.

'We're going through a divorce.'

'I assumed as much,' he said. 'Would you like me to go ahead and open that new account for you now?'

All of a sudden, Bernadine felt confused. Why would he do this to her and the kids? What had she done to him that was so terrible it would make him want to wipe her out, leave her like this? Like it was no big deal. Like her life meant nothing. Were the kids' lives invalid to him too? Was this payback for the cars? And did he find out about the garage sale? But his lawyer had already taken that into account and included it in John's complaint.

'Mrs Harris?'

Bernadine snapped out of it. 'Yes, I'd like to go ahead and open another checking account. Please.'

He handed her the little cards, and she signed wherever there was an X. When Bernadine stood up, it dawned on her that she was broke. 'You motherfucker,' she said aloud this time, and startled the bank officer. She put her blank checks inside her bag, said thank you, and walked out of the bank into the hot afternoon sun.

Bernadine stopped the car and looked at the sign: HARRIS SOFTWARE & COMPUTER SUPPLY. How unoriginal, she thought, as she turned the ignition off and got out of the car. At least they could've changed the damn name. The building itself was dark gray, and the front of the store was black glass. The 'executive' offices, as John called them, were in the back, and behind them, the warehouse. The first person she saw was Lena, standing behind the counter. She looked surprised to see her. 'Hello, Bernadine,' she said. 'And how are you?'

'I'm fine,' she said loudly.

'Are you here to see John?'

What a stupid question, Bernadine thought, but then again, she knew Lena was in an awkward position. Her husband and John golfed together. 'Of course I'm here to see John, Lena,' she said. 'Is he still in the same office?'

'Yes,' she said. 'I'll buzz him,' but Bernadine was already on her way down the hall and had turned the corner when she saw John pick up the phone and put it back down. What a perfect little picture, she thought, as she looked through the plate glass. Kathleen was sitting in front of his desk. Her hair was even blonder than Bernadine remembered. When she saw Bernadine, Kathleen sprang up from the chair. John's hand went up, as if to say, You don't have to leave, I'll handle this.

Bernadine walked inside his doorway and stood stock-still. She looked in Kathleen's face, down at John, and back at Kathleen. Kathleen's face was red. Bernadine's felt redder. Past the boiling point. She was trembling so that she didn't know her arm had flailed up and slapped Kathleen in the face until she saw Kathleen fall against John's desk. Before he could get from behind it, she grabbed Kathleen by the hair and yanked her so close that Bernadine could smell her breath. 'Now. Would you mind terribly if I had a few moments alone with my husband? I won't be a minute.'

John lunged up, pushed his chair to the side, and tripped over his briefcase. Bernadine loosened her grip, and Kathleen fled from the room. When she turned toward John, she clutched her purse and rolled her eyes so tight they looked like slits. He stopped dead in his tracks. Bernadine felt pleased and powerful. 'Don't worry. I don't have a gun,' she said, and sat down in the chair Kathleen had abandoned. 'And you better be glad I don't.'

'You must be delirious or something,' he said. 'You're really testing my patience. You pull a stunt like this again, and *I'm* getting a restraining order. If Kathleen wants to press charges against you, I'll be a glorified witness. What are you doing here?'

'I just left the bank.'

John sat down. 'You're not playing fair, so neither am I.'

He sounded just like a white boy, she thought, which is what he's always wanted to be anyway. 'Why'd you have to do it like this, John?'

'Why'd you burn up all my things? Why'd you

138

sell my fucking car, a car I spent years restoring, for a goddamn dollar? All I'm doing is what I was instructed to do by my attorney.'

'And what am I supposed to do about money?'

'I left you close to seven thousand dollars in the checking account. You've got a job. This should tide you over until we reach some kind of settlement. You really should get a better lawyer. If she'd accepted the amount we offered, we wouldn't have to waste time and money going to court.'

Bernadine was tempted to tell him she knew *everything* he was trying to do, that she was hip to him, but she realized she wasn't supposed to be here. And she didn't want to blow it. 'Look, John. I had to pay my lawyer a five-thousand-dollar retainer.'

'That's too bad. Lawyers are expensive these days, aren't they?'

'And I just paid all the March bills. I've got checks that are going to bounce. What the fuck am I supposed to do?'

'Bernadine, can we be civil about this?'

'Civil? You're the one who closed the fucking bank accounts! The mortgage is due in two weeks. Who's going to pay it?'

'It's your house,' he said. 'If you're willing to reconsider my initial offer, I'd be happy to pay the mortgage and give you fifteen hundred a month until we settle this thing.'

'Fuck you, John.'

'Look, I gave you the damn house. Sell it.'

'Sell it? Today? I will, as soon as I get home. I'll get right on it. Tell me something, when did you take it upon yourself to sell your half of the business?'

'Six months ago.'

'Did you really think you'd get *away* with this shit?'

'I wasn't trying to get away with anything.'

'I hate you, you know that?'

'I'm sorry to hear that, Bernadine.'

'Who do you think helped build this fucking

139

company? Did you really think you could just take the money and run?'

John got up and closed the door. 'The business hasn't been doing as well as you think it has, and don't worry, you'll get something out of it.'

'I'm not worried.'

'Look, Bernadine. Let's not let this thing get any uglier than it already has, OK? I've already given you the house. I'll pay whatever the court tells me to to make sure my kids are taken care of. But I'd be willing to give you three hundred thousand. Today. Cash. And we can be done with this whole thing.'

'You're the one who sounds delirious now. My pussy is worth more than three hundred thousand dollars. And, John, this is already as ugly as it can be.'

'I'd take it if I were you. You'd be saving yourself a lot of money in the long run.'

'Maybe I've been a fool for eleven years. But those days are over, buddy. You want to talk settlement? Have your lawyer call mine.'

'Can I come by on Saturday and get Onika and John?'

'I think not.'

'You can't stop me from seeing my kids, Bernadine.'

'Oh, I can't? Until we go to court, I don't have to let you see 'em at all. You're the one who split. You're the one who abandoned us, or did you forget?'

'I left *you*. I did not abandon my kids. I hope you're not going to try to use them to get back at me.'

'If I wanted to be a bitch, I could. But I'm not a bitch. Where do you want to take 'em?'

'To the movies or something; my place.'

'Your place? Speaking of which, where are you staying these days? With your blond bombshell?'

'I don't want to say just yet.'

'Oh, really. Well, when you get your memory back, that's when you can come and get them.'

'I could be in court on Monday and have visitation rights the same day, and you know it.'

'Look, John. I didn't say you couldn't see 'em, but I'll tell you one thing – you better not even think about taking them anywhere near that white bitch.'

'She's not a bitch,' he said, sounding just like one himself.

'Not yet,' Bernadine said. Then she thought for a minute. 'If I find out they've been in the same room with that whore, you'll regret it for the rest of your life.'

'Are you threatening me?'

'What does it sound like?'

Bernadine put her hand over her purse and stood up to leave. 'You could've at least picked a grown woman, John. But just wait. She may be cute now, but let her have a couple of babies and put up with your bullshit for a few years, and let's see how *cute* you think she is then.'

'Is ten o'clock OK?'

'Honk the horn,' she said. 'They'll be ready.' Bernadine walked over to the door and grabbed the handle, but her hand slipped because her palms were sweaty. Now she wished she had a gun. At least she could crack this goddamn glass.

'Cut it all off,' Bernadine told Phillip. Desiree and Cindy turned to look at her. Both of them hated to see women with long hair cut it, since neither of them had much of her own, but they didn't say a word. Joseph was out on an errand, and Bernadine knew that Gloria was home sick with the flu.

'Are you sure about this, Bernie?' he asked.

'Yes, I'm sure,' she said, while she stared at herself in the mirror. The few folks who were waiting hadn't paid her any attention, because they were busy watching Oprah Winfrey.

'You've got a head full of beautiful hair here, girl-friend, and you know once it's cut it's cut.'

'I know it. But I'm sick of my hair. It's too much trouble, and all I do is worry about what I'm going to

141

do with it. I've got more important things I need to be thinking about besides hair.'

'I hear you,' he said.

'How's Gloria feeling today?' she asked.

'I told you she's got that flu, girlfriend. I had it last week, and it kept me out of commission for five whole days. It's terrible. Going to the bathroom all day long, can't keep your food down, plus a temperature, and you can hardly lift your hand, let alone your body. She's sick as a dog. Tarik's got it too, so you don't wanna be anywhere near either one of them anytime soon.'

'I've gotta call her,' she said, and held up the huge hairstyle magazine that was in her lap. She had marked off a cut she wanted by folding back the corner of the page. 'What do you think of this one, Phillip? Can you do this?'

'Honey, I can cut your hair any way you want it, and you know it, so stop asking silly questions. Give me that magazine,' he said, and snatched it out of her lap. 'Yeah, I can work this,' Phillip said, while he rubbed thick clods of Bernadine's hair between his fingers. 'Your hair feels like straw, girlfriend. Come on back to the sink. We're gonna give you a deep conditioner, then I'll hook you right on up.'

Bernadine followed him. She collapsed in the chair and dropped her head back until her neck fit snugly inside the gap. She looked up at Phillip. His face was brown and oval, blotchy even with foundation on. He wore black eyeliner on his lower lids, and that platinum hair made his head look like a furry moon. She closed her eyes when she heard him testing the water, some of which splattered on her face. He took the nozzle and pressed it against her scalp. The warm, almost hot water felt so good that Bernadine wished she could stay in this spot for ever, especially after Phillip squeezed out large amounts of shampoo and started massaging her head.

When he finished smoothing the conditioner into

her hair and put the plastic cap on her head, Phillip ushered her up front to a hair dryer. 'Fifteen minutes,' he said, and flipped the hood down. The hot air blew out like a shower, and as her shoulders grew warmer, Bernadine felt them drop. The shop was quieter than Bernadine had ever seen it, and she'd been coming to Oasis Hair for years. She could count on one hand the times Gloria actually had to cancel an appointment because she was sick.

Joseph came in the front door, wearing his usual black 'uniform,' and said 'Hey' to everybody. He motioned to his male customer. 'Just let me take one bite of this bagel, and I'll be right with you. I haven't had a thing to eat all day. Oooooh,' he said, when he heard George Michael's 'I Want Your Sex' come on the radio. 'Turn that up.' Desiree, who looked like Diana Ross today, flung her hair away from her face and said, 'I'll do it.'

When the heat stopped, Bernadine lifted the hood. 'Phillip,' she yelled, 'I'm done.' He was in the rear, shampooing another woman.

'Come on back to the sink, and I'll rinse you out.'

Within the hour, Bernadine went from what had felt like pounds of hair on her head to a very short two- or three-ounce style. 'My Lord,' Phillip said. 'I didn't know you were this pretty.'

'I'm hardly pretty, Phillip, but I like it.'

'Look, Bernie. If I say you're pretty, believe me, honey, you're pretty. You just have to learn to appreciate your own face. I think cutting it was a good idea after all, but you're gonna have to come in here at least every four weeks if you want it to keep looking like this.'

'I will,' she said. 'And thanks, Phillip. I like it; I like it a lot.'

'You got it going on, girlfriend. Don't she, Joey?'

'It's working for you, sweetheart,' Joseph said, and took a sip of his coffee. Even Desiree said she liked it. Cindy asked Bernadine if she would let her do her

143

makeup one day, and she looked at her watch, saw that she had a half hour before she had to pick up the kids, and said, 'Is right now too soon?'

Afterwards, one of the manicurists said, 'Now you oughta go ahead and let me do something with those nails.'

Bernadine looked down at them. They were split, chipped, and of various lengths. She could use a manicure, but there was no way she could fit it in now. She'd never consider getting those fake ones. Every other day, Robin would say, 'I've gotta get a fill, girl.' Bernadine couldn't be bothered. 'Some other time,' she said, and handed Phillip and Cindy ten-dollar tips, which made their day.

She walked out of Oasis with a fresh new look. She wondered if Savannah was in town yet. She had left the answering machine on, and she knew Savannah probably wouldn't answer the phone, so there wasn't much sense in calling. When she got into the Cherokee, Bernadine tossed her purse on the passenger seat and checked herself again in the mirror. She did look better, she thought, and reached inside her purse for her cigarettes. Her American Express checkbook fell out. 'Shit,' she said. 'I forgot all about that!' She pushed the lighter in, fumbled around the bottom of her purse for a pen, and, when she found one, wrote herself a check for sixteen thousand dollars.

'Mama, when is Daddy coming back from his trip?' Onika asked, leaning forward from the back seat. Bernadine knew her timing was all off, and she'd been meaning to sit them down to tell them, but everything was happening so fast, the time never felt right. Nor did it now, but she wanted them to know before she got out to her mother's. She had also wanted John to be there, so they could tell the children together, but that seemed unimportant today. She pulled the car into the bank's empty parking lot and turned off the ignition. John junior was playing that stupid Nintendo Game Boy.

'Why are we stopping here, Mama?' Onika asked.

'Because I need to make a deposit.' She got out of the car, filled in the envelope, and dropped it down the slot. John would get the bill at his office, and when he asked her about it, she'd tell him she had taken her half. When Bernadine got back in the car, John junior hadn't even noticed they'd stopped. 'Oh, no,' he sighed. 'I just got killed!'

'Would you put that thing down for a minute?' she said.

He flipped it over in his lap. Bernadine turned around and looked at the two of them sitting there. 'I have to tell you guys something, and it's very important.' Now he was fumbling with a Ninja Turtle. His face was ashy, and Onika's braids were coming loose. 'Do you guys have any idea what a divorce is?'

'Jenna's mom and dad got one,' Onika said.

'It's when you don't live together any more,' John junior said proudly, and dropped his turtle on the seat. For nine years old, this boy was too sure of himself, she thought.

'That's right, John. But do you understand why?'

''Cause you hate each other.'

'That's not true. Who told you that?'

'Zachary told me his mom hated his dad and his dad hated his mom and that's why they got a divorce. There's eight kids in my class who are divorced. And Zachary said everybody is getting divorced because everybody's moms and dads hate each other.'

'That's not true. Don't listen to Zachary. What it really means is that sometimes a mom and dad don't love each other like they used to, and living together is kind of hard.'

'Are you and Daddy getting a divorce?' he asked.

Bernadine wanted to light a cigarette, but she was trying not to smoke in the car when the kids were in it, so she bit her bottom lip and said, 'Yes.'

'Yippee!' yelled Onika, which completely startled Bernadine. 'I can't wait to tell Jenna!'

'You mean Daddy isn't going to live with us any more?' John junior asked.

'I don't think so.'

'Don't you love Daddy any more?' he asked.

Bernadine wanted to say, Hell no, and I haven't for a long time, but she knew better. 'Well, it's a little more complicated than that. Sometimes people still love each other, but they just don't like being around each other as much as they used to. They get on each other's nerves, and then they're always sad or mad and they fight all the time, and it's just better for everybody if they don't live together any more.'

'Where does Daddy live now?' Onika wanted to know.

'Are you getting a new husband?' John asked.

'I think he still lives in Scottsdale, and no, I don't plan on getting another husband anytime soon.'

'Will we get to live with Daddy sometimes, like Jenna does?' Onika asked.

'We haven't worked it all out yet, but you'll get to spend quite a bit of time with your daddy. Weekends, and probably some holidays too.'

'Is that all you wanted to tell us?' John said, easing his Game Boy over and pushing the button to turn it on.

'No. I also want you to know that your daddy still and always will love you guys.'

'When will we get to see him?' he asked.

'Saturday.'

'Are we going to move?' he asked.

'What would make you ask that?'

'Zachary and his mom had to move into an apartment.'

'Well, I don't think we're going to have to move.'

'But I wanna move,' Onika said.

'Why?'

''Cause it would be fun to live somewhere else, huh, JJ?'

'Yeah. Can we move too, Ma? Please?' he begged.

146

'Look, you guys. It's not that simple.'

'Did you say we get to go with Daddy *this* Saturday?' John asked.

'Yes.'

'Yippee!' Onika said.

'But what about my basketball game?'

'Your daddy can take you,' she said, and thought: For once in his life.

'Is Daddy getting a new wife?' John asked.

That struck a sour note with Bernadine, and she didn't know how to answer it, but she blurted out, 'No. It's too soon for him to get another wife, but he may have a friend.'

'You mean a girlfriend,' Onika said.

'Daddy can't have a girlfriend, dummy,' he said.

'Yes he can,' Onika said. 'And I already know who it is.'

Bernadine did not want to hear this. 'Who wants McDonald's?'

'I do. Who?' he asked Onika.

'Kathleen. I want a Happy Meal, Mama.'

'How do you know that, Miss Know-It-All?' he asked.

Bernadine lit a cigarette and started the car up.

'Because.'

'Because why?'

'What do you two want in your Happy Meals?'

'McNuggets and a Sprite,' John said.

'Cheeseburger and a Coke,' Onika said. 'Because I saw her kiss Daddy on the lips. So there.'

Bernadine swung the car around and out on to the street so fast that she ran over the curb. She turned the radio up to blast because she did not want them to hear her crying. She almost choked in the process.

She was sitting in her mother's living room, and the kids were outside. Bernadine had just told Geneva everything that had happened up to today. The only thing that surprised Geneva was that her daughter

147

had chopped off all her hair. 'I never trusted him in the first place,' she said.

'How can you say that, Ma?'

'I've been watching how he operates for a long time. And how he managed to turn you into this sappy woman while he did whatever in God's name he pleased. You've been living like a single parent all these years, so his being gone now shouldn't cause you that much more hardship. All I wanna know is if you're gonna get what's coming to you, so you and these kids won't have to be scrimping and scraping to get by while he lives like Donald Trump.'

'I told you. My lawyer's taking care of it.'

'Well, John better not ever call this house again, 'cause I'll tell him exactly where to go.'

'He hasn't done anything to you, Ma.'

'He's hurt you, and it's the same as hurting me. Look at you. You're a mess. A new hairstyle and a little extra makeup can't hide it, either. Your eyes look sad. And I betcha you've got at least three or four hundred dollars' worth of clothes on your back, and you still look downright haggardly. No man is worth going through these kinds of changes for. No man.'

'Well, regardless, it'll probably be over soon.'

'You don't know how long this mess might take. Everything takes longer than you think.' Geneva reached into Onika's Happy Meal box, got a cold french fry, and put it in her mouth. 'And please don't let him talk you out of anything. He's good for that, you know. And you're just as gullible as the day is long.'

'Ma, give me a break, would you?'

'I will. I don't know how you've tolerated him as long as you have. He is one overbearing son of a bitch. And to think he left you for a white woman!'

'You don't have to remind me, Ma.'

'I betcha she don't know what she's getting herself into.'

'She'll find out soon enough.'

'Anyway, baby, I know this isn't an easy thing to go through. So when these brats get on your nerves and you need to get out, get away, or just need to be by yourself, pick up that phone and call your mother, and I'll take 'em off your hands. Do you understand me?'

'Thank you, Ma. And they're not brats.'

'John junior is, but that's not the point I was getting ready to make. Please don't try to be Superwoman. You're doing too much as it is, working full time – that job uses up too much of your energy, and I don't know how women do it. Go to work, come home and cook and clean, and still tend to the children. And then there's your husband's needs you gotta think about. When do you have time for yourself? Shit, I was lucky, 'cause your daddy worked nights and was there for you all when you got home from school. When I got off that bus, he knew I was tired as a dog, and half the time cooked your dinner. You remember, don't you?'

'Yes, Ma, I remember.'

'But in this day and age, women do too much.'

'You get used to it.'

'Yeah, and have a heart attack before you're forty? It's not worth it. You young people just don't know how to enjoy life. Always in a hurry to do everything and get everywhere. You need to slow down. Relax. When was the last time you and John actually went up to that condo in Sedona that you just had to have?'

'I don't remember.'

'See there. You lied to me about that weekend. I'm not stupid. I knew you weren't going up there for no romantic weekend. You looked like you'd been through the wringer then, but I didn't wanna say nothing. I don't like to interfere.'

'Well, I'm about to make some changes in my life.'

'I would hope so,' she said, and tried to find

another fry in the bottom of the box. 'Like what, for starters?'

'I don't know yet,' Bernadine said. 'But whatever I do, it's going to make the kids' and my life better.'

'You should get out and walk. I get more exercise than you, and you'd be surprised at what exercising can do for your mind.'

'I know, Ma. I've heard.'

'And once this is all over, I hope you quit smoking again.'

'I will.'

'That's all I have to say,' she said, and popped the last shriveled french fry into her mouth.

The kids spotted their toys on the dining room table as soon as they walked in the front door. They were so thrilled that they dashed off to their rooms before Bernadine could make them say thank you. 'Savannah?'

'I'm out here,' she yelled from the patio.

When Bernadine peeked around the door, Savannah was reaching for the handle. 'Girl,' Bernadine sighed, and hugged Savannah hard. Harder than she'd hugged anybody in a long time. 'What are you doing sitting out here in the dark?'

'Thinking,' Savannah said, and sat back down. 'Just thinking.'

Bernadine pulled a lounge chair next to hers and nestled into it. They both lit cigarettes and smoked in silence. Finally, Savannah exhaled. 'Are you scared?'

And Bernadine said, 'Yes.'

'Me too,' Savannah said, and put her cigarette out. She cocked her head to the side and looked out into the darkness. 'You know what I want to know?'

'What?' Bernadine asked.

'How are you supposed to know if you're doing the right thing? I mean, how the hell do you know?'

'Girl, you're asking the wrong person,' Bernadine said. 'I'm trying to figure out how you go about

150

repairing your life after it's been totally ruptured.'

Savannah lit another cigarette, took two consecutive drags, and passed it to Bernadine. 'I don't know,' Savannah said. 'I really don't know.'

When Bernadine handed back the cigarette, Savannah looked over at her. 'I like your hair,' she said.

'Thanks,' Bernadine said, and got up. 'You thirsty?'

'I guess.'

Bernadine went inside and brought back a large bottle of Perrier and two goblets. She set them down on the cement. It was so quiet they could hear the sizzle when Bernadine filled their glasses. They kicked their shoes off, leaned all the way back in their lounge chairs, and sipped. For a while, all they did was stare up at the black sky. Later, they listened to the crickets chirp, watched the lightning bugs glow, and heard the coyotes howl. By the time they finished filling each other in on every single detail of all the recent events in their lives, it was daylight.

Venus in Virgo

I'm not as desperate as I thought I was. Michael is trying. And failing in a big way. He can't fuck, and as his teacher, I can only call him learning disabled. I had to remind myself that he's not the last man on earth. It'd be different if I was completely over the hill and what have you, but I'm not, am I? I mean, Michael is a very nice man and will probably make some woman who doesn't have many physical needs a very happy woman. I wish I could pretend to be one of them.

Maybe I'm a fool. But what am I supposed to do if I can't get it up for him? Life is too short to fake it. And Michael's an even bigger fool than I am. That's what I'm thinking right now. He's lying here next to me, asleep. This is the ninth time we've slept together, and that's about all it boils down to, too. I have never in my life seen a man come so fast. And he's consistent. He also hasn't lost a single pound. As a matter of fact, I think he's put on a few. A week ago, he was taking a bath, and when I looked at him, I realized that under no circumstances would I want to have this man's baby. Who in their right mind would want to walk around for nine months knowing you're going to have a weird-looking baby? Not me. I don't know why I had to get myself all worked up and bothered for nothing.

Me and my big mouth. Me who trusts everybody. Me who doesn't listen. My mother told me a long time ago that a woman should never tell a man the whole truth. She said some things you keep to yourself, because they'll use it against you later. She said a woman should never tell a man how many times she's been in love, how many men she's slept with, and under no circumstances should you give him any details about your past relationships. Well, I forgot.

Now I'm trying to figure out the nicest way to tell Michael that this isn't working out. I want him to get lost. But I also don't want to hurt his feelings, because this fool is definitely in love: gone, hooked. I think Michael's the one who's desperate, which is understandable. He admitted that he's an 'easygoing' kind of guy, and since his last divorce, he's been burned a few times, but 'That's the breaks,' he said. 'I'll keep trying until I get it right.' When you get down to it, he's a sucker. A chump. He's spent more time and money on me in six weeks than all the men I've known put together. Why doesn't that thrill me? He's taken me to the best resorts, restaurants, and what have you, places you need a reservation or a membership to get in. He gave me the money to pay my personal charges on my company's American Express bill and lent me twenty-two hundred dollars to stop the IRS from putting a tax lien on me. He even offered to pay off my student loan, but I didn't want to be indebted to him for ever, so I said no. And regardless of what happens, I plan on paying him back. But Michael doesn't get it. Eighty thousand dollars a year, a house in Paradise Valley, and a 300E can't turn him into a knight.

If I go ahead and get rid of him now, he'll probably think I was using him, but I wasn't. Is it my fault he's so generous? All I've been doing is hoping this could turn out to be a perfect union, but it's not my fault that it hasn't. Is it? I'm glad I had his chart done. Michael's planets are in the wrong houses and not at all in harmony with mine. My Venus is in Virgo, which, in a nutshell, means I'm too critical when it comes to lovers and is the reason I'm still not married. But. According to Frances Sakoian and Louis Acker, it also means that I'm 'a nurturer, capable of sympathy and am helpful when it comes to the sick, and dealing with people who have psychological problems stemming from social maladjustment.' Look how long I put up with Russell. They also claim that if Venus in Virgo is afflicted by Mars, Uranus, Neptune, or Pluto, there can be an overreaction against shyness and social propriety, producing loose living and promiscuity and therefore causing me to make sexual conquests in order to prove my desirability. This shit is not true. And regardless, I've still got to do something about Michael.

I count forty-one gray hairs on his head and finally tap him. 'Michael,' I whisper loudly. 'Wake up.' But he doesn't budge. 'Michael!' I say, louder this time. 'Wake up!'

He rolls over, pulls half the comforter with him, which knocks about ten of my dolls that are piled on top of my hope chest to the floor. The corners of his mouth are white, which I'm not complaining about, because mine are, too, when I wake up. He puts his head in my lap, and I want to push it off, but I don't. Ten minutes go by, and my legs fall asleep. When they're ice cold, I tap him on the back this time. He jumps up like his alarm clock just went off, and when he sees me, he smiles. 'Good morning,' he says, and squeezes my thighs.

'Michael,' I say, 'we gotta talk.'

He sits up. 'Talk?'

'Talk.'

'This sounds serious.' He smiles. 'Can I brush my teeth first?'

'Please,' I say, and when he goes to get up, I feel this burden lift, and the bed springs back into its original shape. I find myself following him over to my bathroom, and my brain is telling me to pretend like there's something in there I need to do. I look for the Visine and squeeze a few drops in each eye. After I do this, Michael reaches over and puts his hand on my behind. I move away from him.

'Oh, it's like that,' he says. 'What's wrong?'

'Michael,' I say, and then stop.

'I don't like the tone of this, Robin. I don't.'

'You want some coffee?' I ask, biting my bottom lip.

'Yes, as a matter of fact, I do. Is this gonna be something heavy?'

'I'm not sure, Michael. I've already got some coffee ready. Come on.' He grabs his blue-and-white-striped bathrobe from the foot of the bed and ties it around his waist, or what would be his waist if he had one. *Stop it, Robin. Just stop it! You're not exactly Vanessa Williams yourself, so just stop it.* I pour us both a cup. We sit down at the kitchen table.

'So what's this all about?' he asks. 'What precipitated this need to talk, although I think I can probably guess.'

'I haven't said a word yet, Michael. Are you clairvoyant or something?' I say. 'I'm sorry. I didn't mean that.'

'I'm still not satisfying you, am I? It hasn't gotten any better for you, has it?'

I don't answer. Instead I take a sip of my coffee.

'I've been trying,' he says.

'I know you have, Michael, and it has been better lately, but that's not the only thing bothering me.' I reach over for the half-and-half. 'I think you're a wonderful man, I really do, and I was hoping that some kind of magic would happen between us so we could live out the fairy tale, but I'm not feeling as excited as I thought I was going to feel, and it has nothing to do with you or your not being a good lover or a wonderful person, because you are.'

'So what's the problem, Robin? Is it Russell? Is he back in the picture?'

'No, he's not. I don't talk to Russell.'

'I'm in love with you, Robin.'

'I know, Michael, and that's what's making this so hard.'

'You mean you want to stop seeing me, is that it?'

'I just think I need a little space is all. Maybe I just need to get a better perspective on you, get some

155

distance. I mean, we've been seeing each other at work and almost every day, and I've got laundry piled up that I could stand to have a little time to do, I haven't cleaned my apartment in weeks, I haven't seen my girlfriends or my parents since I don't know when, and I haven't had a day to myself in so long . . . Do you understand what I'm saying?'

'Do you want to see me any more or not, Robin?'

'I just don't want to see so much of you for a while is all I'm saying. Everything is happening so fast, I'm not keeping up.' This is a real switch for me, I think, asking for 'space.' I wonder if this is what men feel when they ask for it and never come back. Here you are thinking all along that you're ringing their bells, and really they just want out.

'I'm glad we don't work on the same floor,' he says.

'And don't worry, Michael. I have every intention of paying you back.'

'I'm not worried about that money. I just want to know what I can say or do to change your mind.'

'Nothing, right now.' I take a sip of my coffee. 'Michael?'

'Yes?'

I lean forward on my elbows. 'What do you see in me anyway?'

'I've told you plenty of times, Robin.'

'Refresh my memory.'

'I don't want to make a fool out of myself.'

'Believe me, you're not.'

He doesn't say anything for about thirty seconds, and I guess he doesn't have anything to lose, so he says, 'Basically, what I find attractive about you is the fact that we're complete opposites. You're spontaneous and kind of wild – and please don't take that the wrong way. I mean, you do what you want to do and worry about the consequences later. You're unpredictable, smart, and pretty analytical. You're excited about life and all its possibilities, and I just love

156

your sense of humor. And on top of all that, you're beautiful.'

'Wow,' is all I can say. I hadn't looked at myself through somebody else's eyes before, and I was flattered. I'm hoping that somebody else will feel the same way about me, but next time I hope it's somebody who rings my bells.

'I'll say this, and I'll say it again. I love you, Robin. And I would like to marry you. But you take as much time as you need. You go on and date other men, and when you get tired, when you want a real man to take care of you and give you what you need, call me. Would you do that for me?'

'Why are you making it sound so calculated?'

'Because you don't seem to know what you want. I think you still need to till some more soil before you'll be ready to settle down with a man like me.'

'What's that supposed to mean?'

'It means that I've been out here much longer than you have, Robin. You're waiting for a man to come along who'll make you feel fireworks. And he may very well be out there. All I'm saying is that sometimes you have to work a little harder at *starting* the fire, and it may burn a whole lot longer.'

This makes perfect sense, but then again, Michael always makes perfect sense. Which is one of the things that bores me about him. 'I just want to make sure I know what I'm doing,' I say. 'Because sometimes I don't.'

He gets up from the table and puts his empty cup in the sink. 'Do you still want to go the movies today?' he asks.

'I don't think so,' I say, and get up too. 'I'm driving down to Tucson. My mother's having a hard time with my father, and I need to go.'

After he leaves, I feel this incredible sense of relief. I have energy for days. It's only eight-thirty in the morning, so I do my laundry and even fold everything

157

and put it away. I dust and vacuum. I clean the bathroom and take a bath, squeezing out extra bubble bath. I soak for twenty minutes. When I get out, I give myself an organic mud facial and put fresh sheets on my bed. Afterwards, I wash off the facial and put on a pair of denim shorts, a neon-yellow T-shirt, a pair of thick yellow socks, and my Nike Airs. I put one of my handkerchiefs in my back pocket and slip on a Los Angeles Lakers baseball cap because I need to get my hair touched up, then I take my car to the car wash and start the ninety-mile drive to Tucson, with the top down and the music blasting. I put my sunglasses on and sing along with the radio until they start playing nothing but rap. I put on Tracy Chapman, but she's too mellow for me right now, so I pop her out and put on Bobby Brown. I pass through the Gila Indian reservation and, as usual, wonder where they all are. I look out at the dry golden fields, then orange groves with green oranges hanging from their branches. I see fields of cotton and think it's ironic that it's Mexicans now who pick it. I laugh when I pass the sign by the prison that says DO NOT STOP FOR HITCHHIKERS. The mountains that are far away look like someone painted them into the sky. The one that's right here, Picacho Peak, makes me want to stop the car and climb up to the top. One day I will. I pass the Pima Air Museum and once, just once, I would like to turn the car off at this exit to see what's so special about those airplanes. By the time I get to Orange Grove Road, I know I've been trying too hard to make myself not think about what I'm thinking about. For the last eighty miles, I've been trying to appreciate how breathtaking nature can be, how beautiful Arizona is. I've been trying to pay extra-close attention to everything I see, so I won't think about my daddy as much. But now that I'm almost there, the image of him getting worse is wiping everything out.

When my mother answers the door, she looks worn out, sad. She's still losing weight. She never has been a big woman, but now she's too thin, and I know it's because of Daddy. We say hello, kiss each other on the cheek, and she presses her hand to the right side of her face and looks like she wants to say something, but doesn't. Or can't. I see the green and blue veins popping through her skin and remember when her hands used to be smooth and brown. Her hair is still in rollers, and she's wearing a dull floral housedress. Ever since her operations, she still wears a bra but stuffs the cups with foam. When I bend down to hug her, I feel them cave in. It breaks my heart. 'Where's Daddy?' I ask.

She shakes her head back and forth and points. 'In the kitchen, making his lunch.'

I walk through the living room – which is full of the same furniture they had when I was little – to the kitchen, and there he is, with at least ten slices of whole-wheat bread spread out on the counter and a jar of mayonnaise in front of him. He has a plastic case knife in his hand, because my mother's hidden all the real ones. He's a big man, which is where I get my height from, but now he's as thin as thread. His bluejeans sag, his once broad shoulders are round and narrow, his long arms are bonier than mine. My daddy's hair is white, full of tiny curls that lay flat against his head. But I see patches of his scalp, be-cause he's been pulling his hair out. 'Hi, Daddy,' I say, and when he turns around, he nods and keeps on spreading the mayonnaise on a slice of bread.

'What's doing, pumpkin?' he says, and I feel a smile come on my face because he recognizes me this time. He sounds like himself today, because his speech is usually slurred and slower.

'Just came down to see how you and Ma are doing.'

'I'm fine. Just making my lunch here. Getting ready to go to work.'

Work? He hasn't worked since 1981, when he retired from the army. I can't stand seeing Daddy like this. 'You must be pretty hungry today,' I say.

'What's it look like?'

'I was just saying you must be good and hungry, Daddy.'

'Don't get smart with me,' he says. 'I'm minding my own business, making my own lunch, so don't get smart with me.'

'I'm sorry, Daddy. I wasn't trying to get smart.'

'Then leave me alone,' he says, and shoos me with his hands.

I go back into the living room. My mother is sitting there, looking like she doesn't know what to do next. I hate this disease and what it's doing to both of them. A few months ago, when she started feeling really sad because Daddy was getting worse, she took the doctor's advice and joined one of those support groups for people who have family members with Alzheimer's. She took Daddy to one of the meetings, but he embarrassed her so bad she said she couldn't go back. She said he had stood up while someone was talking and just started singing some hymn he'd learned from the Church of Latter-day Saints, and then he started crying and couldn't stop. I remember when Daddy talked her into going to that church. They were the only black people in the whole congregation, but it never bothered him, and when he asked her if she wanted to convert from Catholicism to become a Mormon, that was the first real sign that something was wrong with Daddy.

In the beginning, he forgot little things: like where he put something he just had; or right after my mother asked him to do something, he couldn't remember what it was. Then bigger things: he forgot their address and phone number, and how to tie his shoe, and he got lost going to the store that was only two blocks away. Daddy started doing things he'd never done before and got upset over things that never bothered him before. For the past two years, he's gotten progressively worse, which is the way this disease works.

Sometimes he thinks Ma is his mother, and she said when he's like this, there's nothing she can say or do to convince him otherwise. My parents have been married for thirty-nine years. They used to travel all over the world. Golf. Camp. With his own hands, my daddy built our house in Sierra Vista, but now my mother has to get in the shower with him to help him bathe. He wets the bed, and she changes the sheets. He used to be fluent in French but now can't understand a word. He always thinks somebody is following him or trying to kill him, and sometimes he hides. Ma says that sometimes his anger is so frightening she holds a pillow in front of her to make sure that if he tries to hit or pinch her – which has happened a few times – she won't feel it. What sets him off, she says, is when he's trying to think of too many things at once, or there's an unexpected break in their daily routine, or violence on TV.

When she started getting phone calls from the police in the middle of the night because they found Daddy roaming up and down the streets in his pajamas, she had to change the locks so he couldn't get out. For the last six months or so, his motor skills have deteriorated so much that he can't put his clothes on or take them off. Sometimes he doesn't understand what she says, so she tries to talk in short sentences. Daddy knows he has this disease, but there's nothing he can do, because he can't control his behavior any more.

'Ma, we've gotta do something,' I say.

'I know. But he said he doesn't want to go to any nursing home – he's as clear as the sky about that – and I don't want to put him in one.'

'What about a nurse? I'll help pay for a full-time nurse.'

'Do you know how much it would cost? Twelve hundred dollars a month. You don't have that kind of money, and neither do we.'

She's right, but I can't sit around and watch them deteriorate like this. At the rate they're going, Ma might be the one to go first. She's tired. She's been caring for Daddy now for two years, and it's obvious she can't keep doing this by herself. If I thought quitting my job and moving in with them would help, I would. But Ma doesn't want me to do that. Last year, I offered to take a leave of absence, but she wouldn't have it. 'You've got a whole life ahead of you,' she said. 'Don't stop living because of us. We'll manage.'

'I'll think of something,' I say.

'I better go check on him,' she says, and gets up.

I look around the house, which she's 'childproofed' because Daddy's always losing his balance or getting mad for no particular reason and destroying things. She keeps the hot water turned off in the bathrooms because he almost scalded himself once trying to brush his teeth. And he's always hiding things in the strangest places: his wristwatch in the toilet bowl; his favorite coffee cup under the bed; books he can't read any more underneath dirty clothes in the laundry basket. For some reason, he likes silver. When Ma first noticed her good salt and pepper shakers were missing, then the serving trays and her sterling teapot, she asked him about it and Daddy said he didn't know where they were. Even when she found forks and knives and spoons in the pockets of his winter coats, he insisted he hadn't taken them.

He comes out of the kitchen with Ma. She's holding his hand. She told me once that one of the things that helps is human touch. She ushers him to the couch and goes to get some clothes out of the dryer. As soon as Daddy sees her leave the room, he gets up and starts pacing. 'What time is it?' he asks.

'One-thirty,' I say.

'I've got to go. I'm late,' he says, and heads for the door.

'Wait!' I yell, and jump up.

'Don't scream,' my mother says, and rushes out of the laundry room toward the front door. But Daddy's already outside. 'If you scream,' she says, 'it only makes it worse.'

We both run outside, and since Daddy can't walk very fast, we catch up to him easy. But he won't let us touch him. 'Get away from me!' he screams, and pushes me and my mother away with a strength I didn't know he still had.

'We just want you to come back in the house, Daddy,' I say as softly as I can.

'Come on, Fred, it's gonna be OK. They're waiting for you at work. Your boss just called.'

'He did?'

'Yes, and you need to get dressed. I've got your uniform all laid out for you.'

'Is this a trick?'

'No, Daddy, it's not a trick,' I say, and hold out my hand. He looks at me like he doesn't trust me, and looks at my mother. He takes her hand. This hurts, until I make myself remember that this is part of the disease and not my daddy's will. We head back to the house, both of us holding him by the arm, and when we get inside, Ma locks the front door with her key. Daddy goes into the bedroom, and she follows him. I feel useless and don't know what to do, so I go into the kitchen.

Daddy'd put mayonnaise on every single piece of bread and stacked them all on top of each other. He'd put some instant coffee in a plastic container and mixed the sugar and coffee creamer in with it. He'd taken out a can of frozen juice and put it in a plastic Baggie. I don't touch anything, because I don't want to upset him. I leave everything where it is. I hear Ma say it's time for his medicine, and it doesn't sound like Daddy's putting up a fight.

When I walk back out into the living room, she's turned the TV on and is pouring him a double shot of whiskey.

'That's his medicine?' I ask.

'It works,' she said. 'It settles him down. You'll see.'

So I sit there and watch my daddy drink his whiskey, and I watch him watch TV for close to an hour before I realize that he's closed his eyes and is sound asleep.

'This is what I do all day,' my mother says.

'Don't worry,' I say. 'I'll figure out something. I can't stand to watch you and Daddy live like this. And I won't.'

I end up washing clothes and cleaning up, and I want to take them shopping or to a movie or something, but because of Daddy, we can't. And we can't very well leave him at home by himself. Ma turns the TV to Nickelodeon, a kiddie channel. 'He likes this,' she says, and goes to start dinner. Daddy wakes up, we watch Inspector Gadget and then Looney Tunes. He doesn't utter a single solitary word. When I ask him if he's enjoying the programs, he just sits there, as if he can't hear me or like I'm not here.

We eat dinner, which is pretty uneventful, and Ma gives him his real medicine and reads him a bedtime story. He likes it, because I hear him laugh. He falls asleep before Ma finishes the story. It's only twenty minutes after eight when she comes out of her bedroom with her pajamas on. Now her chest is flat. 'I'm going to bed,' she says. 'You don't have to spend the night, baby. If you've got something better to do, go on home. It's not as bad as it looks.'

'But I want to spend the night.'

'Then let the couch out. If you hear your daddy stumbling around out here, just don't say anything to him and he'll go on back to bed.'

'I won't,' I say, and give her a hug and kiss good night.

It's hard falling asleep. And my daddy doesn't wake up during the night. As hard as I try not to, I keep wondering why he had to get stuck with this stupid disease in the first place. Why couldn't God have given him some other affliction, one that wouldn't wreak havoc with his mind? My daddy has always been a strong man, the one man I respected, the one man I looked up to, the one man I expected all the others to live up to. I've always been his little girl, and I'm still his little girl. And what about my mother? What's she gonna do when he's gone? How's she gonna survive? Her whole life has revolved around my daddy.

In the morning, I feel somebody standing over me, and when I open my eyes, it's Daddy. He's smiling at me. The same way he used to smile at me when I was little. 'You want to know something?' he says.

'Yes,' I say, and sit up.

'I love you,' he says, and thumps me on my head. 'Don't you ever forget that,' he says, and heads for the kitchen.

When I get home, I have one message. From Bernadine. She said that Savannah's been here over a week now, that she found an apartment right down the street from me and wants me and Gloria to meet her, so try to keep Wednesday open so we can go to happy hour somewhere. I know I have to go to Casa Grande that day for a presentation, but I figure I'll be home long before six. I call her back, and Savannah answers.

'Hi,' I say. 'This is Robin.'

'Hi,' she says. 'Well, I've heard a lot about *you*, and I hear we're almost neighbors.'

'Don't believe anything nasty Bernadine tells you about me. When do you move in? And where's your place?'

'I move in tomorrow. It's a complex called the Pointe.'

'I'm less than five blocks from the Pointe! This is too much. We'll definitely be neighbors!'

'Good, because I don't know a soul here except Bernadine.'

'Well, now you know me. I'll get on your nerves, so let me warn you in advance. Bernadine said you're working for KPRX. That's cable, right?'

'Yep. Channel 36, and I start next Monday.'

'Then let's have lunch some time. My office is only about three or four blocks from there.'

'All right,' she said.

'Do you like to go out? You know, party?'

'Who doesn't?'

'Well, the Ebony Fashion Fair is in three weeks. You want to go?'

'That's not really my cup of tea. I've been to one, and it was nice, but once was enough.'

'I hear you. Well, there's some other things going on. But do this. Get my number from Bernadine. And call me.'

'I will,' she said. 'Will we see you on Wednesday?'

'Just name the place ... So are you adjusting to Phoenix?'

'There doesn't seem to be all that much to adjust to.'

'You're right. This is a dull place to live. What made you want to move here anyway?'

'This job. And it can't be any deader than Denver.'

'Well, I hope it works for you.'

'Me too. Hold on, and let me see if I can get Bernie for you. She's helping John junior paint the solar system on his bedroom walls and ceiling.'

'What?' I ask, but she'd already put the phone down.

'Hey, girl,' Bernadine says a few minutes later.

'*What* are you doing?'

'I bought the boy this stencil called Night Sky. When he goes to sleep at night he'll feel like he's outside on a camping trip. But painting it on the ceiling is a bitch. My neck is about to fall off. We're almost finished, thank God.'

'I don't get it, Bernie.'

'When you turn the light out, it looks like a real galaxy. Stars and constellations and stuff. Now I'm trying to find that damn Milky Way. You might want to think about getting one, since you're so into the stars.'

'Go to hell, Bernadine.'

'Anyway, it's about time somebody heard from your black ass. When you're being wined and dined, nobody hears from you. What's up?'

'Nothing. Just got back from Tucson, visiting the folks.'

'How's your daddy?'

'The same.'

'What about your mother – how's she holding up?'

'She's hanging in there. But I've gotta figure out a way to get her some help. It's sad, girl. She can't keep doing this by herself. Daddy's too big for her to be lifting and holding him and stuff. He's almost like a baby.'

'Isn't there any way to get him a home nurse?'

'I don't have the money. And they don't have that kind of money, either.'

'Well, can't you put them on your insurance?'

'I already thought of that, but no.'

'Then what can you do?'

'I don't know,' I say, and change the subject quick. 'Anyway, Wednesday's good for me. And Savannah sounds nice.'

'You'll like her. She's almost as crazy as you.'

'Cool. So how's everything going with you?'

'It's going. My lawyer had me hire a private detective.'

'For what?'

'To check John's shit out. He is one sneaky motherfucker, you know that?'

'Yeah, I knew that.'

'No, you don't know. Anyway, this guy's already found out shit I can't even begin to believe.'

'Like what?'

'Like John's got property all over the fucking place. You know he sold the company, right?'

'No, I didn't know that,' I say. But I was lying. Gloria had told me everything, including that shit he pulled closing all their bank accounts and Bernadine writing that check to herself that John can't do anything about except pay it. Bernadine always gets

167

around to telling me everything anyway, so I figured I should act surprised.

'Yeah,' she says. 'He actually thought he could get away with the shit, but my lawyer knows what she's doing. We had the child support and custody hearing, and my lawyer got it continued until we find out everything. The judge was pissed.'

'Why?'

'Because John's financial statement is packed full of lies, and the judge didn't want to be bothered. Anyway, my lawyer filed some kind of motion that stops him from selling any of his assets, freezes the shit, and if he tries to do anything with it before we reach a final settlement, his ass'll be in big trouble.'

'So when will you know how much you're gonna get?'

'I don't know. We go back to court in six weeks. The judge ordered him to pay me eighteen hundred a month for now, plus he has to pay the mortgage, car payments, and insurance.'

'What about the kids?'

'Until we go back to court, he gets to see them every other weekend and two evenings a week. I'm sick of seeing his ass already. I won't let him come in the house. I make him wait outside in his car.'

'Good. How long do you think the whole thing'll take?'

'I don't know, girl. It could be weeks, months, and then again, it could be years. It depends on what they find and how long it takes 'em to find it.'

'Get out of here!'

'I'm serious. This whole process is deep, girl. And John had the nerve to offer me three hundred thousand.'

'And you didn't take it?'

'I'm not a fool,' she says.

She sure sounds like one. If somebody offered me that kind of money, I'd take it and run.

'Do you know how long three hundred thousand dollars would last in 1990?'

168

'It'd last me awhile,' I say. 'My daddy would have a full-time nurse, I know that much. I'd pay off my student loan and my credit card loan and buy myself a house.'

'Anyway, my lawyer told me to be patient. She said John is slick but he's sloppy. His biggest mistake was selling the business at such a ridiculously low price. So they're checking *everything* out. If I hadn't found out about all his wheeling and dealing, I might've considered settling out of court. But not now. No way.'

'I hear you,' I said.

'I might have to sell this house, though.'

'Why?'

'Because I may need the money if this shit goes on and on and on.'

'You just said you're getting child support.'

'Yeah, but when you get right down to it, it's barely enough to get us by. Do you have any idea how much it costs to *run* a house this size with two kids in it?'

'No, but I know it's a lot.'

'Do you know how much it costs to cool a four-thousand-square-foot house?'

'No.'

'And then there's the gardener, the pool man, and the housekeeper. But I'm not letting her go; I don't care what happens. And we're not even talking about food. John junior's feet are growing an inch a day. Every time I look around, he needs a new pair of sneakers. Anyway, girl, I didn't mean to go off. To make a long story short, the court's making him pay the mortgage for now, but they can't force him to pay it for ever. My lawyer made that clear. So how's Michael?'

'He's out of the picture.'

'Already?'

'He was boring.'

'You know, you sound like a fool, Robin. What is it, you've just got a thing for dogs? From your description, he sounded like a nice guy. So he's a few pounds overweight. Big deal. Even Gloria said she thought

169

he was nice when she met him. He sounds to me like the most principled man you've come in contact with since I've known you.'

Thank God the phone clicks. 'Hold on a minute,' I say, and press the receiver. It's Russell. 'How you doing, Robin?'

'I'm fine.'

'That's good. What you doing?'

'Talking to Bernadine.'

'And how's she doing these days?'

'Just fine.'

'I miss you,' he says.

'No you don't.'

'Yes I do.'

'Since when?' I say.

'Since I've been gone,' he says.

'You've been gone a long time, Russell.'

'I know it. Too long. I do miss you, Robin.'

'Well, you've got a funny way of showing it.' There's a long pause. 'Russell?'

'I'm here,' he says. 'You feel like some company?'

I don't even think about it. I just say yes.

'See you in a half hour,' he says.

I click Bernadine back. 'I've gotta go.'

'Is something wrong?'

'No,' I say. 'What makes you think something's wrong?'

'Well, I *thought* we were in the middle of a conversation.'

'I need to talk to this person, that's all.'

'Is it Russell?'

'No, it's not Russell, Bernadine. And so what if it is?'

'I just asked. Damn. Anyway, I'll see you Wednesday. Wait a minute.'

'What?' I say impatiently.

'The BWOTM meeting's been changed. It's not until April fifth. That's a Thursday. Mark it on your calendar.'

'Gloria already told me.'

'And be prepared to serve on a committee.'

'What this time?'

'I don't know. Come and find out.'

'Bye, Bernadine. And tell the kids I said hi.' I hang the phone up and run to the bathroom. I take a quick douche and thank God for sending me a desirable man tonight. I don't care if Russell belongs to somebody else. I don't care if he has to get up and leave when it's over. And I almost don't care when I look under the sink and my box of Today sponges is empty.

Happy Hour

Bernadine was glad to get out of the house. Gloria prayed she wouldn't be bored to death. Savannah was hoping she'd meet somebody worth giving her phone number to, and Robin kept her fingers crossed that she wouldn't run into anybody she'd slept with.

They agreed to meet at Pendleton's around six-thirty. Robin offered to pick up Savannah when she found out her meeting would be over much earlier than expected. This gave her enough time to zip by Oasis to get a nail repaired and stop at home to change into something flashier.

More than anything, Robin wanted an excuse to see Savannah's apartment. Bernadine had bragged about Savannah's artworks and said she had very good taste. Robin wanted to see for herself. She knew her apartment didn't exactly look like it came out of *Architectural Digest*, but it *was* colorful. When Robin rang her bell, Savannah came to the door wearing a form-fitting orange dress with a wide white belt and orange sling-back sandals. Her hair was cut close on the sides, and skewered-looking curls stuck straight up on the top. It was different from anything Robin had ever seen on anybody down at Oasis. 'Hi,' Robin said. 'I'm Robin.'

'No shit,' Savannah said, and gave her a hug. 'Come on in,' she said. 'Have a seat. I'll be ready in ten seconds. As you can see,' she said, walking down a hallway, 'I haven't had a chance to unpack everything yet, so forgive the place.'

'It looks to me like you've done a lot in two days,' Robin yelled, and sat down on the couch. She ran her hands over the forest-green cushion. This wasn't cheap leather by any means, she thought. There were six mint-green and peach throw pillows strewn along the back. Stacks of boxes were pushed in corners, but there were sculptures sitting on at least four different pedestals, silk flowers on tables, ceramic vases such as Robin had never seen before: copper-colored; metallic green; blackish-silver; each a different shape, and some with blotches of color that made them look like a map of the world. The movers had obviously broken a few, because some were badly cracked, but Robin didn't want to say anything. Savannah already had pictures up on three walls. Robin didn't particularly care for this kind of art, because half of them didn't look like they were finished. The few she *was* able to make out – what they were supposed to be – didn't match anything in here.

'I'm ready,' Savannah said, and came out of the bathroom.

'Your place is gorgeous,' Robin said, standing up. 'Is this a one or two bedroom?'

'One. It's not much to see, but come on back if you want to.'

'I'm nosey,' Robin said, and followed Savannah down the hall.

'This is me,' Savannah said, waving her hand like the women on game shows who show contestants what they can win.

A queen-sized platform bed with four oversized stuffed pillows sat in the middle of the room. Behind it was a picture of a nude man and woman. Next to the fireplace was an ice-cream parlor table with a black and rose floral tablecloth; oak chairs with wrought-iron backs, and more unpacked crates and boxes stacked in a corner. One whole wall looked like the millinery section of a department store. At least twenty hats hung on hooks.

'So I guess you're into hats,' Robin said.

'I am,' Savannah said, and headed toward the living room.

'Well, you should've called. I would've been glad to help you unpack.'

'Girl, this stuff was in storage, and everything was all mixed up. I'm having a hard enough time finding things myself, but thanks.'

'Some people just have the knack of knowing how to put things together, and some don't. I think you missed your calling. You should've gone into interior decorating.'

'Bernadine said your place was pretty nice too. So stop. I wish I could've brought my plants.'

'Why couldn't you?'

'They wouldn't let me bring them across the state border. They worry about bugs. It broke my heart. But it's OK. I've got to get some. I can't stand being in here without live plants.'

'Well, I've got about three, and they're on their last legs.' Robin started rubbing her eyes, because they were itching all of a sudden, and the next thing she knew she was sneezing.

'You're allergic to cats, right?' Savannah asked.

'Yes. Lord,' she said. 'Where is the little sucker?'

'In the back,' she said. 'I'm ready.'

As Savannah reached for her purse and keys, she looked at Robin, particularly her cleavage, which was extremely prominent in that white top. 'You're looking pretty snazzy yourself. If I had legs as long as yours, I'd probably wear miniskirts too. How tall *are* you?'

'Almost five nine,' Robin said, taking a handkerchief from her purse and wiping her eyes. 'I wish I had some of your ass,' she said, and sneezed again.

'Well, in that case, I'd like to borrow about sixteen ounces of your boobs.'

'Then buy you some. How do you think I got these?'

They both laughed, and Robin sneezed again.

'Well, I know one thing. I won't have to worry about you wearing out your welcome.'

'You got that right;' Robin said. 'Now get me the hell outta here.'

174

*   *   *

'What kind of resort is this?' Savannah asked Robin. It seemed as if they had driven through Little Mexico to get here, and the place looked as though it could stand to be remodeled.

'Girl, I don't know. This is my first time here too.'

They were standing in the entry, when a black man in his early thirties came over to greet them. He looked pleased and excited to see them. Robin pinched Savannah, as if to say, 'He's all yours.' Savannah pinched her back, as if to say, 'I don't want him, either.'

'Thanks for coming,' he said. 'Is this your first time here, ladies?'

They both shook their heads yes.

'Well, I'm Andre Williams, and me and a few of my partners have formed the Stock Exchange Group. We're trying to get some exciting things happening in Phoenix, a place where professional sisters and brothers can network and get to know one another in an informal setting and, you know, dance a little, eat a little, and drink a little.'

'Are all of you stockbrokers?' Robin asked.

'No, sister. We just wanted to come up with a catchy, sophisticated name. It's the one we all liked. Do you two ladies have a business card?'

Robin did, but Savannah didn't have hers yet; she hadn't anticipated needing one so soon. The moment this man said 'network,' Savannah cringed. She hated the whole notion. It was as if black folks couldn't get together and have a good time any more unless they were in a position to do something for each other. Whatever happened to good old-fashioned fun? There was a little basket for the cards, and Robin tossed hers in. What were they going to do with them? Savannah wondered. 'I'll bring mine next time,' she said, and peeked around a partition into the adjoining room. There were fifteen or twenty people in it. What a helluva turnout, she thought. It was easy to see

175

that Bernadine and Gloria weren't here yet, so she turned her attention to Robin, who had walked over by the windows, where a woman with long dreadlocks stood behind two tables. One was filled with books by and about black people, the other with various African crafts: silver and brass jewelry, kinte cloths, wooden and soapstone sculpture, handmade cards, T-shirts with Africa on front, as well as little bottles of fragrant oils. There were posters of Nelson and Winnie Mandela, Malcolm X, and Martin, as well as Magic Johnson and Michael Jordan.

Robin had her wallet out and two black bangles already on her wrists. Bernadine had told Savannah that the girl was a die-hard shop-aholic and terrible at managing her money. Savannah smiled at the sister selling the merchandise, eyed one of the soapstone sculptures, but kept her distance. She hadn't come here to shop. Besides, she was now on something she'd never been on before: a budget.

'Come on, Robin,' Savannah said, and headed for one of the forty or so empty tables. When they sat down, it felt as if they were on display, which Robin didn't seem to mind. She liked getting attention, and it showed. There were ten men sitting at the bar, a few of whom turned around and looked at them, and then turned back toward the bar.

'I thought this thing started at six,' Robin said. 'That's what Bernadine told me.'

'This is your world. I'm just in it,' Savannah said.

'I wonder where everybody is. Well, at least the music is good.'

'Forever Your Girl' was playing. 'I can't stand Paula Abdul,' Savannah said. 'She can't sing. Jodey Watley can't sing, and if you want to know the truth, Janet Jackson can't sing, either. I'm sick of all three of them.' But, she thought, if somebody was to ask her to dance right now, she would. But nobody did.

A waitress came over and took their order. Robin ordered a glass of wine, and Savannah, a margarita.

'That must be where you dance,' Robin said, pointing to a wide doorway, and within a minute she had walked over to it, peered in, come back, and sat down. 'Yep, they've got a DJ in there and everything. There's some tables in there too. And not a soul on the dance floor.'

Savannah was staring out the window at the golf course when the waitress brought their drinks. 'I'll buy this round,' Robin said. 'And let's get some of that food over there, girl. It's free, and I haven't eaten.'

They weren't stingy with the food, Savannah was thinking as she filled her plate up with fresh fruit salad, tossed green salad, pasta salad, and buffalo wings. Normally, she never ate chicken in public because it always got stuck between her teeth, and plus, she forgot to put her dental floss in her purse. But hell, nobody worth worrying about was in here.

Robin made two trips to the food table and drank her wine in between plates. On the way here, she had told Savannah her life story, which didn't seem to start until she met Russell. She told Savannah *all* about him. And Michael. And how she wanted to have a baby before it was 'too late.' When she finally mentioned her job as an underwriter and all it entailed, particularly how she sometimes wrote proposals that brought in million-dollar accounts, it sounded to Savannah like the only time Robin used common sense was at work. 'It looks good on paper,' Robin said, 'but I'm still not making any *real* money, and I'm seriously thinking about looking for another job, at a bigger company. The way things stand now, I'm living from paycheck to paycheck and can't even afford to help pay for a nurse for my daddy. That's pitiful,' she said, as if she was talking to herself. 'What the hell did I get a degree for?'

The place was starting to fill up, but there was still no sign of Gloria or Bernadine. Now on her second glass of wine, Robin went back to her favorite subject: Russell. She apologized for his philandering. 'Could he

177

help it if he was so fine that women flocked to him? If I'd been a little more patient and not pressured him, maybe he would've married me,' she said. 'But it's not over till it's over.' Savannah didn't say a word. She just sat there listening to the shit and wanted to slap Robin. Knock some sense into her. Savannah agreed with Bernadine: the woman *was* a little on the dizzy side when it came to men.

Savannah sipped at her second margarita, thinking: This woman is pitiful. Too hard up. But she liked Robin, mostly because she was apparently quite resilient, openly honest, and totally unaware of how dense she was. She ran her mouth a mile a minute, no doubt about that, because Savannah had already smoked three cigarettes in the thirty-five minutes they'd been sitting here.

Now Robin leaned forward over the table. 'If I tell you something, you promise not to tell Gloria or Bernadine?'

'I promise,' Savannah said.

'I let Russell spend the night last Saturday.'

'That's your business,' Savannah said.

'Well, Bernadine always claimed that Russell was nothing but a whore with a dick, so she wouldn't understand, and Gloria had the nerve to tell me that Russell wasn't *stalling;* he just didn't want to marry me. But Gloria doesn't know anything about men, because she's never really had one. It's a shame, if you ask me. She's too pretty to be so damn fat.'

'Every woman wasn't meant to be a size nine, Robin.'

'I know that. But losing sixty or seventy pounds wouldn't hurt her. Anyway, I don't want to talk about Gloria. I'm still optimistic,' Robin said, and leaned back in her chair.

'About what?'

'Russell. Girl, I whipped something on him so tough, he hated to leave.'

'So he spent the whole night?'

'No. He had to take his mother to church early the

178

next morning.' Robin then asked Savannah if she'd heard the rumor going around that Russell was living with some woman who was supposed to be having his baby. Savannah said no. 'Russell said it's not true. And after Saturday night, I hate to say it, but I believe him.'

That's when Savannah could've slapped her again.

'I want him back, girl,' she said. 'And I'm going to get him back.'

'But why would you want him back?' Savannah asked.

'Because I'm never going to meet another man like him.'

'Like what?'

'First of all, he can dress his ass off, he's the best lover I've ever had since I've been in Phoenix, he's fine as can be, and I know he'd make some pretty babies.'

This was too much for Savannah. 'But hasn't he hurt you?'

'I guess, but you tell me what man doesn't hurt you at one time or another. I don't think he did it intentionally. Russell still has some growing up to do.'

'And you want him to do it on your time?'

'Not really. But I think this time apart has done him some good. He does have *some* good qualities.'

'Such as?'

'He's got charisma, and he's a whole lot of fun when he wants to be.'

'And?' Savannah said.

'Like I said, he's a super-deluxe lover, we like to do some of the same things, and we click. And I love him.'

'Well, what makes you think you won't meet somebody better?'

'It's already been close to a year, and all I've met is old dorky Michael.'

'Well, let me ask you this, Robin. What makes you think he *wants* to come back?'

'Because he told me he did.'

'And you believed him?'

'Why shouldn't I?'

Savannah didn't have the energy to respond to that. 'Well, why would you want to be with a man, knowing you can't trust him?'

'I do trust him,' she said. 'People change,' she said. 'And you can't hold a few mistakes against somebody for the rest of their life.'

'This is true,' Savannah said, and licked the rest of the salt from the rim of her glass. It was amazing to her how some women could be so stupid. They make up all kinds of excuses for a man after he's treated them like dirt; apologize for his revolting behavior; and take him back after he's broken their fucking hearts – so he can break them again. And this is supposed to be love? This is supposed to be healthy? This is supposed to be the way to live your life with a man? Not me, Savannah thought, as she listened to Robin move on to what was obviously her second-favorite topic: herself.

'I wish I could just get some plastic surgery and be done with everything,' she said.

'For what?'

'My ass is too flat, my nose is shaped weird, my lips are too thin, and the inside of my thighs won't get firm to save my life. I'm starting to get these bags under my eyes, see?' and she pulled on that area to make her point.

'You look fine,' Savannah said.

'I used to look better. I don't like this getting-old shit, I swear I don't.'

Savannah thought Robin was quite attractive, and she couldn't understand why someone who looked like she couldn't be in better shape was wearing herself out fretting over her age, her looks, and her body. What she needed to do was get rid of that damn weave and stop wearing that red blush, because it was too bright for her dark skin.

'I wanted to have a baby before I turned thirty-six. Don't you?' she asked.

'I'm already thirty-six,' Savannah said, 'and I'm not wasting my energy worrying about it. I'll tell you one thing: I'm not having one by myself, that's for damn sure. Just so I can say I did it? No way.'

'I might,' Robin said. 'If I have to. What sign are you?'

'What?'

'When's your birthday?'

'October fourteenth.'

'A Libra. Cool. I get along good with Libras. I guess you don't know what your rising sign is, do you?'

'No, I don't,' Savannah said.

'Do you know what time you were born?'

'Yes.'

'Good, then I can do your chart for you.'

'I don't want my chart done,' Savannah said.

'It can help you figure out what's going on in your life.'

'I know what's going on in my life,' Savannah said. 'Has it helped you?'

Robin didn't answer, because she spotted Gloria and Bernadine coming through the front door, being greeted by the same man. 'Let me say this, girl. For thirty-six years old, you look good.'

'Thank you,' Savannah said.

'What kind of moisturizer do you use?'

'Aveda.'

'A-who?'

'Come over one day, and I'll show you. I bought it in Denver.'

Bernadine and Gloria came over to their table. 'It took you guys long enough,' Robin said. 'It's seven-thirty. You're missing all the action.'

'We can see that,' Bernadine said. 'So I see you guys have met?'

'We've definitely met,' Savannah said, and Robin gave her a little shove on the shoulder.

'Don't tell me you haven't caught anybody yet,' Gloria said to Robin, and laughed.

'Shut up, Gloria. You look nice tonight,' she said.

'Why, thank you, sugar. You look ravishing, as usual, and so do you, Savannah. Especially your hair, chile. You just have to give me the name of your hairdresser.' Savannah laughed. Gloria had done her hair the day before. Savannah had ripped a picture out of *Essence* magazine and shown it to Gloria. Whatever she did worked, because her hair had so much body that all Savannah would have to do to keep this look was wash her hair and shake it.

'You two look good too,' Savannah said. Bernadine was wearing a tight black dress, and Gloria, a black pantsuit with a red blouse.

'What's so happy about this happy hour?' Gloria asked.

They looked at each other and started laughing. That's when Bernadine spotted somebody she knew at the bar. At first she waved, then she got up and walked over. To a man. Which made Savannah, Gloria, and Robin gasp. A few minutes later, she came back with this handsome specimen, and they wanted to gasp again. 'I want you ladies to meet a good friend of mine,' she said, and introduced them to Herbert Webster, who, they found out a few minutes after he went back to the bar, was a retired football player turned sports agent. He was also married, which caused Robin and Savannah to lose interest immediately. Gloria wasn't fazed. 'He's also active in politics,' Bernadine said. 'He's on the committee that's trying to get the King holiday passed.'

'That's nice,' Savannah said.

'Black Women on the Move is working on that too,' Gloria said. 'You might want to join,' she said to Savannah. 'We do all kinds of things in the community. Last year we gave out ten six-hundred-dollar scholarships from money we raised at the Black Women's Achievement Awards luncheon. We had a Women's Awareness and Self-Help Day so that women who get AFDC could learn how to make extra money without it affecting their checks. Some of the members are lawyers, so we offer free legal advice. And once a year we have this all-day event, with all kinds of workshops: how to deal with breast cancer, incest, sexual harassment on the job, single parenting, financial planning, stress – you name it. Anything that's helpful to black women. Later on, though, we party. We call it Sisters' Nite Out. We get dressed up, play crazy games, have outlandish contests, dance and sing, and there's some pretty good door prizes too.'

'This is *all* women?' Savannah asked.

Robin cut in. 'It starts out with all women, but about nine or ten they let the men in. They usually get a pretty good band. It's a lot of fun, if I do say so myself. It's about the only time in this town you get a chance to *really* dress up and wear sparkly clothes, except for maybe the Ebony Fashion Fair and New Year's. I've been going for the last five years and always have a dynamite time. The food is good too – right, Gloria?'

Gloria rolled her eyes at Robin and waved her hand at her.

'Well, it sounds like fun,' Savannah said to Gloria. 'Who would I call about joining?'

'Me or Bernadine,' she said, looking at Robin. 'We don't have what you call an open membership. There's about fifteen of us, but we do have an advisory board, which you could probably get on. See if you can make it to the meeting next month. That's when we'll be forming committees for Sisters' Nite Out and discussing a few ongoing projects.'

'I'll do that,' Savannah said.

Robin didn't say another word. She hated committee work; it took up too much time: calling folks, trying to solicit money and time from people who for whatever reason could never do this or that. Bernadine was so busy looking around the room – which was now pretty crowded – that she wasn't listening to Gloria's spiel about BWOTM. Besides she knew it all already.

Gloria got up for something to eat, and Bernadine lit

183

a cigarette. 'I'll be glad when you give up that filthy habit,' Robin said.

'I'll be glad when you give up some of your filthy habits,' Bernadine replied, and started rocking her body to the beat of the music coming through the doorway. People were now flocking through it, and Robin and Savannah looked at the other tables, most of which were occupied by women who were also looking around at other tables. 'I feel like dancing,' Bernadine said, and jumped up. She walked straight over to the bar and took Herbert's hand, and the two of them disappeared through the door to the dance floor.

'Is she getting bold or what?' Robin asked Savannah.

'I don't know, but Bernadine is on it tonight.'

Gloria sat back down. Robin was surprised to see that she hadn't piled up her plate. 'I'm on a diet,' she said. 'Just kidding. I had dinner before I got here.'

Savannah and Robin watched Gloria eat and occasionally looked around the room, waiting for someone to ask them to dance. But no-one approached them. Three more songs came and went, and still no-one invited them. Savannah was tempted to ask somebody, but she didn't see anybody she wanted to meet, let alone dance with. If the men in here were a representative sample of what was available in Phoenix, she might as well forget about it.

'No,' Robin moaned.

'What do you mean, "No"?' Gloria said.

'I don't even believe this.'

'What?' Savannah asked.

Robin dropped her head.

'Which one is it?' Gloria said; she'd been through this before.

'Michael.'

'So what's the big deal?' Savannah asked, looking toward the entrance. All she saw was a pudgy, light-skinned man with a nice-looking sister by his side. '*That's* Michael?'

'Yes, and who the hell is that standing next to him is what I wanna know.' Robin's face was now pulsating. She couldn't believe this shit. 'He's supposed to be so in love with me, and here it hasn't even been a whole week since I fired him and he's already out in public with another woman?'

'Take it easy,' Savannah said.

'Don't do anything stupid,' Gloria said. 'You're the one who gave him the ax, so try to act civilized. Whatever you do, don't embarrass yourself, and especially us.'

'I'm not Bernadine, so don't even think it. That little fat fuck.'

Michael had to walk by their table in order to get into the room. When he saw Robin, he smiled and said hello. She didn't say anything. He said, 'How are you?' to Gloria and Savannah, and kept on walking. Robin looked as if she was ready to detonate when Bernadine flopped down in the chair, sweating and out of breath. 'Girl, did you see Michael?' she said.

'What do you think?' Robin said.

'I just asked. You get what you pay for,' she said. 'I'm having a good time. How about you guys? You haven't danced yet? The music is jumping. You guys should be dancing. Shit.'

'We know that,' Savannah said. 'But we're waiting for somebody to ask us.'

'Don't wait for your ship to come in. Swim out to it!'

None of them could believe this was Bernadine. When did she come out of that cocoon she'd been hiding in all these years? Bernadine had never been a real party girl, but she was turning the place out tonight. She sprang back up. 'I need to freshen my makeup. I really needed this,' she said, as she walked away. 'I swear I did.'

Robin sat there as if she was in a trance. Finally, somebody asked Savannah to dance. She didn't care what he looked like at this point, and when she got on the dance floor, she still didn't care. Everything about him was average: height, looks, weight. She didn't look at him until he asked her name, and when he asked her what she did for a living, she told him and, out of courtesy, asked him about his work. When he said he was a mortician, Savannah wanted to crack up. She immediately thought she smelled embalming fluid and was glad she didn't have to hold his hands. They danced through Bobby Brown's 'Every Little Step,' and that's when she saw Robin come out on the floor with a below-average type, and Bernadine was right behind her, holding Herbert's hand. Gloria, who would not walk through that door at all tonight (and really didn't care), was busy thinking about two things: the fact that she was missing *Cagney & Lacey* for this bullshit and whether or not Tarik would have his behind in the house by nine o'clock.

Michael was on the other side of the room, dancing with his date. Robin almost broke her neck trying to find him in the crowd, but she was unsuccessful. After the song ended, the three women went back to their table and sat down. They ordered another drink and took their time drinking it. Every now and then, Gloria and Savannah watched Robin scoping the full room, looking for signs of Michael, who in fact had sat down at a table in the dance room. Although they were right in the center of things, no-one acknowledged them. An occasional man walking by gave them a nod or a half-smile and kept walking. This was not fun.

'How long does this thing last?' Gloria asked.

'Why?' Bernadine asked. 'Are you bored already?'

'You know it. And I'm going home.'

'Me too,' Robin said. 'This is dead.'

'It's only dead because you haven't met anybody and you got your feelings hurt tonight. Can't you be satisfied having a little fun and let it go at that? For once in your life. You don't always have to meet somebody, Robin.'

186

'Shut up, Bernadine, would you? I've got a ton of paperwork waiting on my desk for me in the morning. I had no intention of staying out late anyway.'

'It's not even nine o'clock. What about you, Savannah? Are you ready to leave too?'

'I'm with Robin.'

'You guys are nothing but a bunch of deadbeats, I swear. Go on. Go. I'm not ready to leave yet. I came here to relax and have fun, and that's exactly what I'm going to do.'

'Then do your thing,' Robin said. 'You ready, Savannah?'

'I'm ready,' she said.

Robin didn't have to ask Gloria. She was already heading toward the door. When the three of them got there, the same man who had greeted them popped out from behind the partition. 'Leaving so soon?'

'We have to get up early,' Robin said.

'I heard that,' he said. 'Try to make it back on Friday. It's going to be even better. But we need sisters like you three here to make it that way.'

'Yeah, yeah, yeah,' Robin mumbled, as they walked out into the graveled parking lot. Gloria said good night, got in her car, and took off, leaving a cloud of dust.

'Is this how folks party here?' Savannah asked Robin when they were seated in the car.

'It could be worse,' she said, and turned on the lights.

'You're kidding.'

'I can't believe Michael, girl. I can't.'

'Well, let it go,' Savannah said. 'Just let it go.'

'That's what I thought I was doing, but you want to know what's weird?'

'What?'

'I'm jealous! I can't even believe this shit.'

'I can. You always want what you can't have.'

'But I had it!'

'You know what I mean.'

187

'Yeah, you never know how good something is until somebody else has it.'

'Remember, you're the one who put him on hold, and all men don't have call waiting, honey.'

'Obviously. Anyway, I don't want to talk about him. Did you check out Miss Ginger Rogers tonight?'

'You mean Bernie?'

'Who else? I've never seen her like this.'

'Like what?'

'Didn't you see how she was flirting with that married man? He was the only person she danced with.'

'So what? All she did was dance.'

'I don't know,' Robin sighed.

'Well, you know what they say.'

'About what?'

'About getting divorced.'

'Honey, I have no experience in that department, thank you very much,' Robin said, and finally started the car up.

'Well, they say that some people grieve when they're going through it, and grief can manifest itself in a whole lot of different ways.'

'You mean like flirting with somebody's else's husband and dancing it away?'

'Sort of. Bernadine's going through some heavy-duty changes. You know that.'

'Yeah, I do,' Robin said, and headed toward Tempe. 'John *was* a three-hundred-sixty-degree asshole. A Virgo, honey. A perfectionist from the word go.'

'So you didn't like him, either?'

'He was a selfish egomaniac, and she should've divorced him a long time ago.'

'Well, I hope the whole thing is over soon.'

'I know one thing: if a man of mine ever left me for a white girl, I'd blow him to kingdom come. Simple as that.'

'I'd probably do something, but I don't know about killing anybody. Maybe cut his dick off – something he could remember,' she said, laughing. 'But seriously,

Bernie's always been kind of passive. Right after they moved out here, she told me she was helping John get his computer business started and everything, and once it got going she was supposed to start her own catering business, and—'

'Where is her catering business, thank you very much?'

'I know.'

'I just hope she gets her share out of this deal,' Robin said. 'Because he really screwed her. And Eddie Murphy wants to know why women want half.'

They rode in silence for a few miles.

'You know what? I hate black men who run to white women,' Robin said.

'I don't hate them,' Savannah said. 'But what kills me more than anything is they usually pick the home-liest ones they can find and the ones who don't have shit going for them.'

'I hate the fact that they think white girls epito-mize beauty and femininity.'

'I hear you,' Savannah said. 'But you know what?'

'What?'

'It doesn't bother me all that much.'

'And why not?'

'Because I think people have a right to love who they want to. Who am I to judge?'

'Yeah, but if our men keep running to white women, what does that leave us?'

'When you get right down to it, there really aren't that many who've crossed over. I think we just notice it more because we're black and female.'

'So?'

'So I don't hold it against them. If a black man wants a white woman, that's his business. I've got too many other things to worry about. Like I hope Phoenix isn't going to be a repeat of Denver.'

'Why, was Denver boring too?'

'For a while it was all right, but there weren't very many interesting places to go, and I'm sort of past the bar and club scene, and plus, you never meet anybody when you go to these places. What happened tonight?'

'Nothing.'

'That's my point.'

'I met Russell at a club,' Robin said.

'And look what it got you.'

'Come to think of it, I've met quite a few men at clubs.'

'Have you married any of them?'

'Shut up, girl.'

'You know why I really stopped hanging out at clubs?'

'Why?'

'Because I hate it when men look at me like they know I'm there looking for a man.'

'Why?'

'Because it's true. I'm also tired of going everywhere with women.'

'Well, to hell with you too, Savannah.'

'You know what I'm saying.'

'Yeah,' she said. 'I know exactly what you're saying.'

When Robin pulled up in front of Savannah's complex, she started laughing. 'What's so funny?' Savannah asked her.

'Everything,' she said.

'No, for real, what?'

'I don't know. I don't think I'll be satisfied until I get Russell, even though in my heart I know he's a dog. I just can't seem to get him out of my system. I'm probably living in a fantasy world or something. I like Michael, but I don't want him. Plus, I need to make more money, but I don't even know what my chances are of finding a better job in this town. You ever feel confused?'

'Of course. Everybody does, Robin. Hell, I'm wondering if I made the right move by coming here. I gave up a fifty-thousand-dollar-a-year job for a thirty-eight-thousand-dollar job – and that's before taxes. I don't know how I'm going to keep taking care of my mama if in the next six months I don't get a promotion or find another area to move into at this station.'

'Where's your mama?'

'In Pittsburgh.'

'Is that where you're from originally?'

'Yep.'

'You got sisters and brothers?'

'One sister, two brothers.'

'I don't have any,' Robin said. 'Why can't they help out?'

'It's a long story. They've got their own families, and money is tight everywhere.'

'You don't have to tell me.'

'Anyway, my mama is basically dependent on me. I got her a nice two-bedroom apartment and was thinking about buying her a little car, but I can forget about that for a while. I'm hoping to meet a nice man at the earliest possible convenience, but if tonight was any indication of what I'm in for, I'm in the same boat I was in in Denver.'

'Yeah, well, it sounds like we have a few things in common, girlfriend.'

'I wish we didn't have *those* things,' Savannah said, and bent over and kissed Robin on the cheek. 'See you later,' she said. 'And thanks for driving.'

'Wait,' Robin said. 'Didn't you say you wanted to join a health club?'

'Yeah,' Savannah said, holding the door handle.

'What about tomorrow?'

'Tomorrow sounds good.'

'Then why don't you meet me at Desert Fitness after work. About five-thirtyish. I'll call and tell them you're my guest. It's here in Tempe, and they're in the yellow pages. See you, girl. It's been a real blast.'

When Savannah opened her front door, Yasmine was waiting. 'Hi, baby,' she said, and, dropping her purse on the floor, picked up the cat. 'Mama had a dreadful time tonight. I think Phoenix is as dead as

Denver. And speaking of dead, guess what, Yasmine? I met a mortician tonight. Yes, I did. And guess what else? We're giving Phoenix a year. If nothing exciting happens to us by next year this time, we're outta here.' Yasmine looked at her as if she could care less, and licked Savannah on the face. 'I mean that shit,' she said, and went to wash off her makeup.

The first thing Robin did when she got home was call Michael. He wasn't home yet, so she left a message on his machine. 'That was real cute, what you did tonight,' she said. 'I thought you were a much more considerate person, Michael. But I guess I was wrong. By the way, this is Robin, in case you're having a hard time keeping track of your women.' Click.

She called Russell next. At the number he had given her. When a woman answered the phone, Robin didn't think much of it. She thought it was his buddy's wife, since that's where Russell told her he was staying. 'Is Russell there?' she asked.

'Who's calling him?'

'Robin.'

'Look. Why don't you get a fucking life? Don't call my damn house any more, you got that?'

By the time the voice registered as that of the woman who used to call and harass her, the woman had hung up. He lied to me again, Robin thought. She felt as if she'd been stung twice in one night. She hated this feeling and sat there on the couch for a few minutes with her hand resting on the phone. She was trying to think of somebody else she could call. But she couldn't think of anybody. Because there was nobody.

Gloria lucked out. She had missed only fifteen minutes of *Cagney & Lacey*, and she took off her clothes during the program. She popped herself some microwave popcorn and got in bed and waited for Tarik. She didn't know why she bothered going out with the girls. It was a waste of time, because nobody ever showed an interest in her. Only rarely did anyone ask her to dance, let alone what her name was. It was clear to her that as good as Robin and Savannah looked, they should at least catch somebody's eye, but even they hadn't. What's the problem? Gloria wondered, as she turned out the light. Why are we all out here by ourselves? Are we just going to have to learn how to live the rest of our lives alone or make do with inferiors like Russell and John and maybe even the Michaels of the world? When she heard the front door close, Gloria looked over at the clock. It was ten to ten. She didn't feel like getting up or yelling through the door. He wasn't that late. So Gloria closed her eyes and tried to think of something worth dreaming about.

Bernadine didn't get home until after midnight. She'd had a good time, better than she'd had in years. She couldn't believe the attention she had gotten after her girlfriends left, particularly from Herbert. He walked her to her car and asked if she'd be all right driving home. Bernadine told him she was fine; she'd only had two glasses of wine. 'I'd like to see you again,' he said. Bernadine blushed and, to her own surprise, told him it could probably be arranged. He stood there in the parking lot with his hands in his pockets, and he smiled as she backed out.

On the long, dark drive up to her house, she was thinking: I'm gonna give him some; just because. Just because she wanted him. And just because she hadn't had any in what all of a sudden felt like centuries. The fact that Herbert was married didn't bother her. As a matter of fact, Bernadine thought, as she turned the Cherokee into her driveway and pressed the Genie, she was *glad* he was married, because this way she wouldn't have to worry about what to do with him after she was finished.

Freedom of Expression

It was Monday, Gloria's day off. She was listening to *Take 6*, had just put away nine bags of groceries, and was about to tackle the kitchen drawers, when Tarik walked in and scared the living daylights out of her.

'What are you doing home?'

'The school sent me home.'

'I know you don't mean expelled,' she said, and closed one drawer, then snatched open another one.

'Sort of.'

'There's no such thing as you "sort of" been expelled. What happened, Tarik? And tell the truth, because I'm gonna find out anyway.'

'They accused me of being in a gang.'

'A gang? You mean as in the Crips and the Bloods?'

'Yeah.'

'What would give them that impression?'

'Because me and some of my friends started a club, not a gang, and we wore white handkerchiefs in our back pockets, and so they called us down and told us to stop wearing 'em.'

'Wait a minute. Hold it. Back up. First of all, who is this "we"?'

'Me, Bryan, and Terrence, and a few other guys you don't know.'

'And they're expelled too.'

He nodded yes.

'When they first asked you about the handkerchiefs, why didn't you tell me about this club?'

'Because it wasn't a big deal.'

'But when they asked you to stop wearing them, why didn't you?'

'Because we weren't doing anything wrong. This

is about the First Amendment, Ma. Freedom of expression.'

Gloria's eyes got as big as saucers. 'The first who?' She looked at Tarik and saw that he was serious. 'How many days?'

'Three.'

'And who should I call?'

'About what?'

'About *this*. You think I'm just supposed to take your word about this? I know you've got a piece of paper, something.'

'I did have it in my backpack.'

'Find it, Tarik. Now. Before I slap you into next year.'

'Ma, I didn't do anything wrong, I swear it.'

He reached inside his backpack and handed her a form that described what his offense was and that if she had any questions, she should contact Mr Dailey.

'So tell me something, Tarik. What does your club do? When do you meet? What's the purpose of it? I've never heard you talk about any club until this minute.'

'We don't *do* anything but dress alike. And sometimes we meet under a tree at lunch and just eat together. Other guys don't like that, so they reported us to the principal.'

'And that's it?'

'That's it, Ma. Go ahead and call. They'll tell you that we haven't done anything. It's just because we're black and Hispanic – that's what the real deal is.'

'Don't start that shit.'

'It's true. We're outnumbered everywhere – not just in school but in this entire state. Do you realize that we comprise less than three per cent of the population? Do you know how many Mormons are in this state, how many Klansmen who disguise themselves, and I go to school with their kids? They hate us. Why do you think we can't get Dr King's birthday made into a holiday, like other states?'

195

'Look. I know most of this stuff already, but it ain't got nothing to do with the price of butter. You've been kicked out of school, which means you'll get F's for three days. If you think you're gonna sit around this house all day by yourself, you're wrong, buster. As soon as I find out exactly what's going on, I'll figure out how to handle you. For now, don't even twist your mouth to ask if you can use the car or go any further than that sidewalk out front – for the next three weeks. Do I make myself clear?'

He responded by walking away, going upstairs to his room, and slamming the door. Gloria opened the cabinet, got her bottle of blood pressure medication, and took a pill with some water. Then she yanked out the silverware drawer, grabbed a handful of teaspoons, and dropped them on the countertop. She snatched up the salad forks, dinner forks, and then the knives. By the time she slung the tablespoons on top, at least thirty pieces of silverware had crashed to the floor. It was times like this when she understood how parents could really hurt their children. Also, at times like this, she wished Tarik had a father who lived under the same roof. She was tired of dealing with all this puberty and growing-up shit by herself. She should've had a man in this house a long time ago. Somebody who executed authority much better than she did.

The Love Boat was on. Gloria was watching a repeat, for the zillionth time, when Savannah called to ask if she wanted to go to a party with her and Robin. Gloria flatly said no. 'What about Bernie? Is she going?'

'No,' Savannah said. 'That girl's been busy. I mean hanging out tough. It seems like every time I call her at home, the baby-sitter answers. I don't know what she's up to these days.'

'I bet it's that Herbert man. She better watch her step, that's all I can say.'

'So is everything going all right with you?'

'Yeah. Except that son of mine got expelled from

school for being in a gang. I had to go down and talk to the principal – a real die-hard racist – and I had to cuss him out after he said he wasn't letting any of the boys back in for three days. Tarik is grounded for waiting so long to tell me about this mess. It could've been avoided. Other than that, I'm just watching TV. And I'm tired.'

'I imagine so, standing on your feet all day long. Oh, and guess what? I'm now on the advisory board of Black Women on the Move.'

'Good. Did you meet Etta Mae?'

'Yep. I'm going to a school for unwed teenagers in a few weeks, to talk to them about my job. Etta Mae said they need to see as many black role models as they can. I never thought of myself as a "role model," but anyway, I'm looking forward to getting involved. I think this is a good group. I wish we'd had something like it in Denver.'

'I'm glad to hear this, Savannah. I know we're all busy with our own lives and everything, but I swear, some of these kids out here are just lost, and they need any kind of motivation they can get. If we can help point them in the right direction, then we're doing *something*. So thanks.'

'Thank *you* for telling me about it. Well, anyway, I've gotta go. I'll probably see you some time next week.'

Gloria was surprised when the phone rang again. She had finally broken down and gotten Tarik his own phone, because she was sick of the girls calling every five minutes and tired of being his answering service. She wondered who this could be, since *her* phone hardly ever rang on a Friday night. For a minute, her heart started pounding hard; it probably had something to do with Tarik – but then she remembered he was grounded and up in his room. 'Hello.'

'Gloria, this is Bernie. What you doing?'

'Watching TV. How're you?'

'So-so.'

'Is something wrong?'

197

'Girl, I'm so pissed off, I don't know whether I'm coming or going. One minute I feel like I've got everything under control, and two minutes later, I can't think straight. I'm smoking like it's going out of style. You won't believe what John has gone and done now.'

'What?'

'I got a notice from the bank, saying the mortgage payment is past due.'

'You mean he didn't pay it?'

'Apparently not, so I called the motherfucker, and he said he did pay it, that it must be some kind of mistake. He was lying through his teeth, Gloria, but my lawyer said that right now there's nothing we can do about it.'

'Nothing?'

'Nothing, except wait to see if he does it again.'

'That's a shame.'

'I know, and I can't be sitting in this house worrying about whether or not he's going to be making the payments or if I'm going to come home one day and find out it's being foreclosed. I can't afford these damn payments by myself. I don't know what to do.'

'Well, what about the settlement? How's that going?'

'Girl, it's crazy. They're still trying to get all John's assets figured out, and until that time, I'm in limbo.'

'What about your lawyer? Can't she do something to speed this up?'

'She's doing everything she can, but John's lawyer is just as sneaky and conniving as he is. He's not cooperating, because he's looking out for John's best interests.'

'Well, shit. How long before you get divorced?'

'I don't know, and at this point, I don't care.'

That's when Gloria heard her crying. Gloria couldn't stand it. 'Bernie, are you OK?' She could tell Bernadine was trying to regroup but wasn't able to. 'You want some company, girl?'

'I do and I don't. I don't want to depress you.'

'You're not depressing me. And don't worry about me. Where's the kids?'

'They're here, driving me fucking bananas too.'

'Let me comb my hair real quick, and I'll be over in about a half hour.'

'You really don't have to, Gloria.'

'I know I don't have to, but I'm on my way. Turn on *The Love Boat;* it'll take your mind off some of this stuff. See you in a few minutes.'

She hung up the phone and sank into the chair. Why does life have to be so damn complicated? 'Because it is,' she said. Well, why couldn't God have made it easier? Because then we probably wouldn't appreciate it, she thought, and went upstairs and knocked on Tarik's door.

'Yes?' he said.

'I'm running over to Bernadine's house. I'll be back in an hour or so. If my phone rings, answer it. It'll be me, and you better pick it up. Understand?'

'Yes,' he said, through the door.

When Gloria pulled up in the circular driveway, Bernadine's house looked like Christmas. Every light in the house was on. Gloria turned off the ignition and got out of the car, then rang the bell. Bernadine opened the door, and Gloria gave her a strong hug.

'Thanks, girl,' Bernadine said, and moved so Gloria could come on in. Gloria walked into the middle of the great room and looked around. This place was a mess. She walked toward the kitchen, like she always did when she came over, and there was a trail of ants marching from behind the light switch down into the sink basin. 'Where's the Raid? Did you know you've got ants?'

Bernadine looked surprised, as if she hadn't been in the kitchen in a long time. 'Ants?' she said, and walked over. She reached under the sink and got out some insect spray and started spraying like she was possessed. 'I hate this damn house, you know that?

199

Next it'll be termites. Sit down, girl. Can I get you something to drink?'

'A Coke would be nice.'

'I don't have Coke, just Pepsi.'

'What's the difference?'

John junior and Onika came running out of their bedrooms when they heard another voice. 'Hi, Miss Gloria,' they said in unison. 'Where's Tarik?'

'Home where he belongs,' Gloria said.

'Our daddy doesn't live here any more,' Onika said.

'I know that,' Gloria said.

'You two get back in the room and finish doing whatever it was you were doing. Miss Gloria came over here to talk to me. So please, let grown folks talk to grown folks.'

'Can we have a Pepsi?' John junior asked.

'Yes. Get it yourselves and then scram. I mean it.'

They did just that, while Gloria and Bernadine sat down at opposite ends of the sofa. The TV was off. 'Did you watch *The Love Boat*?' Gloria asked.

'Girl, I couldn't.'

'I was hoping something as stupid as that would help take your mind off of things.'

Bernadine did look a little spaced, but Gloria couldn't tell if it was from those pills or because her friend was stressed to the hilt. 'Are you still taking those pills for your nerves?'

'Sometimes. Why?'

'You're not taking too many of 'em, are you?'

'No, girl. I mainly take 'em at night, so I can get to sleep.'

'Are you sure you're OK?' Gloria asked her again.

'Gloria, I might end up having to sell the house, because there's no way I can pay a three-thousand-dollar mortgage if John keeps this shit up. Just the thought of having to go through more aggravation is wearing me out.'

'What makes you think your only option would be to sell it?'

'Because it's the prize I got for marrying that son of a bitch. He signed the deed over to me. But even though the judge ordered him to pay the mortgage, my lawyer said that by the time we go back to court to enforce it, the fucking house could be in foreclosure.'

'Your lawyer told you that?'

'Yep.'

'Damn. You sure she knows what she's doing?' was all Gloria could think to say.

'Yeah, she knows what she's doing, all right. And my five-thousand-dollar retainer is used up, and you won't even believe how much I owe her now.'

'How much?'

'Thirty-four hundred, and it'll keep on going up until this mess is settled. Plus, I'm paying for a private investigator now too. She knows I don't have this kind of money, but thank God she's a woman. She's being real nice about it. She told me to pay her two hundred a month, or whatever I can afford, until we settle.'

'So sell this damn house and get a smaller place. You don't need all this space anyway.'

'That's what my lawyer told me I should do too. But you know what the market is like for houses like this? Just look at how many For Sale signs you see in the entire valley, not to mention up here in this area alone. I could end up sitting on this house for a long time.'

'Not necessarily, but I wouldn't be worrying about that right now if I were you.'

'Oh, no? What do you think I should be worrying about, Gloria?'

'I don't know. Getting a better job.'

'Getting a better job? Oh, you think I'm in a frame of mind to be job hunting? My marriage is over; I'm stuck in a big-ass house I can't afford and may have to move; my devoted husband has left me for some white cunt, and he's out there having the time of his fucking life, living like a goddamn bachelor, and he's probably fucking his brains out right this minute; and

201

I'm sitting here with my girlfriend on a Friday night, going fucking crazy because I don't know what the fuck is happening to my life and I have no fucking idea what the future holds for me and my kids because I never had to think about so much shit at once until now!'

'Take it easy, Bernie.'

Gloria thought Bernadine would be in tears, but she wasn't. 'I'm sorry,' she said, composing herself. 'I could just kill him for what he's doing to my life. I swear I could just kill him.'

'I agree,' Gloria said, surprising herself.

'Thank God somebody does.'

'What about the kids? How are they handling this?'

'Onika is fine, but John junior is fucking up in school. His teacher has sent two notes home in the last two weeks. She said he stares out the goddamn window when he should be paying attention. She said she tells him to do something, and ten minutes later he can't remember what she said. He forgot his homework two days in a row, and yesterday he lost his good jacket. I know he's going through changes too, so I'm trying not to go off. But shit, all of this is wearing me out. I feel like I'm being split into little tiny pieces and every single part of me has to perform at optimum capacity.'

'They say divorce is harder on boys than it is on girls.'

'Then that theory is accurate in this house. I just have to keep talking to him. That's all I can do.'

'If I ask you something, you promise you won't get mad?'

'What?' Bernadine said.

'Have you been messing around with that Herbert man?'

Bernadine started laughing. 'What makes you think I'm doing anything with Herbert?'

'I was just wondering. Savannah said you've been going out a lot, because you're never home.'

'That's bullshit. I've been out a couple of nights in the past week or two. Savannah doesn't know what she's talking about.'

'So?'

'So?'

'Are you or aren't you?'

'I've spent a little time with him, yeah.'

'Bernie?'

'Bernie, my ass. I can't just sit around here and wither up. I'm a woman, and I've got needs like any other woman, and hell, he's a nice man.'

'Yeah, but he's married.'

'So what? I don't want to marry him. I'm just fucking him.'

'How can you say that?'

'Say what?'

'That you're just sleeping with him for the hell of it.'

'Easy. Men've been doing this shit for years.'

'Yeah, but what if you end up really liking him?'

'I already *like* him, but big deal. I'm not falling in love with his ass, and I'm not trying to take him from his damn wife. It's just nice to know I can get what I need when I need it.'

'You mean sex?'

'No, Gloria. A Tootsie Roll. You should know this shit, I swear. I'm talking about having somebody around to talk to, having somebody put their arms around you and tell you everything is going to be fine and not to worry. Even if the shit is a lie, it still feels good.'

'And how long do you think you can play house?'

'I'm not playing house. I told you, I don't want to marry the motherfucker. Marriage is the last thing on my mind right now. Hell, I'm still married, so as far as we're both concerned, this shit is real safe.'

Gloria just shook her head.

'If it's any consolation, Gloria, the kids don't know he exists, and he hasn't even been in my house.'

'Well, it's your house,' she said. 'You can do whatever you wanna do in it.'

For the next hour, the two of them sat there, watched music videos on VH-1, and said few words to each other. Bernadine chain-smoked and drank two glasses of wine, and when the phone rang, Gloria could tell it was Herbert, because Bernadine's whole attitude changed. She actually sounded like a schoolgirl with a crush, talking on the phone. When she finally hung up, Gloria had gone through a ninety-nine-cent bag of Lay's potato chips and another Pepsi. 'Happy now?' Gloria said. Bernadine simply smiled. 'Would you mind if I used the phone a minute, Cinderella?'

Bernadine handed it to her, still with that silly-ass grin on her face. The phone rang ten times.

'I'll kill him!' she said.

'Who? Tarik?'

'Who else? One day that boy's gonna get my pressure up so high, he's gonna give me a heart attack. I've got to go. I told him not to leave that damn house. He's grounded. And I don't know which is worse, trying to raise a teenage son or dealing with a husband who leaves you for a white woman.'

Bernadine didn't bother to answer that. She was too busy dialing the baby-sitter's number.

Gloria didn't yell out his name like she usually did when she got home. She walked straight upstairs and saw that his door was still closed. Instead of knocking, she barged right on in, and stopped dead in her tracks. She put her hand across her chest and pressed down on it in order to catch her breath. Her eyes had to be lying to her, because her son was sitting on the edge of his bed with his pants down to his ankles, his legs open, and that sleazy little white heffa who lived two doors down the street was on her knees, doing what Gloria didn't want to think she was doing with her face buried between his legs. She didn't notice the look of horror on Tarik's face until after she screamed,

'Get out of my goddamn house!' He pushed the girl away and stood up so fast that all Gloria could do was back away from the door.

She ran down the stairs and sat down in the living room. Her head was spinning. Out of the corner of her eye, she saw a pink blur whisk past her. She heard the front door open and close, and then her son, tall and black, was standing in front of her.

'I'm sorry, Ma.'

Gloria coughed. 'Sorry? Sorry about what, Tarik?'

'That you found me like this.'

'Tarik, how long have you been sneaking this girl in this house like this?'

'Not that long.'

'I told you you were grounded.'

'You said don't leave the house, and I didn't.'

'I'm about sick of this shit, you know that. If your daddy wasn't gay, I swear I'd send your black ass straight to him.'

'If he wasn't what?'

Shit, Gloria thought. Shit shit shit. She forgot just that fast that she hadn't told the boy. Shit. Shit shit shit. Well, shit. It was done now. So to hell with it. 'You heard me.'

'You mean he's a faggot?'

'I don't like that word.'

'Faggot, homo, gay – what's the difference? I *told* you something was wrong with him, didn't I? But you wouldn't listen to me.' He sat down next to Gloria. 'So my *daddy's* a faggot,' he said, and started laughing. 'Well, Ma, at least you know one thing,' he said, and tried to contain his laughter. 'It definitely doesn't run in the family.'

'Watch your mouth,' she said.

'I'm sorry.'

'You're sorry about everything, aren't you, Tarik? You're sorry about your grades. You're sorry about the way you treated your daddy – and I don't care *what* he is. You're sorry about getting expelled from school,

205

and now you're sorry because you're letting white girls come in my house to suck your sixteen-year-old dick. What's next? Will it be drugs? Is that what you'll want me to deal with next? Huh?'

'No.'

Gloria didn't know she'd gone from mad to hysterical. *'Just get out of my face!'*

Tarik got up, walked away with his head down, headed toward the stairs, and stopped. 'How'd you find out he was a homo?' he asked.

Gloria took a deep breath and dropped her head on the back of the couch. 'Just go to bed,' she said. 'Just close the damn door and go to bed.'

Steam

Robin was late again, something I was starting to notice was a bad habit of hers. I was sitting in the steam room, feeling pretty energized because I'd done a whole half hour of aerobics and ten minutes on the Lifecycle. This was a major accomplishment, considering that the first time I came in here I only lasted five.

'Savannah, you in here, girl?'

'Yep, up here,' I said.

She walked in, closed the door, and collapsed on the bottom bench. 'These white folks are trying to drive me crazy, you know that?'

'Why? What's going on?'

'First of all, there's four other underwriters in my office besides me, OK?'

'OK.'

'Well, a few months ago, Marva has a perfectly healthy baby. Her first. She's thirty-nine, but she looks fifty. Anyway, it seems like every other week this baby gets some kind of new ailment, and Marva freaks out, drops everything, and dashes home. So this morning it gets sick again, and of course Marva goes home. She was in the middle of underwriting an account, and guess who got stuck finishing it?'

'You, no doubt.'

'Yeah. I mean, why couldn't they ask Molly or Norman to do it? They didn't have anything pressing. Although it does take Norman all day to do nothing, and I guess I'm supposed to be flattered. Well, I'm not. I want to know when they're gonna stop testing me. I've proven myself a million times over. They know they can count on me when the pressure's on. That's what the real deal is, which is why this just burns me up.

When was the last time I got a raise, thank you very much? I can't wait to see what kind of bonus I get come Christmas. I had to skip my lunch hour, girl, and tomorrow I have to get up at the crack of dawn, be in there no later than seven in order to finish, or we might lose the account. And watch. Marva'll come strolling in the office all set to pick up where I left off; she'll get all the credit or mess up everything I've done.'

'Well, my job isn't exactly turning out to be a thrill a minute, either. Instead of pushing gas, now I have to come up with a bunch of hype about our programs – which are all basically dull. I spend half my time trying to convince magazines, newspapers, and other media to give us coverage. As of next week, I'll have the pleasure of managing the speakers' bureau for the president of the company, the correspondents, and the so-called hotshot anchors. In a nutshell, I'll be a glorified travel agent. Hell, I *live* on the telephone all day long as it is.'

'Your job doesn't sound boring to me.'

'It's fluff work.'

'What isn't, Savannah?'

'Robin, what I do doesn't mean shit to anybody. It's just a glamorous form of propaganda. And I'm already bored with it.'

'If it didn't mean anything to anybody, they wouldn't be paying you to do it.'

'They're not paying me anything. And you want to know why?'

'Don't tell me. Because you're black.'

'That's only part of it. Of all the areas in broadcasting, public relations is the least respected. It's full of women, that's why. The good old boys don't see it as having the same impact as, say, the advertising and marketing departments, because they can't see the money that's generated from our efforts. We don't get any credit, and to top it off, my job has a glass ceiling. There's nowhere to go.'

'So why'd you take the job in the first place?'

'Because it was the only way I could get my foot in the door.'

'To do what?'

'To get into production. I want to do something a little more creative. Shit, I had more fun and made more money working for the gas company. At least there I had a chance to produce a few films. They were instructional and informational, but I didn't care. I still got a charge out of it. I had to come up with concepts, write the scripts, decide what approach we should take and what should go in it, and at the same time figure out how to provide the facts and still make it interesting and appealing to lay people. Hell, gas was boring.' I inhaled a billow of steam and felt it hit my lungs. What a great sensation.

'You know, you don't act like a Libra. I always thought they were more patient.'

'Please, Robin.'

'Seriously, you should let me do your chart. I bet you've got a lot of air in your houses. Your rising is probably in Gemini or something.'

'Who cares?'

'Nancy Reagan does.'

We both started laughing. Robin wiped her face with a towel and pulled her hair – or whosever it was – into a knot.

'And I'll tell you another thing, since we're sitting here. I'm not going to another one of these tired-ass parties with you, either. So don't ask. It was a dud – now tell me it wasn't.'

'Phoenix is not Boston or New York City, Savannah.'

'I didn't say it was. But damn. I felt like I'd gone back in time. Don't these folks know what year it is?'

'You must be getting your period,' Robin said. 'You haven't stopped bitching since I got here.'

'I am. But that has nothing to do with what I'm saying.'

'Well, I was sure glad to see mine.'

'Your period?'

'Yes, my period.'

'Don't tell me you don't use protection, Robin.'

'Of course I do.'

'Then why were you worried?'

'Because you can never be sure. Anyway, I had a *good* time at Loretha's party.'

'Well, I'm tired of getting all dressed up to go out, and then when I do, nothing happens. I did this shit in Denver. I'm not about to go through it here.'

'From what I hear, girl, it's rough everywhere. All you see on the cover of women's magazines every single month is how bad it is. For white women too. They change the titles, but it's always the same stuff. I know most of 'em by heart: "The New Dating Game." "Will I Ever Meet a Decent Guy?" "The Ideal Man: Is He Out There?" "How to Find True Romance." "How to Find Mr Right." "How to Spot Mr Wrong." "How to Avoid the Tender Trap." "One Hundred Places to Look for a Man: In Places You'd Never Guess." And so on and so on.'

'It's not *that* rough. The media want us to believe this shit. I work for 'em. I know how effective it is. The deal is, men are just pussies. They're scared to make the first move because they're too worried we might want their asses and then they'd have to stop playing games, grow up, and act like men. That's what they're terrified of. It's not *us*.'

'Well, Russell definitely falls into that category.'

'I mean, at that party, didn't I look halfway decent?'

'You looked hot, girl. Hot. And speaking of hot, it's getting hot in here.'

'It's supposed to be, Robin. How'd we get on this subject anyway? I get sick of talking about men all the time.'

'Well, you brought it up.'

'Well, now I'm changing it.' I wiped the perspiration off my face, thighs, and arms with a towel, closed my eyes, and leaned forward so the mist could envelop me again. 'You want to know what I really miss?'

'What's that?'

'Not having any male friends. I used to have lots of them. You know, buddies, guys I could just kick it around with.'

'Girl, the older we get, the harder it is. Most of 'em just want to fuck you anyway.'

'I know. And it's sad. But when you get right down to it, the majority of them think that's the *only* reason we're interested in them. And let's face it, Robin, half the time it's true.'

'We're damned if we want 'em, and damned if we don't.'

'Think about it though. When we were teenagers – shit, even in college – didn't it feel a helluva lot easier getting to know them?'

'Yep.'

'I mean, didn't it seem more relaxed?'

'Yep.'

'Don't you get the feeling sometimes that as soon as you meet one, they're already sizing you up, trying to figure out what your agenda is?'

'What agenda?'

I opened my eyes. Now, Robin was lying on the bottom bench. Her boobs were perched on her chest like two brown grapefruits. I think I'll keep my miniatures. 'I mean, it's as if they're automatically assuming they're our next "victim," a target we've picked out, so they act distant, sometimes downright cold, to keep you at bay. Some of them accuse you of being too aggressive or get downright intimidated if you say more than three words to them. I guess they still think it's the fifties, when a man was expected to make the first "move." But hell, if we had to hold our breath waiting for them to say something to us, we'd suffocate. Just the other day I was at the movies and saw this fine brother waiting in the concession line. He looked me dead in the eye, then dropped his head and didn't speak. His girlfriend was with him. But so what? What's wrong with saying hello? I mean, why do they have to get so defensive? I hate it when they second-guess what they think your motive is. Half the time all I'm doing is acknowledging their presence, being courteous, hell, appreciative, but you'd swear I was getting ready to propose in my next breath.'

'I hear you,' Robin said.

'You ever feel like you can't be yourself around them?'

'I don't understand what you mean, Savannah.'

'Don't you feel sometimes like you're straining not to come across as too "down," too serious, or too straightforward?'

'Not really.'

'I mean, don't you find yourself being extra careful about what you say and how you say it? As if you have to be this phony, put on a facade, because you don't want to give them the wrong impression?'

'Not really.'

'Well, I do. I don't feel half as comfortable around men as I do with my girlfriends. And that's depressing. It shouldn't have to be like that. I don't even know how to strike up a generic conversation with a man any more without worrying about a whole lot of other bullshit, like scaring him off. Shit, I used to know men I could call up with no other motive, no pretense whatsoever, and say, "Hey, you wanna go shoot some pool, or go to a movie, or go to this party with me?" and if they weren't doing anything, they'd say, "Yeah." It worked both ways. I *never* had to worry about whether or not I was going to have to sleep with them at the end of the night. It wasn't even about that. For some reason, we knew we weren't sexually attracted to each other and it was no big deal. We still enjoyed each other's company, and could talk about anything and everything. I miss that.'

'This is a crap game we're playing, girl, only no-body wants to roll the dice.'

'A lot of times all I want is somebody to talk to, act silly and bullshit with. Somebody I can trust. He doesn't have to be a candidate for a husband.'

'I hear you.'

'I want to know what it is we can do to get them to understand that?'

'Who you asking? All I can say is that black men can be one big question mark,' Robin said. 'One disappointment after another. Every now and then I wonder if I should go on and date me a white man.'

'Girl, a man is a man.'

'That's not true. I've seen a whole lot of sisters with white guys lately, and they look happy as hell. White men know how to treat you.'

'That's bullshit. They may not come with the same kind of baggage brothers have, but then, white men haven't had to deal with any racial shit either. And if what you're saying was true, then why is it that all these white women's magazines are complaining about the same shit sisters are? A lot of the white chicks in my office are having just as hard a time finding Mr Right as we are.'

'Valid point, Savannah. You ever been out with a white guy?'

'Nope.'

'Why not?'

'Because I happen to love black men.'

'I hear you,' Robin said and sat up. 'But I know one thing: they better hurry up and get their act together or I might be tempted to cross the street like some of these sisters, who don't seem to have any regrets either.'

'Don't let Bernie ever hear you say some shit like that.'

'I'm just talking, girl. But black men play too many games. It feels like they're always testing you. Shit, what do we have to do to pass the test?'

'You tell me.'

'I think life is one long introductory course in tolerance, but in order for a woman to get her Ph.D, she's gotta pass Men 101.'

213

'You are too deep for me sometimes, you know that, Robin?'

'Go straight to hell, Savannah.'

I scooted back, pressed my shoulder blades against the hot tile, and exhaled. 'All I want to do is feel worked up. To be excited about somebody. To have something to look forward to. To meet somebody to fill in the blank. But right now, I do have *one* thing to look forward to this year.'

'What?'

'There's a media conference in November. In Las Vegas.'

'I love Las Vegas, girl.'

'Me too. The station's paying for it. Five whole days. I can't wait.'

'Maybe I'll see if I can make it over there that weekend. You think any brothers'll be there?'

'If I said no, would you still be interested?'

'Maybe, maybe not.'

'Well, in the last four years I've been going, I can count how many I've seen on two hands.'

'Then let me think on it,' she said.

I didn't know how to tell her it wasn't an open invitation, and to be honest, I don't think I want her to come. I like Robin and everything, but she's a little too flashy for my taste, and from what I've seen, when she goes out, she's like a walking billboard: 'Here I Am, and I'm Available.' She could be a bad reflection on me.

The steam had finally filled up the whole room, until you couldn't even see your hand in front of you. We were still the only ones in there. My whole body was dripping with sweat. When I inhaled, my chest felt clean, wide open. Like I'd never smoked a cigarette in my life. I got up, walked over by the door, searched for the silver chain, and yanked on it. Cold water shot out, but it didn't feel cold. When I finished showering, I climbed back up to the top bench. I felt energized. Wholesome. Healthy. I swear, I need to quit smoking.

'What you doing for dinner tonight?' Robin asked.

214

'Eating.'

'You should be a comedian – you know that, don't you? Wanna go get something afterwards?'

'Not tonight, girl. I've got some leftover chicken I'm nuking, and I've got laundry to do. Every pair of decent panties I own is dirty. What about tomorrow?'

'I can't tomorrow.'

'So where were you thinking of going?'

'Home.'

'I thought you just said you wanted to eat out.'

'I do. But not by myself.'

'Not by yourself? Are you serious?'

'Yes, I'm serious. I've never eaten out by myself.'

'Why not?'

'Because it would feel weird.'

'What's so weird about it? I do it all the time.'

'You do? And you don't feel like people are staring at you?'

'What? Why would people be staring at me because I'm eating by myself?'

'Because it looks like you can't get anybody to eat with you.'

'You're for real too, aren't you, Robin?'

'Yeah, why?'

'So what am I supposed to do if I want to eat out but don't have a companion? Stay home? Go to the drive-up window of Taco Bell so I can save face?'

'You're making it sound ridiculous. I'm just telling you that I've never done it because I would feel awkward, like I was on display.'

'On display for what?'

'Everybody would know I don't have a man to take me to dinner.'

'That is the biggest bunch of bullshit I've ever heard in my life. You ought to stop.'

'I can't help it.'

'Yes you can. All you need to do is take your black ass to the restaurant, get out of your car, go inside, sit down, order, and then proceed to eat the

215

goddamn food. This is the nineties, Robin. Eating by yourself is not an admission of loneliness. And who gives a shit if it is. So go.'

'I can't.'

'Try it.'

'I'm too chicken.'

'Then fuck it,' I said.

The steam had disappeared. Now I could see Robin's face, and especially those colossal breasts, clearly. She picked up her towel, tiptoed under the shower, squealed when the water hit her, and jumped back. Her boobs didn't move. I grabbed my towel and walked toward the door. I was at a loss for words. Women who think like her really piss me off.

When I got home, I dropped the mail on the kitchen table and went into the bedroom to see if I had any messages. Two. That's how popular I am. Yasmine was curled up at the foot of my bed. As soon as I walked into the room she stood up on all fours, stretched, and twirled her tail in the air. I listened to the machine rewind, flopped on the bed, and kicked off my shoes.

'Savannah, this is your mother. Haven't heard from you in a while. Hope you're all right. Give me a call. I saw it was a hundred and two degrees there the other day. Are you meeting lots of nice people? Any nice men? Call me. Love you.'

Beep.

'Yeah, Savannah, this is Kenneth. Remember me? I'll be out your way next month for a medical conference and would love to see you while I'm there. I'll call you back later on. Hope you're well. Bye-bye.'

I stood there in a daze for a minute, then rewound the tape to make sure I heard right. Kenneth Dawkins was calling me after all this time? I wondered how he got my number. Mama. I bet it was Mama. When I first told her I was going out with him, she was so impressed that he was a doctor, she said she liked him, and she hadn't even met the man. She was sickening as hell when she did meet him. Cooked him collard greens, corn bread, candied yams, and fried chicken. Kept his glass of Kool-Aid filled. Won him right over. The next thing I know, she's told everybody in the whole family all about him, like I was marrying him in the next few days. I think Mama was more disappointed than I was when I told her I wasn't seeing him any more.

It was after eleven in Pittsburgh, so I decided to call her from work tomorrow. Where it was free. I'd already taken a shower at the gym, so I opened what I called my Victoria's Secret drawer and sifted through all the sexy stuff to find something cute but not so sexy. Lord only knows when I'll get a chance to wear some of this shit. Sometimes I wonder why I bother buying it. They're probably all dry-rotted by now anyway. I decided not to wear anything from that drawer, so I pulled out the one full of old T-shirts, lotioned my body from head to toe, then put one on.

I stuffed my bras and undies inside the lingerie bags and put them in the washer on the gentle cycle. I ate my chicken and some leftover pasta while I flipped through the mail. Nothing but a few bills. I lay down on the couch, punched Power on the remote, and picked up the first magazine I put my hands on, which happened to be *New Woman*. I heard Aretha Franklin singing the score for *A Different World*. I thought about Robin when I saw the article 'What Men Don't Tell Women' heading the table of contents in red. That's when the phone rang.

The deepness of his voice told me it was Kenneth. 'Savannah?'

'Well, this is a surprise,' I said, and put my magazine down.

'You're a hard person to find.'

'I haven't been hiding.'

He chuckled. 'How are you, Savannah?'

'I'm fine. How about you?'

217

'Fair to middlin'. You're the one out there basking in all that sunshine.'

'Where'd you get my number?'

'Your mama gave it to me.'

'My mama,' I said.

'She said you've been out there since February.'

'That's true. What else did she tell you?'

He chuckled again. Kenneth has always been a good chuckler. 'Why, is there something you don't want me to know?'

Then I chuckled. 'No. My mama's got a big mouth. She tells everybody's business but hers.'

'So do you like it out there?'

'I can't tell yet.'

'What about your job? You still in publicity?'

'Yep, at a TV station.'

'That's good,' he said. 'Well, you sound good.'

'You do too. I heard you got married and have a kid and everything.'

'That's what they say. How about you? Why haven't you made some man lucky yet?'

Mama and her big mouth. 'Haven't met Mr Right yet,' I said.

'I'm glad to hear that.'

I didn't know how to respond. 'So are you happy?' I said, and looked around for my cigarettes.

'I'm happy to be a father,' he said.

'I assumed that much, Kenneth.'

'Look, I'm coming out there for this conference next month. Are you gonna be around?'

'When?'

'Well, the conference is the twenty-sixth through the twenty-eighth. But I'm thinking about skipping the last session.'

'I'll be here.'

'I'm staying at the Phoenician. I hear it's a nice hotel.'

'Nice is putting it mildly. It's beautiful.'

'Tell me something: Are you seeing anybody?'

218

'What has that got to do with anything?'

'I'm just curious, Savannah.'

'I just got here, Kenneth.'

'Well, let's have dinner when I come. Is that possible?'

'It might be possible.'

'Good. Have you ever been to Sedona?'

'No; not yet.'

'You have any idea how far it is from Phoenix?'

'I think a little more than an hour's drive. But I could be wrong.'

'I saw pictures of it in *National Geographic*. And man, those red mountains are unreal.'

'It's not that far from the Grand Canyon, that's why.'

'I'd like to drive up that Saturday and see it. Would you go with me?'

'I don't know, Kenneth. Why don't we wait until you get here. I'm not sure what my schedule's going to be like then.'

'I can do that,' he said, and paused. 'So are you still buying all that beautiful art?'

'Not as much as I'd like.'

'Not to change the subject, but to be perfectly honest with you, Savannah, I'm relieved to hear you're not married.'

'Why?'

'Because.'

'Because why?'

'I'll tell you when I get there. I'm just glad to know I'll get a chance to see you. And for what it's worth, Savannah, I have fond memories of you. As a matter of fact, I think about you quite often.'

'*Sure*, Kenneth.'

'Did you get the Christmas card I sent you last year?'

'No,' I lied. I got his card, but what was I supposed to do? Write him a thank you note? Call him up?

'You didn't?'

'Nope.'

219

'Weren't you living in Denver then?'

'Yep.'

'Anyway, there's a lot going on in my life these days. I'll tell you about it when I see you. How's that?'

'Look, I wasn't trying to act like the FBI. I just asked if you were happy.'

'And I wasn't implying that you were. I'm not in a position to talk about it right now.'

'No problem,' I said.

'Well, look, dear. It's late here.'

'Are you still in Boston?'

'I'm over in Brighton now.'

'Oh.'

'I'll call you when I get there. Can't wait to see you. And you take care.'

'Good hearing from you, Kenneth.'

I jumped up to find my cigarettes. My magazine fell to the floor. I hopped back on the couch and sat there for a few minutes. I used to crave this man. God, did he make me feel special! Like I was one of a kind. He said I was stimulating company. So was he. I lit my cigarette. How many Saturday mornings did he call me up and say, 'Let's drive out to the Cape'? And when we got there, he'd have smoked turkey, Brie and crackers, wine and fresh fruit, and a tablecloth stuffed in the trunk of his car. We'd lie on a blanket at the edge of the shore, read articles in *Newsweek* or *Life*, and talk about world affairs while the waves crashed in front of us. He made it feel romantic. We saw a slew of plays and always spent half the night discussing why they worked or why they didn't. He was the only man I ever knew who didn't mind going to foreign films. He told me I was one of the smartest women he'd ever met in his life. And the sexiest. He was also the most sensual lover I've ever had. To this day.

Now that I think about it, Kenneth is probably the reason why I expect so much of men. When I was with him, he treated me like a lady. Once you get used to being treated well, you can't go back to bullshit. I was sure that what we had going would lead to something long-term. But it didn't. Weeks would go by, and I wouldn't hear from him. Then he'd call like we'd just seen each other yesterday. We spent hours on the phone, talking about everything except how we felt about each other. By the time I realized I was in love with him, I was too scared to tell him. I knew what he *thought* about me, but I didn't know how he *felt*. I'd never been in this position before. I didn't know if he was going out with other women at the same time, or if I was considered recreation, a pastime, some temporary form of entertainment. I got tired of guessing. And I didn't feel comfortable questioning him about it. So one day I wrote him a letter and told him I didn't want to go out with him any more. He couldn't understand why. I lied and said I had met somebody else. I haven't heard a word from him until now.

What I want to know is why he wants to see me after all this time. Why did he decide to pick up the phone out of the clear blue and call my mama to find me? Why now? I hope he doesn't think he's coming out here to pick up where we left off or to try to sweet-talk me into anything, because it won't work. He's a married man. I don't care if I was in love with him. I don't care if he still looks like Evander Holyfield, gives me that Pepsodent smile, that make-me-melt hug, and tries to give me one of those sublime kisses. I will not let him put his tongue in my mouth. I will not squeeze him back when he hugs me. I will not look him in the eyes. If I get weak and start feeling nostalgic, I will keep my distance. If I'm not sure about anything else, there's one thing I am sure about: I'm definitely not going to fuck him.

By the time I got to work, I had sixteen phone calls to make, an afternoon presentation for the marketing department that still needed some finishing touches, but I decided to call Mama and get it over with.

She must have been sitting next to the phone, because she answered on the first ring. As usual, after I said hello, she led the conversation. 'Why haven't you called me? I've been worried to death about you. In a strange new city and everything. Are you OK?'

'I'm fine, Mama. I just talked to you two weeks ago, my goodness. Is something wrong?'

'No. Sheila's pregnant.'

'Again! What does she intend to do with four kids?'

'You should keep your mouth shut. And Pookey's home.'

'When'd he get out?'

'Two weeks ago.'

'How's he doing? What's he doing?'

'He's looking for a job. He looks good. Put on some weight, finally. He's staying here with me until he can get hisself together. And as long as he don't start no mess, he can stay here as long as he needs to.'

'Mama, don't let those Section Eight people find out.'

'It ain't none of their business.'

'It *is* their business. They're already pissed because you're living in a two-bedroom. You know they don't like the idea that you've got a daughter who's able to pay your portion of the rent. They could have you evicted if they found out you had somebody living there, so be careful.'

'I will. By the way, I know you just moved and everything, so I was trying to wait to tell you this.'

'Tell me what?'

'My rent is going up.'

'How much?'

'Forty-eight dollars.'

'That's not bad.'

'It is, if you ask me. I just got the new lease, and the housing authority sent me some new forms, so I gotta send 'em to you to sign.'

'Didn't I just sign some kind of papers a few months ago?'

222

'That was for the food stamps. Remember? You had to tell them how much of my rent you was paying. *This* is to verify to the Section Eight people down at the housing authority that you're still paying my part of the rent. That's all.'

'Those people get on my nerves with their forms, I swear.'

'How you think I feel filling 'em out? They're confusing as all hell, and they ask the same questions fifty different ways. Anyway, I'm putting it in the mail tomorrow. Can you send it right back?'

'Yeah.'

'Anyway, Pookey's trying his best to eat me outta house and home.'

'Do you need some money?'

'Who don't? But no. You doing enough for me as it is. I got a letter from Samuel. You know he's stationed in Germany now.'

'No, Mama. I didn't know. Nobody ever tells me anything. How's he doing? When is he ever coming home on another leave? I haven't seen him in two years now. Shoot, sometimes I forget I have another brother.'

'Well, he didn't say nothing about coming home. So I don't know what to tell you. Anyway, how's your new place?'

'It's fine.'

'How's the job?'

'It's fine.'

'That's nice. Speaking of nice, have you met anybody nice?'

I knew it was coming. 'No,' I said.

'You been going out?'

'Yes,' I said.

'Then why haven't you met anybody? You've been there a whole month.'

'Mama, it's not that easy.'

'What's so hard about meeting men?'

'Look, I'm working on it, OK? Speaking of men, why'd you give Kenneth my number?'

'Because he asked for it. What was I supposed to do, pretend like I didn't know my own daughter's phone number?'

'What'd you tell him about me?'

'That you lived in Phoenix.'

'What else?'

'That you still hadn't found that special somebody.'

'I knew it.'

'Well, hell, he asked me if you was married yet. Why, is he coming out there or something?'

'You tell me.'

'He'll be out there on the twenty-sixth of next month. Ain't you excited? You used to like him a lot.'

'*You* used to like him a lot, Mama.'

'Yeah, well, if I remember correctly, you went through a whole lot of changes after you all broke up. He was perfect for you. You didn't have the right attitude. No patience whatsoever, and you ain't changed. That man treated you like he had some sense, but that wasn't good enough.'

'Mama, Kenneth is married.'

'Well, how happy could he be if he went all out of his way to call me to get your number?'

'He's looking up an old friend. I'm not reading anything else into it.'

'Yeah, I got your "old friend." I ain't never been friends with no man after I done slept with him.'

'This is 1990.'

'I know what year it is, Savannah. Some things don't change. And that's one of 'em. Now tell me you don't still have feelings for that man.'

'Mama, I just told you. He feels more like an old friend. I haven't seen Kenneth in four years.'

'So what? I don't care if it's been fifty. Once you love somebody, you don't never stop loving 'em.'

'I gotta go.'

'Call Sheila.'

'Why can't she call me?'

'Because they're adding a new room to the house

and she's trying to watch her money.'

'She's too cheap. She doesn't worry about her phone bill when she's leaving Paul. Tell her to call me.'

'Well, she's worried about you too.'

'Why is everybody always so worried about me?'

'We don't like you being way out there all by yourself, with no kinfolks, no nothing. I don't care how many friends you got; ain't nothin' like being around blood. You've been by yourself for so long, Savannah, we just wanna make sure you ain't lonely.'

'Mama, please.'

'Please, my behind. I'll be glad when you come down off that high horse and stop trying to act like you don't need nothing or nobody. *Every* woman needs a man, and you ain't no exception.'

'I didn't say I didn't need one, but I can't sit around crying the blues because I don't have one.'

'Then do something about it! If you put as much energy into finding a man as you do worrying about promotions and what have you, you'da been married a long time ago.'

'Bye, Mama.'

'Wait a minute!'

'What?'

'Will you send me some pictures of where you live?'

'Yes.'

'And some of the desert?'

'Yes.'

'Especially those cactus.'

'I will.'

'How soon can I come out there and see for myself?'

Shit. She does this every single time I move. 'I'll let you know, Mama. I just barely got here myself. I don't even know my way around this town yet. Maybe by Thanksgiving, depending on what my money situation's like.'

'Is it more expensive living in Phoenix than it was in Denver?'

'No, Mama.'

'If you're having money problems, don't be sending me so much. If Pookey gets a job, he'll be able to help out. You wanna hear something funny?'

I looked at the clock. I'd already talked longer than I'd planned, but that's the way it always is when I talk to Mama. I should've called her last night and paid for the damn call. 'Yes,' I said, 'I want to hear something funny. But make it quick; I have to get back to work.'

'OK, OK. Pookey said when he filled out his application for this job at a gas station, when it got to the part about his education, he lied. He told 'em he'd been to Penn State.'

'That's not funny, Mama.'

'Wait a minute. He said if they catch it and ask him about it, he's gonna say he meant to say the state pen!' Mama was cracking up, and I have to admit I found myself laughing too.

'Anyway, Mama, my money's fine. I have to buy a new car, and soon.'

'You just bought that car four years ago!'

'I know, but I've got eighty-one thousand miles on it. I have to get rid of it before it conks out. It's already worthless.'

'I wish I had a car.'

'I wish I could afford to buy you one.'

'You know I can't drive,' she said, laughing. 'So tell me, do you like it there better than Denver?'

'Mama, I have to go. For real.'

'Well, say it real quick.'

'I can't tell yet. So far it's OK. It's not the most exciting place I've lived.'

'That's part of your whole problem, Savannah. Always looking for excitement. You need to learn how to accept the fact that everything and everybody and everyplace ain't got to be all that exciting for it to be good for you. Slow down. Give the place a chance. Please don't come calling me six months from now talking about you're bored and you're moving again.'

226

'Bye, Mama. Tell Sheila to call me. Tell Pookey I said hi and to call me if he needs anything. How many months is Sheila?'

'Three.'

'I swear.'

'You bet' not,' she said, and hung up.

Control

'That motherfucker thinks he's slick,' Bernadine said to Gloria. They were drinking coffee on Bernadine's patio. It was Sunday afternoon. The kids were with John. They wouldn't be back until six. Bernadine had five more hours of freedom, five hours left to do nothing. A rare occasion.

'You mean to tell me he owns an apartment building right here in town and you didn't know about it?' Gloria said.

'He's got a time share in Lake fucking Tahoe too.'

'No, he doesn't.'

'Yes, he does. And that's not all. It turns out he owned two hundred acres of farmland in California and a goddamn vineyard right here in Arizona. I didn't even know they *made* wine in Arizona! He thought he was being clever by selling them off last year. But it's still considered community property. Listen to this. The son of a bitch owns a Subway franchise. That he didn't sell. I'll tell you one thing: I will never, as long as I live, eat another one of those crab salad sandwiches. He's got all kinds of insurance policies he's borrowed on, a 401K, and a Keogh – you know those retirement plans? I did know about those, but he's been socking money into them left and right. How much, I don't know. And check this out. Today the investigator says he thinks John has bought a house or two in his mama's name!'

'Girl, this sounds like the stuff you see on *Dallas*.'

'How do you think I feel?'

'Like a damn fool. I know.'

'But check it out, girl. An appraiser is getting ready to tear his business records apart. They're going through the taxes for the last five years, phone logs, sales receipts – you name it. My lawyer already got *one* continuance: We go back to court on the thirtieth of April. But now she says she'll probably need to ask for another one. They're going to try to bust his ass. I told you what he sold his half of the business for, didn't I?'

'Yeah, you did. It's unbelievable.'

'Well, any fool could see it was a scam. The judge thought so too. And, girl, the investigator isn't even sure if he's found everything yet. He said John's done a pretty good job of forming a "corporate web" around himself. We're not even talking about stocks and bonds and all that shit. But once they find out everything he owns, they still have to assess the value of it all, then figure out what John's *real* net worth is, before we can even think about a settlement. So this shit could go on for ever.'

'Well, I hope not, for your sake,' Gloria said, and took a sip of her coffee. 'This is enough to drive you crazy.'

'No. This is how women get fucked,' Bernadine said.

'Obviously.'

'But I'll tell you one thing, Glo: This shit won't happen to me again.'

'I hope to hell not.'

'For real. From here on out, I control my own money. I'll never be in the dark like this again. No way.'

'I hear you, Bernie.'

'But then, I'm not ever going to have to worry about this happening again.'

'Why is that?'

'Because I've had time to think about it. I don't care *who* he is, what he does, or how he makes me feel – I will never get married again as long as I live.'

'You're just saying that now because you're going through a divorce, Bernie. Once it's all over, you won't feel this way – watch.'

'I know *exactly* what I'm saying. I'm not that stressed

229

out. Well, I am, but I mean every word I'm saying.'

'Well, I won't lie. I still got my fingers crossed.'

'You can *have* being married. It's not all it's cracked up to be. And believe me, Glo, you're probably better off being single. You just don't know it.'

'*All* marriages aren't bad, Bernie.'

'I didn't say they were, but it's so much bullshit you have to deal with, it's not worth it. Take it from me.'

'Sometimes people marry the wrong person.'

'Yeah, but how the hell are you supposed to know that until after you marry the motherfucker?'

'Good point,' Gloria said.

They finished their coffee. 'You feel like going to the mall?' Gloria asked.

'Why not,' Bernadine said, and put their cups away.

They'd already been in and out of eight or nine stores. Gloria broke down and paid a hundred and fifty dollars for a pair of Air Jordans for Tarik. This was his reward for getting all B's on his report card. Plus, he'd been begging her to buy these damn sneakers for months. Bernadine American Expressed over a thousand dollars on things she didn't want: more makeup, another black purse, another mustard-colored suit for whatever, and a cheap watch. She bought the kids stuff they definitely didn't need: another Nintendo game for John junior and some kind of talking computer for Onika.

'Look who's here,' Gloria said to Bernadine, when she spotted Robin coming out of a lingerie shop. Robin had on a tight red top that crisscrossed in the front. It was cut low, as usual. She was wearing extra-tight bluejeans and a wide red belt. Her shoes were flat and red. Bernadine and Gloria both knew that Robin wouldn't be caught dead in sneakers.

'That girl ought to quit,' Bernadine said, and looked down at her new watch. It was ten to five. 'I'm not letting her talk me to death today. I've got to get home. The kids'll be there in an hour. John is prompt as hell.'

'Hey!' Robin said, when she saw them. She was carrying a tiny white bag. From where they were standing, Bernadine thought Robin could easily pass for a tall Robin Givens, but as she got closer, it was clearly a resemblance that held up only from a distance. 'What are you two broads doing here?'

'Take a wild guess,' Gloria said.

'Look at all the bags! Some of us have it like that, but we peasants don't have the luxury of shopping till we drop.'

'We were just on our way home,' Bernadine said. 'What's up?'

'Girl, you will not believe what has happened to me.'

'What?' Bernadine asked.

'Come over here and sit down for a minute.'

Bernadine and Gloria looked at each other.

'Just for a minute. I haven't seen you sluts in weeks. It seems like all we do is talk on the phone. Come on, just for a minute.'

'All right, Robin,' Bernadine sighed. 'But I've gotta be in my car, driving, in fifteen minutes.'

The three of them walked down the steps into the atrium, where there was a bunch of white tables for patrons of the row of little food shops that lined the wall, offering pizza, frozen yogurt, hot dogs, Greek and Chinese food, and chocolate chip cookies. Bernadine wandered around until she found the smoking section. They sat down.

'I met a man,' Robin said, running her fingers through her hair. When she leaned forward, her breasts plunged out from her blouse, as if they'd been suffocating.

'And?' Gloria said. 'What else is new?'

'Shut up, Gloria. Anyway, he's . . . I swear to God, I can't even hardly describe him.'

'Try,' Gloria said.

Bernadine lit a cigarette.

'His name is Troy. Does the name itself tell you anything?'

231

'What readily comes to my mind is Troy Donahue,'
Bernadine said. 'Don't tell me he's white.'

'Forget you, Bernie. No. He's definitely not white.
He's seriously brown and too fine and he teaches
at South Mountain Community College and he's the
football coach and he's from Atlanta and he's an
Aquarius, thank you, Jesus!'

'So I guess your prayers have finally been answered,
then, huh?' Gloria said.

'Shut up, Gloria.'

'What does he teach?' Bernadine asked, and flicked
her ashes, even though there weren't any.

'Science.'

'That's good,' Bernadine said. 'He's got a brain,
which means you're off to a running start.'

'Is he nice?' Gloria asked, and stood up.

'Nice is putting it mildly. For the last three days I
have literally been intoxicated. Where you going?'

'I think I want to try that frozen yogurt,' Gloria said.
'Anybody else want some?'

'Not me,' Robin said.

'Me either,' Bernie said.

Gloria slipped her purse over her arm and headed
toward the yogurt shop.

'Three whole days, huh?' Bernadine said. 'What are
you doing, Robin, trying to break *The Guinness Book
of Records*?'

'Go to hell, Bernie.'

'So where'd you meet this one?'

'You won't even believe this, girl. At the grocery
store.'

'The grocery store?'

'You heard me,' she said, and drummed her shiny
red nails on the tabletop. 'Buying toilet paper, girl!'

'What ever happened to Michael?'

'He still calls. You know that woman we saw him
with?'

'Yeah.'

'Well, he said it wasn't anything serious. He only

went out with her to be doing something. But I have to give it to him; old Michael said he wasn't gonna sit around the house twiddling his thumbs, waiting for me to tell him what move to make next.'

'Right on for Michael.'

'I still don't want to go out with him.'

'Never burn all your bridges, Robin.'

'Anyway, Troy is like a gift from God. Just what the doctor ordered.'

'So what have you guys been doing, or should I bother asking?'

'Go to hell, Bernie. You're starting to sound like Gloria.'

'Then that means you've fucked him already.'

'What's wrong with that?'

'Robin, I'll be glad when you learn how to control your hot ass. Don't you know how to say no?'

'Why should I?'

'To get to know the man first, damn.'

'Think what would've happened if I had waited before I slept with Mr No-Can-Fuck Michael.'

'Maybe you would've found out you actually liked him.'

'I do like him, but he just doesn't satisfy me. If there's one thing I have learned, it's that you can't teach a man how to fuck.'

'I can't argue with that.'

'Do you know how hard it is to suck a little dick?'

Bernadine started laughing. 'I'm happy to say I don't.'

'Anyway, girl, I think I want to keep this one.'

'How can you even say some shit like this, Robin? You just met him three days ago!'

'You don't know a thing about vibes, do you, Bernie? You've been married too long, that's what your problem is.'

'You're probably right.'

Gloria came back empty-handed and didn't sit down. 'You ready, Bernie?'

233

'Yes, I am,' she said, and picked up her shopping bags.

'Will we see you at the meeting?' Gloria asked Robin.

'I guess so,' she said. 'When is it, again?'

'Thursday, April fifth. I thought you wrote it down.'

'I did, but I don't have my calendar with me, Miss Oasis.'

'Bye, Robin. We'll see you there. I hope.'

'Bye,' Robin said.

On the way out to the car, Bernadine looked at Gloria and started laughing.

'What's so funny?' Gloria asked.

'Robin. She's pitiful.'

'I thought you knew that already,' Gloria said, and took a little container of caramel swirl yogurt out of her purse.

Bernadine's fingers were clicking away on the adding machine. In front of her were at least ten different sets of control sheets. The auditors were coming next week. If she didn't have the figures in order by then, she'd be in deep shit. It was her own fault, for putting it off, but she'd been so swamped, she hardly knew where to begin. One of the secretaries had quit, which was another reason why everything was backed up. Bernadine needed an assistant, but her boss was too cheap to get her one. Part of her job was paying her clients' bills. She wrote the checks – for the IRS, for the payroll, for any maintenance problems that arose at the properties, and for emergencies. She also maintained ledgers of all fiscal transactions and made sure every source of income and disbursements was accounted for. One of the companies Bernadine represented owned a 'chain' of nursing homes. This morning, she'd been informed that they were being sued. Somehow the food at one of the facilities had gone bad, and several of the residents had gotten food poisoning. Two had died. Needless to say, the office

234

was crazy. And today – of all days – Bernadine had a doctor's appointment she couldn't afford to cancel.

Her office was full of smoke. The receptionist buzzed her. 'It's Herbert, on line two.'

What does he want now? Bernadine said to herself. This was the second time he'd called her today. It was only eleven o'clock. She picked up the phone. 'What can I do for you, Herbert?'

'I wanted to see what you were doing for lunch.'

'I'm busy.'

'What about dinner?'

'I'm busy. Don't you ever eat at home?'

'Not if I don't have to. I'd rather be with you,' he said.

'Look, Herbert. I've got tons of work to do, I'll probably have to work late, and I don't know when I'm going to have some free time.'

'What about after the kids go to sleep tonight? Can I come over for a little while?'

'Are you crazy? You know, Herbert, this is getting a little deeper than I wanted it to get.'

The receptionist tapped on her door. 'It's the school. On line one. Onika's sick.'

'Shit!' Bernadine said. 'Herbert, I have to go. Something's wrong with my daughter. I'll talk to you next week,' she said, and pressed the other line. Her heart was pounding. 'What's wrong with my daughter?' she asked.

The school nurse said Onika had a temperature of 103; Bernadine should pick her up as soon as possible and take her to a doctor if it doesn't go down. Pick her up? I can't stop in the middle of this shit and go pick her up. Her first inclination was to call John, but she remembered he was in Mexico, vacationing. She lit another cigarette without realizing one was still burning in the ashtray. Onika's school was twenty-five minutes away. 'I'll be there as fast as I can,' she said, and hung up. She took a deep drag on the cigarette and started coughing because the smoke went down the wrong way. She looked at her desk. Then she looked at her calendar. She'd have to work late every night this week – including the weekend – to get these figures to jibe. Shit. That meant getting a baby-sitter, which pissed her off. Since she started having this little affair with Herbert, Bernadine knew she hadn't been spending as much time with the kids as she should. She was going to have to put a stop to it. Her kids were more important, and besides, Herbert was starting to get on her nerves.

She crushed out her cigarette and grabbed her purse. 'I'll try to get back later if I can. If the bank calls, tell them I'll get back with them tomorrow. If the Utah people call, tell them I've sent the checks. And oh, they're supposed to be putting in new carpet in number eighty-two, at Mission Palms. Call to confirm that it's happened. What else?'

'Go,' the receptionist said. 'If there're any problems, I'll call you at home.'

'I almost forgot,' she said, and ran back to her office. She ripped off a check from the register and brought it back. 'This is for the air-conditioning people. They'll be by between one and two.'

Bernadine walked out the front door, knowing there were a million other things she should've told the receptionist, but she couldn't think. She drove without thinking. By the time she got to the school, Onika's temperature was down to 99. When they got home, it seemed to have stabilized. Onika had a runny nose and a slight cough. She hadn't had any cold symptoms when Bernadine dropped her and John junior off at school this morning. She gave Onika a teaspoon of children's Tylenol, put her to bed, and lay there with her for over an hour. Bernadine felt her head every fifteen minutes, and she didn't get up until Onika had fallen asleep and the fever was gone.

She was sitting on a stool in the kitchen, on the phone with the receptionist, when Onika appeared in front of her, shivering. 'What's wrong?' Bernadine asked her.

Onika wrapped her arms around herself and didn't stop trembling. 'I'm too hot,' she uttered.

Bernadine felt her forehead. It was scorching. She told the receptionist she'd have to call her back. She dialed 911. They said they'd have an ambulance there in about ten minutes. But Bernadine lived up in the goddamn foothills and knew it would take them longer than that to get there. Shit, something was seriously wrong with her daughter, and she couldn't wait. She picked Onika up and carried to the car. 'It'll be all right, baby. Does it hurt?'

Onika nodded her head yes. 'Now I'm cold, Mama.'

'Just a minute,' she said. Bernadine ran back into the house, snatched a dirty bath towel from the laundry room, and wrapped it around Onika. 'Is that better?'

Onika nodded yes, then leaned her head against the glass. Bernadine locked all four doors and backed out of the driveway so fast she ran over the trash can. She left the trash lying there. About six blocks from the house, she saw the ambulance. She laid on the horn. They made a U-turn, and an attendant got out and ran over to the car. Bernadine told them who she was. They lifted Onika out of the Cherokee, put her in the back of the ambulance, turned their siren on, and headed down the hill. Bernadine followed them. She didn't have any idea what could be wrong with Onika. She lit a cigarette. When Janet Jackson came on the radio, singing 'What Have You Done for Me Lately,' Bernadine switched it off and said, 'Nothing, bitch!'

By the time they got to the hospital emergency entrance, Bernadine was a nervous wreck. She jumped out of the Cherokee before the attendant could get his door open. 'Is she going to be all right?' she asked. 'What's wrong with my baby?'

'It's OK, ma'am. It's just an ear infection. She'll be OK. We're going to try to get her temperature down. It's up to 104. If you'd like to go on into admissions and sign her in, we'll let you know how she is in a few minutes. Don't worry.'

Bernadine answered a trillion questions and signed every piece of paper they handed her. She wanted a cigarette bad, but of course she couldn't smoke in here. She waited fifteen minutes, then went outside and smoked one – along with several of the nurses. She came back in and sat down. Another fifteen minutes went by. She went out and smoked another cigarette. Finally, a nurse came outside, told her that Onika was doing fine and Bernadine could see her now. She put her cigarette out and walked briskly down the corridor, into the emergency room. Onika was lying on a white stretcher. She looked much better than she had earlier. 'How you feeling, baby?' Bernadine asked, as she bent down and simultaneously squeezed Onika's hand, stroked her head, and kissed her cheek.

'Good,' she said. 'Mama, I want to go home now.'

A doctor walked up next to Bernadine. 'We're glad you called us when you did. Ear infections can be quite serious. People just don't realize it. Once a child's temperature gets up to 105, they can go into convulsions, and it could cause irreparable brain damage.'

Bernadine stood up. 'But I don't understand how or when this could've happened. When I took her to school this morning, she was fine. Then the nurse called and said she had a temperature of 103. When I brought her home, it was 99. I checked her forehead every fifteen minutes and took her temperature every half hour. It was steady at 99. The next thing I knew, she was standing in front of me, quivering, like she was freezing.'

'They can surface in a matter of minutes. But it looks like we've got it under control now. Tell her what we gave you,' he said to Onika.

'A Popsicle.'

'A Popsicle?' Bernadine said.

'That's it. Is she allergic to any medications?'

'Not that I know of.'

238

'I'm going to give her a prescription for amoxicillin. Make sure she finishes the entire bottle.' He wrote something on a little piece of paper and handed it to Bernadine. 'Her throat looks a bit red. There's a little congestion, but for the most part, she's fine. I think it'd be a good idea to keep her home tomorrow,' he said.

'That's it?'

'That's it,' he said.

'So I can take her home now?'

'Yes, you can,' he said.

Bernadine was relieved. But damn, all this drama was solved by a damn Popsicle? She didn't care. The important thing was that her baby was all right. The next question was, how was she going to find somebody to stay home with her sick child all day? Who could she ask that she could trust? She thought for a minute. Geneva, of course.

Bernadine changed her doctor's appointment to the following week. Her doctor was pissed, but what could she do? For the next five days, Bernadine performed miracles. Geneva took care of Onika on Tuesday, and Bernadine decided not to get a baby-sitter for the rest of the week after all. She took the kids to school, went to work, and broke her neck trying to get to the after-school program before six o'clock. She made it. There'd been too many occasions when her kids were the only ones left in that room. She hated to see them sitting there, trying to entertain each other, and the teacher, clearly pissed and anxious to leave, would give Bernadine the evil eye.

After she picked them up, Bernadine brought the kids back to the office with her. They ate dinner in the conference room: Taco Bell on Wednesday, McDonald's on Thursday, Jack in the Box on Friday, and Kentucky Fried Chicken for lunch and dinner on Saturday. The kids did their homework there. When they needed help, Bernadine stopped whatever she was doing. Seven-thirty was the cutoff she had given herself to stop working. When they got home, she somehow managed to watch Onika take her bath, read her a bedtime story, and tried to stay alert while John junior read her one. By ten o'clock, she was whipped. The most she could do at that point was to go to bed herself.

But Bernadine worried at night. She worried about work. What had to get done the next day. She worried about the kids. How was she going to get Onika to ballet and John junior to soccer practice on time. When would she ever have time to take them to a movie, to the damn park, like they used to? Were they hiding their grief about the divorce? Had they come in contact with Kathleen and were they keeping it a secret? She worried whether or not John was going to pay the April mortgage payment. What if he didn't? What was she going to do? She worried about when this settlement business was ever going to be over. Next month or next year? And what was she going to do with the money, whenever she got it and however much it was? She didn't have the energy to start a catering business at this point in her life. She knew she would quit this job. But what *would* she do then? She also worried about this thing she'd started with Herbert. It was getting out of hand. She worried what would happen if she ended it now. Would she be twice as lonely? Bernadine worried about everything. So much that, lately, she was lucky to get four hours of solid sleep. She often woke up tired. And had to start the whole routine all over again.

Bernadine had just told her doctor all the things that had gone on in her life since the last time she was here, which was two months ago. 'I'm running out of steam,' she said. 'I feel like I've lost my center. I can't concentrate on anything.' Bernadine went on to explain how hard it was getting to keep her mind on one thing at a time. When she did, she couldn't focus on it for long. She said she felt anxious all the time. And sad. And she was always tired. She didn't know how much longer she could keep up this pace. Bernadine also told her doctor that she resented the fact that John was living a carefree life, like a goddamn bachelor. He had no fucking responsibilities whatsoever, other than sending her a check and picking the kids up every other weekend. 'I'm doing everything,' Bernadine said. 'And I'm sick of it.'

Her doctor understood. It was her job to understand. She was a psychiatrist. 'Have the Xanax been helping?'

'Helping me in what way?'

'To relax.'

'I don't take them during the day. They slow me down.'

'How are you sleeping?'

'Some nights it's hard. I've got too much on my mind, but on those nights, I've taken as many as three. They didn't help. So I stopped taking them.'

'Well, how about if I give you a higher dosage?'

'I don't want a higher dosage.'

'Would you like something to help you sleep?'

'No,' Bernadine said. She didn't want any sleeping pills in the house. Not that she didn't trust herself. She'd read about those things. Presumably, you didn't even dream when you took them. Bernadine had two kids. She couldn't afford to be unconscious.

'Well, I think maybe I should put you on an antidepressant. That'll help you to concentrate and generally make you feel better all around. It'll take at least three to four weeks before they get into your system well enough for you to feel their effect. Why don't I give you a prescription for twelve to start out with, and let's see how your body reacts. We can take it from there.'

'OK,' Bernadine said, and didn't ask any questions. She'd heard of antidepressants. Shit, maybe they'd help.

*   *   *

She didn't feel any different after taking the pills for five days. And didn't expect to. On the sixth day, Bernadine woke up with diarrhea and felt nauseous. She thought she'd finally caught that flu that had been going around. On the seventh day, she got out of bed feeling kind of funny. She couldn't put her finger on it, but she felt different – spacey. She got the kids up, went to make herself a cup of coffee, as she always did, but didn't have a taste for it. So Bernadine didn't drink it. On her way to drop the kids off at school, the cars looked bigger, brighter; the traffic lights, greener, redder. At work, she was so self-conscious about everything she did, she backtracked over the same figures five times before she accepted the fact that they were accurate. When the phone rang, she jumped. She was sure everybody could tell she was acting weird, so she worked hard to imitate her normal self.

After she picked the kids up, Bernadine came home and started dinner. That's when it dawned on her that she hadn't eaten a thing in two days. She wasn't the least bit hungry now. She made hamburgers and french fries. She tried to eat one. The burger tasted like rubber. Bernadine couldn't understand why.

That night, she read Onika a story, *Liza Lou and the Yeller Belly Swamp*, helped John junior with his math, and went to bed. She wasn't sleepy or tired, so she lay there and waited for sleep. When it finally came, Bernadine dreamed that a witch was throwing her into a kettle of boiling swamp water. She climbed out over the steel rim. But her body had melted. Now she was in quicksand. An alligator was trying to eat her. He bit a chunk out of her thigh. Somehow she made it to a forest, where she was now stuck at the top of a hundred-foot oak tree. When the tree turned into a green monster, she jumped and landed in a clump of cattails. A gnarled hand reached out and grabbed her. Bernadine woke up, terrified. She ran to the bathroom, because it felt as if she had to throw up. But she couldn't.

She tried to go back to sleep, but she kept hearing things. She thought it was a robber, so she hid beneath the covers. Why was it cold under here? She peeked out and, when she didn't see anybody, ran to the closet and got her bathrobe. She thought one of her shoes moved. Maybe it wasn't hers. Maybe the robber was hiding behind her clothes. She slammed the door and locked it, and ran out into the great room. It was scarier out here. When the icemaker dropped some cubes into the tray, Bernadine screamed. The kids ran out of their bedrooms.

'What's wrong, Mama?' John junior asked.

'Nothing. I thought I saw a mouse. It was just dust. You guys go on back to bed.'

After they left, Bernadine sat on the couch. Maybe she *was* burnt out. Maybe she should check herself into someplace where she could chill for a while. She was definitely out of control, and she didn't like this feeling whatsoever. Was she having a nervous breakdown? Was that what this shit was?

Bernadine went back to bed. When she closed her eyes, she pictured herself in a white room in a white bed in a white nightgown. A white nurse in a white uniform was standing over her. 'All you need is a month,' she said to Bernadine. 'And you'll be able to go back to work. This rest will do you a world of good.'

The next day was worse. Bernadine was paranoid about everything and everybody. She wanted to talk to Savannah, Gloria, or Robin, but she didn't know what she'd tell them. How could she explain these feelings, get them to understand, when she didn't understand what was happening to her herself?

Bernadine didn't say a single word to the kids on the way to school. At work, she paid extra-close attention to the tiniest of details. Everybody in the office knew she was cracking up, she thought. They were just pretending not to notice. They knew she couldn't handle the pressure, but Bernadine planned to fool them all. She became aware of every single move she

243

made. When she went to the bathroom, she counted her steps. She counted how many squares of tissue it took to wipe herself. She counted the number of puffs it took to finish a cigarette. She counted how many movements it took to get in the car and start it. She counted how many lights she had to pass before she made it to the school.

She was too jittery to cook, so she microwaved a pizza for the kids. She had a glass of water for dinner. Bernadine still wasn't hungry. After last night, she was afraid to read Onika a bedtime story and told her she needed a night off. She tried to help John junior with a math problem, but it was too confusing. She told him not to worry about that one and move on.

She went to bed and prayed for a good night's sleep. She didn't get it. Bernadine dreamed she was under a guillotine. John took an ax and split the rope in two. She saw her head roll across the wooden platform. Bernadine turned over, and she saw herself jumping out of a skyscraper window. She hit the pavement. And died. But she didn't want to hit the pavement, so she went back up to the top floor and jumped again. This time, on the way down, other people were soaring through the air too. Bernadine found herself dodging them. She landed at the drive-up window of McDonald's. She ordered two Happy Meals. The young boy handed her the boxes. She opened one. It was full of dead mice. Bernadine threw them both out the window and drove off.

In the morning, she called her doctor. 'What's in this shit you gave me?'

'Are you starting to have side effects?'

'Side effects? I'm one step away from checking myself into a nuthouse. I didn't feel *this* damn bad when I came to see you.'

'Well, this medication affects different people in different ways. For some, it's like magic. For others, it doesn't do so well. Tell me, what are some of the symptoms you're having?'

'For starters, I had diarrhea for two days and kept feeling like I was going to throw up. I've lost six pounds, because I can't eat.'

'This is one of the reasons some people love them. They're great for losing weight.'

'I didn't come to see you because I had a weight problem. When I finally *do* get to sleep, I've been having nightmares. I can't even begin to tell you some of the things I've been dreaming about. And I've been hallucinating. Seeing things crawling when nothing's there. I'm like a damn space cadet. I'm self-conscious about every single move I make, and it's driving me crazy. I'm not taking any more of these pills. That's what I called to tell you.'

'Are you sure, Bernadine? From what you've told me, it's clear that you're clinically depressed. You need *something* to help you get through this. No need to be a martyr. You could try breaking them in half.'

Was this bitch deaf? Had she not heard a word Bernadine had said? 'Look,' Bernadine said. 'I'm not taking any more, OK? And you should be a little more careful about what kind of medication you prescribe. These pills are dangerous.'

'I understand how you must feel, Bernadine. And I'm sorry the medication doesn't agree with you. We could try another kind, if you'd like.'

'I don't think so,' Bernadine said. 'I'll figure out a way to get through this on my own. Just like I've been doing. Thank you,' she said, and hung up.

Bernadine poured the last few pills down the garbage disposal and emptied the rest of the Xanax in too. She turned the faucet on, and the sound of the water made her ears tingle. The grinding noise got so loud that Bernadine forgot all about the water. She listened with such intensity that she had to stop herself. She turned the disposal off, ran over to the phone, and called the doctor back. 'Tell me something. How long will it take for these pills to get out of my system? I want to know when I'll start feeling like myself again.'

'About a week,' she said.

Bernadine slammed the phone down in her face. The bitch didn't know what the fuck she was talking about. First she said it would take three to four weeks to feel their effect, and it'd only been seven goddamn days. Besides, Bernadine already felt like herself. She was pissed off. And knew she had a *right* to be pissed off. 'Fuck being crazy,' she said, and she grabbed a box of Cheerios from the cabinet, poured some into a bowl, and forced herself to eat them.

It Ain't About Nothin'

I opened the door for Troy. Good God almighty. This man is past gorgeous. He was holding a lit cigarette between his fingers. I wish he didn't smoke, but I guess I can live with one bad habit. 'Hey, sugar,' he said. He was wearing a pale-blue polo shirt with some navy-blue baggy pants and Ray-Ban sunglasses, even though it was dark outside. His beeper was clipped to his shirt pocket. Troy does not look at all like he's forty years old. He's in great shape. Hallelujah. His waist is probably the same size as mine, and he moves those narrow hips like he's still twenty.

He gave me a sloppy kiss. It was good. When he went to put his hand underneath my blouse, I thought about what Bernadine had said. The truth was, I didn't know all that much about Troy, and tonight might be a good time to find out. So I backed away.

'What's wrong, baby?' he asked, and took a puff of his cigarette.

'Nothing. Have a seat.' I went to find an ashtray, then sat down on the couch. Troy walked over to my stereo.

'How about some music,' he said, and pressed the buttons on my cassette player like he'd been doing it for years. It was hard to believe I'd only known him three days.

'What would you like to do tonight?' I asked.

'Whatever makes you feel good,' he said. 'This sister can blow,' he said, after Vanessa Williams started singing 'Dreaming.' Troy jumped up, put his cigarette back in his mouth, turned toward me, and pretended like he was slow-dancing with somebody.

'How about a movie?' I said.

'I'm not in the mood for a movie,' he said, and started pacing around the room. 'Ask me what I want to do.'

'What do you want to do?'

'Spend the night making sweet love to you.'

He rushed over to the end table, crushed out his cigarette, and flopped down next to me on the couch. I inched away. 'That's all we've been doing, Troy. I'd like to get out of the house, and I'd like to get to know you better – standing up.'

'Oh, I get it,' he said, grinning. 'We're getting serious, are we?'

'You're not serious?'

'Don't I act serious?'

'I can't tell for sure yet.'

'You mind if I get a glass of wine?'

'I'll get it,' I said, and stood up. I went over to the kitchen, poured us both a glass, brought the bottle back, and set it on the table.

Troy had lit another cigarette. He drank his wine down in one gulp and poured himself another one. 'So what'd you have in mind?' he asked, and got back up.

'Are you nervous about something?' I asked.

'No. Got a lot of things going on, that's all.' His beeper went off. 'Can I use the phone for a minute?'

'Yep. There's one in the kitchen.'

He got up and pulled the cord over by the sink. I heard him say, 'Yeah, man, I'll check on you in a few minutes. I'll have a lady friend with me. She's cool.' He hung up, walked behind the couch, and kissed me on the forehead. I almost died. But I wanted to see if I could control myself. For once in my life. 'I need to run by one of my partners' for a few minutes. You feel like taking a drive?'

'Why not.'

'Cool. He lives in Scottsdale. He's a lawyer. Nice people. You'll like him. Plus, I want you to get to know the kind of people I deal with.'

248

Sounded good to me. 'Can you give me a minute to do my face?'

'You look good enough,' he said, and lit another cigarette.

'It'll only take a minute.' I took my makeup kit out of my purse and went on into the bathroom. I brushed on a little more blush, a coat of lipstick, picked my hair out, and grabbed a fresh handkerchief from my drawer. When I came out and said, 'I'm ready,' Troy looked like he'd just seen a ghost.

His car was deep. It was a 1978 Cadillac. I didn't know he was the Cadillac-driving type. The interior was gray leather, and it smelled good, like jasmine. It was coming from that yellow felt Christmas tree dangling from the rearview mirror. We drove through Tempe and on up toward Scottsdale Road. The closer we got to the hills, the darker the streets got. 'You mind if I crack the window? The smoke is making my eyes water.'

'No. Go right ahead,' he said.

'Whereabouts do you live, Troy?'

'Seventeenth, right off Baseline.'

'Do you live by yourself?'

'Not any more.'

'You don't?'

'No. My mother and son live with me.'

'Oh,' I said. That bit of information put a real damper on things. The man was forty years old. And his mother still lived with him? I bet *he* lives with his mother. Either way, I couldn't believe it. Maybe there was more to this than I understood. Considering I just met the man, I didn't want to get all into his business, but I had to ask something. 'How old is your son?'

'Sixteen.'

'Is his mother here in Phoenix?'

'She's in Detroit. He was having some problems a while back, so I took him off her hands. He's a good kid. Just got mixed up with the wrong people.'

'What about your mother?'

249

'What about her?'

'What's it like, living with your mother?'

'Convenient. She cooks and cleans and basically runs the house. She gets her social security checks, plays a little bingo, and goes to church. I couldn't ask for a better situation, really. She's only sixty-eight but kind of scared about living by herself. She's got asthma. But since she's been out here, she's only had three attacks where she had to be hospitalized.'

'How long has she been out here?'

'Four years.'

'She's been living with you for four years?'

'Yeah.'

'What's that like?'

'I told you, it works out for everybody. She's not all in my business or anything, and I can bring a lady friend home with no problem. You'll see.'

'I will?'

'Yeah. I already told her about you. I want you to meet both of them.'

Well, I thought, how refreshing. Right now I was hoping we'd get where we were going, because I had to go to the bathroom. Bad. We pulled into this long driveway that led to a beautiful Santa Fe house with a big oak door. After we rang the doorbell, Troy bent over and kissed me. 'You'll like Bill,' he said. 'He's real cool people.'

When Bill answered the door, he didn't look like any lawyer to me. He was wearing a Mike Tyson T-shirt, but Mike's face was almost gone. Bill had two gold earrings in one ear, and a raggedy Jheri-Kurl. He was probably handsome at one time, but there were pockmarks all over his face. The sockets under his eyes were puffy, and his lips were chapped. He could stand some dental work. And his bluejeans were clearly too big. He was skinnier than my daddy.

'Come on in,' he said, ushering us. Bill acted like he was in a hurry. He moved so fast, I almost broke my neck trying to catch up to him and Troy on that marble floor. It eventually led to a sunken living room. The whole house was done in black and white, that high-tech look, and he had Kenny G blaring. There were four other men sitting in the family room, and the TV was on, but it didn't look like anybody was watching it. That's when I smelled the reefer and saw the glass pipe sitting on the coffee table, with a flame burning underneath. Oh, shit, I thought, not crack.

I sat down. Bill introduced me to the other four men, whose names and faces I wasn't going to remember. Why didn't he ask me if I did this stuff, or if I minded being around it? Why didn't he give me some clue he was into this? 'May I use your bathroom?' I asked.

'Be my guest,' Bill said, and pointed down the hall.

When I came back out, they were crouched around the same spot, passing the pipe. Troy sounded like he was choking.

'You want a hit?' Bill asked.

'No, thanks,' I said.

'How about some wine?'

'I don't think we have time, do we?' I said, looking at Troy.

'We've got time for a glass of wine,' Troy said, and winked at me.

I sat there listening to them talk about some fight that had been on HBO, while they passed the pipe back and forth. One of the guys lit another joint, and I felt like running out the front door. This was so boring. And these men were old enough to know better.

I drank my wine and then the 'transaction' was done. Troy handed Bill a hundred-dollar bill, and Bill handed him a white piece of paper shaped like a triangle. When Troy said we had to be going, I pretended like it was really good to have met them and looked forward to seeing them all again.

When we got in the car, Troy was wired up. 'You feel like stopping by the Jockey Club and having a drink? I feel like doing something. Didn't you say you wanted to hear some music? I think Patti Williams is singing somewhere tonight. We could get a paper or stop by a phone booth and I could call around to check. She's good. You heard her before?'

'No,' I said dryly. I didn't know where to start, since he obviously didn't feel weird about what I'd just witnessed. But then I blurted out, 'I wanna go home.'

'Is something wrong, baby?'

'I didn't know you were into this kind of thing.'

'I just do it sometimes for recreation, that's all. Does it bother you?'

'Yes, it does.'

'Then I won't do it around you. How's that?'

'I don't usually deal with men who mess around with drugs. Drugs scare me.'

'You're making it sound like I'm an addict or something. All I did was took a few hits, picked up a little package, and to be honest, I don't *have* to do this. I swear. I like you, Robin, and I don't want something like this to come between us when I'm just starting to get to know you.'

'I don't feel good about this, Troy. How can you do drugs, considering what you do for a living?'

'What I do in my private life is completely separate from what I do at work. Look, if I was into this shit that heavy, do you think I'd be in such good shape?'

He had a point, because he was in tip-top shape, which was another thing that baffled me. I was wondering how he could do this junk and work out without having a heart attack or something.

'Look,' he said. 'My mother is barbecuing some ribs tomorrow evening, and I told her I'd bring you over. What time do you get home from work?'

'About six.'

'I'll pick you up about six-thirty. And hey, we can deal with this. It's really not as much of a problem as you're making it out to be. It ain't about nothin'.'

He smiled at me and winked. I knew I was probably being a fool, but no man had asked me to meet his mother in centuries, so I figured *maybe* he wasn't into it so much and *maybe* if we got to know each other better – once he saw that I didn't need drugs to enjoy myself – *maybe* I might be a good influence on him. So I told him yes, I'd love to come over to his house and meet his mother and son.

When we got to my apartment, I let him get back into my bed. We did it for what seemed like hours. Troy didn't act like he was satisfied. He was still hard as a rock, but I was tired and had to call it quits. I had to get up and go to work in a matter of hours. I thought he fell asleep right after I did, but when I heard the phone ring and reached over to answer it, that's when I noticed Troy was gone.

'Hi, baby,' he said.

'Troy?'

'In the flesh,' he said. 'How'd you sleep?'

'Good, I guess. When did you leave?'

'About five.'

'Are you at home?'

'Yep. Just reading and listening to some Coltrane. You ever listen to Coltrane?'

'No, I don't.'

'You should. He's deep, so deep I can't even understand him sometime. How's my baby?'

I didn't quite know how to answer that, but I said, 'Fine.'

'Good. How are those luscious titties of mine this morning?'

'They're mine, not yours, but they're fine.'

'Come on, Robin. Help me go to sleep, baby.'

'You haven't been to sleep yet?'

'I felt like reading. You had me so lit up last night, I couldn't get enough of you. But when I saw you were

253

wiped out, I figured I should just go on home and read and let you get your rest.'

'Thanks for being so considerate,' I said.

'Open your legs for me, baby.'

'What?'

'Open those long brown legs for me and touch yourself until you get slippery.'

'Troy, I don't like this.'

'Come on, baby, do it for me.'

'I'm not doing anything. But what I am about to do is hang up this phone if you don't change the tone of your voice and this whole conversation. I mean it.'

'OK, OK. I was just having a little fun. Damn, I'm hard as ice, baby. See what kind of power you have? See what you can do to a grown man over the telephone? Does that tell you what kind of woman you are?'

'Not really.'

Then the tone of his voice changed. He got serious all of a sudden. 'I'll pick you up at six-thirty. My mother's already made the potato salad. OK?'

'OK,' I said, but I didn't know what I was getting into.

'What should I do?' I asked Savannah. I spent half the morning telling her what had happened. I was at work.

'I wouldn't go. Especially knowing he's into crack.'

'I know. But he said he only does it sometimes.'

'What'd you expect him to say? That he's a crackhead? Give me a break, Robin. Stop being so gullible.'

'What time is it?'

'A little past eleven.'

'I should go ahead and call him and cancel, then, huh?'

'I would, but you do what you want to do. What I want to know is, what's with him wanting you to meet his family, and you haven't even known him a

week? I'd be skeptical if for no other reason besides
that. What have you done with this man besides fuck
him that would make knowing you so deep that he
wants to bring you home to his mama already?'

'I know, girl.'

'Call him, and call me right back.'

'I don't know his number at work.'

'Call his mama and get it.'

When I called, his mother answered the phone.
'Hi there,' she said. 'We're really looking forward to
meeting you. Troy's told me all about you. It isn't
very often that he wants me to meet a lady friend,
so I figure you must be awful special, which is why
I told him I'd have this little barbecue for you. Give
you a chance to meet the rest of the family what lives
here in Phoenix.'

'You mean this barbecue's for me?'

'He didn't tell you? We want to welcome you to the
family. Make you feel at home.'

'That's very thoughtful of you, ma'am. Could you
give me Troy's work number?'

'He didn't go to work today.'

'He didn't?'

'I think he's coming down with a cold.'

'Well, is he there?'

'Nope.'

'You think he'll be back soon?'

'I couldn't tell you, baby. Sick or not, that boy
moves at eighty miles an hour. He don't stop too
long for nothing. If he comes back anytime soon, you
want me to have him call you?'

'Would you? I'm at work. He has the number.'

'I sure will. Looking forward to meeting you. This
ain't nothing fancy, so don't go getting all dressed
up and everything. Just a few of his cousins, his
brother and three sisters'll be here. That's all.'

'Well, I'm looking forward to meeting all of you too,'
I said. 'I'll see you a little later, ma'am.'

'Bye, baby,' she said, and hung up.

What the hell was going on here? I didn't know he'd planned a family reunion. Why didn't he let me in on this? What kind of man was I dealing with? Lord, help me.

I didn't feel like going out for lunch today, so I ordered a ham-and-cheese sandwich from the deli downstairs. When the boy delivered it, I reached inside my purse to get my wallet. It wasn't there. I took everything out and piled it on top of my desk. It wasn't there. I was trying to remember the last time I took it out for something. While I sat there going over this in my mind, Marva realized the boy was waiting for his money, so she lent me four dollars. I paid him. Then I tried to think again, where I could've dropped it, or if I forgot and left it at home.

I walked in my front door at ten after six. I looked between the cushions of the couch, the bathroom, under the bed – everywhere in that apartment – and still didn't find my wallet.

Troy showed up at six-thirty on the dot. His eyes were red, and he smelled like wine. He had a growth of hair on his face. He did not look so hot. He bent over to kiss me, and I wanted to gag. 'You ready, baby?'

'I'm not going.'

'What?'

'I said I'm not going.'

'Why not?'

'Because I don't like this.'

'You don't like what?'

'How you've done this.'

'What are you talking about?'

'Troy. First of all, I don't feel good about any of this. I hardly know you, and you definitely don't know me, or you would've had the common courtesy to ask me if I indulged in drugs, or minded if you did, before you took me over to some crackhead's house, and then on top of that to call me up in the middle of the night talking all vulgar and then giving your mother the impression that we're almost engaged, and here I am thinking I'm going over to your house for a friendly barbecue and come to find out the whole affair's been staged for me.'

'What's wrong with that?'

'I don't know you well enough to be meeting your mother and son yet.'

'Says who?'

'Says me. This is moving too fast for me, and I can't deal with it.'

'Oh, so what am I supposed to tell my mother and son and the rest of my family that's sitting over at my house right now waiting for *you*?'

'Anything you want to.'

'And I'm just supposed to accept this.'

'You don't have a choice. You should've asked me first.'

'I did ask you.'

'No you didn't. You told me.'

'Look. Do you know how many women would love for me to bring them to my house to meet my mother?'

'I can about guess.'

'I want you to come anyway.'

'I said I don't want to, and I'm not going.'

'You know what? You black bitches are all alike. First you complain that don't nobody want your asses or know how to treat you, and then when a man shows a genuine interest in you, you act simple. And y'all wanna know why we go out with white women.'

I guess this was supposed to hurt my feelings, but it didn't. A white woman could have his sorry ass. 'Are you finished?' I said.

'I guess I am,' he said, and turned toward the door. 'You know something?' he said.

'What's that?'

'You need to be more careful about who you pick up in grocery stores.'

When he closed the door, I stood there fuming. I

ran over to the phone, called Savannah, and told her everything. She wasn't the least bit shocked. 'So I guess you know who's got your wallet?'

'You think he stole my wallet?'

'Bye, Robin,' she said, and hung up.

BWOTM

'OK, sisters,' Etta Mae Jenkins said, 'I've got some good news and some bad news.' She'd just finished calling the meeting to order and read Black Women on the Move's Purpose Statement, as well as the minutes of the last meeting, which took forever to get approved. As usual, Dottie Knox objected to just about everything.

Gloria was sitting at the long table with the nine other board members. Bernadine and Savannah sat near the back of the room. Robin hadn't shown up yet. Altogether, there were twenty-two black women, all dressed in tailored business suits, sitting in the conference room of First Interstate Bank, where Etta Mae was a vice-president.

'I'd like you sisters to welcome a new member to our advisory board, Savannah Jackson. Savannah, stand up, sister.'

Savannah took her purple hat out of her lap, handed it to Bernadine, and stood up. Everybody clapped and said hello.

'She comes all the way to us from Denver and works in PR at Channel 36. We're definitely going to be able to use your talents – right, everybody?'

The women laughed and said yes.

'Welcome, sister,' Etta Mae said, and Savannah sat back down.

Judy Long-Carter passed out the treasurer's report, which didn't mean much to anybody until Etta Mae spoke up. 'You see those figures, don't you?'

Everybody nodded.

'Well, let me say this. The Achievement Awards luncheon was a success on the one hand and a

259

disappointment on the other. As most of you know, we didn't get the kind of turnout this year like we did last year, and I firmly believe it had something to do with the speaker we chose. Now, I know there are sisters in here who'll disagree, but right now that's not the issue.'

'I know one thing,' Bernice Mitchell said. 'Next year, we better hire a different caterer. That was the driest chicken I ever had in my life, the beef was tough, and it took them forever to bring out the coffee.'

'I agree,' Mary Collins said, and turned to look at Princess Childs, who headed the Luncheon Committee.

'Look, they had a reputation,' Princess said. 'They'd done the mayor's luncheon and quite a few other functions around Phoenix, and I hadn't heard of any complaints, so don't blame me. I did my job.'

'May I continue, ladies?' Etta Mae said, and kept talking. 'Prior to the luncheon, we had a little under sixteen thousand dollars in our treasury. As you sisters know, we were unable to get the number of corporate sponsors we had hoped and anticipated. The Corporate Sponsorship Committee, which was composed of Janis, Paulette, Marlene, and Winona, did one hell of a job. They went out there and hustled, but we all know how hard it is trying to get companies to donate anything as far as black folks are concerned. They managed to garner a total of five thousand dollars from their efforts. Now, as you all know, it costs us twenty-six thousand dollars to put this luncheon on. Last year, we raised close to fifty. This year, as you can see from the report, we only made about twenty-eight thousand dollars. That's a shame. So where does that leave us?'

'In the hole,' Dottie said.

'Not exactly in the hole, but it means that in order to continue some of our ongoing projects, particularly the Black Family Survival Project and the scholarship program, there won't be a Sisters' Nite Out this year.'

There were moans and groans throughout the room.

'As you know, the purposes of this meeting were to formulate committees for Sisters' Nite Out, to give you a report on the Achievement luncheon, and to briefly get an update on some of our community service projects. Let me start by saying this. For the last two years, we've allocated twenty-five per cent of the proceeds – or a maximum of six thousand dollars – for the scholarship program. We can't change that now. Do you all agree?'

Everybody at the table nodded.

'Shall we take a vote?'

Everybody at the table nodded again.

'All in favor of continuing to use twenty-five per cent, or a maximum of six thousand dollars, of the proceeds from the Black Women's Achievement Awards luncheon toward the scholarship program, raise your hands.'

All ten board members raised their hands. The advisory board wasn't allowed to vote on issues concerning BWOTM itself.

'Would the secretary be so kind as to note that in the minutes.'

'It's done,' Winona said.

'Now,' Etta Mae said, 'we were supposed to set up committees tonight for Sisters' Nite Out, but now that won't be necessary.'

'Don't we usually make money on Sisters' Nite Out?' Gloria asked.

'Yes, but unfortunately we can't afford to deplete our entire treasury to put it on.'

'How much does it cost?' Gloria asked.

'Last year it cost us about seventeen thousand dollars. The hotel and food alone was close to nine, and then it cost us close to four to pay for the band, their airline tickets, and it cost us thirteen hundred to rent their sound equipment, and then we had to feed them. The rest went for publicity. The problem is that the hotel we've used in the past makes us pay up front – not like the civic center for the luncheon, but that's only because Dolores works there.'

'We don't have any connections at *any* of the hotels

in this town, where we could have it?' Gloria asked.

'Unfortunately, no,' Etta Mae said. 'We were also going to need a bigger banquet room this year, one that would hold four to five hundred people.'

'The band was sure good last year,' Robin said. She had slipped in, and she sat in a chair two rows behind Bernadine and Savannah.

Bernadine bent over and whispered in Savannah's ear. 'She was on the entertainment committee last year. She fucked the lead singer.'

Savannah started laughing and turned around and waved to Robin, who then got up and tiptoed next to her.

'Are there any other comments about Sisters' Nite Out?' Etta Mae asked.

'I hope we'll be in better financial shape next year,' Dottie said. 'That's one thing I always looked forward to around the Christmas holidays. Nothing else is usually going on in this deadbeat town.'

'I can't believe they're not having it this year,' Robin whispered to Savannah.

'Now. What I want to know,' Etta Mae said, 'is what happened at the luncheon? Last year we had over twelve hundred black men and women in that ballroom, at least sixty white folks, and this year, less than six hundred altogether. What happened?'

Everybody at the table looked at one another. Nobody had an answer.

Etta Mae wasn't really expecting one, and she went on: 'The big question is: How can we increase our visibility? What do we have to do to be a more viable entity in our community? There's so much apathy in this town, it's beginning to amaze me more and more each year, and I was born and raised here.'

'We're in a recession,' Dolores said. 'People don't have money to spend on this kind of thing.'

'The tickets were only forty-five dollars,' Dottie said.

'Forty-five dollars can mean a whole lot if you're on welfare or all you're bringing home is a few hundred dollars a week and you've got kids to feed.'

'Very few people in this city fall into that category, and you know it,' Dottie said. 'How many free tickets did you get, Dolores?'

'The same as you, Dottie.'

'I only got four, and I understand you got ten.'

'All right, sisters,' Etta Mae said. 'We've got some unfinished business to attend to. Do we want to get to it or adjourn this meeting?'

'For next year's luncheon, I think we ought to try to get somebody like Oprah Winfrey or Maya Angelou,' Dolores said.

'Do you know how much they'd probably charge?' Dottie said.

'Well, it's for a good cause.'

'Why don't we do this,' Etta Mae said. 'I'd like the board members to come up with the names of two speakers they'd like to see at next year's award luncheon, mail them to me, and we'll talk about it at the next meeting.'

'I think we need to push for more sponsorship from companies we've done business with in the past,' Roberta Mason said.

'I think we should target more businesses and employers to purchase exhibit booths for their re-cruitment and vary the price,' Dolores said. 'Jewelry and artwork is one thing, but—'

'What are we going to offer them in return?' Dottie asked.

'Free advertisement in our newsletter,' Dolores said.

'That makes sense,' Roberta said. 'I sent out thank you letters last year to all of them, and this year some of them wouldn't even return my phone calls.'

'Well, apparently they're cutting back,' Dottie said.

'What I'd like to suggest is this,' Gloria said. 'I suggest we do a much better public relations campaign next year, and a lot earlier than we did this year.'

'Getting free advertisement is hard,' Princess said. 'You don't know what I went through trying to get ads

263

in the newspapers and on the radio, and forget about TV.'

'I suggest next year we aim for church bulletins and other organizations, ASU and such,' Dolores said.

'That sounds good,' somebody said.

'We could offer to pay for advertising,' Dottie said, and everybody gave her a funny look.

'Ads aren't cheap,' Dolores said.

'Well, I will say this,' Etta Mae interjected. 'Weren't the workshops well attended?'

Everybody nodded.

'Of the sixteen workshops we had, there were six that had the largest attendance: Cleaning Up Bad Credit, Crack/Cocaine Comes Home, Maturing Gracefully, Single Parenting, Stress and Depression in the Black Female, and Business Alternatives.'

'I think a whole lot of folks just paid for the workshops and not the luncheon,' Dottie said. 'That's why most of them came, and that's why we didn't make any money on the luncheon.'

'Well, we've found a need, and we have to make sure that we keep filling that need,' Etta Mae said, and looked at her watch.

'I think we ought to target a lot more black professionals,' Gloria said. 'They should be more visible and willing to share their experiences and expertise. It doesn't cost them anything except a little of their time.'

'I agree,' Dottie said. 'Some of them live up there in Scottsdale without a care in the world, except for their BMWs, their landscaping, and their annual trip to Hawaii.'

Bernadine looked at Savannah.

'So far our efforts for improving the quality of life have been directed primarily at the young, but senior citizens also need our attention,' Etta Mae continued.

'This crack business is getting a little out of hand, not to mention the gangs in our children's schools,' Gloria said.

'Well, we can't do it all, but we can do our part,' Etta Mae said.

'I think we ought to work on increasing our membership and not continue to keep it closed to board and advisory members,' Roberta said.

'It'd get out of hand. We tried that in the beginning, before you got here, Roberta, and it didn't work,' Etta Mae said. 'Only a handful of sisters showed up on a regular basis. Everybody's busy, got jobs and families, so we decided to keep a board of ten and maintain an advisory board for special projects. I think that's working out, don't you?' she asked the group at the table.

Just about everybody looked as if they agreed.

'It would work a whole lot better if some folks on certain committees did what they were supposed to do when they were supposed to do it, instead of waiting till the last minute to give us their reports, and then they still haven't done what they were supposed to do,' Dottie said.

'I think we need to enlist more volunteers. We need to go to the Urban League, the NAACP, the Chamber of Commerce, and such,' Gloria said.

'I agree,' Etta Mae said. 'Now, does anyone have anything they'd like to report?'

No-one said anything.

'How are the plans for the senior citizens to help out at the Little League games going, Marilyn?'

'Fine. They need forty volunteers, and I've got twenty-six seniors lined up. I'm working on the rest.'

'What about Healthy Mothers, Healthy Babies?'

'Everything's on schedule,' Roberta said. 'I do what I say I'm going to do.'

'And the T-Shirts for Juneteenth? How are they coming?' Etta Mae asked Dottie.

'They'll be ready in three weeks. The posters too.'

'Everybody knows their responsibility for bringing a dish to sell,' Etta Mae said. 'We don't care if it's pie or peanut butter. Just bring something. And by the way, Mount Calvary Baptist has advised me that they *do* want us to help them out over Thanksgiving and Christmas in feeding the homeless, so we're going to need volunteers for that. Not tonight, but keep that in the back of your minds. Some of you are planning vacations, I know, but those of you who'll be here, think about it. Now, do we want to talk about our long-term goals tonight?'

No-one said anything.

'Let me just run over it real quick and give you sisters something to think about until our next meeting, which, by the way, will be on Thursday, May seventeenth. Put it on your calendars. Long-term goals means just what it implies. We want to implement them over a one-to-five-year period. The whole question of what we can do to continue to exist, as well as being able to start changing the conditions of black people here in Phoenix, is our primary objective. We want to continue to brainstorm in doing things that are of concern to and will benefit black women. Without us, there'll be no future for our children, and without our children, there'll be no future families. Now, we've talked about forming a job bank, which would serve as liaison between businesses and the black community. We'd like to establish a permanent senior citizens program, our own Big Brother/Big Sister Program, a day care center, and a mentoring program for inner-city kids. In addition, we'd like to think about starting national chapters of BWOTM. We've got a positive force here, and it wouldn't hurt to spread it around.'

Everybody mumbled something in agreement.

'Well, if there's no other business, at the next meeting I'd like progress reports from those of you who head the special projects committees I just mentioned. I know it's still early, but I need to know what's going on. Any further business?'

Nobody said anything.

'Then this meeting is adjourned.'

Everybody stood up, and quite a few of the women

266

gathered to make small talk. Robin spotted somebody she knew and ran over to say something to
her. Bernadine and Savannah walked outside in the
hallway to smoke a cigarette.

'So how you feeling?' Savannah asked, as she pushed
her hat further down on her head.

'A helluva lot better, and do me a favor, don't
mention this to Gloria or Robin, because I haven't
told them about it.'

'I won't.'

'I will never in my life take any of that shit again, I
don't care how depressed I get. That's all I can say.'

Robin came prancing out. 'Bernadine, Gloria wants
to know if you'll come in for a minute. She said she
wants to introduce you to somebody.'

Bernadine took a few more puffs of her cigarette and
went back inside the room.

'I hope you didn't mention anything about my wallet
and that stuff about Troy to Bernadine, did you?'

'No.'

'Gloria?'

'Nope.'

'Good.' Robin sighed. 'Some things I don't like to
tell them.'

'So,' Savannah said, 'have you heard any more from
Troy?'

'No,' she said. 'But guess what?'

'What?'

'I found my wallet.'

'You did?'

'Yep. I ran over it. It was under my back tire. In my
carport.'

'Was everything in it?'

'Everything except the money. I only had about
forty dollars in it. So it wasn't that much of a loss.
Everything else was there, though.'

'And you think you dropped it out there?'

'I can't remember. I swear I can't,' she said. 'You sure
wear some tough hats, girl. I'd feel stupid in one.'

Just then Gloria and Bernadine came out. 'Hi, Robin. Hi, Savannah,' Gloria said. 'Sorry about Sisters' Nite Out. I didn't know we were going to have to cancel it.'

'It's OK,' Savannah said. 'Shit, we can have our own. Right?' she said to her friends.

'What the hell,' Robin said.

'Why not?' Bernadine said.

'I'm up for it,' Gloria said. 'But right now I'm hungry. I haven't eaten a thing all day. You all can stand out here all night if you want to, but I'm going home.'

'We're right in back of you,' Robin said, and waddled behind her like a duck. Savannah slapped her on the back, pushing her forward. Bernadine was just glad that it all made sense.

Why Are You Here?

I was too anxious. And so nervous I forgot all about the appointment to get the oil changed in my car. I've smoked eighteen cigarettes today. That's almost a whole pack. I've never smoked so many in a day before, and the day's not over yet. If I remember correctly, Kenneth was always punctual. He got in early yesterday morning, but had to go straight to his seminars, which went on all day, into the evening and then he had a slew of them today, too. He's supposed to be here at eight o'clock. It's now seven-thirty, and I still don't know what to wear. I don't want to look too suggestive, by wearing something tight, but then again, I don't want to look like I just got home from work, either. Bluejeans would be tacky, and a dress might be too corny. Shit. I don't know. I called Robin. Why, I'll never know. 'I can't think straight,' I said, 'and this is ridiculous. You'd think I was on my way to my senior prom instead of dinner.'

'Wear something sexy, girl. Let him see what he's been missing all these years.'

'Like what?'

'Wear that orange dress. You look good in that.'

'Maybe I should, huh?'

'And make sure you smell good.'

'Thanks, girl. I'll talk to you later.'

'Get some for me!' she yelled, and hung up before I had a chance to tell her I wasn't planning on doing anything. But just in case, I sprayed some FDS down there anyway, then tried on the orange dress. It worked. I ran into the bathroom again, poured some Plax into my mouth, and swished it around for about a minute. Since I was wearing orange now, I wiped off the fuchsia lipstick and blush and changed it to tangerine. I was searching in the closet for my shoes, when I heard the doorbell. My heart started pounding so hard I could hear it. Now I was hyperventilating. I had to pant, blowing air rings out of my mouth just to get my bearings. By the time I reached for the doorknob, I was poised.

Some things don't change, I thought, as I opened the door and saw Kenneth standing there. He still looked like a black prince. Why and how I let this go, I'll never know.

'Well, are you gonna let me in?' he said.

I started laughing, but he kept a solemn look on his face.

'Why don't you just stand there for a while,' I said, and gave him the once-over. He was wearing a navy-blue suit with a pale-gray shirt and pink tie. He's six two and still looks about two hundred pounds. His hair – even his mustache – had a few strands of gray in it. His skin, which always reminded me of dark chocolate, was still smooth, his nose wide; his lips were full. 'You haven't changed a bit,' I said.

'Well, you have,' he said. 'You look better than I remember. The years've definitely agreed with you, Savannah.'

He gave me a solid hug and then a peck on the lips. I was glad he didn't take my tongue for granted. 'Come on in. Have a seat,' I said.

'I see you haven't lost your sense of style,' he said, looking around the room. 'What are you, a collector now?'

'Sort of,' I said, as he walked around examining my artworks.

'You've got some beautiful pieces in here,' he said. Then he snickered. 'I remember when you couldn't pay your rent.'

'You don't have to remind me,' I said. I wanted to tell him that I'm *still* struggling with the rent. Only now I'm paying it in three different places: here,

270

Mama's, and that stupid condo. But what was the point?

'Wow. Who did this?' he said, looking closer at a signature on an abstract.

'John Rozelle. He's a black painter from Saint Louis. This piece really isn't representative of the kind of work he's known for. He does a lot of mixed-media stuff too, but this is one of my favorites. And one I could afford.'

'You say he's a brother?'

'Yep.'

'I'm glad to hear that. What about these over here? These are incredible.'

'That's a Charles Alston, and that one's by Joe Overstreet. It's called a serigraph. This pastel is by Brenda Singletary. That big collage over there was done by Noah Purifoy. This one here,' I said, walking over and pointing, 'is called a gouache – Joseph Holston did it. The one with the brass masks and kinte cloth is a Frank Frazier, and that abstract is by Lamerol Gatewood.'

'You're helping to alleviate the starving artist syndrome then, huh?'

'I'm trying,' I said. 'If we don't buy their work, who will?' I was glad to be talking about art, something besides me. But I knew it was coming.

'So you're living in Phoenix,' he said, and sat down on the couch. He looked so good sitting there, I had to keep my distance. 'Are you working out these days or what?'

I looked down at myself. 'I just started,' I said.

'You still smoking?'

'Unfortunately, yes, but I'm definitely quitting before 1991 rolls around.'

'Didn't you say that back in '86?'

'Shut up, Kenneth.'

'Do you plan on standing over there until we leave? I don't bite, Savannah. Have a seat.'

I sat down in a chair across from the couch. 'So how do you like the Phoenician?'

'It's pretty as hell from the outside, but the room itself is nothing to scream about. You've been in one nice hotel, you've been in them all.'

'So tell me, Kenneth. What've you been doing with *yourself*?'

He crossed his legs, then clasped his hands together over his knee and leaned forward. 'Well, let's see. I started my own practice.'

'Really? You're not at that hospital any more?'

'Nope. As a matter of fact, I've got a staff of ten.'

'That's great.'

'And I've got a three-year-old daughter.'

'I heard.'

'Who told you?'

'Remember Belinda and Roger?'

'Yep.'

'Belinda told me when I was home last summer. You happen to have a picture of her?'

'I'm sure I do,' he said, and reached inside his jacket for his wallet. He handed me the picture. The little girl wasn't all that cute, but I lied and said she was adorable.

'So what's married life like?'

'It has its ups and downs.'

'Are you happy? Wait. I forgot. I shouldn't ask you that question, right?'

'Let me put it this way. I couldn't ask for a better mother for my daughter.'

'I didn't ask you that, Kenneth.'

He looked up toward the ceiling, like he was deep in thought or something. 'I guess you could say I love her. But it's not that deep *passionate* kind of love. I suppose it's the kind that grows on you.'

'Why'd you marry her if you weren't in love with her?'

'Because she was having my child.'

'You mean you fell for that?'

'I didn't *fall* for anything, Savannah.'

Maybe I said the wrong thing.

'I'd been dating her off and on for about six months.'
I cut him off. 'Like you did with me.'

'No, you're mistaken. You were the one who was going out with quite a few other men at the same time you were going out with me. If I remember correctly.'

'I was not!'

'You were, Savannah.'

'How can you say that, Kenneth?'

'Because the only time we went out was when I called and asked you out.'

'So?'

'So I assumed you were seeing other men.'

'But I wasn't.'

'Then why didn't you ever call and ask me to go somewhere?'

'Because you only seemed to call when it was convenient for you, when it seemed like you could fit me into your schedule.'

'That's not true, Savannah.'

'That's what it seemed like to me.'

'What you're saying is that we both assumed wrong.'

'Maybe. But, Kenneth, let's face it. You weren't exactly the most communicative man in the world. I never knew how you felt about me.'

'Well, I didn't know how you felt about me, either.'

'That's my point. I couldn't keep going out with you and playing a guessing game, and I wasn't about to come right out and ask you, either.'

'Why not?'

'Because I would've felt like a fool. I've never had to *ask* a man how he feels about me. It's usually obvious.'

'Didn't I treat you with respect and admiration?'

'Admiration? I didn't want to be admired, Kenneth. I wanted you to love me. Let me shut up. You just got here. It's been a long time. Forget I just said that. Are you hungry?'

'No,' he said, grinning at me. 'Not now.'

'Don't look at me like that.'

'I'm not looking at you like *that*. Tell me something, since we're clearing the air here. How *did* you feel about me?'

I didn't want to answer that. 'I can't remember.'

'Bullshit.'

'I'll put it this way: I was quite smitten by you.'

'Smitten?'

'What do you expect me to say? That I was madly in love with you?'

'That would be nice to hear.'

'What difference does it make now, Kenneth? We're talking about two thousand years ago. You're sitting in my apartment in Phoenix, Arizona, in 1990, married as you want to be, with a kid, no less, and you want me to sit here and confess?'

'I was in love with you,' he said.

I like to died when I heard him say that. But he was just fucking with me, and I knew it. He was saying this so I'd give him some. He probably had this whole thing planned out. But it wasn't going to work. 'No you weren't,' I said.

'I was too.'

'Then why didn't you act like it?'

'I just told you. I didn't want to make a fool out of myself, either. I thought you were playing it cool, since you were this sexy, pretty young thing running around Boston. I knew you had hundreds of men you could choose from, so I called myself playing it safe.'

'Well, you did a pretty good job of it. And for your information, I have never *dated* more than one man at a time. It's not my style. If I'm sleeping with you, I'm not going to be sleeping with anybody else. I'm a one-man-at-a-time kind of woman. And plus, if we're doing it *right*, I won't want to sleep with anybody else.'

'So *were* we doing it right?'

'Why do you think I used to get so mad at you?' I said, and started laughing. 'I'd be waiting for your black ass to call me, and finally, when you did, you'd talk about some damn article in *Newsweek* and then tell me to have a nice day. Like it was business. I wanted to kill you sometimes, I swear. Can I kill you now, for all the anxiety and heartache you caused me?'

'Come over here and do it now,' he said, and he was actually cackling. I started cracking up too. He got serious all of a sudden. Which I didn't want him to do. I don't think. 'I'm really glad to hear this, Savannah. It's a shame it took so long for me to find out how you felt.'

'It's OK. You live and learn,' I said.

We sat there like fools for about a minute. 'Why'd you want to see me?' I asked.

'Because I haven't seen you in years, that's why. I wanted to see how you were doing. And I can see you're doing just fine.'

'So leave now. Bye,' I said.

He snickered again. 'Aren't you hungry?'

'No,' I said, and I wasn't. Just like the good old days, he could still spoil my damn appetite. At least for food.

'So what else can we do?'

'I'll tell you what we're not going to do.'

'Am I acting like I'm trying to seduce you?' he asked, and leaned back on the couch. 'That's why you're so wired, huh? You thought I was coming over here to try to get some for old time's sake, didn't you?'

'Yeah.'

'And all you're thinking about is the fact that I'm married now, and you have no intention of sleeping with a married man, right?'

'Right.'

'Well, you can relax, Savannah,' he said. 'I just wanted to see you.'

He didn't even want to sleep with me? He's still the same, I thought. Wishy-washy. 'Well, you want to go somewhere and have a drink?' I said.

'I don't care,' he said. 'We can stay here, unless you just want to go out. I'm serious, Savannah. I'm really glad to see you.'

I wish he'd stop saying that. 'There's nothing to do here,' I said.

'We can talk,' he said, and gave me what I thought was a seductive smile. I wish he would stop doing that shit.

'I think I'd feel more comfortable talking to you in a public place,' I said. 'Come on, Kenneth, get up.'

He got up and stood directly in front of me, close enough that I could smell his breath. It smelled good, so good that I backed away from him.

'You feel like driving up to Sedona with me in the morning?'

'Now, that I can handle.'

'Then why don't we do this. I'm whipped. I caught that red-eye out here, I've only had four hours of sleep since Thursday, so I think I'll go on back to the hotel, take a hot shower, and fall out. I'll pick you up about seven.'

'In the morning?'

'Yeah. Is that OK?'

'Why so early?'

'So we can have all day,' he said, and kissed me on my nose.

I wish he wouldn't do that shit, either. 'OK,' I said. 'But just don't get any ideas.'

'I'm full of ideas,' he said, and headed out the front door.

I thought I was going to pass out. Right there on the floor. And of course I was starving now, so I went into the kitchen and called Pizza Hut, ordered a medium vegetarian pizza, made myself a salad, and when the pizza arrived thirty minutes later, I ate the whole thing.

I was taking off my dress when the phone rang.

'Savannah?' Kenneth said in a low voice. I wish he'd stop saying my name like that. 'Are you asleep?'

'No. It's only ten o'clock. I usually don't go to bed until after the news. What's up?'

'I just wanted you to know that I really didn't want to leave,' he said.

I swallowed hard. 'Well, to tell the truth, Kenneth, I didn't want you to, either.'

'You didn't?'

'Nope.'

'Is it too late to come back over?'

'No, it's not too late,' I said. 'I just hope I don't hate myself in the morning.'

'I guarantee you won't,' he said. 'I'll see you in five minutes.'

'Five minutes?'

'I've been sitting down the street in the parking lot of this Circle K store for the last hour and a half, thinking about what we talked about and trying to get my nerve up to call you back.'

'Kenneth,' I sighed.

'Savannah,' he said. I just loved the way he said it.

I'm in deep trouble. I knew I shouldn't have let this man touch me. I'm worse off now than I was four years ago. All it takes sometimes is a touch. A kiss. And I'm right back there again. I wish he wasn't so tender, I wish he didn't make me feel like the Little Mermaid or like I weighed fifteen pounds, and Lord knows I wish he would open up a nationwide school: How to Eat Pussy, so the rest of these men out here can take a crash course. The way I feel right now has nothing to do with the fact that I haven't slept with a man in months. It's *this* man. Any man wouldn't do. When Kenneth first put his arms around me, that alone turned me into mush. He didn't even have to put it in (but I'm glad he did), and now here he is lying in my bed with his arms wrapped around me, and I don't want to move one iota because it feels like heaven. Which is exactly where he took me last night. But I can't go back, because we can't stay there. He's going home to his wife.

'Good morning,' he says.

277

'Good morning,' I say back.

'You're not getting up, are you?'

'It's seven-thirty. I thought you wanted to be on the road about now.'

'I did,' he said, and sat up. I inched closer to the edge of the bed, because if he puts his hands on me one more time, I'll probably give him anything he wants. Why did I have to be so damn fast? Why did I allow myself to fall for the okeydoke and do this shit? I hope I didn't tell him I loved him, but after three or four orgasms, I'm liable to say anything. I swear, I don't remember. Fool.

'You still want to go?' he said.

'To be honest with you, Kenneth, I'm not sure it's such a good idea,' I said, and jumped out of the bed.

'What's wrong?'

'Nothing,' I said. 'Nothing.'

'Did I do something? Say something?'

'No.'

'Talk to me, Savannah.'

'We shouldn't've done this, Kenneth. I mean, it's one thing when you just hop on top of somebody and bang 'em and then get up and go home. But it's quite another thing when you used to love somebody and then they hold and caress you the way you did me. I feel weird. Because I know I shouldn't have done this.'

'What are you trying to say?'

'What I'm trying to say is that sometimes old feelings get rekindled when you do certain things, and sleeping with you is one of them.'

'I'm flattered,' he said.

'I bet you are.'

'What? You think you're the only one who has feelings?'

'I didn't say that. But what was the point of this?'

'The point is that I wanted to see you and I didn't *plan* a seduction. I didn't *plan* to make love to you, or to try to talk you into anything. I swear it.'

'I'm not accusing you of doing that, but you're missing the point. I'm too old for this, Kenneth.'

'Too old for what?'

'To be sleeping with an ex-lover who happens to be very married.'

'I'm working on changing that,' he said.

'That's what you all say.'

'I'm not "all,"' he said. 'My name is Kenneth.'

'So what are your plans?'

'I'm thinking about divorcing her.'

'Thinking about it.'

'Yeah.'

'Why?'

'Because. I'm not happy.'

'What about your kid?'

'I don't know yet. That's the only part of this whole thing that bothers me. What's going to happen to my daughter.'

'I don't want to go to Sedona,' I blurted out.

'Why not?'

'I just told you.'

'We don't have to *do* anything, Savannah.'

'We've already *done* it, Kenneth.'

'I want you to keep me company. I've been looking forward to this for weeks. There's a whole lot more I want to tell you. A lot of things I want to ask you.'

'Tell me now. Ask me now. Go ahead.'

'Look. Didn't you say the drive was pretty?'

'That's what I've heard. But I'm serious, Kenneth. I can't. I'd be doing myself another injustice.'

'I don't want to go if you won't go with me,' he said.

'I can't. I swear, I can't.'

'Can I just spend the day with you? I promise I won't try to lay a finger on you.'

'No,' I said, trying my damnedest to sound like I meant it. 'I think you should get up and take a shower and get in your rental car and drive on up to Sedona

279

just like you planned, and tomorrow go home to your wife.'

'Why do you think I'm here?' he said.

'I don't know. Why?'

'Because I don't want to go home.'

'But you're going home,' I said.

He didn't say anything to that. I put my robe on and went into the kitchen to make some coffee. I made it strong. After he got out of the shower and put his clothes on, I poured him a cup of coffee. But he didn't want it. I walked him to the door.

'So tell me something, Savannah.'

'What's that, Kenneth?'

'What happened last night?'

'Entirely too much,' I said. 'Now go.'

I closed the door on him, but I could tell he was still standing there, because I didn't hear him walk away. I wished he wouldn't do that. When I finally heard his footsteps, I was relieved, in a way. But I have to admit I sat by that door for the longest time, waiting to hear them come back.

Rebounding

Troy had left a message on my machine. 'Robin,' he said. 'I've cleaned up my act, and I'd like to see you. For real. Call me.'

'Get a life,' I said.

Michael left one too. 'Hi, Robin. Where've you been hiding? Don't you return phone calls? I'd love to get together with you this weekend. I miss you. Please call me.'

'Have you learned how to do the nasty yet, Michael? Are you still boring? Are you still fat?'

The last one shocked me, because it was Russell. I'd called him a few times but hadn't heard back from him since *that* night. 'Robin, please, do me and yourself a favor. Would you *please* stop calling me at home. It's causing a whole lot of problems, and my wife doesn't like the idea of my ex calling the house. Sorry to have to break it to you like this. Hope you're well.'

My ears hurt. There was this screeching sound inside of 'em, and I think my heart stopped beating for the next few minutes, and then it started hurting, like somebody stuck their hand inside my chest and started pulling on it. My whole body was throbbing, and I could feel every single vein and muscle getting thicker and thicker until it seemed like I could actually see them pulsating through my skin. Did he just say his *wife*? I replayed his message over and over and cried harder each time. When I got tired of listening to it, I erased all three messages and sat on the couch for what felt like hours, because I couldn't move. My heart had stopped hurting, to the point where it didn't feel like I had one. My whole body was numb. Finally, I saw my hand reach for the pile of mail. There were at least six catalogs. I wish they'd stop sending me these damn things. Married?

This was some rotten shit to pull, Russell. Low. And what did you tell me last time? That you still loved me, that you knew you'd made a mistake and you'd try to remedy the situation. You said, 'Just hold on a minute,' isn't that what you said? You motherfucker. And here I was with your sorry ass for two whole years and you were supposed to be so in love with me and had me believing that shit for the longest. What's Carolyn got that I haven't got? What's she giving you that I didn't give you? How can you be so nonchalant about this whole thing? Call my house and leave a goddamn message on my machine, telling me some shit like this. That your wife doesn't like me calling your house? I don't believe this. I've been a fool too long. But you've taught me a good lesson, Russell. You've taught me in the worst way.

I know I shouldn't give a damn, but I can't help it. Just because you break up with somebody doesn't mean you stop loving them. Looks like it wasn't too hard for you to get over me, though, was it? This is some cold cruel shit to pull on somebody you split up with less than a year ago. And to think I let you live here rent-free for a year. Let you run up my Visa bill, got you some decent insurance, and cosigned for your goddamn car. You still owe me three hundred and eighty-six dollars, you son of a bitch. I wonder if she's having your baby, like everybody said? I could've had *two* of your babies, you simple motherfucker, but you told me you weren't ready to be a father yet. That you needed to get your act together, get your finances in order before you started thinking about getting married, let alone being a father. What has she done for you that I didn't do? Why couldn't you just tell me what I was doing wrong, and I could've fixed it. What was wrong with me, Russell? Huh? What?

I pushed the catalogs to the side and tried to open an envelope. When I realized it was just a bill from Spiegel, I slung it to the side and got up. Music. That's what I needed. I turned on the radio, and Lisa Stansfield was singing, 'been around the world, and I can't find my baby,' which I did not need to hear right now, so I pressed the Play button on the cassette. I didn't know what was in it and didn't care. Prince was singing 'Thieves in the Temple.' Hell no. Not tonight. So I ejected him and put on Paula Abdul.

I was on my way into the bedroom to take off my work clothes, when the phone rang. I answered it. 'Hello,' I said.

'Hello,' some kind of computerized voice said. 'We're conducting a survey— ' I hung up.

It rang again.

'Yes,' I said, thinking it was the computer again, but it wasn't. It was my favorite person, the bitch from the student loan collection agency. 'Hi, Carol,' I said.

'Robin. We haven't received your payment this month.'

'I know that.'

'Why not, Robin?'

'Because I don't have it, that's why.'

'When will you have it, Robin?'

'Next month.'

'What day?'

'I don't know what day. But I said next month.'

'I need a date.'

'Then you pick one.'

'Robin.' She sighed.

'What?'

'Do you know how long we've been going through this, Robin?'

'You tell me.'

'Aren't you tired of these phone calls?'

'No; I love it when you call me and ask me for money I don't have. Really.'

283

'Why don't you just take care of the balance, and you won't ever have to hear from me again.'

'Didn't you hear what I just said? I said I don't have it.'

'Robin, you drive a 1988 5.0, but you can't afford to pay off an eleven-hundred-dollar loan that you knew you were responsible for?'

'What kind of car I drive is none of your business.'

'Oh, yes, it is my business. It's very much my business. You need to get your priorities straight, Robin.'

'Look, my daddy's got Alzheimer's, and I'm trying to help pay for a nurse for him, which is much more important than this stupid student loan.'

'I'm sorry to hear about your father, Robin, but who'll it be next? Your mother? What fatal disease will you give her?'

'You better watch your fucking mouth.'

'No, you better watch your mouth. You've got a Visa card; can't you get a cash advance and just settle this thing?'

'You must be hard of hearing, Carol.'

'Look, I'm tired of this, Robin. My client is tired of this. Either give me a date or I'll have to refer this to our legal department.'

'How about the fifteenth?'

'You have a nice evening, Robin.'

I bammed the phone down. 'Bitch!'

By the time I got my clothes off and hung them up, I didn't know what to do next. I felt antsy and bored and just pitiful. Why did he have to call and tell me this shit? Married? What's wrong with me? Wasn't I pretty enough? Wasn't I sensitive enough, smart enough? Didn't I fuck you good enough? What was wrong with me? Why didn't you want to marry me, Russell? Why?

I put on a pair of old leggings and a big T-shirt and went back out into the living room and turned off Paula and flicked on the TV. Good: *Cheers* was on. I watched it. And watched something else, but I couldn't tell you what it was if you asked me. I went into the kitchen, poured myself a glass of wine, and drank it down fast. Then I went into the bathroom and looked at myself in the mirror. My face was swollen, my eyes were glassy, and I felt my lips trembling. Every cell in my body hurt, and even though I didn't want to and was trying not to, I started crying. What are you supposed to do when you feel like this? What can you do to pretend it doesn't matter? What can you tell your heart to make it stop hurting? What?

I sat down on the toilet for the longest. All my energy was gone. I felt light-headed. Like I wasn't even in this room. In the next second I felt drained, so heavy that I couldn't get up. This isn't right, I thought. That he can pick up the phone and drop this kind of shit on me. Did he expect me to take it like a champ? Did he expect me to not be affected by his little announcement? Married. And then I started laughing. Because there was nothing left to do but laugh.

Finally, I got up. I went back into the kitchen and poured myself another glass of wine. I opened one of the catalogs, and the next thing I knew, I had dialed the toll-free number for Victoria's Secret. When they answered, I realized I didn't know what I wanted to order. So I hung up. Michael. I should call Michael.

I dialed his number. When a woman answered, I knew I had a wrong number, so I hung up and dialed again. She answered again. 'Is this Michael Davenport's house?' I asked.

'Yes, it is. Who's calling?'

'Robin.'

'Robin who?'

'Robin Stokes.'

'Well, Michael's not in right now, but I'll let him know you called as soon as he gets in.'

'Do you have any idea when that'll be?'

'About ten.'

'Thank you.'

'Bye.'

I hung up. I didn't know what to think. I *know* Michael doesn't have a woman living with him. She's probably a relative. Because she was cordial. Maybe she's his sister or something. Who knows? Who gives a shit?

Savannah couldn't believe what Russell had done and the way he'd done it. Bernadine said he was a lowlife anyway, and now maybe I could finally get him out of my system. Gloria said nothing he did surprised her. They wanted to take me out to dinner to cheer me up, but I didn't feel like talking about it. I was too busy trying not to think about it.

I haven't heard from Michael. It's been two days since I returned his phone call. That woman probably wasn't a relative. I don't think she gave him the message. I haven't been seeing him at work, since he's out in the field, so I decided to try him at home again. This time he answered the phone. 'Michael?'

'Robin, how are you? I thought you dropped off the face of the earth.'

'Did you get my message the other night?'

'No, I didn't, as a matter of fact.'

'Who's that woman answering your phone?'

'Oh, that's Gina. She's an old friend who sort of needed a place to stay for a while. She's in between places, and it's a long story, but I'm trying to help her get back on her feet.'

'So she's living there with you?'

'Temporarily. She's a friend, Robin.'

'Where's she sleeping?'

'Robin? I'm surprised at you. If I wasn't hearing right, I'd swear you were jealous.'

'I'm not jealous. Jealous of what? I don't have any reason to be jealous of anybody.'

'I know.'

'How long will she be staying with you?'

286

'Probably through the end of the month.'

'A month!'

He was actually chuckling. 'Robin, take it easy. You're making me feel great, you know.'

'I'm not trying to make you feel great. I thought you wanted to see me.'

'I do.'

'With a woman staying in your house?'

'She's sleeping in the guest room, if that's any consolation.'

'Women creep at night just like men,' I said.

'Robin, look. Let me take you to dinner on Friday, and I'll explain the whole scenario to you.'

'What time?'

'Is seven good for you?'

'Seven is fine.'

'I'll pick you up then at seven,' he said. I could still hear how amused he was.

I don't know why I agreed to have dinner with him, when I really didn't feel like it. Maybe because it was just something to do. Something to break up the monotony. Something to stop me from thinking about Russell's bullshit.

On Friday at seven o'clock I was flipping through my latest Spiegel catalog, waiting for Michael. At seven-thirty I had turned back the corners of at least eight pages of these sexy bras and panties and a sheer silk chiffon nightshirt I pictured myself in. By seven forty-five I picked up the phone and ordered everything from those turned-back pages. I put it on my company's American Express, knowing good and well I couldn't afford any of this stuff. By eight o'clock, I was pissed. Are his fingers broken or something? Couldn't he have called and said he'd be late?

I picked up the phone and dialed his number. That woman answered the phone again. 'Hello, this is Robin. Is Michael there?'

'Yes, he is,' she said. I couldn't believe it.

Michael came to the phone.

287

'Well?' I said.

'Well, what?' he said.

'It's eight o'clock.'

'I know that, Robin. What's wrong? You sound mad.'

'Michael, you were supposed to be here at seven.'

'Damn it! I knew there was something I was forgetting! I'm sorry, Robin. I'm so sorry. Things've been so hectic in my department, it completely slipped my mind. Can I get a rain check?'

'A rain check? You mean you can't make it?'

'I'm eating dinner.'

'With what's-her-name?'

'Her name is Gina.'

'Whatever,' I said.

'Look, Robin. She cooked this meal for me, and it wouldn't be very considerate of me to leave in the middle of it. You can understand that, can't you?'

'Yeah, I understand. But what am I supposed to do while you sit there eating dinner with your *friend*?'

'I said I'd make it up to you. What more do you want me to say?'

'Forget it, Michael.'

'What about sometime late next week?' he asked.

'*Late* next week?'

'I have to go to L.A. for two days on Monday, and when I get back I've got a ton of client meetings. I won't be free until Thursday.'

'Then what day's good for you?'

'How about Friday?'

'Enjoy your meal,' I said. 'I'll see you on Friday.'

After I hung up, I couldn't believe I was actually jealous of this woman. Color me desperate, because nobody was more surprised than I was by my attitude. But next week is next week. What about tonight? I needed somebody tonight.

Troy answered the phone before it registered in my brain that I was even thinking about calling him.

'Robin,' he said. 'It's good to hear from you. I've been thinking about you for weeks. What's happening?'

'What are you doing?' I asked.

'Watching the baseball game. Kicking back. Why, what'd you have in mind?'

'You wanna watch it over here?'

'I'm on my way.'

Killing Time

Bernadine couldn't stand being in this big house by herself. She thought she'd be grateful for the peace and quiet, but when she came home from work, the house felt like a mausoleum. Worse than empty. A house was meant for kids, she thought, and so was she. She couldn't figure out what to do with herself now that they were with John. The weekends had been easy to handle, but it was summer vacation, and they'd been gone for four whole weeks. She couldn't remember the last time she spent so much time by herself, the last time she *had* time to herself. She was trying to remember what she used to do with herself before she got married and had kids. Her mind kept drawing a blank.

And Herbert. What a pain in the ass he turned out to be. She would've been better off if she never fucked him. He'd gotten on her nerves, calling her two and three times a day, wondering where she was when she wasn't with him. She reminded him that he had a wife he should be worrying about, and not her. All he'd done was confirm what Bernadine didn't know was true any more: that she was still desirable, that she still had the power to pull, and that she could still make a man cry out in bed. It took two weeks for Herbert to profess his love for her. Bernadine was more amused than anything. She was actually grinning while her legs and arms were wrapped around him and she was staring out the window at a cardinal perched on the windowsill. He'd done some of everything for her, but she refused to suck his dick. 'Let your wife do that. Or whoever,' she'd said. And Herbert didn't press her.

'But I love you,' he'd said again last week, after Bernadine finally told him they should chill out for a

while. 'You don't love *me*, Herbert; you love the chase.'
Of course he denied this and tried his damnedest to
convince her that he was bored with his wife, that as
soon as his son graduated from high school – which
would be in two years – he would leave her. 'Look,
Herbert,' she said, 'this has been a lot of fun, but I
don't love you. And even if I did, I wouldn't marry
you.' But Herbert didn't believe her. Bernadine thought
he'd made the mistake women were often guilty of:
confusing orgasms with love. 'Why not?' he wanted to
know. 'For two reasons,' she said. 'First of all, Herbert,
you cheat on your wife, which means you'd probably
cheat on me too.' Of course Herbert said that wouldn't
be the case. He loved her and did not love his wife any
more. 'And second of all,' she went on, 'I don't want to
marry anybody. Period.' Herbert didn't believe her.

As far as Bernadine was concerned, they'd had a
good time, so what was he complaining about? The
only thing she wanted from him was between his
legs. She assumed that Herbert must've thought he
was giving her more than that. He was probably hoping
she'd fall madly in love with him and go crazy. But
she hadn't. Herbert didn't have a clue that on those
dry nights when Bernadine needed to get her parts
oiled, she simply knew who to call. She used him.
But so what? That's what they'd been doing to women
for years, she thought. Taking advantage of us.

But Herbert was the kind of man who wouldn't
take no for an answer. He knew the kids were gone.
And he kept calling. Bernadine didn't want to be
bothered, and wanted to make it clear she wasn't
going to break down in a moment of weakness, so
she left the answering machine on to screen her calls
and refused to take his calls at work.

She was sitting on the couch, reading *Essence* magazine. It took thirty-five minutes to finish it. Bernadine
was glad when she had to go to the bathroom; it gave
her an excuse to get up and move. Once she got in

there, she noticed there was toothpaste in the sink, so she got out the Fantastik and started cleaning. Before she knew it, she had cleaned all the mirrors, the tub, the glass shower stall, and inside the toilet. And she wasn't finished. She still had plenty of unused energy and nothing else to do with it. When she saw the handmarks on the wall, she was seriously thinking about going down to Ace Hardware and buying some paint, but they were closed.

Bernadine almost wished they still had Champ, their last dog. But like the eight or nine other pets they'd had – hamsters, gerbils, rabbits, rats, cats, and four lizards – Champ didn't last. He was a Rottweiler. Bernadine had told John that the kids wanted a dog, not a bear, and Champ wasn't the kind of pet they needed. 'They're not pit bulls, Bernadine, my God,' he said. 'They just get big, but they're friendlier than a cocker spaniel. You'll see.'

Champ bit John junior with his 'baby teeth' when he was only four months old and weighed a mere forty-two pounds. Onika slapped the shit out of him every time he acted like he wanted to lick her. She didn't like him, and he didn't like her. They were jealous of each other. If Champ saw Bernadine doing anything with Onika – coloring, reading, helping her clean her room – he would jump up on Onika's bedroom window and paw at it from outside. And he barked. And barked. And barked. It got so that John junior stopped feeding him, because despite the fact that they'd sent him to obedience school, Champ continued to jump up and knock the boy down.

By the time Champ was eight months old, he weighed ninety-five pounds. He liked Bernadine. She was the one who fed him Iams and Science Diet, walked him, rubbed his ears, and scratched under his chin. But Champ hated his leash. One day, after they'd finished their routine walk on the exercise trail, he wouldn't let her put it back on. 'Champ, come,' Bernadine commanded. But Champ wouldn't come. He looked

292

at her and kept walking. 'Champ, come,' she said again, only firmer. Champ kept on about his business: running into other people's front yards, circling their trees to pee, and trampling their flowers. Bernadine put her hands on her hips and yelled, *'Champ, I said come!'* But he just sat down on the sidewalk and started looking around as if he was bored. She walked toward him. He didn't move. When she got right in front of him and reached for his collar, Champ's neck turned with such speed that by the time Bernadine saw his teeth about to cover her hand, she rammed her fist deep inside his mouth, grabbed him by his collar, put his leash on, slapped him on the head, and said, *'Bad dog.'* On the way home, she didn't have to tell Champ to heel, as she usually did. When they got in front of the garage and Bernadine told him to sit, Champ sat. 'You must be losing your damn mind,' she said, 'trying to bite *me*.' Champ looked ashamed and licked her hand as if to apologize.

'Get rid of him, or me and the kids go,' she told John.

'Don't be ridiculous.'

This time, Bernadine didn't wait for his consent. It took three whole days before John even noticed Champ was gone. He was mad as hell, because he'd spent twelve hundred dollars on that dog. But the kids were happy. Happy with their new guinea pig, which lasted all of three weeks before it died of consumption.

Now Bernadine stood in Onika's doorway. Her daughter's bed was still made from the last time the housekeeper was here. She sat down in the middle of it and ran her hand over a bunch of Disney characters. Onika was a pack rat – hoarded everything and hated to throw anything away. Her little table set was over in a corner. Stuffed animals sat in each chair. Each had a tiny plastic saucer with fake food on it in front of them. A big wooden dollhouse was perched on top of her dresser, full of miniature furniture. Next to that, her stove and sink and little white vacuum cleaner. All her doll clothes were in plastic bins. Her room was neat. And Onika knew where everything was. She had ordained herself the artist in the family. Her drawings were everywhere: Scotch-taped to the wall, over her desk, on her doorway, and on her bathroom door. A big green Christmas can was under her desk. It was full of hundreds of markers and crayons she'd kept over Bernadine didn't know how many years. Her easel and paint sets were housed in the garage.

Onika's dolls were sitting stiffly on her bed, lined up in front of her pillow. Bernadine picked one up and looked at it. All except one was black. That stupid Barbie. The first doll Bernadine bought Onika was black. She explained to her daughter a long time ago that she wasn't buying any blond-haired, blue-eyed dolls so Onika would grow up believing that Barbie set the standard for beauty. But last Christmas, Onika pleaded with her for a Barbie, because all her friends had at least one Barbie. Couldn't she have just one white doll? Bernadine gave in. Now she picked up the little comb-and-brush set Onika used to comb her dolls' hair and sometimes tried to use on her own. Bernadine was glad she'd taken the girl down to Oasis and let Cindy French braid it before she left.

She got up and closed the door and was on her way to John junior's room, when the phone rang. She listened to the message. It was a wrong number. John junior's room was just the opposite of Onika's. The housekeeper had said she was not picking up any more toys, and she meant it. He'd been Nintendo-crazy for years now, and Bernadine had bought him at least twenty different games. Which was way too many, and she knew it. But his behavior was improving, and his grades had gotten better. All he ever wanted as his reward was a Nintendo game. And they were everywhere, in addition to those micro machine cars and Battle Beasts and Ninja Turtles and green, purple, and orange men and pieces of the puzzles he'd become fanatical about: he could put a two-hundred-piece puzzle together in under an hour. How he did it bewildered Bernadine. She often tried to sit there and help, but puzzles gave her a headache.

After she picked up every single one of those toys, she put them in the plastic bins under his bed and scanned the room. There was absolutely nothing left to do in here. She went back out into the great room, then into the kitchen, and after putting a TV dinner into the microwave, she sat down on the couch. This isolation was about to drive her crazy. How many times had she prayed for this? To not have to hear 'Ma' for at least one day. She'd gotten her wish, but Bernadine had no idea she'd feel so lonely. So unnecessary. She could eat whatever and whenever she wanted to but found herself stopping at El Pollo Loco and Jack in the Box, even McDonald's – and she despised junk food. She could go anywhere she wanted to, but she couldn't think of anywhere she wanted to go, except the movies. But how many movies could you see? During the last few weeks, she and Savannah had seen just about every movie that was playing. They couldn't wait to see Spike Lee's *Mo' Better Blues*, but that wouldn't be out until next week. And Robin. She was no fun these days, because she'd been depressed ever since she heard about Russell marrying that woman. Bernadine didn't know why Robin was so surprised. Everybody knew he was no good, except Robin. And forget about Gloria. She wished she could give the woman some pep pills, because the only thing Gloria had energy for was Oasis Hair and that sixteen-year-old husband she called her son.

Bernadine heard the microwave beep, took out her Healthy Choice dinner (she couldn't eat another taco or fried hamburger this week), and sat down at the long, empty table to eat it. She picked up her knife and fork and looked around the room. The silence was too loud. She couldn't stand it. She tried to cut into the Chicken Dijon, but it took too much energy, because now she was crying. The knife and fork fell out of her hands. She heard them clink against the Formica. She was not supposed to be in this house without a husband, and now even her kids were gone. She was not supposed to be getting a divorce because her husband decided to cross over that white line. She was not supposed to be sitting in some white folks' office all day long, helping them get rich, then driving home in thick traffic, worrying if she could make it to the day care center by six or whether or not her mortgage payment had been paid. She was not supposed to be fucking somebody else's husband because she no longer had one. She was not supposed to be in this position at all. But she was. She wiped her eyes with her napkin. She was sick of feeling sorry for herself. Still, she ate her meal as though she was in an orphanage.

Maybe she should read a book, she thought, but she couldn't think of any that would hold her interest right now. Maybe she should give herself a manicure. But she always messed them up. Maybe she should call somebody. Savannah, she thought. But she'd already talked to her once today. She damn sure didn't feel like listening to Robin whine. If Bernadine heard Russell's name one more time, she'd scream. And Michael's too. What time was it? She looked at the clock. It was twenty after seven, which meant Gloria was probably watching something crucial on TV. She definitely wouldn't want to disturb her.

Bernadine grabbed her cigarettes and lighter from the table, got up, opened the French doors, and walked outside. The air was warm, but there was a breeze. She looked into the pool and started counting the ripples, until she realized she was counting ripples in the goddamn pool. She looked out at the desert. The mesquite trees appeared to be running toward her, but stopped. The crest of the Superstition Mountains looked like a reclining nude woman. Their peaks covered up most of the purple-and-pink skyline, but the rim of the orange sun wasn't ready to leave just yet. Bernadine lit a cigarette and sat down in a lounge chair until she saw absolutely nothing.

'It's final!' she yelled through the phone to Savannah.

'What?'

'My divorce!'

'Wait a minute. I thought you said you had to go to court again about the settlement.'

'I still do, but John's lawyer asked for this bifurcation hearing, which meant we could get the divorce before we reached a settlement. I'm so happy I could shit!'

'I've never heard of this before.'

'Me either, but I'm glad this part's over. Anyway, can you meet me for a drink, dinner, something? I need to celebrate. I'm a free woman, girl!'

'I wish I could, Bernie, but my friend Kenneth just flew in town.'

'He's back again?'

'Yeah. He surprised me. He claims he's out here looking at new optometry equipment.'

'Shit, this sounds serious.'

'It's not.'

'Well, I still have to celebrate. I have to. I can't sit in this house, that's for damn sure.'

'Did you call Robin?'

'Not yet. She's still tripping over Russell, girl. And Robin is not the kind of company I need tonight. Anyway, you have fun. And get in as much trouble as you want to.'

'I'm not getting in any trouble. If anything, I'll do the same thing you did with Herbert. Fuck him and send him back home to his wife.'

'Why are you saying it like that?'

'Because he's married, that's why.'

'So what?'

'So I can't afford to get involved with somebody who's married.'

'But you're going to see him while he's here.'

'I almost feel like I don't have much choice.'

297

'When was the last time you had some, Savannah?'

'April. The last time he was here.'

'Shit, it's July.'

'I know, and I'm scared.'

'Scared of what?'

'I told you how much I used to love this man, Bernie.'

'That'll make the shit even better. Go for it.'

'I went for it last time and got my ass in trouble.'

'So what? He came back, didn't he?'

'Yeah.'

'Didn't he say he wanted to get a divorce?'

'Yeah, but he's not divorced.'

'Well, shit, you can see from my experience, this shit isn't as easy as one-two-three. It takes time.'

'I know, but I don't know what his agenda is.'

'Why don't you wait and find out. At least he's a good lover, right?'

'Yes indeed.'

'Then go ahead and get some. I wouldn't worry about how you feel until afterwards. How long will he be here?'

'Two days.'

'Then get two days' worth. Enough to tide you over till the next time.'

'I'll play it by ear. Anyway, I'm sorry I can't hang out with you. But I'll take your ass out for a real celebration after he leaves.'

'Bye, girl. I'm gone.'

After she hung up, she called Robin, but she wasn't home. Bernadine was glad. She called Gloria for the hell of it, and Tarik said she was at a BWOTM board meeting and wouldn't be back until after nine. It was six forty-five. Bernadine had to go. Now. But where should she go? she wondered. Most of the nice places she and John used to go to were out of business, which was typical in Phoenix. As soon as a nice place opened where black folks could go to socialize, it lasted a few months, then something happened and it'd close.

Another establishment would pop up in its place, and before long the same thing would happen. But Bernadine didn't care if she saw a black face tonight or not. She was going somewhere.

She took a shower, put on some makeup, and threw on a pink blouse with a blue silk slack suit. When she examined herself in the mirror, she looked boring, so she went through her closet like a maniac, looking for something a little more lively. She found a sleeveless white linen dress with a low neckline. This was perfect.

She ended up at a dinner bar at the Scottsdale Princess, a resort that looked out on to a golf course that Bernadine couldn't see because it was dark. She hadn't exactly planned on coming in here, but it wasn't far from her house. She sat at a table by the window and looked around the place. There was nothing in here but old people. All the women's hair was gray or white and teased to perfection and piled on top of their heads. Bernadine hadn't seen so many rhinestones and sequins since her last New Year's Eve party. Maybe they were going somewhere afterwards, she thought, as she sipped her strawberry daiquiri. The waiter came to her table. She ordered prime rib, a baked potato with sour cream, and green beans with almonds, even though she wasn't hungry. She stirred the whipped cream with her straw. All of a sudden she felt silly. This was no celebration. What was she proving by being here? No-one was paying any attention to her. No-one knew her divorce was final today, so what was the point? When she got his attention, she motioned for the waiter. She asked if it was too late to cancel her order. He said he'd have to check. He came back moments later and said it was too late. Bernadine said she didn't care and paid for it anyway.

She still didn't feel like going home. And didn't know where else to go, so she drove down Camelback until she came to Twenty-fourth Street. When she saw the Ritz-Carlton hotel, a European-styled building that looked pink because of the lights shining on it, she pulled in there.

'Are you a guest?' the parking attendant asked her. 'I'll know in a minute,' she said, and got out of the car.

'I'm sure we have rooms available,' he said. 'This is our slowest season.'

The next thing Bernadine knew, she was standing in the Superior Suite, on the seventh floor, overlooking the whole city. The room was full of antiques. The drapes, bedspread, and sheets were all different shades of blue, and each was a different kind of print. It was beautiful. This was more like it, she thought. Bernadine took the little key and opened the honor bar. It was full of goodies, including little bottles of booze and California wines, but she decided to go downstairs to the bar and have a drink instead. It was still early, and now that she was here, she didn't want to sit in this hotel room by herself.

She found an empty seat at the bar, a very dark, ornate room, and a pianist was playing some kind of classical music, which Bernadine really wasn't in the mood for, but she was here, so she listened to it. She ordered another strawberry daiquiri and looked around the room. More white folks.

'Is anybody sitting here?'

When Bernadine turned around, she was surprised to see a tall, good-looking black man, about her age, in a black suit, standing behind her. 'No, nobody's sitting there,' she said. She was embarrassed because she was sitting by herself at a bar. Bernadine didn't want him or anybody else to think this was what she usually did. She hoped he wouldn't start talking to her. She wasn't in the mood for listening to a line or having a phony conversation with a stranger – she didn't care how good he looked. She was trying to get used to the idea that she wasn't married any more. Which would take longer than tonight.

'My name's James Wheeler. How you doing this evening?'

'Fine. Just fine, thank you.'

'Do you have a name?'

'Bernadine Harris,' she said, and tried not to take her eyes off her drink. He held his hand out to shake hers, so she held hers out too, and when he squeezed hers and shook it, his hand was not only strong but hot. The heat from his hand passed directly into hers. Bernadine was positive she felt some kind of current run from her palm to her arm and straight to her head, and then it permeated her whole body. She didn't know what was going on here. This had never happened to her before. She let his hand go. Then she smelled something sweet and tart, almost metallic, yet soothing. It was him.

'So where you from?' he asked.

'Who, me?'

He smiled at her. Bernadine noticed he was wearing a wedding band on his left hand, which made her relax. He was so well-groomed, she figured he had to be a lawyer, or maybe even a model or something. 'I live in Scottsdale,' she said.

'And you're staying here at this hotel?'

'Yep.'

'So it's like that,' he said, and took his right hand and ran it over his hair.

'Like what?'

'I'm being fresh. I apologize,' he said.

'It's OK,' she said, and took another sip from her drink. Bernadine didn't know what to do or say next. It was obvious that he was going to keep talking, and since her drink was half full, she couldn't very well hop up and leave without looking foolish. For some stupid reason, she felt like talking now. 'I just went through a divorce, and today it's final and I'm celebrating,' she blurted out.

'Well, congratulations,' he said. 'If congratulations are in order.'

'They're definitely in order.'

301

'How long were you married?'

'Eleven years.'

'Whew,' he said, and took a sip of the beer he had ordered.

'What about you?' she said.

'Five.'

'Happily?'

'At one time,' he said.

'Where do you live?' she asked.

'In Virginia, right outside D.C.'

'What brings you to Phoenix?'

'Well, I had to come out here to get some background on a case I'm working on. I'm a civil rights attorney.'

'So how long have you been here, and how long are you staying?' She couldn't believe how nosy she was being. Bernadine blamed it on those daiquiris.

'For four days now. I leave tomorrow.'

'Have you had a chance to see the city?'

'You mean "town," don't you?' he said, grinning.

He had the most incredible smile. Sexy, when she got right down to it. And that mustache, boy, was it shiny, even in this dim light. And those bushy eyebrows, and those luscious lips, and the way he moved, as if his bones were lubricated. Bernadine was positive the booze was responsible for these impressions, these sensations she was having. She'd never felt aroused by a complete stranger before, and now that she was aware of it, she was starting to feel uncomfortable. She couldn't remember feeling these kinds of sparks when she met John. Or any man. 'You're right,' she said, trying to keep her mind on what he'd just said and not on him. 'Even though there're a million people here, it really is just a big town.'

'I've seen enough to know I wouldn't want to live here. It's too hot, for one thing, and what's there to do?'

'Nothing.'

'I have to admit,' he said, 'you're the most stunning thing I've seen in the four days I've been here.'

302

'Thank you,' she said. Bernadine's face felt flushed, and she knew that if she were white, she'd be red.

'So is this the extent of your celebration?' he asked her.

'It looks like it,' she said.

'You're not celebrating alone, are you?'

'Well, you're sitting next to me now,' she said, and wanted to bite her tongue for saying it. Was this flirting? Bernadine wondered. Or was she making a fool of herself?

'You're right,' he said. 'I hope you don't mind.'

'So far I don't.'

He started laughing and asked if she'd like to sit at a table, where he could see her face when they talked. Bernadine got up, leaving her drink at the bar.

'Would you like another one?' he asked.

'I think I've had enough. Maybe a club soda,' she said, 'with a twist.'

James ordered two of them and brought them back to the table. Over the next three hours, they learned more about each other than some people do who've known each other for years. Bernadine didn't know what to do with this information – how to process it – now that she had it. It turned out that James was thirty-seven years old, and his wife, who was white (which didn't bother her tonight, for some reason) and only thirty-two years old, had some rare form of breast cancer. She'd been hospitalized at least six times this past year. As Bernadine listened to him, she could tell he wasn't making it up. This wasn't the kind of shit you made up. He didn't have any kids but said he always wanted some. His wife didn't, which was a major cause of their problems. Three years ago was when she had noticed a big bruise on her left breast. James said she told him she hadn't bumped into anything that she knew of. When they had it checked out, they discovered it was the kind of breast cancer that even a mastectomy wouldn't help. James told her that they'd been planning to

303

divorce, but he couldn't leave her like this. They had a respirator at home, and for the last year she'd literally been living on morphine. Now they were just waiting for it to happen. He said he was drained. Watching her suffer like this was the worst thing he'd ever been through in his life.

Bernadine told him her whole history with John, and even the recent incident with the pills. James said she was brave. The way she was going forward with her life, raising two kids by herself and working full time. Even the way she came into this bar alone tonight to celebrate. He said he had seen her when she checked in, and confessed that he'd hoped she wasn't meeting anybody here. He said he had his fingers crossed that she'd come back down to the bar for a drink. And here she was.

He also said John was a damn fool, like so many men. 'We take entirely too much for granted,' he said, 'when we shouldn't. We abuse what we should be doing our damnedest to protect. We hurt the people who love us, and then wonder why our lives are so fucked up – excuse the language.'

'You don't have to apologize,' she said. 'I totally agree.' As a matter of fact, Bernadine agreed with just about everything he'd said during these three hours. As they talked, James became more and more enchanting. Bernadine wondered how men did that. How they could say the right things at the right time and just look better, become so much more alluring. How they could move a certain way, look at you a certain way, and make you yearn for them. James had done that and more. She couldn't remember the last time she actually sat down and talked to a man who had an opinion about so *many* things. She could've sat there and listened to him all night.

'Can I help you celebrate your new freedom?' he was saying. He was holding Bernadine's hands, which by now she felt perfectly comfortable with.

'What do you mean?'

'Let me ask you this first. Haven't you ever wanted to do something like this?'

'Something like what?'

'Meet somebody and feel so attracted that you don't waste time pretending because you just want to be with that person, you want to feel that person so bad that it's more like a need, so you go for it and don't worry about what'll happen afterwards?'

Damn, Bernadine thought. It sure sounded good. And even though she'd had that fling with Herbert, that was some superficial shit compared to this. She and Herbert never talked, they just fucked. 'Well,' she said, 'I've been married for so long I never thought about it.'

'Let me be your comfort zone tonight,' he said, and looked her in the eye. This man was serious.

'Well, it's been *comforting* just talking to you,' she said. 'But to tell the truth, I'm game.' She got nervous right after she said it. But fuck it. She wanted to see what doing something like this was like, before she came to her complete senses and changed her mind.

James got up from the table and helped Bernadine out of her chair. He went over to sign for the drinks, turned around, and looked her in the eye again. Damn, Bernadine thought. She watched every move he made. His shoulders were so wide, she had to inhale. She couldn't wait to get inside them. When James put his arm over her shoulders, she felt that same current pass through her body all over again.

They caught the elevator to her floor. Bernadine could hardly get the key in the door. James could tell she was nervous, so he reached over her head and took the key from her. 'It's OK,' he said. 'Relax. Let me do this.' She could feel his chest against her back. She wanted to fall just so he could catch her. Instead Bernadine stood stock-still. When the door opened, the cool air flooded the room and hit them in the face. She set her purse on the bed and walked over to the picture window. Now that he was here, she didn't know what to do. She was scared to get too close to him too soon. But James followed her. They both looked out at the view of the city, which was lit up and spectacular. She'd had some pretty good dreams before, but nothing came close to this.

'You feeling OK?' he asked.

'Nervous.'

'I know,' he said. 'It's pretty obvious you've never done anything like this before.'

'You're right,' she said.

'I like that,' he said. 'Having second thoughts?'

'I'm having all kinds of thoughts,' Bernadine said.

'Well, if it's any consolation, I've never done this before, either.'

'I bet,' she said.

'I don't lie,' he said. 'It's just a temporary solution to a permanent problem, which always comes back.' James bent down and kissed Bernadine on her head, her cheeks, and then her bare shoulders. She felt them drop. 'I know it sounds corny, but I feel like I've known you all my life,' he said, and kissed her on the lips. 'You want to know something else?'

Bernadine could barely hear him. He tasted so good. 'What?' she finally said.

'I haven't slept with a woman in six months.'

Bernadine heard that. 'Now, this I don't believe,' she said.

'It's true,' he said.

'Why haven't you?'

He just looked at her. 'Tonight I want to make you feel like the most beautiful woman in the world,' he said, and kissed her again.

Bernadine looked in his eyes and smiled. It sounded good, so good that she took a deep breath, looked at *all* this man standing in front of her, and dropped her guard. After all, she wasn't married any more. She had protection in her purse. And she *was* a grown woman. Free to do whatever she wanted to do. Wasn't she? Hadn't her heart given her permission to do this? If

306

so, why was it changing its mind in midstream? Now it was telling her that she shouldn't be here. That what she was doing was low and sleazy and the kind of shit she should've gotten out of her system in her twenties, not her thirties. But she was starving for *real* affection, for *real* tenderness, and Bernadine needed a *real* man to give it to her. She *wanted* James to hold her. She *wanted* him to tell her over and over again that she was beautiful, until she believed it. She wanted him to tell her that everything would work out, that her life would be OK. But she wanted it to be the truth.

James said it had been ten years since he'd held and kissed a black woman. It had been ten years since he'd been able to talk to a woman without any pretense. He said he was grateful to be standing here. He put his arms around Bernadine and held her so close for so long that Bernadine started crying. James told her to go ahead and cry. And she did. And it felt good.

They stood there, in front of that big window, until they both felt strong enough to give each other another kind of comfort. By six o'clock the next morning, James Wheeler and Bernadine Harris were in love. They both knew, they said, that this kind of comfort was a temporary thing. James thanked Bernadine for easing his pain. Thanked her for trusting him. And thanked her for her honesty. He thanked her for everything, but especially, he said as he got in a taxi, for restoring his faith in black women. Bernadine checked out of the hotel, got in her Cherokee, and drove home. In the house, she sat down on the couch and, out of habit, reached for a cigarette. But she didn't have the desire or the need, and didn't smoke it. She sat there smiling, replaying the past night in her head for hours. It didn't matter if she never saw him ever in life. It didn't matter at all. She was alive again.

New Territory

Gloria heard the sound of a big truck outside her bedroom window. She knew it wasn't trash day, so she got up and peeked out through the miniblinds to see what and who it could be. There was a big moving van pulling into the driveway across the street. And then a navy-blue Buick sedan pulled up in front of the house. A black man, who appeared to be about fifty, got out of the car. He was wearing a bluish-gray uniform. Gloria figured he worked for the transit authority. If she wasn't mistaken, that was the color of their uniform. His hair was almost totally gray, and he was getting bald. His skin was a reddish brown. He looked about five nine, maybe ten, but she couldn't tell for sure. She also couldn't tell how good-looking he was, but from where she was sitting, for an older man, he didn't appear too bad.

Finally, she thought, some black people in the neighborhood. Gloria was excited. She and Tarik were tired of being the only ones on the whole block. She couldn't understand why more black folks hadn't moved in here. It wasn't like these houses were all that expensive. And it wasn't like they were out in the boonies.

She sat there for another fifteen or twenty minutes, watching the movers unload box after box after box. Gloria was wondering where the wife was. Maybe she'd go there later and introduce herself, take them a bottle of wine or something. No. Maybe they were religious people and didn't drink. She wouldn't want to offend. Then she remembered she had a half-baked sweet potato pie in the freezer. She could thaw it out and take it over.

Maybe now she'd have somebody to have coffee with, at least talk to. Even though Gloria's other neighbors were friendly when she met them at the mailbox, they weren't all that neighborly. They said hello and usually waved from their cars when they saw her out in the yard (although sometimes they didn't), but not once had any of them invited her over for a drink, or dinner; then again, neither had she. The truth be known, she didn't feel she had all that much in common with them. All of them were white. And most of the women were housewives. The height of their excitement seemed to be going to the K Mart or the malls or the Price Club, or cleaning their houses all day.

Gloria couldn't tell if these new people had any kids. She hadn't seen the movers unload any children's furnishings or toys or bicycles. Maybe they had a teenager. Or maybe their kids were grown. This *was* the smallest house in this subdivision, the only one-story, two-bedroom on her street. Still, it was a very nice house, only five years old. Except that the people who lived in it before put an atrocious dirty-brown carpet in there and had the nerve to put some loud orange tile in the foyer and the kitchen. Gloria knew this because she'd peered in every single window right after that family moved out. She also knew that this new family had gotten a deal on the house, had paid only about $95,000 for it, because like everybody else in the neighborhood, she always read the realtor's listings that were inside the tube below the For Sale sign. The house had been on the market almost nine months. Gloria was so used to that sign being there, she hadn't noticed when the Sold sign replaced it.

Finally, she closed the miniblinds, got up from the chair, and went downstairs to make herself a western omelet. Then she'd get ready to go down to the shop. Lord knows, she didn't feel like facing those folks today.

*   *   *

The shop was empty. Which was strange: Phillip was always there before her. Desiree was invariably late, and Joseph didn't take appointments before ten. Cindy had to register for court-reporting school today, so Gloria knew she wouldn't be in until noonish. She went over to the machine to check the messages, and that's when she saw the note from Desiree, saying she'd quit. Gloria's head jerked up, and she looked over at Desiree's station. It was spotless. No ponytails anywhere. When did she decide to do this? But Gloria was glad the heffa was gone.

The machine beeped. 'Gloria, this is Phillip. I didn't want to tell you like this, but I've got some bad news, girlfriend. I'm sick. I've got a rash. It's called shingles. It's a virus. Like the chicken pox. Only it's not. I'll be out of action for at least a month, maybe longer. Don't worry about me. I'm OK. I hope this don't mess things up down at the shop. I'm staying with a friend, so you can't call me. I'll call you. Love you, sweetheart.'

Shingles? She'd never heard of anything called shingles before. And he'd be out at least a month? What was she going to do, with two stylists gone? Gloria reached inside her purse and got out one of her blood pressure pills. As she went for some water, Gloria prayed this didn't mean Phillip had AIDS. She wished, too, that she could call him. She wanted Phillip to be straight with her. Tell her the truth about this shingles. Maybe she could ask somebody. But who? She turned on the ceiling fans and the stereo. There was a sudden chill. A void. The shop was empty. It was all wrong.

Bernadine was early. 'Hey, girl,' she said from the front door. She was wearing a red baseball cap, which meant her hair was probably a bird's nest underneath. It was. Bernadine had canceled her last two appointments, so it was no wonder she was trying to hide it. But she looked fresh, downright spry, like she was excited

310

about something, and Gloria couldn't wait to hear what it was.

A few of Joseph's and Cindy's customers had already arrived and were pouring some of Gloria's weak coffee, stirring in what she thought was entirely too much of her creamer. She wanted to tell them to ease up on the sugar, but Phillip wouldn't approve.

'So,' Bernadine said, and hopped up in Gloria's chair. 'What's been going on, girlfriend?'

'You tell me,' Gloria said.

'Girl, I've been having so much fun, I can't even believe it. You see my hair, don't you?'

'Yeah, I see it,' Gloria said. 'I can't believe how fast this mess grows. Tell me you got your settlement.'

'I wish. Every week it's something else. It seems like my lawyer is subpoenaing the world. I'm almost ready to say forget the whole thing. Take some money and run. I don't mean that shit. But it's taking for ever to get the records for everything she's asking for. And sometimes these people send the wrong shit. Anyway, I'm not worrying about it any more. It's out of my hands.'

'What about the house?'

'I had the realtors put the sign up yesterday.'

'You did?'

'Yep.'

'Has John been late with any more payments?'

'I haven't gotten any notices, so I assume he's making them. I think my lawyer scared him to death when she told him his ass could go to jail.'

The three customers who'd gotten their coffee looked up when they heard the word 'jail.' They were totally involved in this conversation, and when Bernadine realized they were listening, she lowered her voice.

'Anyway, girl, I've met the nicest man.'

'I know one thing, you're about the only one I know who's not having any problems in that department, I swear.'

'He's a tenderoni.'

'You mean he's younger than you are,' Gloria said.

'Very much so.'

'How much younger?' Gloria asked. The three customers were all ears again.

'Ten years.'

'You mean he's only twenty-six?'

'You don't have to say it so loud, Gloria. Damn.'

One of the customers, a woman maybe in her late fifties, was grinning from ear to ear, flipping through *Ebony*. It was pretty obvious she wasn't reading it.

'What are you doing, Bernie? You've already got two kids; what you want with another one?'

'He's very much a man.' She added, 'I'm just playing.'

'Does he know you're playing?'

'Well, you know, that's the problem. He's serious as cancer. I told him I was too old for him, but he said he didn't care how old I was. The kids like him too.'

'You mean he's met the kids?'

'What's wrong with that?'

'You better watch yourself. You shouldn't be letting the kids meet every man you decide to go out with. What are they supposed to think?'

'You act like I've been breaking *The Guinness Book of Records* or something. What they *think* is that he's a friend of mine, which is true, and that he's nice. Can I help it if he wants to take them to the park and the zoo and the movies and kite flying? Their daddy never spent any time with them, so why should I deprive them? We even went to church together, girl.'

'What does he do?'

'He's got a normal job. He's an airplane mechanic.'

'That's good,' the older lady said, and got Bernadine and Gloria's attention. 'I'd go ahead and enjoy myself if I was you, baby. These younger men treat you better, they got more energy, they ain't set in their ways, and they ain't half as stingy.' She giggled and went back to pretending she was reading her magazine. She had a look on her face as if she hadn't said a word.

Bernadine and Gloria looked at each other in the mirror and cracked up. 'Come on back to the sink,' Gloria said. 'What's his name?'

Bernadine waited until she got to the rear of the shop, knowing the folks up front couldn't hear her without straining, and said, 'Vincent. Vincent Gresham.'

'Lean back,' Gloria said, and put a little more pressure on Bernadine's head than she should have.

'I met him at the bank a couple of weeks ago. We were standing in the same line, and he started talking to me about something, I can't even remember what it was. Anyway, all I was thinking was that this young man was as cute as a button, and to make a long story short, he asked me for my phone number and I gave it to him. And then he called and took me out to dinner and so on and so on and so on.'

'And?' Gloria said, massaging the thick shampoo into her scalp.

'That's it.'

'So what's he like?'

'What's he like? Just like any other grown man, Gloria. Damn. The way I figured it, if this "baby" was bold enough to ask me for my number, then I wanted to see what a "baby" could do. He's turned me out, girl. Hey, where's Phillip and Desiree today?'

The customers looked up, waiting to see what Gloria was going to say. 'He's sick,' she said, and let it go at that. 'And Desiree quit.'

'What's wrong with him?' Bernadine asked.

'I don't know. But he'll be out for a while.'

'When did Desiree quit?'

'This morning, I guess. And I'm glad she's gone.'

'Will you be able to replace her?'

'Who knows?' Gloria said.

Joseph and Cindy came in one after the other and said their hellos.

'You talked to Robin lately?'

'Not since she was in here last week, getting a fill. Why?' Gloria started rinsing her out.

313

'That girl's going to get herself killed one day, I swear she is.'

'What's she doing now?' Gloria asked.

'Guess.'

'No, she isn't?'

Joseph was ushering the older woman to the sink next to theirs. You could tell she was happy to be within earshot. When she sat down and leaned back, she closed her eyes.

'The kids spent the night over there last Friday. Vincent and I went to a movie, and, girl, I almost had a heart attack when Russell answered the door.'

'No, he didn't.'

'Yes, he did.'

'What about his . . . you know?'

'Check this out. They're separated.'

'But they just got married a few months ago!'

'She put his ass out, girl.'

'You're lying, Bernie.'

'I just said he answered her door, didn't I?'

'I heard you,' Gloria said, and started putting the conditioner in.

'Can you believe it?'

'I can believe anything Robin does. That girl just don't have a drop of sense and no pride whatsoever. Why don't you talk to her, Bernie?'

'And say what? "Why don't you stop being such a damn fool and leave that parasite alone?" She's about as dense as they come. I love her to death, but you should've seen her. She wasn't the least bit embarrassed. As a matter of fact, she was just as happy as a little lark. Like she got lucky or something. I can't talk to her, Gloria. She's past the point of no return, if you ask me. But she ought to stop.'

'You don't think she let him move back in, do you?'

'I'm scared to ask,' Bernadine said. 'But Robin doesn't know how to keep her mouth shut. She'll tell it, and when she does, I'll act like I don't care one way or the other. This is her life, not mine.'

'Come on,' Gloria said, pushing Bernadine out of the chair. 'Let me get you under the dryer.'

'Better than the soaps, huh?' Bernadine said to the lady at the next sink.

Tarik was practicing his saxophone when Gloria got home. He'd been playing it a lot more regularly, and Gloria hadn't heard him play so much in ages. Now that he was a senior, he seemed to have gotten more serious about everything. His report card had improved almost a hundred per cent. Gloria told him five hundred different ways how proud she was of him. That she knew he could do it. He hadn't said another word about the gang business and had stopped seeing that white girl. For some reason, all the girls he brought home seemed to have the same thing in common: they had long hair and light skin and were pretty. She asked him if these traits were a prerequisite, and Tarik said no. He just knew what he liked.

Gloria didn't want to remind him that all he was doing was picking girls who looked white. What was this obsession all about? And where'd he get it? What was wrong with black girls with dark skin and short, nappy hair? Didn't he think they were pretty too? But Tarik kept telling her: he knew what he liked.

His horn stopped. Gloria was disappointed. She loved hearing him play. She had taken the pie out of the oven and was ironing his shirt. He was getting his senior pictures taken tomorrow. Tarik came in and sat down at the kitchen table. 'Can I talk to you about something, Ma?'

Gloria was thinking: Please don't let it be some bullshit. We've been on a roll, Tarik; don't mess it up now. 'I'm listening,' she said, and sprayed starch on the sleeve.

'Remember I was telling you about Up With People?'

'Yeah.'

'Did you read all the stuff I gave you?' he asked.

'Yes, I did.'

315

'What'd you think?'

'Well, it seems like a good opportunity for a young person, no doubt about that.'

'I want to apply.'

'Tarik.' She sighed and put the iron down. 'I thought we'd already decided you were going to ASU.'

'First of all, I don't think I'm ready for college yet, Ma. I don't have a clue about what I want to do with my life. But,' he said, 'when I do go, I want to go to Morehouse.'

'That's all the way in Atlanta!'

'I want to go to a black college, Ma. Since I was little, I've been going to all-white schools. I'm sick of being the only blood in the class. I want to know what it's like being around people my own color. Anyway, I can get college credits from the U of A if I get in. Just think. I'd get to travel all over the world, performing for a whole year!'

'And you think you could handle living with people you don't know for a whole year?'

'Yeah, I do. But it's more to it than that, Ma. Don't you think that doing things for the community . . . You saw the kinds of things they do in the brochure, didn't you? They perform in nursing homes, do benefits for abused women and children, and a whole lot of other stuff. All over the *world*! Don't you think this would be a good educational experience for me?'

'Of course it would.'

'I don't have to be all that good a musician, either, but it won't hurt. So please let me go for an interview.'

'The brochure said you need to go to one of the performances.'

'There's one in two weeks, at ASU. I checked already.'

'You haven't said a word about how much this would cost.' But Gloria already knew that. She'd read all the literature and had even called and talked to the administrator about how this whole thing worked. She had to admit, she was impressed. Seven hundred kids, seventeen years old to twenty-five, from twenty-five countries would be broken down into five different 'casts.' They would spend the first five weeks in Tucson, rehearsing, learning the music and choreography, and judging by the pictures in the brochure, the performances looked pretty spectacular. The handbook also said these kids would get a chance to participate in seminars, debates; meet and hear various leaders in the arts, business, government, and education, in the United States as well as abroad.

'Well, I think it's only about eight thousand dollars, but they have scholarships too, Ma.'

'Oh, *only* eight thousand dollars.'

'Ma, if I get in, I can do all kinds of fund-raising stuff, and I can try to get sponsors. That's what a lot of people do. But depending on how much money you make, I might qualify for a scholarship.'

'I can afford some of it,' she said. Gloria had always made sure Tarik didn't know how much money she made or how much she had. After she sold her parents' house, she used part of the money to open Oasis and put the rest in a savings account and, later on, in CDs. She didn't ever want him to take her for granted. Didn't want to raise a spoiled-rotten brat who'd grow up thinking he could have anything he wanted without earning it. When Tarik asked her to buy him something, Gloria often told him they couldn't afford it, or she'd just plain say no. Sometimes, though, she'd surprise him, which she thought made him that much more appreciative.

'How much?' Tarik asked.

'I said *some* of it,' she repeated, knowing she could afford the whole amount. 'Let me just say this. If you get accepted, you need to try to earn as much on your own as you can.'

'I'll do anything,' he said. 'I wanna go, Ma, I do. I've been thinking about it all summer. And remember Bill up the street, who graduated last year?'

'Yes.'

'He couldn't sing or anything, and he got accepted, and he said it was great. He went to Finland, France, Frankfurt, Germany, and all over the U.S., even New York City! And guess what else, Ma? He met the queen of England – can you believe it?'

'You don't have to convince me of anything, Tarik,' she said, and sprayed more starch on the front of the shirt. 'All I'm concerned about is you getting a college education. You can play that saxophone and sing and dance all over the world if you want to, but without that piece of paper, you won't have much of a future. But you already know this.'

'Bill's a freshman in college right now.'

Gloria put the iron down.

'I'd only be nineteen when we finish touring, and a lot of times you can get accepted to a college and defer it for a year. I'd do that, I promise.'

'Well, why don't we wait and see if you get in?'

'Bet. But I'm getting in,' he said. 'Didn't you always tell me to think positive?'

'I did.'

'So that's what I'm doing,' he said, and stood up.

Gloria could swear the boy had grown three or four inches in the last few months. He had to be at least six foot four now. He had the body of a grown man. 'I'm proud of you, Tarik,' she said, and squeezed the handle of the iron.

'Why are you proud of me, Ma? I haven't done anything.'

'Because you haven't given me any trouble. At least not the kind some of these teenagers are getting into out here. Drugs and all that. I'm very lucky to have a son like you.'

Tarik walked over to her, pressed his hands down on the shirt – the part Gloria had just ironed – bent down, and gave her a peck on the forehead. 'Thank you, Ma,' he said. 'Now, can I have a piece of pie?'

'No,' she said. 'It's for our new neighbors.'

'What new neighbors?'

'A black family moved in this morning. Right across the street.'

'Get outta here,' he said. 'It's about time,' and then he did some kind of dance backward out of the kitchen. A few minutes later, Gloria heard him playing his horn again. She couldn't wipe the smile off her face if you'd paid her. This was the kind of son she wanted to raise: confident, responsible, with a sense of direction. Today Gloria felt she was batting a thousand.

The garage door was up and the car was inside, so she walked across the street with the cooled pie, wrapped in aluminum foil, and rang the doorbell. The man answered the door. 'Well, hello there,' he said.

'Hello,' Gloria said. He was definitely good-looking up close, she thought. Definitely. And then she forgot what she'd been about to say. How was that possible? She had never been at a loss for words in front of any man, let alone an older one, and one she didn't even know. 'I'm Gloria Matthews,' she said, remembering her name. 'I live right across the street. And I just wanted to welcome you and your family to the neighborhood.'

'Well, thank you,' he said, with some kind of southern accent. 'That's sure nice of you,' he said. 'Come on in for a few minutes,' he said, motioning with his hands.

'Well, I don't want to intrude,' she said, still standing there. 'I just wanted to introduce myself. Is your wife at home?'

'I'm afraid I don't have a wife,' he said. 'She passed away, going on two years now. It's just me here.'

'Oh,' Gloria said. 'I'm sorry to hear that.'

'Thank you,' he said. 'What you got there? Some kind of pie?'

'Sweet potato.'

'Who don't love sweet potato pie?' he said, and started laughing. 'Why don't you come on in and have a seat for a few minutes? I wasn't doing nothing but fiddling. My daughter was supposed to come help me

319

get some of these boxes opened, but she said something about being late getting her kids from the day care, so I'm just in here tinkering with the refrigerator, trying to get the icemaker going. You're welcome to come on in.'

'Well, I'm just getting my dinner started and wanted you to have this pie.'

'Then I'll have this for dinner,' he said, and laughed again.

He had such a hearty laugh, Gloria thought, and such a warm disposition, she really wanted to come in, but she knew it wouldn't look right, and plus, she didn't want to give him the wrong impression, considering he lived right across the street and all. 'You don't have to do that,' she said. 'I could have my son bring you over a plate. All we're having is leftovers, to tell you the truth. I've got some greens and corn bread over there, some candied yams, a little potato salad, and a few slices of ham.'

'Sounds like a feast,' he said. 'I'm not one to turn down a home-cooked meal. Thank you, Gloria,' he said. 'I haven't eaten a thing today. What's your son's name?'

'Tarik.'

'Tar-what?'

'Tar-reek.' She pronounced it for him.

'Oh, one of those African names. I like that one. Only two syllables. And how old is Tarik?'

'Seventeen.'

'A teenager.'

'Yes, Lord, a teenager.'

'My kids are grown and gone. Thank goodness.'

'Well, he'll be gone in June, I think.'

'College?'

'Sort of.'

'How can you sort of go to college?' he asked.

But Gloria didn't answer him right away. She was too busy trying not to stare at him. But she *was* staring at him. Looking him dead in the eyes. For a minute, she thought he'd put a spell on her or something, because she didn't hear a word he'd just said. She saw his lips move, but she was too busy thinking: If you *are* fifty, you *sure* look good. Fifty isn't all that old, is it? And your skin. As smooth as any thirty-five-year-old's. Looks like you've taken good care of yourself – or somebody took good care of you. And to think you live right across the street. From *me.* 'I'm sorry,' she heard herself say. 'What did you just ask me?'

He had a sly grin on his face. 'I think I said, How can your son *sort* of be going to college?'

'Well, he plays the saxophone, and he may get a chance to travel all around the world with this organization called Up With People. But I don't know.'

'Let the boy go,' he said. 'How's his daddy feel about it?'

'His daddy lives in California somewhere,' Gloria said, and didn't know what made her tell that barefaced lie.

'So you're divorced, then, are you?'

'Yes,' she said, because once again, Gloria didn't want to give him the wrong impression.

'Well, look, Gloria. If you ever need anything done around the house, don't hesitate to knock on my door. I can fix anything,' he said proudly, and laughed again. 'And I truly wouldn't mind. Not one bit.'

'That's awfully kind of you . . . you know, I didn't get your name.'

'Marvin. Marvin King,' he said.

'Well, it's nice to meet you, Marvin,' she said, finally handing him the pie. 'And welcome to the neighborhood. I'll warm the food up and send that plate right over by Tarik.'

'Thank you so much, Gloria. I hope to be seeing you again real soon,' he said.

Gloria said, 'I sure hope so,' under her breath, and started walking back across the street. She was trying to be as poised as she possibly could. Something told her he was watching her, so she turned around to see if she was right, and sure enough, there he was, still standing in the doorway, waving at her. She waved back, tickled as she wanted to be, because no man had ever waited to watch her cross a street before, no man had ever volunteered to fix anything for her, and no man had ever made her feel this giddy. Gloria liked the feeling. She liked it so much, she felt her knees grow weaker with each step she took. Her heart was actually fluttering as if it had wings. That was a brand-new feeling too. All of this was new territory to her, and Gloria had no idea that feeling attracted to somebody could make your body go limp. She closed her eyes for a second and asked God to please help her make it to her front door without falling and to her surprise, this time He answered her.

Closer to the Bone

I'm so glad Russell's back. Well, he's not all the way one hundred percent back. Yet. Most of his stuff is still over at his other house, but it's been kind of hard for him to get it, since she changed the locks. It didn't take long for her to find out he was over here, and she had the nerve to call and cuss me out. 'You're one *dizzy* bitch,' she said. At first I was planning on bamming the phone down in her face, but then I sort of wanted to hear what she had to say, so I kept the phone to my ear and didn't say a word. 'How could you let that son of a bitch back in your house, let alone your bed, knowing he walked out on you and came running over here to me? I'll tell you one thing, you must be one hard-up broad 'cause Russell ain't worth two cents, and you more than anybody should know that by now. You ain't doing nothing but setting yourself up for more disappointments. How old are you anyway? You must be obsessed, possessed – something – 'cause I swear, I can't understand for the life of me why you'd wanna put yourself through more hell, knowing he ain't nothing but a slimy, sleazy no-good whore who doesn't know how to control his own dick. But you know what? You can have the sorry motherfucker! *Keep him! I* don't want his ass. And you wanna know something else? You better pray to God he don't give you herpes, like he did me. So watch yourself.' Click.

Herpes? This was a scare tactic, that much I knew. Russell didn't have any herpes. If he did, I'd never seen it before. I was fuming after I hung up that phone. Who did she think she was, calling my house, talking all this mess? I wished I knew what sign she was, so I'd at least

323

know what element I was dealing with. Probably an Aries, because they're totally into revenge. And just when was Russell supposed to have gotten herpes? Women'll do anything to keep a man. I don't know why they always attack the other woman when they should be jumping on *his* case.

I did not, however, want her to think she could just pick up the phone anytime she felt like it and call me whenever she wanted to blow off steam, and I damn sure didn't want her calling Russell, so I had my phone number changed to unlisted. I didn't tell Russell she'd called until a few days later. That's how mad I was.

'What'd she say?' he asked.

'She was very nasty,' I said.

'I know that. But what'd she *say*?'

'Why? Is there something I should know?'

'Nothing you don't already know,' he said.

'She said you gave her herpes.'

'What? And I suppose you believed that shit?'

'Well, is it true?'

'Do I look like I've got herpes?'

'It's not a *look*, Russell. Do you have the shit or don't you?'

'No, I don't have no damn herpes, and if I do, then she gave it to me,' he said, and he turned on ESPN and pretended like he was hypnotized by some football game.

That night I checked for myself. It was still as smooth as it always was. And so was Russell.

I bet Bernadine, Gloria, and Savannah are probably talking about me like a dog behind my back, but I don't care what they might be saying. Not a one of 'em have been in love for centuries, so they can't say what they'd do if they were in my shoes.

Russell literally begged me to give him another chance and told me he'd made the biggest mistake of his life, leaving me the way he did. I wanted to correct him, and tell him, You didn't leave me – I put you out.

Remember? But it's OK. All men have bad memories.

Anyway, when he first got here, we had a long talk. He told me he only married Carolyn on a whim, and now he was sorry he ever met her. He said she kept tabs on him. He couldn't walk out of the house without her asking where he was going and what time he'd be back. And she was bossy. Always telling him what to do and how to do it, and it eventually got on his nerves. He also said that right after she had the baby (which I finally found out was real, and it was a boy), she changed. He said Carolyn got lazy and fat. She never cooked, the house was always a mess, and he just couldn't stand it any more.

Well, color me jealous, because the sound of her name made my skin crawl, which is why I told him never to say it in front of me again. So now, when he mentions her, he refers to her as 'Her.' Which is cool.

He also finally admitted that he'd been a fool for treating me the way he did, and actually said he was sorry. Would I please forgive him? I didn't want to say yes right there on the spot, but he sounded so pitiful and so sincere and all that I couldn't help but give in. You get the best loving in the world when a man is begging. Afterwards, he said, 'Can I stay here with you for a minute?' I told him I wasn't sure if it would work. He rolled over and gave me some more. 'I'm not sure if I'm ready to come back yet, but the only way I'll know is by being here. Would you give me that opportunity, at least until I can figure out what I'm doing?' he said, and kept touching me in places he knew would make me say yes to anything.

Later on, I was thinking about asking him what really happened over there, but to tell the truth, I didn't much care. I didn't need to know all the details. The important thing was this: He had a hundred other places he could've gone, but Russell came here, to me, which – as far as I'm concerned – is where he wanted to be: closer to the bone.

* * *

Right now I'm going a little bizonkers, because he's over there negotiating with Her about how they can end this marriage without getting a lawyer. Russell said he didn't want a whole bunch of legal hassles. He said he was willing to pay Her whatever child support was reasonable. As a matter of fact, he took one of those little do-it-yourself forms you get at the stationery store for her to look at. I heard there was a drive-up window somewhere in Phoenix where you could hand them that form and be divorced in a matter of minutes, as long as you didn't have any property. Everything Russell owns is on his back, in a closet, or parked in a garage.

I'm just glad he was honest and told me where he was going, which tells me that he's finally maturing. Learning how to tell the truth when you're not used to it is definitely a sign of maturity, if you ask me. All I can say is this: It's about time.

He's been gone close to three hours, and I want to know what's taking him so long. I was trying to pay attention to what they were doing on *Growing Pains*, but I couldn't, so I switched to *Unsolved Mysteries*, and that was too eerie for me, so I decided to call my mother to see how she and Daddy were doing. One thing I hate about Alzheimer's is that you can pray all you want to, but once that disease takes hold of you, that person doesn't get any better. I keep hoping my daddy's condition will improve, but the last time I was down there, he could hardly utter a word. He babbled and didn't seem to know where he was or who I was from one minute to the next. He went to the bathroom on himself, even though Ma got him one of those wheel-chairs with the toilet right in the seat. Daddy refused to sit in it and bit her on her arm when she tried to force him.

Not long after Daddy was diagnosed, the doctors told us we should start our grieving process now. How can you grieve for a person who's not dead?

326

we both wanted to know. The doctors warned us that all of Daddy's good personality traits would vanish, one right after the other. But we didn't believe him. He'd always been spirited and spunky and smart to us, and we couldn't imagine him otherwise. It didn't take long for us to see that the doctors had been right. But we didn't know how to grieve ahead of time. We were too busy trying to keep Daddy happy.

I knew there was a chance she might already be in bed. It was almost nine o'clock. But she answered the phone right away.

'Hi, Ma. Did I wake you up?'

'Nope. I'm up. Can't sleep,' she said.

'What's wrong?'

'Well,' she said, and let out an exasperated sigh.

'Is it Daddy? Has something else happened? He's not in the hospital, is he?'

'No, he's not in the hospital,' she said, and her voice trailed off.

'Ma?'

'I'm here, dear.'

'What's wrong.'

'Well, I had to go see a lawyer.'

'For what?'

'About me and your daddy's assets.'

'Why?'

'Hold the line a minute,' she said.

I held the phone to my ear so tight I could feel the oil from my skin making it slippery.

'Robin?'

'I'm here, Ma. Why'd you have to talk to a lawyer about your and daddy's assets is what I want to know.'

'Well.' She sighed. 'He thinks I should divorce your father.'

'You should do what?' I didn't think I heard her right. What she just said sounded crazy. Maybe she was under too much pressure and didn't know what she was saying. But I know my mother. She's got more strength than any woman I've ever met. I figured it would be best to hear her out.

'I've got to put him in a facility, Robin. I can't manage any more. He can't pick up a fork, he can't get out of bed, and I have to turn him over every two hours. He's lost ten pounds in two weeks. You wouldn't recognize him if you saw him. I'm using flash cards to get him to understand me, and he doesn't know who I am. I don't know, sweetheart, I just don't know.'

'I understand, Ma. But why does the lawyer think you need to divorce Daddy? What's that supposed to do?'

'Well, let me say this. Your father worked very hard all his life to make sure we'd be comfortable when he retired and we were both up in age. So we've got money put away, but it'd all be gone if I were to use it to pay for a nursing home. Right after he was diagnosed, your father told me to swear I wouldn't use our savings to care for him if he became incapacitated. He was worried about what would happen to me more than himself. So the lawyer said that if I divorced your father, that would separate our assets and make it so that the state would pay for his care at the nursing home. All on his own, Fred wouldn't be able to afford it.'

'How much does the nursing home cost, Ma?'

'Twenty-five hundred dollars a month.'

'What? I know this may be a stupid question, but how do you feel about doing something like this?' After I said it, I thought it might make her cry, but it didn't. I wanted to find out how she was dealing with the whole idea.

'I married your father for better or for worse.'

'I know, Ma.'

'As Catholics . . . I know you're not a practicing Catholic any more, Robin, but I am. I don't think I can go through with it. Divorce is a sin.'

328

'I know, Ma. I know.'

'It would feel like I was abandoning your father. I swore before God I'd never do that.'

'I know, Ma.'

'If he knew I was even considering doing this, he'd be angry, so very angry.'

'I know, Ma.'

'From the beginning, Fred said he'd rather I pull the plug on him before letting him go to a nursing home. If he knew I'd have to use up all our savings and go bankrupt in order to do it, he'd be enraged. I know he would.'

'So what can we do, Ma?' I asked, knowing she didn't have an answer. I wish Russell – or somebody – was here, somebody that could help me think of what to do. I wish somebody was here who could put their arms around me and her, too, and make everything all right. I wish somebody would stop my daddy from dying the way he is, make all his pain go away. And I wish I was ten years old again and we were still living in Sierra Vista and everything would be like it used to be. Like it should be: normal.

'I've got to think about this a little longer, although the lawyer told me I don't have much time. If I'm going to do it, it had better be soon, so as not to look suspicious.'

'I truly wish I had some way of helping, Ma. I don't have anything that's worth anything. Which is embarrassing. At my age, I should be in a position to help you and Daddy. But I'm not.'

'You're doing the best you can, Robin, and don't worry. We'll figure something out. We'll figure something out.'

'Is he asleep now?'

'Yes, he is.'

'I wish I could take tomorrow off, but I have a meeting with these transportation people, an account I've written the proposal for, and it's a biggie – a ten-million-dollar account. I think we may get it, so I have to be there. And if we do get it, I'll probably get a raise. Let me think. Tomorrow's Thursday. I'll take off Friday and drive down there. How's that?'

'You don't have to miss work, Robin. Saturday'd be fine.'

'If I could, I'd come right now, Ma. I feel so helpless. I don't want you down there by yourself, dealing with all this. As a matter of fact, I think I'll take next week off. That's what I'll do. Longer if I need to. You'll be sick of me.'

I heard her smile through the phone.

'Do you have anything around there you can take that'll make you sleep?'

'Yes, but I can't take it. It knocks me out, and I have to be able to hear your father. Don't worry, I'll doze off pretty soon. I always do.'

'You sure?'

'I'm sure.'

'I love you, Ma. Kiss Daddy for me and tell him I love him too.'

'I will, and I love you too, baby. Good night.'

After I put the phone in its cradle, I sat there thinking about what my mother must be going through. I'm the one who feels disabled, because I can't do anything to make the situation better. I wanted to tell her Russell was back in my life, but I knew it wasn't appropriate. Plus, Daddy never liked Russell. He said Russell was too pretty, dressed entirely too flashy for a man, and a woman should never trust a man as pretty as he was. Ma couldn't accept the fact that he hadn't asked me to marry him, that we were sleeping together and living in sin, which was the main reason they never came to visit the whole time we lived together.

I was watching *Quantum Leap* when Russell walked in the door.

'Hi,' he said.

'What took you so long?' I asked, and then wished I hadn't said it like that. I didn't want to sound like Her.

'I wasn't gone that long,' he said, and went straight into the bathroom.

I got up and followed him.

'Well?'

'Well, what?' he said, taking his clothes off. He turned on the shower and stood there as if he was waiting for me to leave.

'What happened?'

'Nothing.'

'What do you mean, "nothing"?'

'We talked.'

'I assumed that much, Russell. Is she going to sign the divorce papers or what? That's a simple question. I'd appreciate a simple answer.'

'We talked about it.'

'Talked about it?'

'Yeah, that's what I went over there to do,' he said, and got in the shower and started lathering his body. 'You don't just decide to divorce somebody and then they sign on the dotted line and it's over. It's not that simple.'

It was getting so steamy and hot in there, I decided to wait until he got out before I said another word. I wanted to tell him about my daddy and the predicament my mother was in, but for some reason I didn't think he'd be all that sympathetic.

I put on a silk nightshirt and waited for him on the bed. When he came out of the bathroom, he stopped in the middle of the room, butt naked. 'Where'd you put my pajamas?'

'Why?'

'Because I wanna put 'em on, that's why.'

'What if I don't want you to?'

'Come on, Robin. I've had a rough day, a long-ass night, and I'm not in the mood for screwing tonight. Just tell me where they are, so I can go to bed. I've gotta be in Yuma at seven.'

'They're in the bottom drawer, where they always were,' I said. 'And what's with the nasty tone? I haven't done anything to you.'

'I know it,' he said, in the same tone. 'I'm just not sure about this shit.'

'What shit?'

'Me being here under these circumstances and all, when what I really need to do is be by myself so I can think straight. I can't take coming in here and being pressured about what I'm doing or not doing with my wife.'

'I'm not pressuring you, Russell. I just asked you a simple question, which I think I have a right to have answered. Don't you?'

'Look. I'm trying to work this out, OK?'

'OK,' I said. 'Now come on and get in the bed.'

He looked in the bottom drawer and put his pajamas on, then got under the covers.

'I'm going to Tucson on Friday morning. I'm staying down there all next week.'

'Is it your daddy?'

'Well, really it's my mother. She's not doing so good. Anyway, I need to be there.'

'Is there anything you want me to do while you're gone?'

'Just water the plants.'

'I can do that. Good night,' he said, and gave me a bullshit kiss on the lips with no tongue, then rolled over to his side of the bed. A few minutes later, he was snoring so loud, I couldn't even think about sleeping.

The phone rang. I knew who it was. 'Hello,' I said in a low voice.

'Robin, what's up?' Troy said.

'Nothing,' I said. 'I'm in bed. Can I call you tomorrow?'

'Yeah,' he said. 'Say something sexy to me, baby?'

'I can't.'

'Why not? You got somebody over there?'

'No.'

332

'Don't lie to me, Robin.'

'I'm not.'

'Then say something nasty.'

I hung the phone up. I figured he'd get the message.

'Who was that?' Russell said, scaring the daylights out of me.

'Savannah.'

'I suggest you tell your boyfriends not to call here after eleven,' he said, and rolled back over.

He's jealous. That's a real good sign. I felt a grin emerge on my face, and I sat there for at least another fifteen or twenty minutes. Then I had to go to the bathroom, so I got up. I closed the door behind me. Russell's clothes were still on the floor. I threw his jeans over my arm, and when I picked up the shirt I smelled something. I brought it to my nose and sniffed. The whole right side of the collar and the sleeve smelled like Eternity. I didn't want to, but before I knew it, I grabbed his briefs and turned them inside out. I looked at the crotch. There was no sign of anything unusual. I smelled the shirt again. It was Eternity, all right, and I don't wear Eternity. I threw all of his clothes back to the floor and kicked them into a corner.

I flushed the toilet, got back in bed, and looked over at this asshole. I'm so glad I didn't tell Michael that Russell was back. I can see he's not serious. He's trying to pull the same old shit. But I'm not taking it this time. I mean it.

Wait a minute! Hold it! Don't be so stupid, Robin. She was probably crying on his shoulder or something, being melodramatic. Begging him to come back. That's why his shirt smells like this. Could he help it if she got close to him? She probably did this on purpose, knowing I'd smell it when he got home. That I'd be pissed off and maybe he'd go running back to Her. Well, I wasn't falling into her trap.

I turned on my side and pressed my breasts against Russell's back, dropped my arm over his torso, then

333

wrapped my hand around his right wrist. I could feel his bones. When I gave his wrist a little squeeze, I thought he'd feel my body heat and snuggle a little closer, but instead he lifted my hand up, put it back on the sheet between us, and moved closer to the edge of the bed. He must really be tired.

Drunk

'We should drag her butt out of the house,' Robin said.

'I dare you to try it,' Savannah said, then laughed.

'You know we can't get her fat ass to go anywhere, so why don't we take a few bottles of champagne over to her house, get a birthday cake, order a pizza or something, and help her celebrate.' This was Bernadine. Miss Levelheaded these days.

'Sounds good to me,' Savannah said. She took one last sip of her coffee and put her cigarette out. They were having lunch indoors at a sidewalk café. Savannah couldn't believe that it was the end of September and 103 degrees outside. It was humid as hell, but it beat the frost that was probably on the ground in Denver right now.

'You're still not smoking?' Savannah asked Bernadine.

'Nope. Haven't had a cigarette in almost three months. And don't want one, either.'

'How'd you do it?' Savannah asked.

'I just quit.'

'This girl in my office went to an acupuncturist,' Robin said.

'Did it work?' Savannah asked.

'She hasn't had a cigarette since. She swears by it. So,' Robin said. 'Does this mean we're having a hen party?'

'Why, will it kill you?' Bernadine said.

'Go to hell, Bernie. I just asked.'

'Have you guys noticed how weird Gloria's been acting?'

'I have,' Robin interjected. 'Ever since Phillip got

those shingles. I think something's up. Whatever it is, she's not talking about it.'

'Let's go in one car,' Bernadine said.

'Yeah, let's go in your BMW!'

'Fuck you, Robin,' Bernadine said, and started laughing.

'Are we splitting this check or what?' Robin asked.

'No, we should make you pay it,' Savannah said.

Robin looked at the bill. 'Ten apiece.'

Bernadine and Savannah put their money on the table. Robin picked it up, put it in her wallet, and dropped her company's American Express card on the table. 'I'm broke,' she said. After the waiter took care of it, they all got up and walked out into the hot sun.

'Wait!' Robin yelled at Savannah and Bernadine, who'd gone on ahead of her. 'What about birthday presents?'

'Oh, shit,' Bernadine said. 'I forgot all about that. Yeah. Let's each get her something. And, Robin, please wrap it.'

'Go to hell, Bernie,' she said. 'How old is she gonna be?'

'Thirty-eight,' Savannah said. She and Bernadine turned past a building into the parking lot.

Robin stepped off the curb and got into her car. She removed the window shade and turned the radio on. Paula Abdul was singing. I don't care what Savannah thinks, she thought. This girl *can* sing.

They had begged Gloria not to be at work, the grocery store, the mall, or any other place except home by eight o'clock. She knew they had something up their sleeve. Gloria could use a little pick-me-up. She'd been depressed ever since Phillip got sick. She still didn't have a replacement for Desiree, and yesterday Cindy had told her she was accepted at court-reporting school. She'd be going full time, starting in January. Gloria was trying to deal with all this. Trying to figure out how she'd get three replacements. She and Joseph wouldn't be able to run the shop by themselves for too long. She didn't know if and when Phillip was coming back. Nor did she want to talk about this with her girlfriends. It was her problem, not theirs.

Her pressure was up too: 190/140. Almost stroke level. She'd gone to the doctor three days before, and Gloria swore up and down she felt fine. The doctor told her there weren't usually any symptoms. He said exactly what Gloria anticipated he'd say: that she needed to lose some weight, needed to stop eating salt and foods high in sodium, and to avoid cholesterol altogether.

Tarik said he didn't want to be in a house full of old women. He asked if he could go to the arcade with Bryan. 'Midnight,' Gloria told him, 'and not a minute later.' He promised he'd be back before then and kissed her on the cheek.

This morning he had knocked on her bedroom door. She told him to come in, since she was under the covers. 'Happy birthday, Ma,' he said, and handed her a package she could tell somebody else had wrapped. She was glad he remembered. She opened the package and he'd done one of those numbers where there were four boxes, one inside the other, until she finally got to the smallest one. In it was a pair of mother-of-pearl earrings shaped like birds. They were pretty. Gloria never wore this kind of jewelry, but she slipped them in her ears and told Tarik she'd always wanted some like these.

Now she was waiting for her girlfriends to show up. They'd told her 'not to do a thing.' Leave everything to them. Gloria was trying, but she couldn't sit still and do nothing for ten minutes, let alone a half hour, so she started reorganizing bottles of cologne on her dresser. She moved the Paris in front of the Ysatis. When she noticed a bottle of Anaïs Anaïs was almost empty, she threw it in the trash. She had dusting powders galore, because she sweated so bad. She decided to

337

take them into her bathroom, then changed her mind and brought it all back and put them where they originally were. 'This is ridiculous,' she said, and went down to the living room.

She heard a car pull up, and she heard the music. Sometimes Gloria couldn't believe her girlfriends were all around the same age as she was. She felt much older than they were – especially Robin. Maybe because she was the only one with a teenager. Sometimes they acted like they were still in their twenties. She didn't see anything wrong with having so much energy, and Gloria often wished she had their spirit. But that was something you either had or didn't have. Gloria knew she didn't have much. She opened the front door and walked outside to meet them.

'*Happy birthday!*' they yelled in unison.

'Thank you, thank you, thank you,' Gloria said.

They were pulling bags out of the trunk. Marvin was watering his grass. He waved from across the street.

'Who's that?' Robin asked.

'That's my neighbor. Marvin.'

'Watch out!' Robin said.

Gloria spotted a white box that she knew had to be a cake. This was so thoughtful of them, she thought, as they led the way inside. She followed them but first checked to see if Marvin was still there. He was. Gloria waved again.

'Where's the party?' Robin asked, once they got inside.

'Where's the music?' Savannah asked.

'Let's get this party moving,' Bernadine said.

Savannah made another trip to the car, came back with three presents and another grocery bag. She dropped the bag on the coffee table, pulled out birthday hats, little horns, and party favors. Gloria was tickled.

'Well, what are you waiting on, Gloria? Go get us some glasses,' Robin said.

Savannah was fumbling with Gloria's stereo. She'd brought her latest CDs, and the girl only had a tape

338

deck. 'You mean to tell me you own your own hair salon and you're too cheap to break down and buy a CD player?'

'I've got tapes that sound just as good as a CD. Why should I waste my money?' Gloria yelled from the kitchen.

'Gloria, this is the nineties, girl. Get with it. Let me see what kind of tired music you have down here.'

Savannah and Robin both got on their knees and started going through one old tape after another. 'Wait a minute,' Robin said. 'Look at these. Real albums! When was the last time you bought some music?'

Gloria came back in with four wineglasses. 'I don't know. Tarik buys most of the music. He keeps it in his room. But I don't touch his stuff.'

'Well,' Robin said, 'I haven't made Tarik any promises.'

'Every tape the boy has is rap or hip hop. I have to listen to that shit enough as it is, so I'd appreciate a break from it tonight. Especially since it's my birthday!' she said.

'Now you're getting some life into your big ass,' Bernadine said.

'We started to get one of those male strippers,' Savannah said.

'Why didn't you?' Gloria said.

'Because to tell the truth, we'da probably raped his ass, considering our condition.'

'Your condition couldn't possibly be as bad as mine,' Gloria said.

'I think my pussy's dead,' Bernadine said.

'What happened to Vincent?' Gloria asked.

'Who's Vincent?' Robin asked.

'Nobody,' Bernadine said. 'I had to get rid of him. He turned out to be a big baby.'

'Well, mine is mad at me. Once again, I broke down and gave Kenneth some. For the last time, I swear to God,' Savannah said, looking at Bernadine. Bernadine eyed her back, as if to say, 'So what.'

'Well, mine is in good working condition,' Robin said. 'I try to get a tune-up at least once a week.'

'From who?' Gloria asked. 'Or should we take a wild guess?'

'Not from Russell. He's out of my life. For good.'

'Bullshit,' Bernadine said. 'Anyway, let's pour some of this champagne and toast to Gloria's thirty-eighth birthday.'

Savannah tried to pop the cork.

'Oh, oh, ladies! You won't believe this. Guess what I found over here?' Robin said.

'What?' Savannah asked.

'Rick James!'

'Then put the shit on,' Bernadine said.

'And she's got Teddy Pendergrass, no less, and Aretha and Gladys and The Temptations! Gloria, you've got all the oldies over here, girl!'

'Put Rick on first, with his nasty ass,' Savannah said.

'I would love to have given him some,' Robin said.

'That nasty motherfucker!' Bernadine said. 'Be serious.'

'I am serious. He could've got some of this. I swear. You check out those lips? And that little tight ass of his and that bulge in his pants? Now tell me the truth. If Rick James came over to your house and offered to do it to you, you'd turn him down?'

'Yes.'

'That's bullshit.'

'I went out with a musician once,' Savannah said. 'Never again.'

'Why?'

'They're whores.'

'What man isn't?' Robin said.

'All men are not whores, Robin. But musicians can get women in every city they play in. We're like pit stops.'

'That's why God invented condoms,' Bernadine said. 'No man, and no amount of dick is worth dying over.'

As quiet as is kept, Robin hadn't exactly been using them as often as she should've. At least not with Russell. And if she got pregnant, she'd already decided to keep it.

'Toast!' Bernadine said, after she'd poured all four glasses.

'Wait,' Savannah said. 'Where's the hats and shit?' She dumped the bagful of birthday paraphernalia on to the floor, and everybody grabbed something and put on a hat. 'OK, OK,' she said. 'I've got a good one. Gloria, I just want you to know that you're the best hairdresser in this town and I'm glad I met you and I hope turning thirty-eight is your best year yet!'

'That was tired,' Robin said, and stood up. 'I hope you find true love and get some that's so good it'll make up for all the years you didn't! Now.'

'Happy birthday, girlfriend,' Bernadine said. 'Here's to finding genuine happiness and peace of mind.'

'Thank you,' Gloria said, and they all drank up.

Bernadine poured everybody another round. 'I love this shit,' she said. 'Champagne makes me silly as hell.'

'You're already silly as hell,' Robin said.

'I'd rather be silly than dizzy,' she said.

'Go to hell,' Robin said.

'All right, let's not start this shit,' Savannah said. 'Turn the music up. Where's the cake?'

'In the kitchen,' Gloria said. 'I'll go get it.'

'You ready to blow out the candles already?'

'No, I can wait,' she said.

'Let's order the pizza. Domino's guarantees it'll be here in thirty minutes.'

'Please no pepperoni for me,' Savannah said.

'I can't eat it without pepperoni,' Robin said.

'I don't care,' Gloria said.

'Then let's get two. One with and one without.'

'Minnie Ripperton *and* Smokey Robinson!' Robin yelled.

'Put them aside,' Savannah said. She sat down on the

floor next to Robin. They were looking through about a million albums, putting the best ones to the side.

'Stevie and Roberta, girls. Wait! The Emotions! We're going back in time tonight, sistahs. Hey. Let's go *all* the way!'

'I don't want to hear *nothing* that'll make me cry,' Bernadine said.

'I do,' Robin said, and started laughing.

'I don't, either,' Savannah said.

'Does this turntable work?' Robin asked.

'Of course it works,' Gloria said, and downed her entire glass of champagne.

'OK,' Robin said. 'Check this out. Tell me who it reminds you of, and don't lie.'

The three of them sat there frozen in place, their ears geared up, all set to recognize the first few chords of the song. That's all it ever took.

'Oh, no!' Savannah yelled, and fell on the floor.

'Shit,' Bernadine said.

Robin had put on Teddy Pendergrass, singing 'Turn Off the Lights.'

'Why'd you have to play that shit?' Savannah said, and took her cigarettes out of her purse and lit one.

'Go ahead. Cry, girlfriend! Let it out!' Robin yelled.

'Don't you have any M.C. Hammer, or Bobby Brown?' Bernadine asked.

Gloria was laughing, then got a sad look on her face as she poured herself another glass of champagne. She got up and refilled everybody else's glass. 'I don't have anybody to remember for that song.'

'Girl, please,' Robin said. 'I was in love with this creep. That seems to be a pattern I have, now that I think about it. Falling in love with creeps. But anyway, his name was . . . Damn, what was his name?'

'I was in love with John for real back then,' Bernadine said, looking all starry-eyed and swaying her head to the beat of the music.

'I was going out with this guy named Al, and Lord, could he do the wild thing. That's all we did was fucked, but it was worth it! He had the biggest dick in the universe. I was strung out on the shit too. I don't even want to think about it. Turn out the lights!' Savannah yelled. She started snapping her fingers and closed her eyes. But she wasn't thinking about Al at all. She was thinking about Kenneth. 'Hey,' she said, 'let me play something.' Savannah put on another album. 'This should do it to you ladies!'

The doorbell rang and scared everybody half to death. 'It's the pizza,' Gloria said. She hunched up her shoulders and started giggling. She thought the shit was funny. 'Who's got the money? I'm not paying for this birthday pizza. Church up, ladies.'

'Did she just say "church up"?' Bernadine asked. 'Gloria, you've got a teenaged son; get your language together, girl. Nobody says that tired shit any more!' Bernadine started laughing, stopped long enough to guzzle down her champagne, then reached in her purse and got out two twenties. 'I feel like it's my birthday!'

'OK! Listen to this!' Savannah howled. She'd put on 'One Hundred Ways' by James Ingram. But now even she thought maybe it was a bad move. It wasn't hard to place that song. She was living with Raymond. Damn. She was trying to remember what made them break up. Her mind was too cloudy, so she poured herself another glass of champagne.

'Anybody ready for pizza?' Bernadine asked.

Savannah and Robin shook their heads no. They were too into the music. Gloria didn't bother to answer but took the boxes into the kitchen, where she immediately opened one, looked at the pizza, and said out loud, 'No.' She put them both in the oven, turned it on warm, then started popping her fingers and rejoined her friends.

'You know what I want?' Savannah was saying.

'No. What do you want?' Robin asked.

'I want to feel like this goddamn record. I want a man to find a hundred ways to love me.'

343

'Keep dreaming,' Bernadine said.

'I don't get it,' Savannah said.

'Don't get what?' Robin said.

'Why can't we ever feel like the record? Like these: "Just once, let me be your angel."' She was flipping through them, forming a giant pile. '"Be the best of my love," and oh shit, this! "Can't hide love" by Earth, Wind and fucking Fire!'

'*Stop!*' Bernadine said.

'Fuck you! "When doves cry" by that weird-ass Prince, but it worked, right? *Ow!* "The first time ever I saw your goddamn face" by Roberta Flack! And my man Al Green, "Let's stay together." I want to roll all these songs up and feel like this for the next thirty years. Is that asking for too much? If it is, why do they make these damn songs to make you think and believe and dream that you *can* feel like this? Huh? Somebody had to have gone through this shit in order to write it and sing about it, don't you think?'

'You're going off, Savannah,' Bernadine said.

'I am not. I'm a little drunk, and I'm glad to be drunk,' she said. 'But let me ask you sistahs something. And tell me if I'm crazy. What is it we all have in common?'

'We're black and female,' Gloria said, and started with the giggling again.

'Funny Fanny. I'm serious.'

'Don't go getting all deep on us,' Bernadine said.

'I'm not getting deep. Yes I am. Maybe that's what's wrong with us: we're not deep enough. We need to get deeper.' Then she shook her head back and forth as if she was trying to rattle her brains. 'I'm getting off-track. What was I saying?'

'Something about what we have in common,' Robin said.

'Yeah. Anyway, you know what we have in common? And it's a damn shame?'

Everybody waited for this revelation.

'None of us have a man.'

'I don't want one, either,' Bernadine said.

'So what?' Gloria said. 'Men ain't everything. When are you gonna realize that? I'm having a good time sitting here acting silly with you guys, and do you think if any of us had a man we'd be here doing this?'

'That's precisely my point,' Savannah said. 'If. But we don't. And let me say this up front. If I had a man and it was your birthday and you were going to be over here by yourself all lonely and shit and Robin and Bernie called me up to come over here to help you celebrate, I'd still be here, girl. So don't ever think a man would have that much power over me that I'd stop caring about my friends. And that's the truth, Ruth. Did you see that movie?'

'Do the Right Thing?' Gloria asked.

'Yeah.'

'No, I didn't see that one yet.'

'I saw it twice,' Robin said. 'Spike Lee is serious.'

'I think he's sexy,' Savannah said. 'Anyway, we're getting all off on another subject here.'

'Gloria, your turn to play a record,' Bernadine said.

'There's nothing in particular I want to hear.'

'Well, that makes a statement too,' Bernadine said, and dropped her head. 'You know what? I'm mad.' She was slurring, but nobody even noticed.

'About what?' Robin asked.

'About every goddamn thing. I gave that bastard eleven of the best years of my goddamn life, and he leaves me for a trifling scabby-ass white bitch! And now here I am over the hill and shit—'

'You're only thirty-six, damn, and don't ever let me hear you say some simple shit like that,' Savannah said. 'You – hell, we all look better than some of these chicks out here in their twenties. Now tell me I'm lying. And I know I'm not a ten.'

'You are a ten, bitch, and you know it. Your false modesty kills me,' Bernadine said.

'Well, I'm a six,' Robin interjected.

'We're all tens,' Bernadine said, laughing. 'It just depends on who's judging us. Right?'

'Well, thank you, sister,' Savannah said, and lit a cigarette. 'Anyway, as soon as I give up these cigarettes, it'll take a few years off me. Look at Gloria. Her ass is as big as a house, and she's still pretty. I just wish I could put your behind on a diet and stop you from eating all them hog maws and shit. Fifty less pounds, and your whole life would change.'

'That's bullshit,' Robin said. 'I don't need to lose any weight. What's *my* problem?'

'Don't let me get started,' Bernadine said.

'Go to hell,' Robin said. 'Am I not a good catch or what?'

'We're all good catches,' Bernadine said.

'Why are we all such good goddamn catches?' Savannah asked, leaning forward on her elbows and motioning for the other bottle of champagne.

'Because we've got good hearts and we're good lays and we're nice people. Isn't that enough?' Bernadine said.

'Well, since you know so damn much, why are we having such a hard-ass time meeting Mr Wonderful?' Robin asked.

Nobody had the answer to that one.

Bernadine gathered her thoughts and spoke as carefully as she possibly could. 'Because you want one too bad. That's why.'

'What's wrong with that?' Robin asked.

'Look, I've got a whole lot of other things on my mind besides men,' Bernadine muttered.

'We know that,' Robin said. 'I do too. Shit, my daddy's dying.'

'My mama's rent went up,' Savannah said. 'And thanks to President Bush, my younger brother's over in the fucking Persian Gulf, waiting to find out if he's going to be in a goddamn war. I'm getting down to the wire on the cash level. And my mama depends on me. If you want to know the truth, I hate my

346

job,' Savannah said. 'So men *aren't* the only thing on *my* mind either. It just seems that way because we talk about 'em all the time.'

Robin took another sip of her champagne and let her eyes roll up in her head as if she was pondering over something. Then it was as if a light bulb went on in her head. 'We're all stupid.'

'Speak for yourself,' Bernadine said.

'I'm serious. The ones that are good for us we find dull and boring, like Michael, for instance, and then we pick the assholes, like Russell, the ones who won't cooperate, the ones who offer us the most challenge and get our blood flowing and shit. Those are the motherfuckers we fall in love with.'

'Thank you, Mrs Nietzsche,' Savannah said. 'But I don't think I fall into that category personally. I just haven't met the kind of man I need.'

'Which is what?' Robin asked.

'Well, I'll put it this way. I fell in love with Kenneth because he was his own man. He was smart and witty and vital, and I knew one day he was going to make a difference in people's lives. He was honest and charming and sexy, and he respected me. Wasn't intimidated by me in the least. Shit, that was enough.'

'So what happened?' Robin asked.

'Don't ask.'

'I think it's a lot of stupid men out here too,' Gloria said. This shocked everybody.

'Speak, Dr Ruth, speak!' Bernadine said.

'I'm serious. A lot of them *are* stupid. They don't know what they want and don't know how to treat a woman.'

'Can I get a witness?' Savannah said.

'You got a point,' Bernadine said. 'That asshole I was married to sure didn't. Speaking of assholes, I should call him.' She got up and went to the phone.

'*Are you crazy, girl!*' Savannah said, and snatched it away from her. 'You don't have anything to say to him tonight that can't wait until you're sober.'

'Well, let's call the bitch!' she said.

'Kathleen?' Gloria asked.

'Yeah.'

'Hand me the phone,' Robin said. 'I'll call the whore.'

Savannah handed the phone to Robin, and Bernadine – to everybody's surprise – knew her number by heart.

Robin's heart was pounding with excitement. This was so much fun. And she thought it was going to be a regular old hen party! This was the lick! When she heard a Shirley Temple voice answer, she hadn't thought about what she'd say, so she hung up.

'What happened?' Bernadine asked. 'Give me the damn phone.'

'No, give me the phone,' Savannah said, and took it. 'What's the number again?' Bernadine rattled it off. Savannah dialed, and the woman answered on the first ring. But Savannah hung up.

'What happened?' Bernadine said.

'This is childish and stupid.'

'Thank you,' Gloria said.

'Well, fuck it!' Bernadine said. 'Put some more music on! It's a party over here!'

'Where's the pizza?' Savannah asked.

Gloria got up to take the two pizzas out of the oven. 'I need some help!' she yelled. Bernadine came into the kitchen. 'Get some plates from up there,' Gloria said, pointing with her head, 'and the hot sauce.'

'Hot sauce? On pizza?'

'You're right. Never mind.'

Gloria and Bernadine walked back into the living room. Now Savannah and Robin were playing Isaac Hayes' 'By the Time I Get to Phoenix.'

'Well, we're already here, Isaac,' Gloria said, giggling.

'Hey!' Savannah said. 'If you were an instrument, which one would you be? Come on. Robin?'

Robin let her eyes roll up inside her head. This little

quirk was beginning to get on Savannah's nerves. 'A soprano saxophone.'

'Why?'

'I don't know right now. Go to the next person.'

'Bernadine?'

'An upright bass.'

'Why?'

'Because they're always in the background, but they carry the whole beat.'

'What about you, Gloria?'

'A flute.'

'And?'

'Because it's pretty and soft.'

'I'd be a harp,' Savannah said. 'For the same reasons Gloria wants to be a flute.'

'Now that we've got that over with, let's eat the pizza, shall we?' Bernadine said. Everybody picked up a slice.

'Is there some more champagne in the refrigerator?' Robin asked.

'Yep. Go get it,' Savannah said.

'And then let's sing "Happy Birthday."'

'You don't have to sing "Happy Birthday,"' Gloria said.

Everybody looked at her as if she was crazy.

'Seriously. This is nice. Just like this.'

'And bring the cake too, girl,' Bernadine said, and reached inside her purse for the little package of candles. Robin came back with the bottle and the box, which she set on the coffee table. Bernadine put candles on the cake. 'Can we dim these lights?' she asked.

'Wait!' Savannah said. 'I've got a song already picked out.'

'We're getting ready to sing "Happy Birthday," Savannah,' Bernadine said.

'I know, but let's be unorthodox here. Tradition can be boring. Break the rules. Here we go,' she said. She put the record on, and Bernadine lit the candles.

It was Stevie Wonder's birthday song to Dr Martin Luther King. All four of them started singing along with Stevie, clapping, then they all stood up and started dancing. When the song was over, the three women screamed 'Happy birthday' at the top of their lungs. Gloria had tears in her eyes. It took two tries before she blew out all the candles.

'Thank you, you guys,' she said.

'Time for the presents,' Robin said, and lifted the packages off the chair. 'Before you say it, we know we didn't have to, but we did. So shut up and open 'em.'

Gloria was laughing again. She picked up one and opened it. Her mouth dropped open. Savannah had given her a sexy orange nightgown.'

'I hope it fits,' she said. 'If you were my size, I could've given you a whole drawerful of this shit. I damn near own Victoria's Secret.'

'Don't tell me you don't wear it?' Bernadine said.

'Some of it, but not the real drop-dead shit. I'm waiting for a reason.'

'Girl, you better wear that shit. You can't wait on a man, or you'll never get a chance to wear it. Wear it for yourself! I sleep in silk nightly,' Bernadine said.

'Yeah, well, you've got it like that,' Robin said. 'Open mine.'

Her box was small. Gloria knew it was some kind of jewelry. She wanted to burst into laughter when she saw the same earrings Tarik had given her. Robin obviously didn't know her very well, either, but she pretended she loved them. Robin looked pleased. Then Gloria opened Bernadine's box. She knew it was going to be something expensive. It was one of those big black Coach purses she loved. 'Thank you you guys for being so good to me. Really.'

'I hope the party's not over *now*,' Robin said. 'I'm just getting worked up here.'

'Hey, why don't you all spend the night?' Gloria said. 'As a matter of fact, I don't think any of you should be driving, with all this champagne in your system.'

'She's right,' Robin said. 'So let's get sloppy drunk!'

'Where's my glass?' Savannah asked.

Robin gave everybody a refill. For the next hour, they played old records and got so drunk they couldn't laugh anymore. By the time Robin managed to get Smokey Robinson's 'Tracks of My Tears' on, they all had their heads down. 'I told you I didn't want to cry,' Savannah said. 'I'm so sick of this shit, I don't know what to do. Can somebody tell me what we're doing wrong?'

'What are you talking about now?' Bernadine asked.

'I want to know why I'm thirty-six years old and still single. This shit is not right. What ever happened to the good old days?'

'What good old days?' Gloria wanted to know.

'You know. When a man saw you in a crowd, smiled at you, flirted, and came over and talked to you. Not one has asked me for my phone number since I've been here. Why not? There's nothing wrong with me. Shit, I'm smart, I'm attractive, I'm educated, and my pussy's good, if I do say so myself. What happened to all the aggressive men? The ones that aren't scared to talk to you? Where the fuck are they hiding?'

'They're not hiding. They're just scared to make a damn commitment,' Robin said.

'They're with white women,' Bernadine said.

'Or gay,' Gloria said.

'Or married,' Savannah said. 'But you know what? They're not all with white girls, they're not all homosexuals, they're not all married, either. When you get right down to it, we're talking five, maybe ten per cent. What about the rest?'

'They're ugly.'

'Stupid.'

'In prison.'

'Unemployed.'

'Crackheads.'

'Short.'

351

'Liars.'

'Unreliable.'

'Irresponsible.'

'Too possessive.'

'Dogs.'

'Shallow.'

'Boring.'

'Stuck in the sixties.'

'Arrogant.'

'Childish.'

'Wimps.'

'Too goddamn old and set in their ways.'

'Can't fuck.'

'Stop!' Savannah said.

'Well, shit, you asked,' Robin said.

Savannah reached inside her purse in slow motion. She was trying to find some Kleenex, because something was in her eye. She wasn't successful. Robin handed her a handkerchief. 'Here, girl,' she said.

'And stop crying,' Bernadine said. 'This is too pathetic.'

'I'm not crying. Something's in my damn eye. Shit, I can't help it if I'm sick of *being* by myself, *doing* everything by myself, and I don't know what to . . . Oh oh,' she said, and struggled to get up.

'Get her to the bathroom,' Gloria said. All of them helped Savannah up, dragged her to the bathroom, and as soon as she got inside the door, she threw up all over the floor.

'That champagne'll do it every time,' Robin said. 'Who's gonna clean this mess up?'

'I will,' Gloria said.

'Not on your birthday,' Bernadine grumbled. 'Get me some old rags, and lay her down on the couch.'

Bernadine cleaned the floor on her hands and knees. By the time she finished, she couldn't get up, let alone stand, so she crawled back into the living room. Savannah had long since passed out on the couch. Gloria went to the laundry room to empty the pail.

She'd planned to get Savannah a blanket, but she was moving so slow by the time she dropped the pail in the utility sink, she had to stand there for a few minutes to get her bearings. She forgot what she was getting ready to do next.

Robin and Bernadine heard a key in the front door. A burglar with his own key. Now, that was a good one, Bernadine thought, and wanted to laugh, but she'd lost the ability. Robin's eyes were half closed, but she could tell it was Tarik, who was shocked to see his mother's friends sprawled out on the living room floor and one – unconscious – hanging over the edge of the couch. The room was a total disaster. Albums and tapes were everywhere. At least five empty bottles of champagne were on the coffee table, as well as plates of dried-up, half-eaten slices of pizza. 'Hi,' he said, with some reservations.

'Hi, Tarik,' Robin and Bernadine mumbled.

'You're getting taller by the day,' Bernadine whispered, and let her head drop.

Tarik could see they were all toasted. 'So you guys did it up, I see.'

'You only turn thirty-eight once,' Robin muttered.

He looked at the cake. It hadn't been cut. 'Where's my mother?'

Bernadine and Robin looked at each other. 'Isn't she in this room with us?' Bernadine said.

Tarik realized this was a waste of time. 'Well, good night,' he said, and on his way toward the stairs, he saw his mother feeling her way through the kitchen. Tarik started laughing. He could see she was drunk too. He tried to wipe the smirk off his face, but Gloria didn't even see him. 'Yo, Ma. You all right?' he said.

Gloria waved her hand toward the floor and said, 'Un hun.'

Tarik ran on upstairs. Gloria finally remembered what she was supposed to do. Once she found the linen closet, she fell inside it and grabbed some blankets. When she got back to the living room, somebody had dimmed the lights – at least they looked dim. Robin and Bernadine were on the floor, dead to the world. Gloria dropped a few folded blankets on top of her friends and headed for the stairs. She stopped at the foot and looked up. At first it looked like an escalator, but then the steps stopped moving. She blinked, grabbed hold of the banister, and looked up again. Not tonight, she thought, and found herself an empty spot near the front door. She made a pillow out of a stack of albums, pulled her dress up over her shoulders like a blanket, and went to sleep. Gloria didn't feel the cold tile against her legs and thighs or the spider crawling over her right foot. She didn't hear Smokey Robinson, either, still singing his heart out.

Monsoon

Bernadine was watching *Married with Children* when she heard John's Porsche pull up. As usual, he was right on time. He still wouldn't come into the house, which was fine with her. He also hadn't said a word about the For Sale sign. The house had been on the market for two months now, and not a single realtor had been by to show it.

A gust of wind blew in the front door right after Onika, who was wearing a dress Bernadine had never seen before. 'Guess what, Mama? Daddy and Kathleen got married!'

John junior walked in, carrying both of their backpacks, and closed the door. Bernadine kept pressing the button on the remote to turn down the volume on the TV. 'What did you say?' But she had heard her daughter loud and clear. She tossed the remote on the coffee table, then watched it slide to the edge, where half of it hung over. She waited for it to fall off. But it didn't.

'Kathleen and Daddy got married!' Onika yelled again, as if she'd rehearsed it.

'So when did all this happen?'

'Today,' John junior said.

'Today? And where were you guys?'

'We were right there,' he said. 'It was totally boring.'

'When he picked you guys up on Friday, he didn't say anything about getting *married* this weekend, and if he had, I would've at least packed something dressy for you to wear.'

'He didn't even tell us until yesterday,' John junior said.

'And when'd you get that dress?' she asked Onika.

Of course she knew John had bought it, but she was trying to change the subject. The scroungy bastard. The only reason he did it this way was to fuck with her, to keep rocking her world. But it wasn't going to work.

'Kathleen taked us shopping yesterday. She pickted this one out. Isn't it pretty, Mama?'

Bernadine wanted to get the scissors and cut every single stitch of that dress off her daughter. 'It's very nice,' she said. 'And, Onika, you know how to talk. It's took, not taked, and picked, not pickted.'

'She buyed me three dresses, but Daddy told me to leave them at their new house.'

What new house? Bernadine wanted to ask.

'She bought me Megaman Two and Rescue Rangers,' John junior said.

Bernadine wanted to say: You know whose money she's spending, don't you? From the beginning, she had promised herself never to say anything nasty about Kathleen or their daddy in front of the kids. So far she'd kept her promise, but it was getting harder and harder. 'Well, that was nice of her to be so generous,' Bernadine said, and sat down on the couch. A cigarette would be perfect about now, she thought. 'What does their new house look like?'

'It's big. Way bigger than ours,' Onika said.

'I like our house better,' John junior said.

'So was it a nice wedding?'

'I told you, it was boring,' John junior said.

'I was the flower girl,' Onika said.

'Where was it?'

'I don't know what you call it, but it wasn't a church,' he said.

'How many people were there?'

'Let me think,' he said, and started going over in his head how many people had been in the room. 'Six, I think. Seven, if you count the minister.'

Onika threw in this: 'Daddy said now Kathleen can spend more time with us too.'

'Oh, he did, did he?'

'Yep. So now we have two mamas.'

'No we don't,' John junior said.

'We do too!' she screamed.

'We don't!' he yelled.

'And guess what else, Mama?'

'Why don't you shut up!' he said. But Onika refused to pay him any attention. She liked the idea of being the bearer of good news, which was why she had dashed out of the car to beat John junior to the house.

'Kathleen's having a baby!' she said. 'And we're gonna have a brand-new baby sister or brother in seven months!'

'I'm really glad to hear all this,' Bernadine said, and lunged up from the couch. 'This is the best goddamn news I've had all day. It's just great! And I hope your sorry-ass daddy is happy with that white whore!' Her voice cracked, and her hands were trembling. She stormed out of the room, slamming her bedroom door behind her. Bernadine wished she had a Xanax in the house. No she didn't, she thought, after she fell across the bed. She lay there, listening to the wind rattling the windows, but the kids were talking so loud, she could hear them too.

'See what you did, you little bitch!' John junior said. 'You made her cry.'

'I did not!'

'You did too!'

'I did not!'

Bernadine heard John junior slap Onika. 'That's for having such a big mouth! You think she's supposed to be happy knowing that white lady is having a baby with our daddy?' She didn't hear Onika respond. She must be in shock, Bernadine thought, and started laughing. Served her ass right. She needed to be slapped. Onika ran her damn mouth too much sometimes. Said the first thing that came to her mind. And he called her a bitch! Now Bernadine was grinning. It was good to know her son was on her side.

'If you go near her room,' Bernadine heard him say, 'I'll slap you again, only harder.'

Bernadine got up, cracked the door, and peeked through it.

John junior was pacing around the couch as if he had a lot on his mind. 'Now sit your little ass down on this couch, and say, "I talk too much," five hundred times. And don't even think about getting up until I tell you to!'

Onika started to oblige.

Bernadine covered her mouth to stop from laughing out loud. She had closed the door before Onika made it to fifty-six.

It was raining. Bernadine was lying in bed under crisp white sheets and a forest-green comforter. The French doors to the patio were open. A cool breeze rushed in through the screens. It was falling so hard, and the raindrops were so big, it sounded as if somebody was pounding a million nails into the skylight in her bathroom. She could see the water in the pool splattering. This was unusual weather for October. She was even more surprised when she heard thunder. The monsoon season had long since passed. When she looked out the window, she saw lavender-and-yellow lightning bolt across the Superstition Mountains. The 'wash' behind the house, which was usually a big dry gully, was now a gushing river. Her flower beds were drenched. The patio was flooded.

She remembered Onika once saying that when it rained like this, it was really God crying. Today it made sense to her. The ceiling fan spun slowly. The lamp was on, but a gray haze filled the room. Bernadine had a book in her lap, a book she hadn't opened. Two fat pillows lay beside her. She'd been trying not to think about John and Kathleen all week long. The idea that he was married to somebody else bothered her. It wasn't that she still loved him. Because she didn't. It wasn't that she was jealous. She wasn't. It was just . . . it was just that he'd always been *her* husband and now he was somebody else's. And here she was, on a rainy day, all by herself. Bernadine wished somebody were here to console her.

She thought about James. James James James. Whenever she felt lonely, she thought about James, and that night. Whenever she felt disenchanted, she thought about James. And that night. Whenever she felt ugly and old, she thought about James. And that night. And whenever she needed to remind herself how good a man could make her feel, she thought about James and that night.

Bernadine closed her eyes. She let her mind drift backward until she could smell his cologne, feel his chest against her back, feel the heat from his hand, hear his laughter and every word he'd said. Her pillow became his shoulders, his chest, the side of his neck, his mouth. She dug her face so deeply into it that the feathers flattened.

She was almost ready to call out his name, when she heard a little knock on her door. Bernadine sat up, ran her hands across her face, blinked extra hard, and said, 'Come in.'

Onika was hiding something behind her back. 'What you got back there?'

'Guess?' Onika said, grinning. Her hair was sticking out like black wire, making her face look too small for her head.

'I can't even begin to guess,' Bernadine said.

'You have to try, Mama. Please?'

'OK, OK. The newspaper?'

'Nope.'

'My purse?'

'Nope.'

'A picture you made me?'

'Nope.'

'What color is it?'

Onika looked up toward the ceiling. 'Some are white and some are brown.'

'Is it candy?'

'Nope.'

'I give up. Just tell Mama what it is, please?'

'It's the mail!' she said, and flung her arms around the front of her body, causing six or seven envelopes to fly all over the floor. Onika said she was sorry and started picking them up. Then she handed them to Bernadine. It was easy to tell which ones were bills. She hurled those to the floor. One was a letter. Addressed to her. From the Ritz-Carlton. Why would they be writing me? she wondered. Bernadine opened it as fast as she could. Another envelope was inside. The letter wasn't from the hotel. It was from James. The mind *is* a powerful thing, she thought.

'Mama, is "freak" a bad word?' Onika asked.

Dear Bernadine: I guess you don't like to write or call, huh? I don't want to think you threw my business card away, and since your number's unlisted, I couldn't call, and you never told me where you worked. (I still have your card. But what was I supposed to do with it? And I *had* to change my number, because that asshole Herbert wouldn't stop bugging me.)

'No,' Bernadine said. ' "Freak" is not a bad word.'

I've waited as long as I could to contact you, and since you never gave me your address or anything, it took me the longest time to think about trying the hotel. I know you probably thought that night was just something frivolous, but like I told you before I left, it meant more to me than that. Much more.

'Elizabeth said it was a bad word.'

'It's not a nice word, but it's not a bad word.'

'Can I say it?'

Paragraph. *I buried my wife back in August, and for her sake, I'm glad she's not suffering any more. I've also sold the house, and just about everything in it. I don't need all the memories, and definitely don't need the space.*

'No, you can't say it.'

'Why not?'

'Because it's not a nice word.'

I want to see you again, Bernadine, and not for another one-nighter, either. If there's any truth to what's known as a 'soul mate,' then you're as close to it as I've ever come. I've tried to forget you, believe me, I've tried. But I can't. That alone tells me something. I'm not interested in playing games, or starting something I can't finish. I play for keeps, and I'm not some dude just out to have a good time. (Oh, Lord. He wants to see me again!)

'What does it mean?'

'What does what mean?' Bernadine asked.

'Freak.'

'It means weird.'

Paragraph. *I know you're thinking that I'm probably grieving and feeling sorry for myself, and there may be some truth to that. But I knew I was in love with you long before we ever turned the key to that hotel room. I'm not asking you to make me any promises or any kind of commitment. All I'm asking is if you'd be willing to explore this relationship further.* (Explore? I like that word. And love. That one sounds good too. Shit. The man *was* serious.)

'You let me say "weird," so why can't I say "freak," Mama?'

'Because I said so, that's why.'

Paragraph. *I'll be waiting to hear from you. Here's my number again, just in case. I hope you and your kids are doing fine. I really hope I get the chance to meet them at some point. Love, James. P.S. If there's anything you need, call me first.*

'Damn,' she said out loud, and took a deep breath.

'You just said a bad word, Mama.'

'I'm sorry.'

'Mama, what are you reading?'

'A letter.'

'From who?'

'A friend.'

'Can I try to read it?'

'No.'

'Why not?'

'Because it's a letter to me, that's why.'

'Were you taking another nap, Mama?'

'Yes, I was.'

'Why come you're smiling like that?'

'It's "how come."'

'How come you're smiling like that?'

'Because I feel good.'

'You look weird,' she said.

'So do you,' Bernadine said, and pulled Onika's nose between her fingers.

'Can I take a nap with you?' she asked.

'I'm getting up in a few minutes,' Bernadine said. She had energy now, but she patted the empty side of the bed. 'Come on, jump in.'

Onika plunged into the bed beside her mother and snuggled up so close that Bernadine's book fell to the floor. 'God stopped crying,' Onika said, looking outside at a scarlet sun.

The monsoons were weird like that, Bernadine thought, as she kissed the letter, folded it, and put it in the drawer of her night stand. She inhaled the scent of rain and looked out at the turquoise sky. Now there was a double rainbow. She put her arms around her daughter and squeezed. 'I don't know,' she said. 'I don't think those were God's tears at all. I do believe they're just His way of making sure everything He made keeps growing.'

As soon as Onika fell asleep, Bernadine called Savannah and read her every single word of the letter.

'Girl, that's beautiful,' Savannah said. 'I could almost cry.'

'I know, girl,' Bernadine said. 'It's deep, huh?'

'Did you call him?'

'Not yet. I just got the damn letter.'

'Well, what are you waiting for? Ask him if he can get here by fax or Federal Express.'

'This is some scary shit, Savannah.'

'Everything worth doing in life is scary, Bernie. You know that. What do you have to lose? You're always telling me that shit.'

'Yeah, but it was only *one* night, Savannah.'

'So what? I've read about people who fell in love at first sight, and some of them have been happily married for a million years. What do your instincts tell you?'

'To go for it.'

'Well, then.'

'Savannah. I was married for eleven years. I feel like I'm out of practice. You saw what happened right after my divorce was final.'

'You went man-crazy.'

'Not really. I wanted to test the water. To see if my shit still stunk.'

'And?'

'It still stinks. But this is different. I really liked James. That's what's so scary. I didn't plan on liking *anybody* too tough for a long time. I just got out of one bad situation.'

'Look, girl. All men aren't as fucked up as John, so don't go putting them all in the same category. There's still some good ones out here. *I* haven't met any lately, but it sounds to me like you may have lucked up.'

'I know.' She sighed. 'I don't know how much weight I should be putting on what I felt that night – that's all I'm saying. My divorce was final that day, remember? I was on a high.'

'Yeah, I remember. That's when Kenneth was here.'

'What do you think I should do? For real, Savannah.'

'I just told you. But why don't you do this: Take a few days to think about it, but *definitely* tell him to come on out. For at *least* a week. You need to spend some time with this man. And he should *definitely* stay at a hotel. Tell him what your fears are, and see which way it goes.'

'I guess that makes sense,' she said.

'I mean, how do you feel when you think about him?'

'I'll put it this way: I haven't been able to wipe that night out of my mind to save my life, in spite of the little escapades I've had. I've never in my life felt the way James made me feel. Not even with John.'

'Then call the man when you feel comfortable. But I'll tell you one thing: I wouldn't wait too long.'

Geneva was sitting on her daughter's couch, sipping on a gin and tonic and braiding Onika's hair. Bernadine thought it was kind of strange when she asked if she could come over. Her mother hated that drive from Sun City, which was why Bernadine knew something was up. Geneva looked so nice in her pink jogging suit (although she didn't jog), and her hair glistened like steel wool.

'Be still,' Geneva was saying to Onika. For some reason, the child hadn't shed a tear. She was sitting and coloring, watching *All Dogs Go to Heaven* at the same time. Onika was *never* like this when Bernadine did her hair. 'I'm moving back to Philadelphia.'

'What?' Bernadine said. She was standing in front of the stove, squeezing fresh lime juice over a skillet of sizzling scallions and veal shanks.

'You heard me.'

'But why?' Bernadine asked, wiping her hands on a dishtowel.

'Because,' her mother sighed, 'I'm bored to death out here. I don't have any friends, and I'm tired of all these white folks. Don't get me wrong; it's not that I don't like 'em, but I'm tired of not being around my own people. I'm so sick of playing bridge and pinochle and shuffleboard and doing that damn water aerobics class, I don't know what to do. I'm lonely out there. And it's too damn hot. At first I thought I'd get used to it, but my electric bill is always so high, I might as well be paying for heat.'

'Well, when did you decide all this?'

'I've been planning it since June. I wanted to make all the arrangements before I told you, 'cause you've been going through enough changes yourself this year. I didn't want to add nothing else to it. And plus, I didn't want you to talk me out of this.'

'Why would I do that, Ma? You know what's best for you. To tell the truth, I never knew how you could stand it out here in the first place.'

'I'm moving in with Mabel.'

'Aunt Mabel?'

'Yep,' she said, and patted Onika on the head. 'There, baby, you look jazzy now.'

'Thank you, Granny,' she said. Onika got up from the floor and trotted off to her room, her braids flopping back and forth.

'Why would you want to live with Aunt Mabel?'

'Don't say it like that. I know she can be an evil old bitch, but she's still my sister. And ever since Milton passed away, Mabel's lonely as hell too. We could keep each other company. And I know how to make her laugh. She finally sold that raggedy-ass house. So me and her went in together and bought us a two-bedroom condo right in the heart of town, where it's clean and safe and we'll be close to everything.'

'Well, damn. When are you planning on moving?'

'We closed yesterday. I'll be out of here by the fifteenth of November.'

'That's less than a month away.'

'I wish I could leave today. I've got a million things to do between now and then. And I want my grandkids to spend a weekend with me before I leave. Not their daddy's weekend, of course.'

'They'd like that,' Bernadine said, lying. She knew she'd have to blackmail them to go.

'Whatever that is you're cooking sure smells good.'

'It's veal. There's rice in this pot, zucchini in here, and I'm about to make a quick salad. If you'd be kind enough to set the table, we'll be ready to eat in about twenty minutes.'

'You think the kids'll be mad if I don't go roller-skating with you all after we eat?'

'It only lasts about an hour, Ma.'

'I know, but you know I don't like being on the highway at night.'

'Then don't worry about it. John junior wants to try out his new Rollerblades. I've been so busy these past few months, I haven't been spending enough time with the kids. This was my bright idea.'

'Are you planning on skating too?'

'Yes, I am.'

'When was the last time you been on roller skates?'

'I can't remember. Some things you don't forget how to do.'

'Well, I hope the next time I see you, you ain't got no cast on your leg,' Geneva said, and started laughing. She took a sip from her drink. 'Has anybody been by to look at the house?'

'Three people, two days ago. All in the same day.'

'Any of 'em seem interested?'

'I don't know yet. I haven't heard anything back from the realtors.'

'Well, I sure hope somebody buys this sucker, and quick.'

'Me too,' Bernadine said.

'What you gon' do if it don't sell anytime soon?'

'I don't know,' Bernadine said. 'I'll cross that bridge when I get to it.'

'I called him!' Bernadine said to Savannah.

'And?'

'He's coming.'

'When when when?'

'Early next month.'

'When next month?'

'November fourth.'

'Shit, I'll be in Las Vegas at a conference. How long is he staying?'

'At least a week. He's leaving his ticket open, girl.'

'Get out of here!'

'I'm not kidding. I'm so scared I don't know what to do.'

'That's a good sign,' Savannah said. 'A real good sign.'

'What if I don't feel the same? What if I don't even like the way he looks?'

'You're starting to sound like Robin. It's how he makes you feel that counts. Not how he looks. You liked the way he looked the first time, didn't you?'

'Yeah.'

'So don't worry about it. I think this is so exciting.'

'I need to get a pedicure. My heels are crusty as hell.'

'Then do it,' Savannah said.

'And get my teeth cleaned.'

'Call the dentist today.'

'And I need to . . . Shit, girl, I can't even think straight.'

'Well?' Savannah groaned.

'Well, what?'

'Aren't you going to wish me happy birthday?'

'Birthday? Did I forget your birthday? Is it today?'

'It was yesterday.'

'Yesterday? Shit! I'm sorry, girl. Why didn't you remind me? Damn. What'd you do to celebrate?'

'Took myself out to dinner.'

'You mean you went by yourself?'

'Yeah.'

'Why didn't you call some damn body?'

'Because I wanted to be by myself.'

'That's messed up, Savannah.'

'It wasn't so bad. I went to the gym first, then to dinner, came home, gave myself a manicure and a facial, and went to sleep.'

'You should've at least called *me*, damn.'

'Girl, on my birthday, I like to think about what I'm doing with my life. What I've done so far. And what I should do next.'

'And what's the verdict?'

'Last year I made this stupid New Year's resolution.'

'Which was what?'

'That I wasn't spending another birthday or major holiday by myself.'

'Well . . .'

'Well, I spent the Fourth of July with you and the kids, Labor Day with you and the kids, and you know the rest. Anyway, I told myself I was going to meet Mr Right before 1991 kicked in. But fuck it. Since I left Denver, I haven't met a soul I'm crazy about. Nothing but a few no-name creeps. So I made up my mind, girl.'

'About what?'

'That I might have to get used to the idea of being by myself.'

'This doesn't sound like the optimistic Savannah I know.'

'I'm not being pessimistic; I'm being realistic. I have to accept the fact that there's a chance I may not ever get married or have a baby. If I do, cool. But I can't spend the rest of my life worrying about the shit or waiting for it to happen. I'm serious. I did get a few cards, and a dozen roses from Kenneth.'

'He sent you roses?'

'Yeah. But I'm not impressed.'

'I don't see why not. Have you talked to him?'

'He left a message on the machine. I told you, I'm not getting involved with that man. One more trip out here, and we'd be having an affair. I had to stop the shit before it went any further.'

'He said he wanted to leave his wife, Savannah.'

'They all say that, Bernadine.'

'John left me for Kathleen, didn't he? So it's not like it can't happen.'

'It's too complicated.'

'Well, look. I know you'll meet somebody. You haven't even been here a year.'

'I know that, but I've also been alive for thirty-seven.'

368

'Birthdays can depress the hell out of anybody.'

'I'm not *depressed.* As a matter of fact, I feel pretty damn good. And I mean that. To be honest with you, I do believe in my heart that I will meet *him*. I just don't know when. I know it won't be until I honestly accept the fact that I'm OK all by myself. That I can survive, that I can feel good being Savannah Jackson, without a man. I'm not holding my breath any more, looking around every corner, hoping *he*'ll be there. If *he*'s out there, we'll find each other. When we're *supposed* to. That's all I'm saying.'

'You haven't met *any* decent men since you've been here?'

'Yeah, I've met some *decent* men but none that light my fire.'

'I hear you.'

'Anyway, I can't put my life on hold, waiting for a damn man. And by the way, I got offered a shot at this assistant producer's job at the station.'

'Really? What's with you, Savannah? Why're you keeping everything such a big damn secret all of a sudden? What took you so long to tell me *this* shit? I tell you *everything.*'

'I wanted to make sure it was in the works first. Have you seen that black talk show called *The Black Board*?'

'Girl, that show comes on at six o'clock on Sunday mornings, doesn't it?'

'Yeah.'

'No. I can't lie. I haven't seen it.'

'Well, I don't care what time it comes on. They're letting me coproduce a show on a trial basis.'

'No shit?'

'No shit. Apparently nobody watches the damn show, so they're trying to restructure it.'

'So what'll you have to do?'

'Well, first of all, I have to develop new ideas for a better format, which is no problem. I've watched about eight videos, and it is tired. Basically, they want me

369

to come up with a list of potential guests that I think would be interesting to black folks. For my trial show, I'm only supposed to pick one. I'm thinking about asking some of the *board* members – no pun intended – from BWOTM. Gloria's on the top of my list.'

'That sounds real good.'

'So I have to write a script, figure out what questions the host should ask – you know, let the viewers know the kind of stuff they're doing, that kind of shit. I think it'll be fun.'

'What's your chances of getting the job?'

'I don't know. There's two other people, from other stations, that were asked to do the same thing I'm doing. We'll see. If it's meant to be, it'll be.'

'Well, shit, I'll keep my fingers crossed for you, girl. Sounds promising at least. What about Robin and Gloria? You heard from them?'

'I haven't talked to Gloria in a few days, but Robin's in Tucson.'

'Her daddy's not in the hospital, is he?'

'I don't think so. But he's not doing so good.'

'I bet they'll have to go ahead and put him in a nursing home. It's like a nightmare, what her mother's going through. Robin's been dealing with it pretty good, if you ask me.'

'Yeah. It's sad, though. I don't know what I'd do if something like this was to ever happen to my mama.'

'I thank God mine is still in good health and has all her faculties.'

'Mine too,' Savannah said. 'As a matter of fact, I'm sending her one of my frequent flier tickets. She's been bugging me to death about coming out here. She wants to come for Thanksgiving, but I volunteered to go down to that church with BWOTM to help feed the homeless, so Christmas'll be better. Three thousand more miles, and I was going to London. But fuck it. I haven't seen my mama in over a year. She could use a break from my brother, and I could use the company around the holidays.'

'Well, mine is moving back to Philly, girl.'

'No shit?'

'Yeah, she said she's had it with Arizona.'

'I can't much blame her.'

'Damn. And I missed your birthday. I could kick myself in the butt. I'll tell you what. Leave Saturday open. I'll take you to dinner. Get your ass drunk.'

'That'll work.'

'Well, let me tell you about *my* other latest development.'

'What?'

'I had to go see my lawyer today. The shit has hit the fan for real, girl.'

'What happened?'

'She finally got all the information we need. And guess what?'

'What?'

'The accountant went through all John's taxes and company records. What tipped him off were all the different codes on the cash transactions, and, girl—'

'Would you get to the point, Bernie?'

'OK, OK. I'm trying. Anyway, to make a long story short, they ended up comparing some figures against his taxes, and they didn't add up.'

'You mean he's been cheating on his taxes?'

'Deeper than that. He's not only been putting money in his own pocket but swindling his partner too. He put all kinds of stuff on his expense account, girl. The Porsche and my BMW! They've found out so much shit, I can't even believe it.'

'Well, you don't mess around when it comes to the IRS.'

'Tell me about it.'

'So what does all this mean?'

'It means I could drop a dime on him and get his ass for fraud.'

'Would you do that, Bernie?'

'Of course not; I'm not as low as he is. Plus, my lawyer said that since I signed our joint tax returns,

I could get in trouble too. We'd both be responsible for repaying any penalties, so I'm keeping my mouth shut. All I want is my money, so I can be done with this whole thing. But my lawyer's still going to threaten him with this, just to call his bluff. The settlement conference is next week.'

'Damn,' Savannah said.

'Damn is right,' Bernadine said. 'But if all goes well, this could finally be over.'

'Have you talked to him at all lately?'

'Yeah, but not about this. My lawyer told me not to discuss anything except the kids with him. Did I tell you we had to have the visitation stuff modified since he got married?'

'No, you didn't.'

'Yeah.'

'I still can't believe he didn't tell you.'

'It's OK. Because you know what?'

'What?'

'I can't wait to see if that white bitch still *loves* his black ass when he's driving a Hyundai instead of that goddamn Porsche.'

To Heaven and Back

'Savannah?'

'Yeah, Mama?'

'You 'sleep?'

'I was,' I said, and sat up. 'What's wrong?'

'Oh, nothing much.'

'So why're you calling me so late if nothing's wrong?' I said, and reached for a cigarette like I always do when she calls.

'I'm just a little worried.'

'About what? Nothing's happened to Samuel, has it?'

'Naw. He called yesterday. He said there's probably gonna be a war. And if it is, because of his job, he said he won't be on no front lines or nothing like that. He told me not to worry.'

'So what's going on, then?'

'Well, I got a little problem.'

'What kind of problem, Mama?'

'Well, it ain't a *big* problem.'

'Mama, talk to me. It's not Pookey, is it?'

'Naw, he's fine. Moved in with some girl. Still working down at that gas station.'

'Did Sheila have the baby? Is something wrong with it?'

'Naw. She's not due for a few weeks. They're just waiting.'

'So what is going *on*? You call me up in the middle of the night like something's wrong, and then you beat around the bush.'

'I need you to write me another letter.'

'What for now?'

'My food stamps.'

373

'Why? What happened to the other one?'

'I gave it to 'em.'

'So why do they need another one?'

'Well, Savannah. A few months ago, they made me fill out some more forms. I just had finished filling out the Social Security papers to get my check to go straight to the bank. And let me tell you, I was seeing double. I ain't as quick as I used to be. So anyway, I accidentally made a mistake and checked off the wrong box. And' – she let out a long sigh – 'they cut my food stamps.'

'To how much?'

'Twenty-seven dollars.'

'A month?'

'Yeah.'

'Mama, you're lying.'

'I wish I was.'

'When did this happen?'

'Back in August.'

'August!'

'Yeah.'

'You mean to tell me you've been getting twenty-seven dollars' worth of food stamps a month since August?'

'Yeah,' she muttered.

'Why'd you wait so long to tell me? It's November, Mama.'

'I know, Savannah. But you ain't getting paid as much as you did at that job you had in Denver, and you still ain't sold that condo. So I know your money's gotta be tight too.'

'And just how do you know all this?' I said, although of course I already knew.

'Sheila told me.'

'Sheila's got a big mouth,' I said. But I was the one who opened *my* big mouth and told her, back in April, right after Mama told me she was pregnant. Why, I'll never know. 'Well, tell me this, Mama: Have you been eating OK? How've you been living?

Has Pookey been helping? Does Sheila know about this?'

'Well,' she sighed. 'At first Pookey was giving me a little change, but then the landlord started asking me who he was, and I didn't wanna get in no trouble with the Section Eight people, so that's when he moved in with that girl. I been eating OK. More soup than anything. And Sheila. She's got enough to deal with with this new baby coming, and you know Paul got laid off from IBM.'

'What?'

'You didn't know that?'

'No. Nobody tells me anything.'

'They got computers to do his work now. He found some piecy job, but he ain't making half as much money as he was. It's just temporary, until he can find something better. They say there's a recession going on. I'm beginning to believe it. Everybody's having a rough time. You should call Sheila. She ain't in the best of spirits.'

'Damn,' I said, and took the portable phone into the kitchen and got myself a glass of wine. 'So, Mama. How've you been getting by? For real. Do you have any money?'

'A little.'

'How much is a little?'

'Eighteen dollars.'

'Eighteen dollars!' I said. 'I'll wire you some tomorrow.'

'Twenty is plenty.'

'Mama, *please*.' I took a sip of my wine and another puff from my cigarette. 'Tell me this: What exactly do you have to do to get . . . what's it called?'

'Reinstated. I just need another letter from you, saying the same thing you said last time. That you pay three hundred and ninety-six dollars a month of my rent. They already know Section Eight pays the rest.'

'Who do I send it to?' I asked, and went back to the bedroom.

'You can send it to me.'

'I'll Federal Express it in the morning. Unless you need it sooner.'

'Naw, that's quick enough. My appointment ain't until next week. And thank you, baby. I'm sorry if I upset you. I didn't mean to. I been trying to deal with this on my own. I get tired of asking you for everything. But food is so high, and my check goes so fast, I'm lucky to pay my phone bill. It's already starting to get cold. And you know this place is all electric.'

'Yeah, Mama. I know. But don't worry. Be down at Western Union first thing in the morning. You understand?'

'I will.'

'And do me a favor?'

'What's that?'

'Don't *ever* keep anything like this from me again.'

'I won't,' she said.

'And from now on, *whenever* you get low on cash, you pick up that phone and call *me.* When you need something, you call *me.* I don't care if it's for a knitting class, a girdle, or a new toaster. You don't have to be too proud. You're my *mother.* And I'm your daughter. I don't ever want you sitting in that damn apartment with no lights, no heat, or going hungry because you're too embarrassed to ask me for help. Do you hear me, Mama?'

'Yeah,' she said.

'Twenty-seven dollars a month, huh? These people just don't care what happens to you when you get old, do they? You could've been in there starving to death. Now I see how people end up living on the streets. And you're trying to live off of four hundred dollars a month?'

'Four hundred and seven.'

'Whatever, Mama. The point is, they don't give a damn. Do they?'

'I guess not.'

'Well, you won't have to worry about it. I guarantee

it. I'll write your letter. But these motherfuckers ought to stop.' I didn't mean to say 'motherfucker,' but shit, I was mad. Mama obviously didn't care, either. Normally, she'd say something.

'Anyway, baby, so you're doing all right, then?'

'I'm fine, Mama. Just fine. I might have a new job.'

'You didn't quit this one already, did you?'

'No. I'll tell you more about it in a few weeks. It'd still be at the same television station, though. More like a promotion.'

'You and your promotions.'

'Anyway, I have to get up early. I'm going to Las Vegas in the morning.'

'Well, that sounds exciting.'

'I'm going to a conference. I don't know how exciting it's going to be.'

'Well, put a dollar in one of those slot machines for me, and if you win anything, you can Federal Express it.' She giggled. Which was good.

'I'll do that, Mama,' I said. 'I love you.'

'Love you too, baby.'

'See you Christmas,' I said.

'I can't wait. Now go on back to sleep.'

'I will,' I said, and hung up.

It took me for ever.

In the morning I mailed my absentee ballot to cast my vote for the King holiday, cashed in my last five-thousand-dollar CD, wired Mama five hundred of it, Federal Expressed her that letter, and felt a whole lot better by the time I got on the plane. I'm going to get this job. I feel it. I've earned it. And it's supposed to be mine. I'm convinced. God *wants* me to be able to help my mama. I'm scared to think of what'll happen to her if I can't. Plus, I owe her. She's worked hard all her life. She's the one who busted her ass to take care of us. And now that she's old, and all by herself, she needs help. As her firstborn, I'll do whatever I have to do to make things easier for her. I want the rest of her life to be pleasant. Happy. I don't want her worrying about how she's going to pay this or pay that, stressing herself all out.

There's one thing I already know. The first program I'm going to propose will definitely be about the lack of concern for the elderly. How poorly they're treated, how their needs are being ignored by the government, how they too often get pushed aside by their own families, and what can be done to change the situation. I don't have all the answers, but I've got a few ideas. I'll know in three weeks if I'll get the chance to make them known.

Las Vegas made me feel lit up. Like something exciting was about to happen to me. I'm sure everybody feels like this, but you can't help it. All the flashing lights and the thousands of people walking from one casino to another in such outrageous clothes; all the cars and honking horns and, inside Caesar's Palace (which is where I'm staying), the sound of hundreds of slot machine levers being pulled, bells ringing, and people screaming at the top of their lungs when they hit the jackpot – it had me wired for sound.

I had barely hung up my clothes when I rushed downstairs to put my first twenty into that dollar slot machine and stood there waiting for more to drop. They didn't. I sat down at a blackjack table for an hour, won fourteen dollars, went back to the quarter slots, and won my twenty back. By then I was tired, so I decided to go up to my room and soak in that Caesar's bubble bath. Which is exactly what I did.

The actual seminars were at the convention center, about a ten-minute drive away. When the shuttle bus pulled in front of the hotel the next morning to pick up a group of us, I got on. The first vacant seat I came to was next to a black man. He *would* have to be handsome. That rugged kind of handsome – my kind of handsome. I was scared to sit down, but it would've looked too obvious if I'd kept on walking.

I sat. He immediately turned toward me. 'Hi,' he said, in a baritone voice. 'Charles Turner, KXIP-TV, San Francisco. How you doing?'

'Savannah Jackson, KPRX-TV, Phoenix. Nice to meet you, Charles.' I couldn't tell what the rest of him looked like, but from what I could see, he looked like a complete package.

'Hey,' he said. 'KPRX is our sister station.'

I nodded and smiled. I didn't know what else to do or say.

'This is my first time at this convention. And you?'

'My fourth,' I said.

'Is it worthwhile?'

'It all depends. You'll get to hear a lot of stuff you probably already know. You'll meet some hotshots from other stations that'll try to court you, but this, of course, is only after they've thoroughly checked out your bio in the back of your station's program booklet. They'll spend half the day walking around looking for your name tag. You'll go home with tons of business cards, and of course you'll never hear from them.'

'So why'd you come?'

'You want the truth?'

'Nothing but.'

'I needed a vacation. And it's free.'

He smiled. 'I hear you.'

'The real fun is at night.'

'So does that mean you're going to the party tonight?'

'I'm considering it.'

'Is something better going on that I don't know about, or are you planning on hitting the casinos?' He pretended to give me a scornful look.

'It just depends on how beat I am at the end of the day.'

'I hear you,' he said again. 'So what seminars are you going to *today*?'

'I was planning to go to the NewsCenter exhibit first.'

379

'I'm going to that too.'

'Oh, really,' I said, and threw him a sarcastic look. 'Then I was thinking about sitting in on the minority-journalists seminar.'

'Me too,' he said.

'Are you serious?'

'I kid you not. Look what I've circled on my schedule.'

I glanced down at it. He was telling the truth. 'I see you're going to the one for program producers. Is that what you do?'

'Yep. What about you?'

'Right now I work in publicity, but I might get a chance to coproduce a community affairs show. I won't know for sure for a few weeks.'

'Well, good luck.'

'Thanks,' I said.

'So,' he said, and tried to stretch his legs. 'Looks like we might be stuck with each other most of the day, then, huh?'

'Looks that way,' I said. And thanked the Lord. I couldn't think of anything else to say, and hell, I was nervous. I looked out the window and saw a billboard for the Nevada State Lottery. A man was thinking about what he'd do if he won. It said: 'I'd still work every day . . . on my tan!' I cracked up.

'What's so funny?'

'Did you see that billboard?'

'No, I didn't.'

I told him what it said. He chuckled. By now we were in front of the convention center. All forty or so of us got off the bus. There were six or seven other buses in front of ours. After we registered and got our respective packets and name tags, we went to the exhibit. Charles and I talked through the whole thing. The production seminar was so crowded, we had to stand up. It was even more boring than the one for minority journalists. We knew most of this stuff already, and we spent half the time looking at the clock.

Charles ran into a person from his station who

wanted to introduce him to somebody from another station. They were halfway across the room. He'd been over there about twenty minutes. I intentionally hadn't looked in that direction. When I finally did, Charles was looking at me, pointing toward the door. I got up and walked out. A few minutes later, he appeared. 'I didn't think he'd ever stop talking,' he said. 'What's next on the agenda?'

'I don't think I can take another seminar today.'

'Me either,' he said. 'So tell me. How're you planning on spending the rest of your afternoon?'

'I was thinking about going swimming, to tell you the truth. It's warm enough.'

'At the hotel?'

'Yep.'

'Mind if I join you?'

'Not at all,' I said. Was this a dream or what?

'Great,' he said. 'I'll run up to my room and change real quick, and I'll meet you by the pool. How's that?'

'That's fine,' I said, and tried hard to contain myself.

Since none of the buses were there yet, we took a taxi. I told Charles I needed about a half hour. I didn't tell him why. I wanted to shave that ugly crotch hair and whatever new growth was under my arms. When I got in my room, I couldn't decide which bathing suit to wear: the one that made my breasts look bigger, or the one that made my ass look smaller.

I felt like I was on speed. I couldn't remember the last time a man made me feel this excited. Yes I could. Kenneth. Only this man wasn't married. He'd told me that at the exhibit. So I could afford to get excited. I also didn't care what did or didn't happen. I liked this being spontaneous shit. Besides, I just wanted to have some fun.

I showered and shaved and put on some lipstick. I decided on the fuchsia-and-chartreuse two-piece: not bikini; two-piece. It was loud, but it still made my ass look smaller and hid the few stretch marks I have on my hips. The top had pleats, which gave my boobs a 3-D look. I put a big T-shirt on over it and slipped on a pair of flip-flops. The elevator couldn't get there fast enough.

I hope I like him, I thought, as I walked through the doors that led to the pool. And I hope he likes me. Wouldn't that be ironic? To come to a conference on business and end up meeting the Man of My Dreams. Here you go again, Savannah. Dreaming out loud. But fuck it, I thought. You only go around once.

I put my canvas bag between two empty lounge chairs and walked over to get some towels. By the time I came back and took off my T-shirt, I heard that voice. 'I'm trying not to stare,' he said. When I turned to look at Charles, he was wearing some Hawaiian-looking boxer-type trunks. Thank God. I couldn't have stood to see much more of him out here in broad daylight. There was an abundance of hair on his chest. I could tell he pumped iron, because his arms had these hard muscles bulging up. His thighs and legs looked like a runner's. His skin was a mouth-watering shade of brown. 'Can you believe this weather?' I said, for lack of something more profound to say.

'It beats San Francisco. We never see this kind of heat up there, except in October, when it's Indian summer.'

'Are you *from* San Francisco?'

'Nobody's *from* San Francisco. I'm originally from Chicago.'

'Did you go to school there too?'

'Yeah. North-western. After I graduated, I worked as a newswriter for six years, then moved into production. I got burnt out on Chicago, though, so I decided to try the West Coast. But I hated L.A. Only lasted a year there. So when I got this offer in San Francisco, I jumped on it. I've been there for – what – close to two years now.'

'How old are you, if you don't mind my asking?'

'Thirty-three. And you?'

'Thirty-seven.'

His eyebrows went up. 'I figured you to be thirty-one, thirty-two at the most.'

'Well, I'm thirty-seven,' I said again, proudly.

'You *sure* look good.'

'Thank you.'

'You know something? When you got on the bus this morning, I was hoping you wouldn't do like some sisters do and pretend like I wasn't there.'

'Why would I do that?'

'For some reason, when black women see me by myself, they not only don't speak but usually won't even make eye contact.'

'I find that to be true of a lot of black men.'

'You've gotta be kidding. As fine as you are?'

'Look at you!'

'If you're giving me a compliment, thank you. But I'm serious. I get more cold shoulders than you can imagine.'

'Well, I can be at a restaurant, a bar, a club – you name it – and black men hardly ever look my way, let alone talk to me.'

'I find that hard to believe. I mean, let's be real. You're attractive – beautiful, really – sexy, and obviously smart.'

'Thank you, Charles. But how do you know how smart I am?'

'If you handle publicity for a television station, been asked to produce a television show, how dumb could you be?'

'I didn't say I was dumb. But you can't tell how smart somebody is by looking at them.'

'I beg to differ with you,' he said.

'Well,' I sighed. 'Now that you mention it, you've got a point.'

'Would you like a drink?'

'Iced tea,' I said. 'Thank you.'

He got up and walked over to the outside bar, and I rubbed some suntan lotion over my thirty-one-year-old body. Charles came back with two iced teas and set them down on the little table. 'So you feel like going in?'

'Why not,' I said. 'Let me take one little sip before I get dehydrated.'

He took a sip too. We went to the edge of the deep end. Charles dived in, as beautiful as Greg Louganis ever has. He had form. And so much grace. I watched his brown body glide through that blue water like a torpedo. When he came up, he stood in the shallow end and watched me. My diving isn't the greatest, but for some reason, today it was perfect. I blew bubbles under water until I saw his legs come into focus. I stood up in four feet. He was standing in three.

'You can come a little closer,' he said. He must be crazy, I thought. I saw how the sun was making his mustache, his muscles – hell, everything on him – glisten. I didn't budge. We both stood there as if we were considering each other. He smiled at me. I grinned at him. It was pretty obvious: we had started something. I couldn't wait to see what happened next.

We sat by the pool and talked until it was almost dark. Charles gave me all kinds of tips, pointers, and suggestions for the show. Told me not to be intimidated by the idea of it. Just do it. He shared some of his experiences with me. The good and the bad. He said this was a hard business for black men to break into. But he wasn't whining. Charles said that white men didn't like being upstaged by black men. But that was too bad. He was on a mission: to be one of the best black television producers in the country. He had loads of ideas. My adrenaline accelerated just watching how worked up he got explaining some of them to me. It was almost as if nobody'd ever taken the time to listen to him before. Charles also said that his so-called good looks often worked against him. He tried to downplay them as much as possible, which was one of the reasons why he liked being behind the scenes: where it didn't, or shouldn't, matter what he looked like.

By the time he walked me to the elevator (I didn't want him to come up to my room yet), he told me how refreshing it was to meet a black woman on the same 'wavelength.' I was honest and told him I felt the same way. What was also rare was how sobering and solemn he was. He had a philosophical answer to everything. He told me he had a little book he wanted to give me. Said he'd bring it to the party.

Right now, I'm trying to figure out what to wear to this damn party. I always get like this when I've been roused. Why do some men have the power to get you like this, and some don't? Who knows? Who cares? I thought, as I pulled all the evening clothes I'd brought out of my garment bag, spread them on the bed, the couch, and over the chair. I'd meant to bring my black lace dress. That would've been perfect. I looked at everything again. I'll wear the white dress. It's sort of Diane Keatonish, but with much more pizzazz. It's long, has a drop waist, this thick gold embroidery stuff all around the hemline, kind of low in the front but not too revealing, which of course wouldn't reveal all that much on me anyway. I was staring at myself in the mirror when the phone rang. It had to be him. Nobody else had this number. I was tempted to let it ring three times, but what was the point? 'Hello,' I said, after one ring.

'Are you ready to boogie?' he asked.

I liked his energy. His spirit. I swear I did. He was the first black *professional* man I'd met in a long time who wasn't stuffy. And Charles hadn't forgotten he's black. From what he talked about this afternoon, he still knew where he came from. 'I'll be right down,' I said.

He was standing in front of the elevator when the doors opened. He looked outstanding in a tailored blue suit, yellow shirt, and yellow-and-orange print tie. I smiled at him like I was still in high school. Charles looked at me and shook his head. 'You ought to be against the law,' he said.

'Thank you,' I said. 'You look pretty snazzy yourself.'

He took me by the hand. Had I really just met this man this morning or what? Why did I feel so comfortable? Like I *knew* him? How does this shit happen so fast? I wondered. But right now I wasn't trying to come up with any answers. I didn't care how it happened. I was just glad *something* was happening.

When we got outside, Charles asked if I wanted to take a taxi or walk. I was wearing flat shoes, so I told him I didn't mind walking. 'Good,' he said. 'I feel like I could walk ten miles.'

'What'd you have for dinner?' I asked.

'Nothing. What about you?'

'I had the same thing you had.'

'Why didn't *you* eat?'

'Wasn't hungry,' I said.

'Me either,' he said. 'You're spoiling my appetite, Savannah. Throwing me all off kilter. I only brought two suits, but I had one hell of a time trying to decide which one to wear. If I don't learn anything while I'm here, it'll be your fault.'

'Stop it, Charles. You're embarrassing me.'

'Good. I want you to feel as giddy as I do.'

'I think I do,' I said, and locked hands with him.

We started walking down the strip, passing couples who were also holding hands. I finally felt like I could identify. Charles must've sensed what I was thinking, because he gave my hand a squeeze. It felt good. I squeezed his back.

When we got to the hotel where the party was, we walked into a room full of hundreds of white folks. You could count the number of black people in here. We found a table, but before we sat down, Charles asked if I wanted to dance. I said yes. So we danced. He danced like a man who was sure of himself. He watched me. I watched him. He smiled at me. I smiled at him. I don't know how many songs we danced to, but when we finally went back to our table, somebody had taken it. We didn't care.

'I like you,' he said.

'What?'

'I said I like you. I like who you are. I like what you're about. I like how you think. I like what you do. I like what you talk about. And I love the way you move. I really enjoyed this afternoon.'

'Well, you're a breath of fresh air too,' I said.

'So does this mean we can *talk* some more?'

'I'm all *ears*,' I said, and gave him a mocking look.

'Would you dance with me one more time?' He pretended like he was pleading.

'Just one more, and that's it,' I said.

'But you know what? I'm starving. Aren't you?'

'You didn't hear my stomach growling out there?'

'Nope. I wasn't close enough to you. You think you could hold out a few more minutes? They have to play some kind of ballad after an hour of nonstop rock and roll. I can't stand it. I want to see how you feel.'

'You don't have to wait for a slow record to see what I feel like.'

His eyebrows went up. 'I don't?'

'Nope.'

'Let me be cool,' Charles said. 'I'd love to put my arms around you right now and smother you with kisses. But. If nothing else, I like to think of myself as a gentleman. I'll just have to let my curiosity drive me crazy over dinner. Shall we?' he said, and held out his arm.

I slid my arm through his, and off we went.

I ate like a bird. Afterwards, we were walking through the casino at Caesar's Palace, and Charles asked if I liked to gamble. 'I'm gambling right now,' I said. He gave me a peculiar look. I didn't know what had gotten into me, what was making me so bold. But hell, my heart was on cruise control. And I was loving every minute of it.

'What's your game?' he asked.

'I don't have a *game*,' I said.

'I'm glad to hear that,' he said. 'Me either.'

When I heard somebody scream, I looked to my right and saw a red siren on top of a slot machine flashing. 'Somebody hit the jackpot!' I yelled.

'I think I have too,' he said.

'Wait a minute. There's two ways I can take that, Charles.'

'You know exactly what I meant, so don't play *that* with me,' he said, and sat down on a stool in front of a machine.

'OK, then. For real. Do you feel lucky, or do you think you just "got lucky"?'

'You're not hearing me, Savannah. If you think all I want to do is sleep with you, then you've got it all wrong.'

'Oh. So you don't want to sleep with me. Is that it?'

He reached into his pocket, took out a quarter, dropped it into the slot, and pulled the lever. We waited. He got one cherry. Two quarters dropped out. 'Now, that's luck,' he said, and handed the quarters to me. 'Of course I want to sleep with you. I'd be lying if I said I didn't. I'd be worried if I didn't. You're holding the winning quarters. You tell me when.'

'Follow me,' I said, and led him toward the elevator. An old couple got on at the same time. As soon as the doors closed, Charles eased me back into a corner and looked down at me. 'I'm glad I met you today,' he said, and kissed me on the lips. I almost slid to the floor. 'So very glad,' he said. When the doors popped open, the old couple tried to pretend they hadn't seen what we were doing. As we got out, they yelled after us, 'Enjoy your honeymoon!'

I apologized for my room before I opened the door. As soon as I got inside, I started picking up all the clothes. Charles *was* a gentleman. He didn't try to 'get to it.' He sat on the couch, pulled out a little red book from the inside of his suit jacket, flipped to a page he had folded back, and watched me put everything away.

'When was the last time you sang to yourself?'

'What?'

'When was the last time you sang to yourself?'

'I don't know. Is that the book you wanted me to see?'

'Yeah. I'll leave it with you. It's pretty interesting. It makes me think about things I never would've dreamed of.'

'What's it called?'

'Ask Yourself,' he said. 'If you could change one thing about the world, what would it be?'

I was folding a bathing suit, and stopped. 'There's a whole lot of things I'd like to change.'

'I only want one.'

'Well, one of my biggest hopes is that people in general, but all colors specifically, treat each other with kindness and respect. But. I wish I had the power to wipe out poverty, and especially drugs.'

He nodded. 'If you could live anywhere in the world, where would it be?'

'I don't know.'

'What are you striving for most in life: security, love, power, excitement, or money?'

'All five,' I said. 'But I have to say love, which I hope would make me feel more secure and powerful and excited than I do already. I'd also like to think I wouldn't be poor.'

'If you could wake up tomorrow having gained one ability or quality, what would it be?'

'Willpower. Enough to quit smoking.'

'I didn't know you smoked.'

'I do, believe me.'

'What was your most enjoyable dream?'

'I'm not telling.'

'Your worst nightmare?'

'That I killed somebody. Except I woke up scared that I'd done it for real, so I made myself go back to sleep so I could redream the whole thing, and I changed it.'

'Would you be willing to have horrible nightmares every night for a year if you would be rewarded with extraordinary wealth?'

'No.'

'If you could use a voodoo doll to hurt anyone you chose, would you?'

'No.'

'Are there people you envy enough to want to trade lives with them?'

'No.'

'It's a hot summer afternoon, you're walking through a parking lot at a large shopping center. You see a dog suffering badly from the heat inside a locked car. What would you do?'

'Break the window and let him out.'

'What do you look for in a man?' he said.

'Is that question in there?'

'No,' he said, and closed the book.

I paused for a minute. 'Respect, honesty, sincerity, a sense of humor, a sense of self, sensuality, intelligence, energy, and . . . I'll stop there.'

'Do you believe in God?'

'Of course I believe in God.'

'Do you believe in love at first sight?'

'I'm not sure what you mean by "first sight".'

'Don't worry about it,' he said. 'One last question.'

'What's that?'

'What would constitute a perfect evening for you?'

'This,' I said.

Finally, the man got up, walked over to the bed, where I was now sitting, and kissed me. I'd never had this kind of foreplay before, but I liked it. I liked it a lot.

'You've got the sweetest lips,' he said.

'Well, you're *such* a good kisser,' I sighed.

He started kissing my fingertips. One at a time. The next thing I knew, he ran his hands over my dress, down my legs, and started sucking my toes. I was glad I wasn't wearing panty hose, glad I took a shower before I left, and even gladder that I'd put Shower to Shower in my shoes.

I was floating. But I wanted to make him feel as good as he was making me feel. I reached out for him, but Charles pressed my hand down on the bed. 'Don't move,' he said. So I let him go right on about his business. Somehow he lifted my dress over my head in one smooth motion. By the time he finished kissing my belly, I felt liquid. I thought I'd dissolved. This *had* to be heaven. Charles made the mistake of kissing my breasts in slow motion for so long that I couldn't control myself. I screamed out his name in somebody else's voice. 'Why'd you have to do this to me?' I said.

'Do what?' he said, and kissed me on my lips. 'Do what?' he said again.

But I couldn't answer.

I rolled over and unbuttoned his shirt, and then his trousers. I kissed him on the chest. I wanted to do *everything* to him. But I couldn't. Not yet. So I stroked him. Moistened the inside of his thighs with my tongue, kissed his knees, slid my body over his, and kissed him up and down his spine. 'Savannah,' he said. 'Come here.'

Charles squeezed me tight, and then let me go. He squeezed me again, and let me go. Then he clung to me like I'd vanish. By the time I felt him ease inside of me, I felt like screaming again. So I did. He danced. I followed. I danced. He followed. Until we couldn't dance any more.

'My goodness,' I finally said.

'My goodness is right,' he said, and wrapped his arms around me so tight, I felt like I was underneath an electric blanket. I wanted to go back to heaven. Just one more time. But I didn't want to be greedy. 'I wish I could keep you,' he said, and stroked my hair.

'Maybe you can,' I said, and closed my eyes.

The next morning we took a long, hot shower together.

Charles ordered croissants and cappuccinos and billed it to his room. I hadn't smoked a cigarette since yesterday, and didn't want one now. We didn't go to the conference. We went sightseeing instead, ate lunch, then dinner, and while we lay by the pool, I asked him some of those questions from that book. I appreciated his answers. We spent that night in his room, and the next two in mine. On the last night, we admitted that this was ridiculous. We couldn't stand the thought of separating, but we didn't have much choice.

'How soon can you come to San Francisco?' he asked.

'As soon as I find out if I get the job,' I said. 'Will you come to visit me in Phoenix?'

'Any way I can,' he said. 'As soon as I can.'

I called Bernadine, Gloria, and Robin as soon as I got in the front door. Told them the whole story. Blow by blow. Robin tried to act like she was excited for me, but they were putting her daddy in a nursing home the next day, so she wasn't in the best of spirits. Bernadine was another story. She was in her own new world. James was still here. She said *she* was in seventh heaven. And Gloria, of all people, had the nerve to say that her neighbor that lived across the street was getting friendlier by the day. She said he was fixing everything around her house that was broken. I wanted to say, I hope he started with you, but of course I didn't.

I couldn't wait to get home from work, but decided to stick to my routine and went to the gym. When Paula Abdul came on over the sound system, I sang right along with her.

I got home after eight. To my surprise, I didn't have any messages. I was hoping he'd call soon. I messed around the apartment until well after eleven. The phone didn't ring once. He's probably busy, I thought, and went on to sleep.

The next day came and went, and I still hadn't

heard from him. I was going crazy and decided to go ahead and call him at work. I wanted to know if something weird was going on. I got his voice machine, so I left a message. 'Hello, Charles,' I said in my office tone. 'This is Savannah. I hope everything is going OK. Call me when you get a chance. Here's my number, in case you lost it.'

By the end of the week I was a nut case. Bernadine said something probably happened. Gloria said that I should stop worrying, that based on everything I told her, Charles sounded legitimate. Robin told me to call him again. I didn't want to come across as desperate, over-anxious, or paranoid, but I also wanted to know what was going on. I mean, you don't spend a hundred and twenty hours with somebody, breathe them in and out, talk about everything under the sun, and then poof, don't call. I sat by that phone for over an hour, trying to decide whether to call or not. I didn't want to make a fool of myself, but I kept remembering everything we'd done together, everything he'd said to me. I played the videotape over and over again in my head. Hadn't he gotten the Bible out of the drawer next to the bed and read his favorite passages to me? The ones he said mirrored his philosophy about life? Hadn't he looked in his closet one morning to figure out what to wear and couldn't think straight, so he asked me to decide for him? Hadn't he actually jumped up in the air and kicked his heels together to show me how good I was making him feel? Hadn't he told me that he just found out last year that his daddy was a heroin addict, that his sister was dying of AIDS, and hadn't he asked me to promise not to act like I knew it when I met them? Hadn't he sung to me on three different occasions, even though he couldn't sing?

I didn't call. I waited. Another week went by. Still not a word. My period was due in four days. I thought I was dying. For real. I sat on the floor in my bedroom with my back against the wall. For three solid hours, I literally could not move. I just sat there staring at the lamp plug sticking out of the socket on the other side of the room. I had no appetite and couldn't sleep. Didn't have enough energy to go to the gym. I went to work like a zombie, came straight home, fed my cat, and sat in front of the TV until it was time to go to sleep. I'm sitting there right now.

I know I'm not going to hear from him. And I hate the thought that I made a fool of myself. That I spilled my guts. Made my most intimate feelings known. How could somebody who acted so sincere be so insincere? How could he play with my feelings like this? I would *never* do this kind of shit to *anybody*. Never.

I turned the television off, turned the CD on, and fell across the bed. Tracy Chapman was singing one of my favorite songs, 'This Time.'

I let Tracy sing. She was giving me strength. I pulled the spread up to my shoulders and looked at the ceiling. I wondered what Charles was doing. Probably lying in bed with his woman, fucking her brains out, and not the least bit concerned about what he's done to *me*. How bad I might be feeling. Even if he is concerned, *I* can't feel it. It doesn't change the fact that he has caused me pain. That he's made my heart feel as if it's been crushed. I don't care if it was barely a week. What gave him the right to do this to me? Doesn't he know this shit is *wrong*? Doesn't he know he'll pay for this one day? Doesn't he believe what he reads in the Bible?

Charles has scarred my heart, my fucking world. This is not the kind of shit you forget about in a few weeks. You don't just get over it. You can't wake up and pretend it never happened, because it *did* happen. I've got feelings. And right now they hurt. And he's the cause of it. All I want to know is this: What happened to all the pride, the tenderness, the love and compassion, black men are supposed to show *us*. I thought we were supposed to be a prized 'possession.' How are we supposed to feel beautiful and loving and soft and caring and gentle and tender and compassionate and

394

sensitive, when they treat us like shit after we surrender ourselves to them? Would somebody tell me that?

After Tracy sang 'All You Have Is Your Soul,' I turned her off, wiped my eyes on the corner of the sheet, and tried to get myself together. I know one thing. I will not put myself on the line like this again. I can't. I'm too old for this shit. And I'm tired. Tired of playing these sick-ass emotional games with these simple-ass men who don't care about anybody but themselves. I'm tired of these have-their-cake-and-eat-it-too motherfuckers. I'm through. Finished. From here on out, my pussy will be much harder to get, my heart no longer on display. It's going to take a whole lot more than a juicy dick, a sparkling swimming pool, some iced tea, a thick mustache, a pretty body, a handsome face, Bible class, smooth conversation, and a serenade to get me to drop my guard. I can't afford to do this shit any more. It costs too much. And besides, being lonely has *never* made me feel this damn bad.

Still Waves in It

Phillip wouldn't let Gloria come see him. He called at least once a week, asking about his clients. Had So-and-so been in? Were her ends splitting again? What about her roots? What was everybody saying about him? Were they gossiping? Did any of them even care that he was sick? Gloria lied and told him they were all deeply concerned. The truth was, most of her customers were glad Phillip didn't work at Oasis any more. Gloria corrected them. 'He still *works* here. And as soon as he's better, he'll be back.' They didn't want to hear that. 'He won't be doing my hair,' somebody said. Gloria called them ignorant. 'Don't you people read? Don't you watch TV? You can't catch it from somebody doing your hair?' And Sister Monroe – Miss Holy Christian herself – was the ringleader. 'I don't care what the newspapers and television say. I don't want to be in the same room with nobody with AIDS, so you know I ain't even thinking about letting Phillip put his hands on my head.'

Phillip didn't sound all that good, either. He said his whole body was covered with blisters. He was in so much pain – itching and everything – that it'd be at least another month before he could think about coming back to work. Gloria hated the thought of Phillip – or anybody – suffering. Right after Phillip got sick, he finally admitted that he'd been HIV positive for three years. 'Well, it's a good thing you've got insurance,' she said. But Phillip told her he *didn't* have health insurance. Gloria asked him why not. He said he couldn't get any. Gloria asked him why not. Phillip said because he had what insurance companies considered to be a fatal preexisting condition. Gloria was furious. Outdone. Hurt. She went and withdrew four hundred dollars of Tarik's tuition money and mailed it to Phillip. 'I hope this helps,' she said. Phillip said, 'Everything helps.'

Since he'd been gone, Gloria was handling too many customers. Putting in twelve- and fourteen-hour days for the past month and a half. She couldn't keep doing this. Her pressure was up. Her feet were always swollen by the time she got home, and she hardly ever saw Tarik. She'd had the sign STYLISTS WANTED in the window for so long now, the sun was turning it yellow. She knew this wasn't the smartest way to go about it, but she'd already notified several of the beauty schools around town, and the young girls that came in weren't good enough yet. It was just hard to find established black stylists in Phoenix. Quite a few white ones had come in to enquire too. They claimed they'd been trained to 'work' with black hair. But they'd be too much trouble. Some of Gloria's customers had already told her, 'I ain't letting no white person mess with my hair.' They said they wouldn't trust somebody white giving them a perm. How would they know how to do it without burning up their scalp? And how would they know how to cut their hair if it didn't hang straight when it's wet? And forget about a Jheri-Kurl.

Joseph, who had assured Gloria that all of his tests had come back negative, went so far as to prove it. He showed her the results. He missed Phillip too. The whole mood in the shop was dreary these days. Cindy's morale wasn't exactly high, because it was almost December and her days here were numbered. Desiree was going to be the hardest to replace. The demand for weaves was high, and not very many people in town could do them as well as she could. Gloria also had to consider the possibility that Phillip might not come back.

Some mornings, she actually entertained the thought of selling the shop. Moving back to Oakland. There were plenty of black stylists there. But hell, they had that big earthquake last year, and from what she'd heard and read, Oakland had changed. It was drug and gang infested, almost as bad as L.A. Tarik would graduate in May. He'd had that interview with Up With People, and now was just waiting for his letter. The admissions lady told him it looked good. Gloria wouldn't have any *real* reason to stay in Phoenix, she thought. She would sell the shop if she had to, but all she could do now was wait and see what happened.

She was ready to pass out. It had been a rough day. It started out bad. Phillip called her at six-thirty in the morning and said he thought it'd be best if he didn't come back to Oasis. There was nothing Gloria could say to change his mind. Then her toilet overflowed. She saw a mouse run across the canned goods in her pantry. The garage door came off the hinges again. The sprinkler system was on the blink. Tarik rear-ended somebody in the Safeway parking lot, which meant her insurance was going to go up. And the washing machine wouldn't stop spinning. To top it off, Sister Monroe, who sweated more than Gloria, picked today to drench herself in that nasty, stinking White Shoulders.

But one good thing had happened. Right before Cindy left to go home, she pulled Gloria to the side and told her that she'd been thinking. She'd feel bad leaving Gloria in this kind of jam. 'You've been good to me,' Cindy told her. 'You gave me a job when I needed one. I'll stay until you get some more help. Court-reporting school'll be there,' she said. 'I can go anytime. And to be honest with you, Glo, I could use the money.'

Gloria was glad Savannah's hair was short. Glad she didn't need to perm it or blow-dry it, and glad as hell she didn't have to curl it. She hadn't eaten all day. And why she had indigestion, Gloria didn't know. She was sweeping up Sister Monroe's red hair when she heard Savannah come in.

'Hey, girl. Where is everybody?'

'Home. Where I need to be.'

'Well, don't sound so excited,' Savannah said and took off her red Stussy cap.

'Girl, I'm tired as a dog. So let's get started.'

'Wait a minute. How tired are you, Gloria?'

'You tell me,' Gloria said, and she put all two hundred and ten pounds on one foot and placed her right hand on her hip. Sweat beads lined her forehead. Savannah could see where she had wiped off some of her makeup.

'Well, I won't die if I don't get my hair cut tonight.'

'I don't do business like that.'

'I'm your friend, Gloria, not some *customer*, so don't worry about it,' she said, and put her cap back on.

'It won't take but a minute.'

'That's what I'm afraid of. I don't do anything well if I'm tired, and I damn sure don't want you clicking those scissors on my head if you're beat. Seriously, I can wait another week.'

'Well, thank you, girl. You ever get gas pains in your chest so bad it feels like you're having a heart attack or something?'

'Yeah. Why? You having chest pains?'

'Like you wouldn't believe.'

'You got any Rolaids or anything around here?'

'I've got some Mylanta in the car. But I'm so hungry I could eat this chair. That's what's wrong with me.'

'Then let's go get something to eat.'

'I have to get home.'

'Why?'

Gloria thought about that. She didn't know why she needed to rush home. Tarik was doing volunteer work, delivering meals to shut-ins. Ever since his interview, the folks at Up With People told him that the more community service work he did, the better his chances were of getting in. So he was always busy. At first Gloria scolded him for not having done this kind of stuff on his own. Tarik said that until Up With

People gave him a list of all the different organizations that needed volunteers, he wasn't aware of how much help they needed. He admitted that at first his motives were purely selfish, but now Gloria could tell he was getting something out of it. He visited the elderly, helped feed the homeless, and some nights Tarik came home so excited, he spent hours describing how the kids responded to him at the hospital after he read them stories, or how good it felt when he helped a handicapped person get out of a wheelchair to go to the bathroom.

Gloria realized she was just used to going straight home after she finished at the shop. It was part of her routine, and now Savannah was asking her to break it. It wouldn't hurt to do something spontaneous for a change, would it? Tarik wouldn't be home until eightish anyway, and shoot, he could fend for himself. 'You're right,' she heard herself say. 'Where you want to go?'

'Anyplace that doesn't have a drive-up window, where we can sit down at tables that aren't Formica, and where they're not wearing paper hats.'

Gloria snickered. 'Let me turn everything off. I'll be ready in a minute.' She emptied the dustpan full of hair, turned the air conditioner down, got her purse, turned on the alarm, and doused the lights. 'Let's do it,' she said, sounding like Tarik. 'I'll follow you.'

'This is your town,' Savannah said. 'Why don't I follow you.'

After Gloria got in her car, she reached inside the glove compartment to find her Mylanta, popped two in her mouth, and prayed the pain would go away. She promised herself not to eat anything greasy or heavy. It would only aggravate the situation.

She drove two blocks and pulled into a Denny's. Savannah honked her horn and shook her head – No, please? – and gave Gloria a signal to keep driving. When Gloria came to Chinese Paradise, Gloria lifted her hands off the steering wheel, as if to ask, 'Is this

OK?' Savannah nodded, and parked her Celica next to Gloria's Volvo.

The tables were Formica. Savannah didn't mention it. Neither did Gloria. After they sat down, Gloria was glad the pain in her chest had stopped. She had already decided what she wanted before Savannah looked at the menu. The waitress asked if she could get them anything to drink. Gloria said she was ready to order. Savannah flipped the rim of her cap up, then looked at her. 'Could you chill out a minute, Gloria? Please?'

'I'll have a Sprite,' Gloria said.

'I'll have a glass of white wine,' Savannah said.

The waitress said she'd be back in a minute to take their order. 'So,' Savannah asked. 'What's been going on?'

'Working like a maniac since Phillip's been gone.'

'That disease is ruthless, isn't it? There's so many folks getting it, and not just gay people, either.'

'Yeah, it's something,' Gloria said. 'Phillip's not coming back.'

'He's not?'

'Nope, he called this morning and told me. Said he didn't want me losing any business because of him, and of course I tried to talk him out of it, but he wouldn't listen. He said he's feeling much better, though. He's gonna work out of his house.'

'So what are you going to do?'

'I don't know, to tell you the truth. Yesterday I interviewed this girl to take Desiree's place, but I couldn't tell if she was an alcoholic or on drugs.'

'What made you think that?'

'She acted like she was on something. But she could do the hell out of some weaves. I told her I'd call her. And I will, some time this week. If she looks sober, I'll hire her.'

'What about Joseph?'

'Joseph is a lifesaver, girl. He's not going anywhere, and he's definitely not sick.'

'And Cindy?'

'She's staying too. Said she'd wait until I hired somebody. Wasn't that nice?'

'That *was* nice. So relief *is* in sight.'

'It looks like it. Thank the Lord.'

'Well, when are you going to ask me about my job?'

'You got it, didn't you?'

'I damn sure did.'

Gloria reached over the table to give her 'five' and knocked over a glass of water. 'Hot damn! When'd you find out?'

'Yesterday.'

'Did you tell Bernie?'

'You know I did. I left a message on Robin's machine. She's in Tucson, you know. Her daddy's got pneumonia, girl. They don't know how long he's going to last.'

'I've been praying for that man as hard as I can. I hope he gets to see our Maker soon, so he can stop going through this.'

'Me too,' Savannah said.

'So anyway, tell me the details.'

'Well, they liked the trial show on BWOTM. A lot. I'll actually be an assistant producer and won't really go on board until after the first of the year. But it's cool.'

'What about the money?'

'The money is sweet. I'll be making close to fifty thousand, which is what I was making when I left Denver. Hallelujah!'

'Right on, Savannah. See how things turn out?'

'You're telling me. I did some of Robin's shit. I pictured myself doing that job, girl. I wouldn't let that image go for anything. Now I'm just hoping my condo sells. This job is going to take a whole lot of pressure off me, let me tell you.'

'Isn't your mama coming out here for Christmas?'

'Yep. You know something, Gloria? Why haven't I ever heard you talk about your parents?'

'My mother and father died back in 1975. Less than a month from each other.'

'How?'

'My mother had a heart attack, and my daddy fell asleep behind the wheel, driving to Alabama. I moved here right afterwards. I couldn't handle it.'

'I'm sorry to hear that, Gloria.'

'I know. What happened to that waitress?' Gloria said, and waved her hand until she got the waitress's attention. She came right over and took their order. Gloria broke her promise. She ordered twice-cooked pork, Mongolian beef, and Yangchow fried rice. For an appetizer: one order of pot stickers and two orders of foil-wrapped chicken. Savannah asked for sesame chicken with steamed rice and an egg roll.

'Do you ever take vacations, Gloria?'

'Do I ever take what?'

'A vacation.'

'Girl, I can't remember the last time I've been anywhere. When you run your own business, it's hard to get away. By the time you try to explain how everything is done, you might as well do it yourself.'

'Everybody needs a vacation every once in a while, Gloria.'

'Once Tarik graduates, I might be able to take some time off.'

'What's Tarik got to do with it?'

'Well, I *am* a mother, you know.'

'Everybody knows that, Gloria. You act like you've got four kids instead of one.'

'What's that supposed to mean?'

'Don't you ever get lonely?'

'Of course I do. Who doesn't?'

'Do you ever want a man in your life?' Savannah asked.

'Of course I do. But looking at what you, Bernie, and Robin have been through, I don't know. I don't want the kind you all had, I know that much. I'm not interested in going through any heartache. Look at what that Charles character did to you.'

'*All* men don't cause pain, Gloria. Just because one fucked up doesn't mean they all fuck up. To be honest, I don't blame Charles for what happened. It was my fault. *I* was the one who made the decision to open up my little heart. I was the one who said, "Here, go ahead and have some. Here, go ahead, take it." I've accepted responsibility for what *I* allowed to happen to me. I gambled. And I lost. But it wasn't the end of the world. I survived.'

The waitress set the egg rolls, foil-wrapped chicken, and pot stickers on the table. She put the red sauce, plum sauce, and hot mustard next to it. Gloria dug in. 'You want to know who I love?' she said.

'I can't begin to guess,' Savannah said.

'My son. So far he's the one *man* who hasn't broken my heart. I've tried to raise him so he won't grow up to be as trifling and irresponsible as some of these fools running around out here parading as grown men. I've tried to teach him to treat people with respect, and that includes girls. I've tried to teach him to be giving and unselfish, to not be afraid of his feelings, to be honest in everything he does, so he won't grow up to be another Charles or John or Herbert. And what was that guy's name that captured you on the freeway and then turned into a werewolf?'

'Lionel,' I said, and started laughing.

'I'll tell you something else. A lot of men don't want to go out of their way for you, but they want you to go all out of your way for them. But Marvin, he's different.' Gloria pushed her chopsticks to the side and picked up her fork.

'Who's Marvin?'

'My neighbor. He lives across the street. I told you about him, Savannah.'

'Is he the one who got the cracks out of your driveway?'

'Yeah,' Gloria said, blushing.

404

'Was he the one who fixed your garage door and did something wonderful to your swimming pool a couple of weeks ago?'

'Yeah,' Gloria said, and continued to blush.

'Oh, *that's* Marvin,' Savannah said, and pierced a pot sticker with her fork.

'Go to hell, Savannah.'

'Has anything major happened yet?'

'No,' Gloria said, laughing. 'He's just being neighborly. But he's real nice. He's older. Widowed. He's been helping me fix a whole lot of things around the house.'

'That's all?'

'That's enough.'

'Don't lie, Gloria.'

'Why would I lie?'

The waitress brought the rest of their food. There was hardly any room left on the table.

'Well, tell me something, Gloria. What are you going to do when your son graduates and leaves home?'

'Just what I'm doing now.'

'Which is what?'

'Living.'

'You know what I mean. What are you going to do then that you don't do or haven't done up to now?'

'I might sell my house. Get a condo or something. I'm tired of the upkeep. What about you?'

'What about me?'

'Yeah, you. Now that you got this job, does that mean you're planning on staying in Phoenix for a while?'

'I guess so.'

They ate their dinner in relative silence. They had already said what they had to say, and now they just wanted to eat. Gloria finished first and told Savannah she needed to be home before nine o'clock, because *Moonstruck* was coming on. It was already a quarter to eight. And plus, Marvin was coming over at eight-thirty to hook up her new CD player. Gloria said she wanted to at least 'freshen up' first. She left her

405

money on the table and took her fortune cookie with her.

She got home in ten minutes flat. She was surprised to see Tarik in the kitchen, doing his homework. She said hello, asked him how his day went, and Tarik said, 'Excellent.' Gloria headed on upstairs to take off her dress. When she got inside her bedroom, she saw she'd left the sliding glass door to her deck open. She walked outside. There was no breeze. The air was perfectly still. Gloria could actually see hundreds and hundreds of tiny stars. Some twinkled. A big yellow moon dominated the middle of the black sky. This was one reason Gloria loved Arizona. She looked down at the pool. The water was a magnificent sparkling turquoise. Gloria, who rarely got in her pool, took her dress off, got her bathing suit out of a drawer, and put it on. It was too tight, but she didn't care. All she wanted to do was take a quick dip.

She walked down the steps from her deck, stood by the pool, and looked into the water. It was beautiful. So beautiful that Gloria jumped right in. She immediately came back up to the top, treaded water to the edge of the deep end, then pushed off and floated on top of the water until she got to the shallow end. Gloria shook her hair and got out. She was finished.

After she dried herself off, she went back upstairs, the same way she came down, and stood out on the deck. It was so quiet, she couldn't hear anything. She looked into her neighbors' backyard. The house was dark. Gloria knew they'd gone camping. The folks to her right were watching TV. She could see the square light through their kitchen window. She looked down at the pool again. There were still waves in it. She looked up at the sky. The moon seemed bigger.

This was the kind of night for people in love, Gloria thought. A quiet night. A still night. The kind of night when you should drink a glass of wine, take a hot bath, lie across the bed, and roll over on each other.

But Gloria knew she'd probably never get a chance to do anything like that. She knew she'd locked herself inside an emotional prison, had done a fine job of building a wall around herself. And although she didn't know how to, Gloria wanted to get out of it. She thought about what Savannah asked her. 'What are you going to do when your son graduates and leaves home?' Gloria really didn't know. But Tarik would be gone in less than a year, wouldn't he? Even if he didn't get into Up With People, he'd still be gone. And she'd be alone. She felt a pain shoot through her chest and bent down to pick up her towel. She closed the sliding glass door, then went to the bathroom to get the Mylanta out of the medicine cabinet. When Gloria reached for the bottle, a pain, sharper than any she'd felt before, cut into her heart and turned.

Unreasonable Requests

After Gloria left, I waited until I got in the car to read my fortune cookie. 'Your happiness is intertwined with your outlook on life,' it said. 'No shit,' I said, and pulled out of the parking lot. I stopped for a red light, pushed the gear into first, pressed my foot on the accelerator, and the car died. I tried ten different times to start it, but it wouldn't start. I was blocking traffic, and people were honking their horns at me. I stood in the middle of the street, trying to figure out what to do. Finally, some guy in a red Jaguar asked if I wanted to use his car phone. I called AAA. They came and towed my Celica away. It turned out that my engine had blown up. I'd thrown a rod. I'd forgotten to put oil in the damn car.

When I got home, it was almost ten o'clock. I had two messages: from Kenneth and, of course, from Mama. She didn't sound upset or anything, so I waited until after I changed my clothes before calling her.

'Hey, hootchy-kootchy woman,' I said.

'Well, Sheila went and had another big-headed boy. Can you believe it? A house full of boys?'

'When'd she have it? I mean *him*.'

'Two hours ago. I called you from the hospital.'

'What'd she name him?'

'I can't hardly pronounce it. Jaheed, Jaleel, Jamal, Ja-something. Call her and ask her. She's in Saint Augustine's.'

'So how much did he weigh?'

'Eight pounds, nine ounces. He's a big one.'

'How's Pookey?'

'He's doing all right. Staying out of trouble.'

'Heard from Samuel?'

'Not lately.'

'So what else is up?'

'Did you buy my ticket already?'

'I don't have to buy it. I'm using one of my mileage-plus coupons. Why?'

'Well, would your feelings be hurt if I didn't come?'

'No. But I thought you wanted to see Arizona.'

'I do. But Sheila could really use my help around here during the holidays.'

'Are you sure about this, Mama?'

'Yeah, I'm sure. She's got her hands full. And,' she said, with her usual sigh, 'there is this class coming up on how to make wreaths and centerpieces that I would just love to take.'

'How much?' I said.

'Sixty dollars.'

'Is that what you want for Christmas?'

'Do I have a choice?'

'No,' I said.

'So anything exciting going on your way?'

'I'm just trying to do some homework for my new job.'

'What kind of homework?'

'Well, I spend hours combing the newspaper, trying to come up with ideas for the show. Things I think would be relevant to black people.'

'Heard any more from Kenneth?'

'Mama, I wish you'd stop. Once and for all.'

'I just asked.'

'No, I haven't heard from Kenneth. I told him to stop calling me.'

'I thought you said he sent you some roses for your birthday.'

'So what.'

'Ain't no man never sent me no roses.'

'He could afford it.'

'You can really be a bitch when you want to, you know that?'

'I guess I can, Mama.'

409

'That's your whole problem. You're too hard. Ain't no man gon' want you if you don't loosen up. This man is doing everything he can to let you know how he feels about you. Why don't you give him a chance?'

'Mama, look. I am *sick* of you telling me what my problems are. Why don't you let me deal with them my way, since they're *my* problems, OK? Until you can offer some good solid constructive advice, I'd appreciate it if you'd keep your little snide remarks to yourself. I am thirty-seven years old, Mama. And I'm tired of listening to you tell me what I'm not doing right or what you think I should be doing. And more than anything, I'm really sick and tired of you asking me about the men in my life. *I don't have any!* OK? And you know what? I don't give a shit!'

'Take it easy, Savannah. Damn. I didn't mean to upset you. And I'm sorry if I did. You're right.'

Mama has *never* apologized to me for anything. 'What did you say?'

'You heard me. I said I'm *sorry*. And you're right. But you're still my oldest daughter, and I just want you to be happy. That's all.'

'Mama, I *am* happy. I'm as happy as I *can* be right now. When I get any happier, believe me, you'll be the first to know. Can we leave it at that?'

'We can leave it at that.'

'Good. I love you. Now let me call Sheila.'

'Wait a minute!'

'What now, Mama?'

'What'd you do for Thanksgiving?'

'I spent it at church.'

'Church? Since when did you start going to church?'

'I helped feed homeless people.'

'Well, that was a nice thing for you to do,' she said. 'I'ma let you go, then. Bye, baby.'

I was just about to unplug the phone, when it clicked. Please don't let it be Kenneth, I thought, while I lifted the receiver. 'Hello,' I said.

'Yeah, Savannah, how you doing?'

'I'm fine, Kenneth. And you?'

'So-so. Look, I wanted to ask you something.'

'What's that?'

'I'm coming out to Palm Springs for a conference in two weeks, and I was wondering if you could meet me there.'

'I can't.'

'Why not?'

'Because I don't want to. That's why.'

'I need to talk to you.'

'I've got the phone to my ear. Talk.'

'In person.'

'About what, Kenneth?'

'About us.'

'Us? Get real, would you.'

'I am being very real,' he said. 'I've been thinking about what you said last time. And I'm getting ready to make some major changes in my life.'

'Then why don't you do this: Why don't you invite me to Palm Springs *after* you've made those *major* changes in your life. How's that?'

'Savannah, I'm not asking you to *do* anything. I just want to see if we could spend some time together, to see if what we have is something we might want to pursue on a more permanent basis.'

'That's sweet, Kenneth. Really it is.'

'Look. All I'm asking you to do is meet me in Palm Springs, at my expense, of course, for a few days, so we can get reacquainted. To see if what we had is still as strong as *I* feel it is. What's wrong with that?'

'Fuck you, Kenneth, and the horse you rode in on,' I said, and hung up.

Of course, he called right back.

'What's wrong with you, Savannah? What, did somebody break your heart since the last time I saw you or something? You sound bitter.'

'I'm not bitter. I'm better. Can I ask you something?'

'I'm all ears.'

'Have you filed for your divorce?'

411

'Not yet. We're talking about it.'

'I figured as much. But you want me to meet you in Palm Springs so you can fuck my brains out for three days and then go home to your wife, and a month or two later, you'll call me up all pitiful and probably say something like, even though you *love* me to death, you can't leave your wife right now because you'd feel too guilty about leaving your kid, or it's too much money involved, or whatever other excuses you motherfuckers always manage to come up with.'

'You obviously don't know me very well, Savannah. That's not what I'm planning on doing.'

'You *all* say that shit, Kenneth. I know you have good intentions, but if you're that damn unhappy, why can't you leave your wife on your own and keep *me* out of the picture?'

'Because I want to know if you're going to be a part of the picture.'

'Look, Kenneth. I'm thirty-seven years old. I've got enough shit going on in my life right now to deal with, without putting my life on hold waiting for you to divorce your wife, OK? Why do you guys always pull this shit? You claim you're miserable, so you fuck around on your wife and then expect the other woman to wait for you to finalize your goddamn plans. You must be nuts. Now, I'm sure there's plenty of women out here who'd probably jump at this chance. Because I guess you fit in that category of what's commonly known as a "good catch." But I'm not one of them. I'm not that desperate.'

'I'm not accusing you of being desperate, Savannah. All I'm asking is if you're willing to see what we have. I thought you felt as strongly about me as I do about you. Am I wrong?'

'You're not listening, Kenneth.'

'I *am* listening. To every word you're saying. But life isn't all black and white, Savannah. It's not as cut-and-dried as you'd like it to be. I would *love* to

412

tell you that we've already signed the papers and it's over, but that's not the case.'

'Tell me about it,' I said.

'Look, I can see we're not getting anywhere,' he said. 'So why don't I do this. I'll call you back in a few days. You give it some thought. Some serious thought. And let's talk again. Would you at least give me that courtesy?'

'Would you give me a courtesy, since we're talking courtesy here?'

'What's that?'

'Leave me the fuck alone.' I hung up. And this time I unplugged the goddamn phone. I felt good. So good that I jumped in the air and kicked my heels together. Exactly the way Charles had.

I told my boss what happened to my car and explained why I'd probably be out most of the morning – maybe the whole day. I also had a doctor's appointment. I finally got up my nerve to go to see that acupuncturist. But that wasn't until noon. I'd planned on going during my lunch hour. I was also secretly getting a jump start on my new job. I'd already lined up folks for the show on the elderly. As a matter of fact, right after I found out I got the job, I went through some of my back issues of the *Arizona Informant* – the black newspaper here – and cut out articles on topics and issues I wanted to explore. One that struck me in particular was about black children who faced longer stays in foster care. I called the Black Family and Child Services to get more information, but the woman in charge was too busy to talk to me. She suggested I come down to see her, which was what I was planning to do today. Since my car was gone, I called to ask if I could come a little later. She was pissed but said OK.

I took a bus to the Nissan dealer. I got there at five minutes after nine. By eleven, I drove off the lot in a black 1991 300 ZX. My first payment is due on January 15. I get my first decent paycheck the very same day.

I smoked a cigarette on the way to the acupuncturist's office but refused to flick the ashes in my new ashtray. He took me into a small room, told me to lie down on this bed that was just like the kind you see in a regular doctor's office. Then he stuck these long wirelike needles into my wrists and right below my knees. It didn't even hurt. 'This detoxify you,' he said, and closed the door. I lay there for forty-five minutes, thinking, This shit isn't going to work. When he took the needles out, I felt exactly the same, except I had this disgusting taste in my mouth. I felt like I needed to brush my teeth. The doctor gave me some kind of tea to drink and said, 'You no smokey no more.' I threw my cigarettes in the trash, stopped by Walgreen's and bought some mouthwash, ate lunch, and went to talk to the adoption lady. It was after three, and it didn't make much sense for me to go to work. Normally, when I'm out of the office for an extended period of time, I call in for my messages. But what was the point? And since I was only a few blocks from Oasis, I decided to stop by so I could show Gloria my new car.

Friendship

Gloria thought she was dead. At first she couldn't see or move her lips, because something was covering her face. It was an oxygen mask. But Gloria didn't know that. Her skin felt clammy. She also wanted to know why those tubes were in her arm. Her chest hurt like hell, too. She remembered that somebody'd been beating on it. Her vision was less blurred now. Gloria wondered who all these people were. And what were they doing here? She couldn't hear them talking, but some of them were wearing white. They must be doctors, Gloria thought. And this must be a hospital. 'Where's my son?' she said. But no-one seemed to hear her. 'What the hell is going on around here?' she said. Again, no-one seemed to hear her.

It wasn't until much later, when Gloria was more coherent, that the doctor told her she'd had a massive heart attack. She was ready to have another one, just hearing it.

She fell asleep. When Gloria woke up, there was a crowd of people standing around her bed. 'Who's all here?' she asked, but no-one could hear her yet. Somebody'd been holding her hands for a while now. When Gloria looked to her left, she saw a tall, dark figure standing over her. She knew it was Tarik. 'Thank God you're all right,' she said. But he didn't hear her.

'You're gonna be OK, Ma,' Tarik said. He sounded like he was crying. Gloria still couldn't see his face all that clearly. She turned her head to the right, to see who was holding her other hand. She saw another dark figure, who wasn't as tall. 'That's Marvin over there, Ma. He's the one who gave you mouth to mouth resuscitation and called the paramedics. When I heard you hit the floor, I was so scared, I didn't wanna leave you.' Gloria squeezed Tarik's hand. 'It's OK, baby,' she said, but he couldn't hear her because even though Gloria thought she was talking, she wasn't.

Marvin squeezed her hand. 'Me and Tarik are gonna take good care of you when you get out of here. So don't you worry about a thang,' he said. 'Not a doggone thang.'

Gloria heard other familiar voices. Bernadine. Savannah. And Robin. Now it seemed like everybody was rubbing different parts of her body: her legs, feet, arms, and shoulders. But her feet were still cold. Why were her feet so cold? Gloria wondered. It then occurred to her that maybe she'd almost died. But she wasn't dead. 'I'm not dead!' she thought she yelled. But no-one could hear Gloria.

When the cardiologist came back into the room, he asked who the responsible party was. Tarik spoke up. 'She's my mother.'

'And I'm her husband,' Marvin said. 'I'm this boy's daddy.' Tarik looked at Marvin. Marvin looked at Tarik. Then they both smiled.

'I think we're all responsible for her,' Bernadine said. 'She's our sister. Please tell us she's going to be all right.'

The doctor looked at all three women. He knew Bernadine was lying. But he was used to this.

'Well, she's got a clogged artery, and since we didn't know what her heart looked like before this attack, we can only tell you that there appeared to be blockage in her anterior artery. That artery apparently went into a spasm, which chokes the blood flow to the heart. We're doing everything we can to stabilize her heartbeat. There's been some damage, but she's almost out of the woods now. Those first four hours were critical. She's lucky someone was there to give her oxygen and got her here so quickly. Right now she's doing fine.'

The doctor then told everybody to leave. Gloria felt lips touching her face and forehead, her hands and

416

arms. She didn't know who all was kissing her, but it sure felt good. She also didn't know what was going through those tubes that were sticking out of her arms. And didn't much care. Gloria looked at all the machines hooked up to her. She noticed what she assumed was her heartbeat on a little screen. At least it was moving, she thought. But her chest still hurt. It felt tight. The muscles inside ached. And her left arm was sore. She didn't know that every two minutes an automatic blood pressure cuff was squeezing it. Gloria wished she could get up out of this bed and find herself an Advil.

She pressed down on the button near her right hand. A nurse walked in and asked if she was in pain. Gloria nodded yes. The nurse squeezed the end of another tube, which took the pain right away. Gloria grabbed the nurse's hand, looked at her with desperation, and pointed to her heart.

'You're going to be fine,' she said, but Gloria was asleep before the nurse finished the sentence.

By the fourth day, Gloria felt much better. Even that stupid blood pressure machine was only socking it to her every fifteen minutes. Most of the machines and tubes had been removed. She was grateful for her very first meal. When the nurse came in to move her to the progressive care unit, Gloria heard the applause. Her three best friends were standing next to the doctor and nurse. Tarik whispered in her ear. 'Yo, Ma. I'm Up With People.' He made a fist and swung it in the air.

Gloria smiled.

'You better hurry up and get your ass out of here,' Savannah said. 'My hair still needs to be cut.'

'Yeah,' Robin said. 'And I want this weave cut out of mine. I'm sick of it.'

'Gloria!' Bernadine said rather loudly. 'You've got some nerve, having a damn heart attack when you knew good and well Onika was coming in to get her hair permed. Is that why you did this shit? Tell the truth?'

Gloria was laughing so hard, she couldn't say anything.

'Sister Monroe's here,' Bernadine said.

Oh, Lord, Gloria thought. She sat straight up; a look of terror loomed on her face.

'Just kidding,' Bernadine said.

'So this is what it takes to get your big ass to go on a diet, huh?' Savannah said.

Gloria shook her head.

'That's all right,' Robin said. 'We'll still love you when you're skin and bones.'

'Where's Marvin?' Gloria whispered.

'I'm right here,' he said, and came through the doorway. 'I hope you don't go losing too much weight on me, gal. I like my women big.'

Gloria smiled and looked around the room one more time before she closed her eyes. Everybody she loved was here.

The Weight of All Things

My daddy died in his sleep yesterday morning. Even though he wasn't really aware that we'd put him in a nursing home, my mother said he knew it. Which was why *he* decided to leave us when he did. The way he did. She's taking it pretty good, all things considered, and I'm still numb. This whole ordeal has drained us both, but at least my daddy's at peace now. We don't have to watch him act like somebody else any more. I know he's in that place where he can be the way he used to be.

And this baby I'm carrying. I'm keeping it. Russell can do whatever he wants to do. But I'm keeping it. I haven't told him yet, but I will. When it's too late to do anything except have it. I don't want him to leave his wife. I'm not going to do anything stupid to try to hold him accountable, either. This is *my* decision. Russell couldn't say enough, he couldn't do enough, to make me even think about taking him back. If he divorced his wife today, I wouldn't take him. Baby or no baby. I don't want him. He's no good. Rotten to the core. That I've finally realized. I've let him hurt me too many times. And I'm tired of being a fool. Tired of giving him so much power. Over me. Over *my* life. I'm tired of letting him get away with everything. Even fools get tired of being fools at some point. If death teaches you anything, it has taught me to cherish life, to value myself. Something I haven't exactly made a habit of doing.

And guess who came to console me and my mother when I called to tell him about my daddy? Michael. And guess who told me he doesn't care if I'm carrying Russell's baby or not, he still wants to marry me? Michael. I told him I couldn't do that. I don't love Michael, and he knows it. I told him he's a wonderful man but not for me. As much as I want to get married, I realize that just because I want to settle down doesn't mean I have to settle. I'm going to have to learn how to stand on my own two feet. Learn how to rely on Robin. The answers aren't in any astrology book. It's not hidden in a number, or in my psychic's palms, either. The answer to everything is inside me. Still, it is so very comforting to know that there's at least one decent man in my life who cares about me.

I'm thinking about taking a leave of absence from my job, at least for a month. My mother needs me. And I'm pretty sure I need her. I haven't told anybody at work that I'm pregnant, but I will. My mother wasn't exactly thrilled to hear it, but she's already making a quilt.

And they finally gave me my raise. They didn't have much choice, though. I wrote up that ten-million-dollar account I'd quoted a few months ago. I know how good it is to book a premium this size this late in the year. It means we don't have to worry about paying for any losses. Binding it is what made my position that much stronger. My boss told me I could look forward to getting a pretty big Christmas bonus too. I asked him how big. He said somewhere in the neighborhood of five to ten thousand. I could pay off my student loan, but it depends on how I feel.

The doctor said the baby's due about the fifteenth of June. I don't care what sign this child is, as long as it's healthy. I was also advised to get that amniocentesis test. They said I could find out what sex the baby is, if I want to know. But I don't want to know. I don't care what it is. I don't care if it's pretty, either. If I don't do anything else right, I'm going to do this right. I'll finally have somebody I can love as hard as I want to. Somebody who needs *me*. Hopefully, I'll have at least eighteen years to get used to the idea. And whenever I have any questions, or any doubts, I can always ask Gloria or Bernadine. They always know what to do.

Back to Life

Bernadine sat at her desk, pretending to move her fingers on the adding machine keys. Her phone rang. Finally. She prayed to God it was her lawyer. She'd been waiting all morning to hear from her.

'Well,' Jane Milhouse said, 'it's over.'

Bernadine's heart was pounding so hard she thought it was going to explode. She took a deep breath. 'And?'

'How does nine hundred sixty-four thousand sound to you?'

Bernadine exhaled. Her hands fell on top of the keys. 'Did you say nine hundred and sixty-four thousand *dollars*?'

'That's what I said.'

'That's almost a million dollars!'

'That it is,' Jane said.

'John must be in his grave by now,' she said.

'He could be, but that's not our problem, now is it?'

'No, it isn't,' Bernadine said, and swallowed hard. 'And you're absolutely, positively sure about this?'

'I just left his lawyer's office.'

'Was John there?'

'No, he wasn't.'

'Nine hundred sixty what?'

'Nine hundred sixty-four thousand. You'll also be entitled to half of his pension when he retires. And since you're already aware of our legal fees, we can talk more about the details of the settlement later.'

'Thank you,' Bernadine said. 'Really.'

'You're quite welcome. Now. When would you like to come in?'

'You tell me.'

'Well, they've got twenty-four hours to deliver a certified check to my office. How's day after tomorrow?'

'I'll be there,' she said. 'And thank you again.'

Bernadine hung up and immediately called Savannah. After she told her the good news, she asked Savannah if she could meet her, Gloria, and Robin for dinner the next day. She wanted to take everybody out to celebrate. Much to Bernadine's surprise, Savannah said she had a date. 'A what?'

'You heard me. A date.'

'With who?'

'This painter I met.'

'Where'd you meet him?'

'At that new black gallery that just opened.'

'Any potential?'

'Girl, I'm not even going to guess. Let's just say he's nice. But I'll cancel. For you.'

Bernadine was flattered. 'And you're still not smoking?'

'Hell no. Whatever was in those needles worked. I lost the craving. But I won't lie. I did go back for a booster, just in case.' Bernadine laughed. Savannah was the most resilient woman she knew.

'Do you need anything?' Bernadine asked.

'Like what?'

'*Anything?*'

'I can't think of anything.'

'Stop lying, bitch,' Bernadine said. 'After all *we've* been through, we *both* could use a vacation. And you know what? We're spending New Year's in London. And don't argue with me either. Didn't you always say you wanted to go to London?' She didn't give Savannah a chance to answer. 'You tell those folks down at Drum Beat or whatever the name of that show's called – tell 'em you're going to see the queen of fucking England. It is time,' she said. 'It is time.'

'You're crazy,' Savannah said. 'But I'll start packing tonight. They've got the best hats in the world in

London. And I'll buy as many as I can squeeze in the overhead compartment.'

'Speaking of hats. Let's all wear one tomorrow, Savannah. And put on your best shit. Nothing glittery, but do get clean. Remember when we said we'd have our *own* Sisters' Nite Out?'

'Yeah.'

'Well, it is time.'

'I hear you,' Savannah said.

'What you doing for Christmas?'

'Spending it with you and the kids.'

'Don't forget James,' Bernadine added.

'Oh, shit. I forgot. I don't have to stay all day. I'll drop the kids' presents off, have some eggnog, and make like a banana and split.'

'Savannah, give me a fucking break, would you? I want you to spend the damn night. Help me play Santa Claus. Shit, help me cook. James is a *real* man, girl. Nothing like John. So bring your flannel jammies.'

'I'll do that,' Savannah said. 'A million fucking dollars, huh?'

'And that's the truth, Ruth. Bye.' Bernadine blurted out: 'I love you, girl.'

Next she called Robin. After Bernadine told her the good news, she gave Robin the same instructions for dinner, right on down to the dress code. Robin was so excited for her she said she was going to pee on herself. 'I don't have any hats,' she said.

'Well, buy one,' Bernadine said. 'Seriously, Robin. How's everything going?'

'Everything's fine, girl. I'm sick as a dog, though. Eating crackers like it's going out of style.'

'How's your mother?'

'She's doing good. Got me down here making quilts again.'

'Good. Keep your ass out of trouble. Any word from Russell?'

'Yeah. You want to hear what that bastard said?'

'What?'

424

'He said how's he know this baby's his.'

'No, he didn't.'

'Girl, I'm not thinking about Russell.'

'Well, fuck him,' Bernadine said. 'Me, Gloria, and Savannah'll help you do everything but breast-feed the little rug rat when it's born. And for your information, when you get closer to your due date, I'm giving you the biggest goddamn baby shower in history. Now get your pregnant ass in the car and drive on up here tomorrow. And don't forget to wear a hat.'

'What's with the hats, Bernie?'

'Because we're stepping out, that's why. And it is time,' Bernadine said again. 'And speaking of time, have your black ass at my house *on* time. Seven o'clock sharp, Robin. No bullshit.'

'I will I will I will,' she said. 'Bye, you rich bitch!'

Bernadine was still laughing when she called Gloria. By now, of course, Savannah had already called and told her Bernadine's news. 'Savannah's got a big mouth,' Bernadine said. 'So, Glo. Tell me. Do you need any extra cash for Tarik?'

'Nope,' Gloria said. 'We've got everything under control. He's working his behind off. Cleaning up people's yards, painting fences, you name it.'

'Gloria, the boy is going around the goddamn world.'

'I know that! But I'll tell you something, since you're in such a generous mood. You *could* send Phillip a few dollars.'

'Consider it done. Just give me his address. How's he doing anyway?'

'He's much better. He's not doing as much hair as he hoped. He'd really appreciate it. Especially coming from you. Phillip always liked you.'

'You don't think he'd be offended, do you?'

'No.'

'Did you ever get anybody to replace Desiree?'

'Miss Black America came back on her hands and knees. Begging me for her job back.' Gloria was clearly being sarcastic.

'Did you slap her for old time's sake?'

'No,' Gloria said, laughing. 'I told her to go ahead and set up her station, whip that hair out of her plastic bag, and get busy. As long as we don't say too much to each other, we'll get along fine.'

'You sure you don't need *anything*, Gloria?'

'I've got everything I need.'

'Meaning what?'

'Well, me and Marvin've got a "thang" going on,' Gloria said, and was actually *giggling*.

'You mean to tell me you finally did the nasty?' Bernadine said.

'No. We haven't done the nasty yet,' Gloria said. 'I'm still recuperating, girl. But he did kiss me.'

'Kissed you?' Bernadine moaned.

'Yeah. A kiss is worth a whole lot. He's being *so* good to me. Ain't nothing in this house broke any more. When I'm fully recovered, don't worry, we'll do the nasty, and I'll call you up while we're doing it, to let you know how it's going. How's that?'

'Fuck you, Gloria.'

'You ought to stop saying that word so much. It doesn't become you.'

'Fuck you, Gloria. Do you think you could possibly squeeze me in tomorrow? I need to get my hair done bad. Maybe get some of those acrylic nails too. Wait. Never mind. I'm wearing a hat, shit. And forget about the nails. I won't be needing anybody's long fingernails for what I'm about to do,' she said.

'Which is what?'

'You'll see soon enough,' she said. 'Don't forget, Gloria. Wear a hat. You're a churchgoing woman, so I know you've got a closetful. Just don't come out looking like Sister Monroe.'

'Fuck you, Bernie.'

After she hung up, Bernadine knew her girlfriends were just as elated about her settlement as she was. She could hear it in their voices. Hell, they'd been waiting as long as she had. Now it seemed as if they'd *all* won

426

the lottery. And as far as Bernadine was concerned, they had.

She looked at the control sheets spread out on her desk, then glanced down at the adding machine. Bernadine was trying to remember where she'd left off. It was damn near impossible. She couldn't wait to get home to tell the kids. But what would she tell them? She hadn't figured that out yet. And then a light went on in her head. She'd tell them their daddy wanted to be extra nice, so he gave her a little *extra* money. Out of habit, Bernadine reached for a cigarette, then she shook her head. She inhaled deeply. Then slowly exhaled.

Now that she thought about it, Bernadine herself owned only one decent hat. She'd stop by the mall on the way home. After she picked up the kids. No. She couldn't do that. She'd promised she'd take them to see *Home Alone* tonight. She'd broken enough promises. The hat she had would have to do.

Bernadine sat there a few more minutes, drumming a pencil on her desk. She was thinking. About all this. She could definitely quit this damn job. But not until after the first of the year. If she quit now, she'd leave them in a bind. That wouldn't be right. Like Robin always said, good karma was a good thing to have. She'd finally be able to spend more time with her kids, which made Bernadine smile. She'd be the first mother there after school. Every single day. She'd sit in before that bell rang. No more rushing in rush hour. No more leaving at dawn, getting home when it was dark.

She also wouldn't have to worry about selling the house now. But Bernadine wasn't taking that fucker off the market. She'd drop the price. And she'd send a nice check to the United Negro College Fund, something she'd always wanted to do. She'd help feed some of those kids in Africa she'd seen on TV at night. She'd call that toll-free number she'd written down on a piece of paper that was stuck under a magnet on the refrigerator. Maybe she'd send some change to the Urban League and the NAACP, and she'd definitely help out some of those programs that BWOTM had been trying to get off the ground for the last hundred years. At the rate she was going, Bernadine had already given away over a million dollars. But she sat there, still trying to think of who else might need her help.

And James. The man had backed up everything he said, and then some. Bernadine was still love-struck. And planned to stay that way. He'd be there for Christmas. He'd already found an apartment. His next step was setting up his law practice here. James said he wanted to see what *he* could do to help get the King referendum passed in this racist state. Once and for all. He'd already joined a coalition to stop the liquor board from allowing so many liquor stores in the black community. Savannah was even planning to do a show on it. The man was for real. James promised he wouldn't rush her. That he'd be patient. But now, Bernadine wanted to be rushed. She wanted to get this show on the road. Hell, she had her life back. The one she'd lost eleven years ago.

And now that she'd have the money to start her catering business, Bernadine didn't want to be bothered. She'd had a better dream. One that would see the light. Since these white folks were making a fortune selling these damn chocolate chip cookies, she'd open up her own little shop. Sell nothing but sweets, the kind black folks ate: blackberry cobbler, peach cobbler, sweet potato pie, bread pudding, banana pudding, rice pudding, lemon meringue pie, and pound cake. She'd put it in the biggest mall in Scottsdale. Serve the finest gourmet coffee she could find: cappuccino and all those other ridiculous coffees everybody couldn't live without these days. She already had the name picked: Bernadine's Sweet Tooth. That sounded good. Yeah, she thought. It's got a real nice ring to it.

THE END

Disappearing Acts
by Terry McMillan

'A love story waiting to explode'
New York Times Book Review

Franklin's tired of women, tired of trouble. He's young, he's
six-feet-four and he likes to pump iron. But his ex-wife's riding him
for money to keep their two children, and there's no security in
construction work. Not in New York anyway, and especially not if
you're black. All Franklin really wants is to stay together, stay in
work and, most of all, stay out of love.

And Zora. She's a music teacher, fresh from Ohio, looking for
that one big break as a singer-songwriter. She's going to get an
apartment, get fit, and get her first songs down on a demo tape. The
last thing she needs is to disappear into another relationship, and
wind up with another broken heart.

But when Franklin sees Zora and Zora sees Franklin, none of
it means a damn. Everything – their pasts, their independence,
their plans – evaporates in the electric charge of one of the most
passionate, turbulent and memorable affairs in contemporary
fiction . . .

'Out of the growing tradition of black American women writers comes
the exceptionally vibrant voice of Terry McMillan. *Disappearing Acts*
is fluid, sexy and thoroughly engaging'
Louisa Saunders, *Elle*

'Funny, earthy . . . McMillan gives her work a voice that is her own,
one tough enough to speak across colour and class lines'
Newsday

'Sparkling fly-on-the-wall stuff . . . compelling'
Isabel Appio, *20/20*

0 552 99449 9

BLACK SWAN

Mama
by Terry McMillan

'A remarkable first novel . . . brilliant . . . a winner'
Peter Grosvenor, *Daily Express*

For all the men in her life – including three husbands –
Mildred Peacock, mother of five of Point Haven, Michigan,
never found one she could rely on. No-one could figure out
where she got her strength. True a few bottles of rye came out
of the welfare cheque, and she needed those nerve pills to
keep going. But motherhood meant everything to her, and she
had great hopes – especially for her beloved eldest daughter
Freda. It broke her heart when Freda moved to LA.

That was in the 1960s, when most folks in Point Haven had
hardly even heard of Martin Luther King. But on the West
Coast it was different. There, Freda learned that being black
was beautiful, and when she sent for Mildred to join her, the
tempestuous drama of their family life, and of the special and
fascinating intimacy of their relationship, resumed as forcefully
as ever.

A powerful story of struggle and survival, Terry McMillan's
highly-acclaimed debut novel MAMA is equally as moving
and immediate as her extraordinary bestseller DISAPPEARING
ACTS.

'An unforgettable combination of compassion and sass'
Maureen Freely, *Observer*

'A rich, gutsy portrait'
Madeleine Kingsley, *Company*

'Engaging and funny . . . paints a moving picture of Black
America before it became politically conscious'
Rana Kabbani, *Literary Review*

0 557 99480 4

BLACK SWAN

Sugar Cage
by Connie May Fowler

'A beautifully constructed novel in which each character is drawn with sympathy and humour and the momentum of the plot increases irresistibly . . . If she wrote nothing else, this book should make her famous'
Sue Gaisford, *Independent*

Married on the same day, by the same judge, the Looneys and the Jewels have been neighbours – best friends and best enemies – since meeting on their honeymoons at the Coquina Motel on Florida's north-east coast. Rose and Eudora are marked – nearly destroyed – by their consuming love for their husbands; while Charlie and Junior are haunted by their pasts – both real and imagined. It falls to Emory Looney, exiled by his angry father to the harsh discipline of the sugar-cane fields, to grow to love the sensual, mysterious Soleil Marie Beauvoir, Haitian migrant worker and voodoo *mambo*.

Right at the start, Inez Temple saw the sugar cage at the bottom of Rose Looney's glass, its deceiving bars glittering like white sand under the sun. Was there, she wondered, a way to dissolve that sugary curse?

SUGAR CAGE is a mesmerising, magical first novel springing from the great tradition of storytelling in the American South.

'Relentlessly readable and never less than beautifully written'
Nick Hornby, *Sunday Times*

'Filled with love and humour, desire and rejection and above all, a great story – Read it!'
Company

'A soaring and operatic book . . . Connie May Fowler writes with tenderness of eye and an ear extraordinarily attuned to the cadence of language'
Kathryn Mead, *Sunday Telegraph*

0 552 99488 X

BLACK SWAN

A SELECTION OF FINE WRITING FROM BLACK SWAN

THE PRICES SHOWN BELOW WERE CORRECT AT THE TIME OF GOING TO PRESS. HOWEVER TRANSWORLD PUBLISHERS RESERVE THE RIGHT TO SHOW NEW RETAIL PRICES ON COVERS WHICH MAY DIFFER FROM THOSE PREVIOUSLY ADVERTISED IN THE TEXT OR ELSEWHERE.

☐	99198 8	THE HOUSE OF THE SPIRITS	*Isabel Allende*	£6.99
☐	99313 1	OF LOVE AND SHADOWS	*Isabel Allende*	£5.99
☐	99488 X	SUGAR CAGE	*Connie May Fowler*	£5.99
☐	99169 4	GOD KNOWS	*Joseph Heller*	£6.99
☐	99195 3	CATCH-22	*Joseph Heller*	£6.99
☐	99409 X	SOMETHING HAPPENED	*Joseph Heller*	£6.99
☐	99208 9	THE 158LB MARRIAGE	*John Irving*	£5.99
☐	99204 6	THE CIDER HOUSE RULES	*John Irving*	£6.99
☐	99209 7	THE HOTEL NEW HAMPSHIRE	*John Irving*	£5.99
☐	99369 7	A PRAYER FOR OWEN MEANY	*John Irving*	£6.99
☐	99206 2	SETTING FREE THE BEARS	*John Irving*	£5.99
☐	99207 0	THE WATER-METHOD MAN	*John Irving*	£5.99
☐	99205 4	THE WORLD ACCORDING TO GARP	*John Irving*	£6.99
☐	99384 0	TALES OF THE CITY	*Armistead Maupin*	£4.99
☐	99086 8	MORE TALES OF THE CITY	*Armistead Maupin*	£5.99
☐	99106 6	FURTHER TALES OF THE CITY	*Armistead Maupin*	£5.99
☐	99383 2	SIGNIFICANT OTHERS	*Armistead Maupin*	£5.99
☐	99239 9	BABYCAKES	*Armistead Maupin*	£5.99
☐	99374 3	SURE OF YOU	*Armistead Maupin*	£4.99
☐	99449 9	DISAPPEARING ACTS	*Terry McMillan*	£5.99
☐	99480 4	MAMA	*Terry McMillan*	£5.99

All Black Swan Books are available at your bookshop or newsagent, or can be ordered from the following address:
Corgi/Bantam Books,
Cash Sales Department,
P.O. Box 11, Falmouth, Cornwall TR10 9EN

UK and B.F.P.O. customers please send a cheque or postal order (no currency) and allow £1.00 for postage and packing for the first book plus 50p for the second book and 30p for each additional book to a maximum charge of £3.00 (7 books plus).

Overseas customers, including Eire, please allow £2.00 for postage and packing for the first book plus £1.00 for the second book and 50p for each subsequent title ordered.

NAME (Block Letters) ....

ADDRESS ....

....